BLACK SAND

Books by William J. Caunitz

One Police Plaza
Suspects

BLACK SAND

WILLIAM J. CAUNITZ

CROWN PUBLISHERS, INC.
NEW YORK

Copyright © 1989 by William J. Caunitz

Published by Crown Publishers, Inc., 225 Park Avenue South, New York, New York 10003

CROWN is a trademark of Crown Publishers, Inc.

Manufactured in the United States of America

Design by Jake Victor Thomas

Library of Congress Cataloging-in-Publication Data

Caunitz, William J.
  Black sand / by William J. Caunitz.
    p.   cm.
  I. Title.
PS3553.A945B54   1989
813'.54—dc19   88-37372
                                                                   CIP

ISBN 0-517-57132-3

10 9 8 7 6 5 4 3 2 1

First Edition

In loving memory of a Greek mother,

ANNA INTZEKOSTA

Far-stretching, endless Time
Brings forth all hidden things,
All buries that which once did shine
The firm resolve falters, the sacred oath
is shattered;
And let none say, "It cannot happen here."

Sophocles, *Ajax*

BLACK SAND

1

Voúla, Greece
May 1987

Takis Milaraki sat on his fourth-floor terrace, gazing at the islands, recalling those boyhood days when he and his friends used to row out to the two specks of land and spend hours pretending they were valiant members of Alexander's Shield Bearers, defending Greece against Darius's hordes.

A long time ago, he sighed, patting the roll of fat hanging over his belt. He missed those carefree days almost as much as he missed his friends, most of whom had left Greece to seek their fortunes in the United States or in other parts of Europe.

But not Takis. He had remained in Voúla. He could never bring himself to leave his village, or his two islands. They were the places that gave meaning and energy to his life; those places, and his family, were world enough. A lighthearted wind brushed across the terrace. Takis reached out and picked up the cup from the glass table. Sipping the syrupy liquid, he returned his gaze to the wine-dark sea.

After staring at the sea for several minutes, he reluctantly finished his coffee, returned the cup to its saucer, and got up. Moving into his apartment, he paused to identify the different smells coming from the kitchen. Lamb. Okra. Mary, his wife of twenty-three years, was already busy preparing for the midday meal. After doing that, she would clean her house, do the laundry, go shopping, have tea with her girlfriends, and then return home to her kitchen.

Walking up behind her, Takis realized that today was Tuesday, the twelfth of May. His name day was two days away; he wondered what surprises his wife had planned. Watching over her shoulder as she chopped fresh basil on a cutting board and brushed it into a pot, he slid his arms around her waist, pressing her close. "I'll try and come home after the midday rush."

"Make sure that our sons are not here."

"Our boys are already at the beach trying to screw tourists. Both of them will rush home at one, gulp down their food, and rush back to the beach." He kissed her neck. "Remember how we met?"

She smiled. "Go to work."

At exactly eight A.M., Takis Milaraki unlocked the doors of the Elite Café in the center of Voúla's main square and began to put out the tables and chairs. After he did that, he would make the espresso, arrange fresh pastries in the display cases, and await his first customer of the day.

In an apartment on Voúla's seafront, a couple lay entwined, each aware of their racing hearts. The bed was soaked with the tallowy smell of lovemaking; the sounds of the sea rushed into their second-floor bedroom.

"Eighteen years of marriage," Andreas said, gasping, "and I still can't get enough of you."

Breathing hard, Soula Vassos stroked her husband's damp hair. "I love you so."

"I wish that I were ten years younger so I could start right up again."

She bit his chin. "I'm patient."

Andreas Vassos pushed himself up so he might look down into her saffron eyes, drink in her beautiful face. She tightened her legs around her husband and rubbed her body against his. In a gesture of marital intimacy, she turned her head, showing him what she wanted him to do. Obligingly, he caressed her ear with his tongue, gliding it around the rim, sucking on the lobe. At the same time his hand roamed her body, causing her to moan with delight.

She relaxed her grip on his body and whispered, "Taste me."

He kissed her and slid down on her body until his face was between her legs. His finger went into her slowly and softly. She groaned and gently pressed his face to her. Suddenly the bedroom door burst open. Five-year-old Stephanos plunged into the room. "Mommy. Daddy. Let's hurry to the beach. All the *tendas* will be taken."

Andreas Vassos jackknifed into a sitting position.

Soula Vassos grabbed the sheet and covered her nakedness.

Stephanos hurled his little body on the bed, his all-seeing eyes fixed on his father. "Daddy, what were you doing to Mommy?"

"Well, I . . . I . . . was . . . looking for my ring. See?" He held up his hand so that his son might see the golden ring. "It came off during the night . . . and I was searching for it. See, I found it."

Soula Vassos yanked a pillow across her face and laughed.

A long line of buses stretched along the south side of Athens' National Gardens. People queued at the waiting stations. Fumes from the corn vendors' charcoal blended with the clean, sharp smell of wisteria. The sun rose higher in the sky. George Sanida walked from the dispatcher's shack and, shielding his eyes with his hand, looked up at the sky. It was going to be a perfect beach day. Carefully examining the line of female tourists waiting to board, Sanida thought: maybe I'll get lucky today.

He opened the door, climbed into the driver's seat, and turned to watch the boarding passengers file past him, making sure that each one deposited the thirty-drachma fare. He studied each of the foreign women as they passed, sneaking a look at their bouncing tits and cute asses.

A blond woman in her early twenties stopped in front of the box and opened the drawstring of her beach bag, searching for her fare. She was dressed in bikini bottoms and an oversized, lightweight white cotton shirt. A blue nylon rucksack was strapped to her back, pulling her shirt taut in front, accentuating her large, unhaltered breasts. Her nipples stuck out: big brown rings.

Sanida unbuttoned two more buttons on his shirt so that she might better see the hair on his manly chest. He smiled at her. She smiled back, dropping in her fare and moving to the back of the bus. He watched as she shrugged off her rucksack and set it down on the floor between her legs. She saw him watching her and smiled at him. Yes, today might be his lucky day, Sanida thought, closing the door and turning to check the side mirror for traffic.

Takis Milaraki was engaged in a heated political argument with his communist friend, Dinos, when the police car drove headlong into the space in front of the Elite Café. Two policemen got out and ambled over to the newsstand a few meters to the right of the café. Takis realized that it was time to roll down the awning. While he was unfurling the canopy, Takis noticed that the policemen were loafing around the newsstand. One was sucking on an ice cup while the other talked on the telephone, probably to his girlfriend, Takis thought as he secured the awning clamps.

Looking across the street, Takis saw a group of boys straddling their Japanese motorbikes. The Greek Rambos were trying hard to impress the admiring girls gathered around them. Takis smiled. He had seen them all grow up from babies; he enjoyed watching them play out their adolescent mating games under the stern eyes of Voúla's black-mantled gossips who spent their days cooking, praying, and leaning out windows. No matter how many tourists came, village life would never change completely.

Golden sand swept up from the rolling sea, melting into a lush savanna where people reclined on sun chairs. Boys played soccer; girls talked while lolling on the grass. Fifteen meters from shore swimmers dove off anchored platforms while several men cut through the blue-green sea on jet sleds.

Major Andreas Vassos, Security Division, Athens Station, lay on his back under the tenda's cloth roof. The past five months had been difficult ones for Vassos. His section had been conducting several major investigations into terrorist activities and narcotics networks operating in the Athens area. He had put in long hours and had not had a day off in six weeks. He loved his career and the excitement that went with being a policeman; he even enjoyed the meticulous attention to detail that his work demanded. But he did not enjoy being able to spend so little time with his family. He had seen too many of his colleagues give up their family life for the department. It was not going to happen to him; he was going to be there to watch his son grow into manhood.

Several days ago Vassos had slapped leave papers down on his boss's desk and announced, "I've rented an apartment in Voúla, near the beach. I am taking my family there on a ten-day holiday. I won't have a telephone—and you won't have my address."

Colonel Dimitri Pappas spread his hands in a pleading gesture. "Andreas? So many of our important cases are just coming together. Put off your holiday a little while. Till June. As a favor to your colonel."

"I'll see you in ten days, Colonel," Vassos said, backing out the door with a slight bow.

Vassos stretched his lean body under the dark green cloth of the sun shelter. It was wonderful to be doing nothing.

At forty years of age Andreas Vassos was a handsome man whose receding hairline complemented his olive complexion and majestic nose. He had a cleft chin and unusually dark blue eyes. Soula was fond of calling his eyes her Mediterranean pools because by day they appeared to be a deep blue, and by night, inky black.

I'm a lucky man, he reflected, watching his son build a mud fort at the water's edge. His gaze slid to Soula, who was sunning herself on a straw mat next to the tenda. She was wearing the brown-and-white bikini that he liked so much. Her arms were outstretched, her legs slightly apart as she lay on her back. He pushed himself out from under the shelter, resting his head on his wife's flat stomach.

"My other child is here to pester me," she said, opening her eyes.

"I didn't seem to be pestering you this morning," he said, tilting his head so that he could see down the front of her bikini bottom.

She playfully hit him. "Don't be fresh. And next time make sure the bedroom door is locked. Our son rushes into our room and discovers his father doing that to his mother."

"He has to learn sometime."

"Don't be disgusting."

Stephanos ran over to his parents, spraying sand over them. "Mommy, I'm hungry."

Soula sprang up off the mat. "Can't I ever relax?"

Stephanos jumped up and down. "Mommy, please, can't we go into Voúla. I want ice cream. And I want to ride in the spacecraft. Oh, please, Mommy, please."

"We can have ice cream here at the beach, it's less money," she said.

Andreas took his wife's arm. "Let's go into Voúla. It's a short walk—and the Elite Café has wonderful pastries."

She smiled sternly at her husband and his sneaking passion for sweets. "You're a big baby, you know that?"

Ten minutes later the Vassos family strolled into Voúla. Soula had wrapped her slender body in a beach sarong and her husband had slipped into an oversized brown T-shirt.

"Mommy. Daddy. The spacecraft," Stephanos shouted, breaking away and dashing for the mechanical ride in front of the Elite Café.

Andreas swung his son up into the cockpit. He dug a five-drachma piece out of his handbag, inserted it in the slot, and stepped back to watch as the toy sprang to life.

"Major Vassos," a voice called out.

Andreas Vassos looked up and groaned inwardly when he saw the policeman approaching them, a glow of recognition lighting up the officer's face. He immediately regretted the decision to come into town. Now the local cops would know he was in Voúla and would feel that a visiting dignitary had to be entertained. Just once, Vassos thought in desperation, I'd like to be a private citizen on vacation with his family.

It was a little after eleven o'clock when the No. 122 bus lumbered out of the winding streets onto Voúla's main plaza. About a dozen passengers remained aboard; the rest had gotten off at the beaches along the route. George Sanida drew the bus to a stop at the light. Glancing up into the mirror, he saw the blond tourist sitting in the back. She was studying a map spread open across her lap. A black Ford Escort pulled alongside and stopped. Sanida looked down into the car and saw two men. The driver was sitting alone while another man sat in the back. They're not Greeks, Sanida thought. Greek men sit up front with the driver; to do otherwise is rude.

He could not see the driver clearly. The passenger was a fat man with bulging cheeks; he wore a watch with a heavy gold band. Americans or Germans, he thought, looking back at the traffic signal.

The light turned green.

The Ford bounded ahead.

Sanida maneuvered the motor coach around the maze of parking medians and into the bus terminal, which was on the edge of a vacant lot bordered by walnut and cypress trees. The last stop.

Passengers began to file from the bus. The blond tourist remained in her seat, studying her map.

Sanida slid out of his seat and, moving to the back of the bus, sat down beside her. *"Parlez-vous Français?"* he asked.

"No, I'm Canadian. From Vancouver."

Shit, he thought, knowing his English was bad. "I help you?" he said, pointing to the map.

"Would you, please? My girlfriend told me there was a wonderful pay beach here in Voúla that only costs fifteen drachmas to get in."

Shit, the only damn words he understood were beach and drachmas. He smiled, nodding understanding, moving in close to study the map, admiring the fine blond hair on her legs. She was blond all over, he thought, and felt his blood stir.

"Beach," he said, stabbing the map with his finger.

"Pay beach? Drachmas?" she said, brushing two fingers against her thumb to indicate money.

"Yes, yes, pay money."

"How . . . me . . . get . . . there?" she asked, walking two fingers in front of her.

He struggled to give directions in English. She shook her head, not understanding. Realizing he was not making himself understood, he took her hand and led her up to the front of the empty bus. He began to point the way to the pay beach. While he was doing this he saw the Ford Escort was double-parked alongside the police car in front of the Elite Café, just a block away from the terminal. The passenger in the back of the car picked something up from the floor and passed it over the top of the seat to the driver. George Sanida stopped talking, wide-eyed with disbelief. The driver of the Ford got out and stood by the open door looking around. The fat man rolled down the window and pointed the barrel of a machine gun at the outdoor café.

The driver stuck his head into the car and said something

to the man in the backseat. The fat man lowered the weapon and sat back.

George Sanida shouted at the tourist.

"I don't speak Greek," she said, unnerved by his sudden change of tone.

"Look! Look! They have guns," he shouted, jabbing his finger against the windshield.

She shrugged her shoulders, smiled nervously.

Frustrated at not being understood, the bus driver grabbed the back of her head and forced her to look in the direction of the Ford Escort.

"I don't know what you want me to see," she said, noticing the man one block away who was standing by the open car door.

"Look!" he shouted in Greek.

Her face showed utter confusion. She saw the man standing by the open door reach inside and slide something off the front seat. A fat man got out of the backseat of the car. When she saw what both men were holding in their hands, she clutched her chest and gasped.

"Nai! Nai!" Yes, yes, he shouted, using both hands to mime the firing of a machine gun.

Takis Milaraki was wiping off a table when the sound of a blaring horn caused him to look up from his work. His eyes drifted to the bus depot. A blond woman was leaning out the front door, shouting, gesticulating. Someone had his hand pressed down on the bus's horn. Takis looked around. People were taking their late-morning coffee, eating pistachios. A waiter made his way among the tables, carrying a tray laden with desserts. Everything seemed normal. He looked back to the bus. What the hell was that crazy woman doing? The bus was backing out of the depot, but she was still leaning out the front door. She appeared to be stabbing her finger in the direction of the police car. His gaze darted to the police car and then he saw the two strangers moving up onto the side-walk. "My God!"

He had heard him lecture on methods of interrogation at the Police College, the policeman told Vassos. The major smiled, thinking of how he was going to get rid of the pest. Then frightened screams startled Vassos; distracted, he stopped watching the policeman. Suddenly a curiously muf-fled sound of gunfire echoed across the square.

Andreas Vassos hurled himself at his wife, throwing her down on top of the toy spacecraft and protecting her and son with his own body. The policeman to whom he had been talking had his revolver out when a chunk of lead plowed into his face, causing him to topple backward.

The officer by the newsstand dropped the phone and made a grab for his weapon as a spray of bullets stitched its way across his chest, hurling him back into the stand where he slumped awkwardly to the ground.

Panicked people ran screaming in all directions; others flat-tened themselves on the ground, playing dead, praying for deliverance. Vassos could hear his wife saying calming things to their son. He raised his head and saw the dead policeman. His eyes focused on the nearest officer's revolver. The two killers were heading for a double-parked car. Vassos reacted instinctively. "Stay down," he shouted. He slid off his wife and got on the ground; he crawled toward the revolver. Grab-bing it, he got to his feet and, running crouched, put some distance between himself and his family before he threw him-self behind an upturned table and fired two rounds at the departing killers.

The tall, thin man whirled around, enraged by the chal-lenge. "You cocksucker!" he screamed, leveling his weapon at the prone crowd.

The slow-moving but curiously graceful fat gunman turned and shouted at his partner, "Frankie, don't! Let's get the fuck outta here."

Heeding him, the other man raised his weapon and turned to run for the car.

Vassos fired two more rounds double action. The thin man stumbled into a Citroën and slumped to the ground, blood staining the back of his shirt. The other, furious at the sight of his wounded friend, ran back, firing bursts of parabellum bullets into the helpless victims lying on the terrace of the café. Hysterical people leaped up off the ground and made desperate dashes for safety only to be cut down by the lethal spray of bullets.

The wounded gunman propped himself up against the Citroën's front wheel. The fat killer ran back to him and, clutching him under the shoulders, helped him up off the ground.

Vassos, crouched behind the table, opened the cylinder of the revolver to check on how many rounds he had fired; two live ones were left. He closed the cylinder.

The fat one held his partner in one arm as the two men backed away together toward their car, their weapons pointed in the direction of the carnage. Vassos popped out from behind the table and fired his last two rounds at the retreating killers. The wounded man sagged in the other man's embrace. The fat man, with his wounded friend in tow, continued to back up toward the car while responding with a deadly burst of fire.

Vassos picked the table up by its metal leg; using it as a shield, he charged the killers. The fat killer fired at him. Bullets impacted on the table, striking the metal base and hurling the shield up into Vassos's face, knocking him unconscious.

The still-untouched gunman pushed his badly wounded partner into the front seat of the Ford and ran around to the driver's side. He had just gotten behind the wheel when George Sanida rammed the car broadside with his bus, wrapping the Ford's frame around the rear of the police car. A burst of gunfire from inside the Ford hurled the blond tourist up out of the door well, splaying her body over the dirty floor.

"Murderers!" Sanida screamed as he ground the transmission into reverse and then roared back, aiming the shattered grill of his bus at the smoldering Ford. The bus shot forward, crashing into the Ford. Metal twisted. Glass shattered. The force of the impact pushed the scraping mass up onto the sidewalk. Bodies lay among the upturned tables and chairs. Bewildered people tottered from doorways. And a young woman in a beach sarong lay limp over a dead child inside a toy spacecraft while her unconscious husband lay in a pool of blood.

Sirens screamed in the distance.

George Sanida was sprawled across the steering wheel, listening to the steam billowing from the mangled grill. His body was soaked in sweat and a stream of hot urine coursed down his leg. He struggled up out of the jump seat and stumbled over to the dead tourist. He knelt beside her, crying silently. He brushed her hair from her face, mouthed the words "thank you," then bent and kissed her stilled lips. Her lifeless legs were spread in an unladylike way, so he reached out under the driver's seat, pulled out an oil-soaked blanket, and covered her. He became conscious of people outside the bus screaming curses. Pushing himself up off the floor, he looked out the window and saw an angry crowd hurling maledictions at the wreckage.

A thin man, covered in blood, was struggling out of the car's shattered window. A large flap of skin hung down over his jawbone.

The crowd watched. Waited.

Sanida found himself cheering the man's efforts. He watched as he wiggled his way on top of the wreckage and fell to the ground. The wounded man tried to get up, only to fall backward onto his haunches. He looked up, his hard eyes glaring at the crowd, a strange expression of contempt curling his lips. Sanida grabbed a wrench from the emergency tool chest under the driver's seat and leaped down off the bus. Plunging through the crowd, he pushed his way up to the killer and began beating him with the tool.

The crowd surged forward.

Takis Milaraki lay on his back, his hands feebly pressing a slimy mass back into his stomach. Dimly aware of the noise around him, he blinked several times in an effort to make out what it was that he saw in the sky. A vaguely familiar form was floating down toward him. He squeezed his lids tightly closed to clear his vision. Now he could see clearly. Drifting in the sky were his beloved islands. They were silhouetted against a blue canvas, beckoning him. "I'm coming," he moaned, and then he died.

2

olonel Dimitri Pappas sat behind his spindle-legged
desk on the fifth floor of 173 Leoforos Alexandras,
studying field reports on the recent consolidation of
the gendarmerie and the city police into one national
department, the Hellenic Police. Each report stated
that the unification was an unqualified success. Pappas knew
better; it was cover-your-ass time in the department. The
politicians wanted one national police force and the officer
corps was not about to go against the politicians who had the
power to approve or disapprove their promotions. It was incredible to Pappas that, under the new system, the mayor of
Athens—or the mayor of any city or village—would no
longer have any say in the running of their local police. A
bad omen. It reminded Pappas of the days of the junta; the
dark, bloody days of the colonels.

Dimitri Pappas commanded the Athens and Salonica Security Prefecture, which encompassed the plainclothes and
intelligence forces of Athens, Voúla, and Glifádha. He had
begun his career in the gendarmerie thirty-two years ago. At
that time the city police force was responsible for Athens,
Patras, and Corfu; the gendarmerie policed the rest of the
country.

Pappas had broad shoulders, narrow hips, and a mane of

silver hair. His chin had long ago merged with his neck, leaving his chin with no definition. He loved wearing jacketlike Greek shirts but, when forced to by the occasion, he would don his uniform. This morning he wore a light blue shirt with gray slacks and brown shoes.

Pappas had just reached for another report when his door burst open and his adjutant, Lieutenant Sokos, blurted, "There's been a massacre in Voúla."

The wop-wop-wop sound of the helicopter's main rotors became Voúla's death dirge as Pappas and his adjutant left the craft and ran through a whirlwind of dirt and paper toward the waiting police car. The sergeant who met Pappas delivered his report as they drove to the scene. The initial investigation showed eleven dead, eighteen wounded. Two of the dead had been policemen; they died with their guns drawn.

A cordon of police had sealed off the village from the rest of the world; all domestic and international flights out of Athens had been grounded; ferries and hydrofoils leaving Piraeus had been ordered to remain at their docks. Security Division investigators had been rushed to Voúla and a temporary headquarters had been established in the Ionian and Popular Bank of Greece across the street from the Elite Café.

Looking out the window of the car, Pappas could see policemen struggling to restrain grieving relatives and friends. The crime scene had been roped off, a frozen zone established. A shaken driver sat on the ground next to his bus answering investigators' questions, still unsure of exactly what had happened. Lieutenant Sokos rushed up to Pappas. Looking at his adjutant's ashen face, Pappas thought: he does not function well under pressure. "Well, are you going to tell me the result of the preliminary or do I have to drag it out of you?" Pappas growled.

Sokos's head made small nervous shakes. "Most of the witnesses confirm that the two killers stood on the curb and without warning fired into the crowd. They used Ingram model two submachine guns equipped with sound suppressors."

"What have we found out about these brave killers?" Pappas asked, staring grimly at the café's pockmarked facade.

"They're Americans."

"What did you say?"

"Americans," repeated the adjutant, handing the colonel two passports.

Pappas examined the photographs pasted inside the official documents. Frank Simmons, age 32, born New York City. George Cuttler, age 34, born New York City. Both passports had been stamped by Athens customs control. The killers had entered Greece five days ago. He noted that both passports had been recently issued and that they bore no other country's admittance stamp. They came here to kill, Pappas thought, looking over at the body bags awaiting transport. At that moment Pappas knew that the reason for the massacre would be found only in New York.

Sokos was talking. ". . . Simmons tried to escape. The people ran after him, there was a struggle, and Simmons was killed."

Pappas gave his adjutant a long, hard look. He's learning how to lie, maybe there's some hope for him. "And this George Cuttler?"

"He was rushed alive to the hospital in Glifádha."

"Where are the rest of the wounded?"

"Some are here in the hospital, and some went to Glifádha, and the rest to Vouliagméni."

The adjutant stopped and swallowed nervously. "We also found four thousand dollars U.S. and two first-class tickets on Olympic Flight 411 leaving Athens at twelve fifty-five today."

Tapping the passports against his palm, Pappas said, "I don't think our American friends are going to make their flight."

The lieutenant handed Pappas four grainy photographs. "These were taken from Simmons's body."

Pappas opened the evidence bag and took out the pictures. They showed two men relaxing in a taverna. "Who are they?"

"The one on the right is Tasos Lefas, and the one on the left is Lakis Rekor. They're the two policemen who were killed here this morning."

Pappas looked at his adjutant. "What else?"

The lieutenant paled. His eyes fell to the roadway. "Sir, Major Vassos was on the scene when the shooting began. He picked up one of the dead policemen's guns and shot Frank Simmons. The major was hurt, but . . ."

"But what, Lieutenant?"

"Major Vassos's wife and son were killed, sir."

Pappas gasped, his face sagging in anguish. He sucked his lower lip into his mouth and dug his teeth into it.

The rotors were winding down when the door opened and a tall man rushed down the large helicopter's steps into Voúla's main square. Colonel Pappas waited outside the blades' arc. Antonis Vitos, the Minister of Public Order, walked over quickly to meet his old friend.

"It looks like we have a bad one on our hands," Vitos said, shaking the colonel's hand.

"Yes, it does," Pappas agreed, leading the minister away from the aircraft, noting the black pouches under his eyes and the disturbing raspiness in his voice. Vitos had aged a lot since they joined the gendarmerie together so many years ago. But then, I guess I've changed too, Pappas conceded.

"What facts can you give me, Dimitri?"

"I'm afraid that we don't have very much to go on, yet, Minister."

"I have to tell Papandreou something," Vitos said, walking beside the colonel.

"You can tell the prime minister that there were two of them, and that they were both Americans."

A mask of disbelief froze on the minister's face. "Are you sure?"

"Yes. We found their passports."

"Were they terrorists?"

"I don't believe so. The evidence so far suggests that they came here for the sole purpose of killing two policemen."

"Bastards," Vitos said, lighting up a cigarette. "What do we know about the policemen?"

"I've sent to Athens for their folders." The minister watched three policemen struggle to restrain a hysterical woman. His thoughts seemed to wander.

Pappas waited.

Suddenly Vitos was roused from his lethargy. "What have you told the press?"

"Only the barest of facts. And nothing about the Americans or the two dead policemen."

"Good. Don't tell them anything."

"I've taken it upon myself to have telephone service in and out of Voúla cut off, except for to and from the bank that we're using as our headquarters."

"A wise precaution, Dimitri."

"Do you want to inform the American embassy?"

"Not yet. Wait until we know more." Vitos softened. "What about the woman who was killed helping the bus driver?"

"Her name was Debra Wright. A schoolteacher from Vancouver. She was twenty-four years old."

Vitos threw his cigarette down and ground it out with his heel. "Bastards. Have you notified the Canadians?"

"Yes."

"See to it that her body is sent home as quickly as possible. Cut all the red tape. And Dimitri, I want an honor guard of *evzones* to accompany her body home."

"I'll see to it, sir."

They moved over to the crime scene and watched in silence as body bags were solemnly lifted into the back of an ambulance.

"It is unbelievable that such a thing could happen here," Vitos said.

Pappas sighed and said quietly, "With all the terrorist attacks and the assassination of ten PLO members in Athens over the past six years, our people are learning to live with violence."

"Every one of the incidents you've just mentioned was directed against foreign nationals. But this?" He swept his hand across the crime scene. "This was aimed at Greeks. Why, Dimitri? Why?"

"We don't know yet," Pappas answered, the cries of wailing women catching his attention. His fists clenched tightly. "But I promise you that we will know and that the people responsible will be made to pay dearly." His face clouded. "Major Vassos was here in Voúla with his family on vacation. The major's wife and son were killed."

Vitos grabbed his friend's arm and spoke in a low tone of warning: "Be careful how you handle this case, Dimitri. There are foreign nationals involved. We don't want any problems with the Americans."

"I understand."

"Good. Has anyone questioned the injured American?"

"I'm going to Glifádha now," Pappas said. "I've already sent a man ahead to ask the hospital to keep him conscious. I'm anxious to have a chat with our Mr. Cuttler."

Vitos placed a hand on his classmate's shoulder. "Dimitri, please remember what I told you; no problems with the Americans. Be discreet when you question Cuttler."

"I'm always discreet, Antonis."

Pappas sat in the passenger seat of the small, unmarked police car. His driver, a corporal, was a skinny man with a thick nose that had been broken in three places when a husband had unexpectedly returned home and the corporal found it necessary to dive out of an upstairs bedroom window. Pappas told his driver not to park on the hospital grounds. There was a lot of traffic inside; the colonel did not want to have his official car boxed in as a result of the Greek penchant for parking anywhere and then taking the keys with them. He might have to leave in a hurry.

The Asklipeion Hospital in Glifádha was on Miramare Street, just off the coastal road, on the same corner where the No. 122 bus made a left hand turn into the village of Voúla. The main building had two wings coming out at forty-five-degree angles from the central structure and was partially hidden behind a screen of cypress and eucalyptus trees.

Pappas got out of the car. Turning around, he stretched his arms out over the car's roof, gazing across the road at the sea. A cruise ship glided across the horizon; a barkentine followed in her wake, its sails billowing. The beach was crowded. Yachts tugged gently at their anchors and the masts of boats swayed to the lap of the waves. Sucking in a mouthful of sea air, he turned and hurried past the hospital gate onto the grounds.

A detail of one sergeant and five policemen had been rushed to the hospital to maintain order and to guard the prisoner, Cuttler. Much to his annoyance, Pappas discovered the sergeant, a fat, slovenly man about forty, standing outside the emergency room entrance smoking a cigarette.

The sergeant saw Pappas hurrying up the path and quickly tossed the butt away.

"Where is your prisoner, Sergeant?" Pappas asked, looking down at the burning cigarette.

"He's in examining room D, Colonel."

"And am I safe in assuming that someone is guarding him, or have your men also abandoned their posts?"

Flustered, the sergeant answered, "He's guarded, sir. I only stepped outside for a minute or two."

"A minute or two is all it takes, Sergeant. If anything has happened to that prisoner, I'll personally see to it that you end your career teaching the Syrtaki to Albanian tourists."

"It won't happen again, sir," the sergeant said, rushing to open the door.

Doctors rushed up and down the corridors examining charts, holding hurried consultations. Walking into the emergency room, Pappas told the sergeant that he wanted to speak to the doctor who had treated the American. The sergeant hurried off, returning within a matter of minutes with the doctor.

"I'm Dr. Christopoulos. As you can see, Colonel, I'm a bit busy this morning."

"I only need a few seconds of your time, Doctor," Pappas said, slipping his arm through the doctor's and leading him off to the side. "How is this Cuttler?"

"He has compound fractures of both arms and both legs. His right shoulder is crushed, as are most of his ribs. Several of his ribs have punctured his lungs and there is internal bleeding."

"Has he been operated on yet?"

"As you requested, we waited until you got here. And, he has been given only mild sedation."

"When do you expect to operate on him?"

"There are only four operating rooms in this hospital— they are all full of Greek citizens. There are many who are more seriously wounded than the American. But, he should be under the knife in about forty minutes or so."

Pappas leaned in close to the medical man and whispered, "There is no rush, my friend. Take care of our people first."

The doctor wiped his arm across his brow. "I agree," he said, and walked away.

Colonel Pappas pushed the curtain aside and motioned the policeman from the room.

"See that I'm not disturbed," Pappas commanded the departing officer.

George Cuttler lay naked on a gurney, a sheet neatly folded across his groin. A tube ran from his arm up to a bottle that hung from a steel pole. His head was propped on a small

rubber pillow. Both his knees were skewed over the sides of
the gurney; shards of bone protruded from scarlet fissures on
his arms and legs. His shoulders were awkwardly positioned
and his eyes were closed.

Pappas noticed that his ears were small and clove-shaped;
he watched the waves of fat roll over Cuttler's hairless body
every time he breathed. He looks more like a circus freak
than a professional killer, Pappas thought, moving up to the
hospital trolley. "How do you feel?"

Cuttler's eyes fluttered open, focusing on the stranger.

"How do you feel?" Pappas repeated in flawless English
while his eyes surveyed the tiny, bare cubicle.

"They gave me a shot for the fucking pain, but it's wearin'
off," Cuttler groaned.

Pappas moved up to the cream-colored medical cabinet
that was against the wall. "I'd give you some more, George,
but unfortunately, we're running somewhat short this morning."

"Where'd you learn your English?" Cuttler asked as his fat
face grimaced in pain.

Studying the contents of the cabinet, Pappas said, "When
I was a young man I worked as a waiter on cruise ships. I
learned to speak English, French, and German." He opened
the cabinet door and, reaching inside, removed two plastic
bottles of peroxide. He put the bottles down and lightly
touched Cuttler's leg.

Cuttler let out an anguished howl.

Pappas snatched his hand back. "Oh, I'm sorry, George. I
didn't realize that you hurt there."

Wincing, Cuttler said, "Don't touch, okay? That painkiller
is wearing off." His eyes widened with suspicion. "Who are
you, anyway?"

Pappas picked up one of the bottles and unscrewed the cap.
"I'm Colonel Dimitri Pappas, Security Division, Athens Station, Hellenic Police." Tossing the cap aside, he leaned over

the American. "George, I've been a policeman for most of my adult life. And during that time I've seen a lot of people do a lot of stupid things. But what you and Frank Simmons did this morning is memorable in its imbecility." He shoved his face close. "Did you really think that you could slaughter our people and then calmly waltz your ass onto the next flight back to the States?"

Cuttler turned his head away. "I wanna see someone from the American embassy. I got my fucking rights."

Pappas smiled. "Ah, yes, your famous American rights. Well, I really don't have the time to discuss them with you. So, I'm going to ask you a few simple questions, and you will give me a few simple answers. Who paid you to kill the two policemen? Why did that person want them killed? Who was your contact in Greece? And anything else that you might want to tell me."

"Fuck you. I wanna see—"

Pappas calmly poured peroxide over the shard of bone protruding from Cuttler's left leg.

A piercing shriek exploded from the prisoner. Waves of fat heaved over his body as it levitated up off the gurney and cartwheeled onto the cold floor. Screaming, Cuttler rolled from side to side, shards of bone hitting against the floor, the wheels of the gurney.

Two policemen rushed into the room. Pappas calmly shooed them back outside. Grabbing the other bottle, Pappas knelt down beside the writhing prisoner and began to unscrew the cap. "Are you going to tell me, George?"

Pappas then appeared to have second thoughts; he reached under his shirt jacket and slid out his revolver. Gripping the weapon by its barrel, the colonel slammed the butt of the weapon against the bone jutting from the prisoner's left leg.

Thirty-seven minutes later, Pappas stuck his face out of the cubicle and motioned the policeman back. "See to our guest. He slipped off the trolley."

■   ■   ■

The green unmarked police car turned onto Cathedral Square. The five-kilometer trip along the coast road from Glifádha to Athens had taken a bit over a half hour, with the blue roof light on.

"Do you want me to go with you?" the corporal asked Pappas.

"I want you to stay with the car and radio Lieutenant Sokos to meet me here with those folders. I'm anxious to see what we can find out about our two dead heroes."

The corporal reached out for the handset. Pappas shoved open the door and squeezed out of the car. Walking across the tiled square, he came to the twelfth-century Byzantine Church of Aghios Eleutherios, which nestled in the shadow of the cathedral. He stopped and examined the old marble walls and the frieze of the Attic festal calendar, the bas-reliefs of symbolic beasts and heraldic designs, wondering as his eyes ran over them if life was any simpler then.

Walking across the plaza toward Plaka, the old city of Athens, which was tucked away on the northern and southern slopes of the Acropolis, he spied the huge red-and-white banner stretched across the street, proclaiming in English: WEL- COME TO FLEA MARKET OF PANDROSSOU STREET. We've become the damn flea market of the tourist world, he thought, moving into the narrow streets lined with shops. The windows of jewelry stores sparkled with gold trinkets. Shills beckoned from doorways.

When he reached the corner of Kapnikareas Street, Pappas turned left and stopped in front of number Forty-three. The peeling gold letters on the glass door spelled: ORHAN ISKUR, OBJETS D'ART. A dirty shade covered the other side of the door. Pappas checked the time. 2:11. Siesta time throughout Greece. But not here in Plaka. Here the rhythm of life was determined by the ebb and flow of the tourists. Pappas tried the door and was surprised to find it was open. The overhead bells tinkled as he slipped inside. The store was empty; quiet save for the monotonous hum of three ceiling fans. Horse-shoe-shaped display cases filled with copies of antiquities lined the walls of the shop. Rugs and kilims covered the wood floors.

There was a door behind the display case. Pappas went behind the counter, reached out, turned the doorknob, and pushed the door open. He stepped into a cluttered storage area. There were boxes of *calyx kraters* and wine jugs, racks of silver-plated bowls with handles in the form of human heads, and there were funeral *stelae*, ranks of *amphorae*, and rows of Euphronios kraters. It was a junkyard of obvious and rather crude imitations.

Two cats darted out from behind the amphorae and disappeared behind cartons overflowing with plumed helmets. Cats, used before refrigeration to protect the meat from rats, now overran Greece. There was a short hallway that led from the storage area to a door. Pappas moved cautiously along the passage, sliding his revolver out from under his shirt jacket. He reached the door and stopped; listening as he quietly worked the knob. Finding it unlocked, he hurled the door open and fell into a combat stance. "Shit!"

The body lay on its back with the feet protruding from behind an ornate desk. A high-backed chair lay on its side close to the head. A trickle of dried blood ran from the small hole in the dead man's eyebrow. The mouth was open, revealing many gold teeth; one eye was open, one closed. A shocked expression had congealed on the dead man's face. An armchair stood in front of the desk. The killer must have been sitting there when he shot him, Pappas reasoned.

Orhan Iskur knew his murderer, trusted him; Orhan Iskur did not trust many people.

Pappas knelt next to the body and placed his hand on the forehead. It was cold, clammy. The beginning contractions of rigor mortis had stiffened the head and neck. You made one deal too many, Pappas thought, lifting up the right hand, examining the inch-long pinkie nail. A Turkish affectation, a man wore that nail long to demonstrate that he made his living by using his brain rather than his hands. He dropped the wrist.

Pappas's first contact with Orhan Iskur had been in October of '71. Rubens' *Christ on the Cross* had been stolen that past September in Liege, Belgium. Interpol had sent an all-stations flash to Athens advising that they had confidential information that Iskur was negotiating for the sale of the stolen Rubens with a German collector. Pappas did a fast check on Iskur and discovered that he was a man of Turkish origins who had acquired Greek citizenship and presently lived and worked in Athens. Iskur had been one of the many former Allied operatives who after World War II used their old boy intelligence network to deal in stolen and plundered art works.

When Pappas questioned the Turk, Iskur denied any knowledge of the stolen painting. He was a mere dealer in tourist trinkets, he had reassured Pappas. Iskur was put under tight surveillance for several months. No illegal activities were observed and the stakeout was terminated.

Pappas had concealed his surprise when George Cuttler told him that he and Frank Simmons had been met at the airport by a Turk named Orhan who had gold teeth and a long pinkie nail on his right hand.

It had been Orhan, Cuttler told Pappas, who supplied them with the weapons, and it had been Orhan who got them the rooms in the Orion Hotel in Athens; Orhan who gave them the photographs of the policemen and got them the black Ford and gave them the emergency telephone number that turned out to be the one at his own store. Iskur had also set up a very clever escape route for them.

Pappas removed his handkerchief and carefully put it over the billfold lying next to the body. It contained sixteen thousand drachmas and a great many credit cards. Jade worry beads strung on a gold strand lay next to the body. Pappas picked them up and fingered them. He liked the way they felt; he dropped them into his shirt pocket. The appointment book on top of the desk contained only blank pages; Iskur obviously carried his schedule in his head. The desk drawers were stuffed with invoices and worthless artifacts.

Pappas stood in the center of the room staring at the cartons of swords and helmets stacked on the leather sofa. A painting on silk of a fish hung on the wall. Pappas recognized Dvogvos's bold signature. He searched the closet and looked behind paintings and under rugs. He rummaged through cartons. Finding nothing, he stared down at the body. Gray nylon socks had collapsed around the corpse's marble white ankles. Damn, Dimitri, do this the right way. He covered the handset of the telephone with his handkerchief, lifted it, and dialed Athens headquarters.

Lieutenant Kanakis, a tall gangling cop with a boyish face, led the search team that screeched to a stop ten minutes later in front of 43 Kapnikareas Street. Orhan Iskur's store was methodically taken apart by the Security Division's special team. Electrical fixtures and plates were removed from walls and ceilings; moldings were pried from baseboards; floor coverings were taken up; rugs and furniture were vacuumed, the fibers carefully deposited into plastic evidence bags. All the papers were removed from drawers and cabinets and then indexed and cross-referenced. Photographs were taken; fingerprints were lifted.

Pappas moved about, supervising the operations, his hands behind his back, fingering his newly acquired worry beads. He watched as plastic bags were placed over the hands and tied around the wrists of the corpse in order to preserve any scrapings that might be wedged under the nails or in the crevices of the hand.

Outside, Security Division investigators moved up and down the street, canvassing for witnesses. Uniformed officers maintained a security zone in front of the shop, chasing away the curious. Shopkeepers grumbled; they were losing business. Lieutenant Sokos appeared in the doorway with two folders tucked under his arm. He looked a bit like a very worried accountant, an impression reinforced by his prematurely graying hair. "Here are the files on the dead officers," he said, handing them to Pappas.

Looking around the store for some quiet place and finding none, Pappas went out into the street, using the folders to shield his face from the sunlight, and crossed the street to his adjutant's official car. It was parked half up on the narrow sidewalk, blocking the front of a clothing store whose owner was locked in argument with a nearby policeman. Pappas slid into the rear of the car; Sokos got into the front. The lieutenant told his driver to go grab a smoke; draping one arm over the seat, he turned and watched the colonel study the files on the two murdered policemen.

Fifteen minutes later, Pappas looked up into his adjutant's blank face. "Have you studied these?"

"Yes, sir, on the way here."

"And your conclusion?"

Sokos hesitated. "Well, I'm not really sure. I . . . ."

"Damn it, Spiro," Pappas said, using the adjutant's first name in order to take some of the sting out of the admonition. "You must learn to make judgments on the given facts. You read their folders. Now tell me what you think."

"I think that both officers lived above their means. They both recently bought apartments in an expensive neighborhood, and—"

A knock on the car's roof interrupted them.

"Yes?" Pappas said to the sergeant who was staring into the car.

"Lieutenant Kanakis sent me to get you, sir. He's found something."

Pappas got out of the car and returned to the cool, dark interior of the shop. Kanakis's head and shoulders were visible above the amphora. He was kneeling before a row of the tall, two-handled storage jars, examining one.

WILLIAM J. CAUNITZ ════════════════════ 29

"What have you found?" Pappas asked, edging carefully along the row. Kanakis looked past the colonel and nodded hello to Lieutenant Sokos. "I think this amphora might be real, Colonel."

Pappas looked at the storage vessel and made a dismissive grunt. "Junk, the same as the rest of them."

"I don't think so, sir," Kanakis insisted.

Pappas's face showed impatience. He knelt next to the lieutenant. There *was* a spirited freshness about this amphora. The oranges were bright; the blacks were the pitch-black of night, and the blues, the blue of a Greek morning. The scenes depicted were alive, real. Ancient times were reborn.

"I studied art history, Colonel," Kanakis said in a low voice. "I'm no expert, but I think that this piece might be the real thing."

There was a strangely regal quality about it, Pappas admitted to himself as he slid his hand over the side and up to the rim. Kneeling upright, he stretched his arm down into the vessel. His fingers encountered a cold, granulated substance. Scooping up a handful, he held his palm up to show the lieutenant.

"Black sand," Pappas said.

A priest chanted the litany of prayers for the dead. Women clustered in front of the grocery store making keening, howling cries, crossing themselves. The sounds were as ancient as the chorus from *Agamemnon*. The stairway was crowded with milling people; the elevator was stuck on the fifth floor.

Pappas shouldered his way up to the third floor. As he pushed his way into the dead policeman's apartment on Euphorinos Street, the air pressed in on him. He glanced at the time. Five P.M. Had it all begun a bare six hours ago? He thought of the fishing boats returning to their berths at Piraeus. He was going to miss the *Peripato*, the habitual evening stroll around the harbor. There would be no cold *demestica* to wash down the eels and crayfish. Not this evening; this evening Pappas would be looking for the truth.

A dazed woman was slumped into an armchair in the living room. Other women stood around her trying to comfort and console her.

Lakis Rekor's widow, he concluded, knowing that there was no way that he would be able to question the distraught woman, at least not for a while. He noticed the doilies on the backs and arms of the furniture and wondered why women loved to crochet them. He moved unnoticed through the crowded apartment to the open door that led out onto the terrace. Two men were sitting at a table, drinking, smoking, picking at the plates of snacks, seemingly oblivious to the commotion going on around them.

Stepping outside, Pappas lowered himself into a chair, saying, "I'm looking for Thanos and Kostas Koukoudeas."

"And who are you?" one man asked abruptly. His hair was black, and he had thick, dark eyebrows over deep-set, somber brown eyes.

Pappas introduced himself. "I've come to offer my condolences."

"I'm Thanos," the one with the brown eyes said. "This is my brother, Kostas."

Pappas figured Thanos to be the younger of the two brothers. Kostas, his heavily jowled face and gleaming, shaven head supported by a thick neck, was a man in his middle forties. The colonel poured ouzo into a glass and added water, watching as the clear liquid turned milky. "Your brother-in-law was Lakis Rekor?"

Both brothers wore open-collared shirts and were watching the policeman with troubled expressions.

"Yes. He was married to our sister," Kostas Koukoudeas said.

Pappas ripped off a piece of bread and swept it across the *taramosalata*.

"Your brother-in-law was a good policeman. A brave man," Pappas said, and tossed the bread into his mouth.

Kostas's worried eyes fixed on Pappas. "Lakis always wanted to be a policeman."

"Yes, most of us do," Pappas said, digging a chunk of bread into a bowl of *gigantes*, pushing the huge kidney-shaped beans onto the bread. "We know that we'll never be rich, but it's a way of getting out of the village and securing a steady job with a pension. And, of course"—he stopped and ate the gigantes—"there is always the chance of making some fast money."

The brothers shifted uneasily in their seats.

"I have to ask you a few questions," Pappas said.

"Of course, we'll do anything to help," Thanos said.

"I thought you might," Pappas replied, taking out his notepad and flipping it open. He read aloud the dead policemen's official biographies. Both of them had come from the island of Kos. They were appointed to the gendarmerie together on June 1, 1979. They went through recruit school together; they did their probation together on the island of Crete, after which they were assigned together to the duty station on the island of Thíra. On October 9, 1984, both officers submitted form E 6c Request For Transfer. When the police force was consolidated they were reassigned to the Athens patrol district. "From the record they appear to have been close friends," Pappas said, looking up from his notes.

"They grew up together," Kostas said. "Both were best man at the other's wedding."

Pappas scooped up some *mezedakia*. "Yes. I've noticed many similarities between them." He ate. "And their families."

The Koukoudeas brothers became guarded.

"How's that?" asked Thanos.

"Well," Pappas said, carefully wiping his fingers on a paper napkin, "it appears that there was a sudden infusion of money into the Koukoudeas and the Lefas families. And this sudden good fortune took place around the same time that Lakis and Tasos requested transfer off of Thíra. Both officers bought expensive apartments in Athens. And all on a salary of fifty drachmas a month. Their wives must be wonderful managers."

Thanos stole a look at his brother.

"We wouldn't know anything about their finances," Kostas said.

"Wouldn't you?" Pappas said, sipping ouzo, checking his notes. He read aloud. "Thanos Koukoudeas, worked as a waiter in Pappa Spiros until November of 'eighty-four. Kostas Koukoudeas, worked as a tour guide for Atlas Tours until December of 'eighty-four. Both brothers left good-paying jobs to open the Taverna Apollo on Tripodon Street in Plaka." He watched the brothers closely. "It takes considerable money to open a taverna in Plaka. I have to assume that you both had the good fortune to marry financial wizards."

"We saved our money," Thanos insisted, taking a long sip of ouzo. Drink your courage, my friend, Pappas thought, you're going to need it.

The dirge from inside the apartment grew more intense. The widow ran screaming out onto the terrace and threw herself across Thanos's lap.

"Lakis! They murdered my Lakis!" she wailed.

Both brothers comforted her, helping her up onto her feet and escorting her into the waiting arms of several women. The brothers walked back out onto the terrace. Kostas slid the glass door shut. "I don't know why you're standing on our balls, Colonel. Our sister's husband has been killed in the line of duty, and you're treating us like we're criminals."

"Criminals?" Pappas said with a mock amiability. "You're not criminals, you're businessmen who've had a sudden windfall; unfortunately you've neglected to pay any taxes on that windfall. I believe that you owe our government some money." He sipped his drink, his stare fixed on the two brothers. "And then, of course, there's the small matter of your brother-in-law's pension. I hope that your sister gets it." He drank some more ouzo.

"What do you mean by that?" demanded Kostas.

"Well, you see, police regulations prohibit policemen from engaging in outside occupations or from having a proprietary interest in any business." A frown, a slight shrug of the shoulders. "We know, of course, that many policemen do work on the side and have businesses in their wives' names, or in the name of a family member, such as a brother-in-law."

Beads of sweat suddenly popped out at Thanos's hairline.

"Most of the time," Pappas continued, "the department looks the other way, but when there is a problem, then we must investigate. I believe that Lakis Rekor and Tasos Lefas came into a lot of money while they were assigned to Thíra. And I also think that they used their families to invest that money in businesses. It was Lakis's money that opened the Taverna Apollo." Pappas reached out and pushed aside some of the bottles so that he could have an unrestricted view of the brothers. "We have evidence that shows us that the policemen were the intended victims of the Voúla massacre. And I think that you both know why and who is responsible."

"We don't," Thanos blurted. Even in the half-light, his nervous pallor was obvious.

"Withholding evidence and hindering a police investigation is a very serious matter. Compounded with your tax problems and the loss of your sister's pension, I'd say that you had a few problems that you had better resolve."

The Koukoudeas brothers exchanged nervous looks.

Kostas asked, "Have you spoken to anyone in the Lefas family?"

"Not yet," answered the colonel.

"And if we do tell you what we know?" Thanos asked, a deep flush reddening his ears.

"Then I think it would be safe to assume that some accom-
modation would be reached that would protect your sister's
pension and save your business from the greedy tax collectors."

Kostas wiped his damp hands on his trousers. "It all
began . . ."

3

The measured treads of the evzones echoed over the Tomb of the Unknown Soldier. Clusters of tourists kept a respectable distance, watching the tall soldiers, resplendent in their white tunics, white skirts, white stockings, and heavy, tassled shoes, stride with military precision across the marble pavement of the national monument.

Colonel Pappas had directed his driver to let him out at Syntagma Square so that he might watch the Sunday morning changing of the guard. The Minister of Public Order had called an emergency meeting for 10:00; he had a half hour to spare. The last five days had been hectic ones. The massacre continued to dominate the media. A brutal act of terrorism had been the official lie. Unconfirmed reports hinted that Turks or Cypriot nationals might have been behind the massacre. Disinformation goes a long way in helping to keep the lid on things so that the police can devote their energies to solving the case—or so Pappas had argued.

Damn cloud, Pappas thought, wiping his eyes as he glared at Athens' perpetual shroud of pollution. Making his way along one side of the National Gardens toward the Presidential Palace, Pappas checked his sleeve to make sure that the stain was gone. When Anna, his wife, had pressed his uniform that morning, she'd discovered the spot. "It won't do, Dimitri," she announced, wiping it with a wet rag. "You must look your best when you are with Vitos. Especially when the rest of the wolf pack is going to be there too."

The evzone guards presented arms as Pappas passed them. The colonel returned their salute and hurried into the cream-colored palace. Pappas paused outside the first-floor conference room to tug down the front of his uniform blouse and smooth his thick white hair. He opened the double doors and entered a large room filled with the haze of cigarette smoke. Middle-aged men sat around a polished oval table; a manila folder was in front of each one, as was a silver tray with a glass and a bottle of mineral water. The crystal ashtrays were already filled.

Antonis Vitos, the chief of the Public Order Ministry, chaired the conference; he was at the head of the table. On his right sat Lieutenant General Constantinos Politopoulos, the commanding officer of the Hellenic Police. Politopoulos had a peasant's strong, squat frame and a warm, heavily lined, and intelligent face. His olive drab uniform was exquisitely tailored; the thick wrists and stubby hands sticking out of its sleeves seemed incongruous. The tall, thin older man who sat on the minister's left seemed to carry his own chill with him. His unblinking, reptilian eyes watched everything that was going on without betraying the slightest hint of emotion. This was the mysterious Major General Philippos Tsimas, the head of the Central Information Service, Greece's unpublicized but quite effective intelligence organization. The one man who seemed definitely the odd man out in this gathering was a frail, elderly, and distinguished-looking man with snow-white hair who rested his hands on the curved top of a cane and gave Pappas a single, dignified nod of greeting.

"Talk to me, General Politopoulos," beseeched Vitos. "Tell me what our excellent police have discovered. Prime Minister Papandreou is crawling over my ass for answers, and I'm about to climb over yours, General."

The general clasped his hands in front of him. "Minister, I would prefer to have Colonel Pappas of the Athens Security Prefecture make the report. The investigation is his direct responsibility." You socialist goat fucker, Pappas thought. You're always looking to crawl out from under.

Antonis Vitos looked down the table at his old classmate. "Dimitri, let's hear your report."

CIS smiled. Vitos's use of Pappas's first name did not go unnoticed.

Pappas glanced surreptitiously at his sleeve and began his report, beginning with the when, where, who, what, how, and why of police work used the world over. Cuttler had confessed to participating in the massacre along with his dead accomplice, Frank Simmons. Both men had been approached in New York City by a man known to them as Denny McKay who frequented a bar in New York City called, The Den. McKay had offered them fifty thousand dollars each to come to Greece and kill two policemen, then fly out the same day. They were each to be paid another fifty thousand dollars upon their return to New York.

Cuttler told Pappas that Orhan Iskur had met them at the airport, provided them with the weapons, and given them the photographs of their intended victims. Orhan also provided them with the policemen's addresses and work schedules. "When I asked Cuttler who wanted the policemen killed and why, he told me that he did not know. He and Simmons had never bothered to ask," Pappas said.

"And you believed him?" Vitos asked, an edge of disbelief in his voice.

"Yes, I did," Pappas answered. "Professional killers do not ask why, they only want to know who and how much."

"Do you think that this Denny McKay could have been the source of the money?" Vitos asked, lighting up another cigarette.

"I don't think so," Pappas answered. "I believe that McKay was the contact man. Cuttler told me that McKay, to the best of his knowledge, had never traveled outside the United States. I had our records checked and discovered that the two policemen had never been to the United States. In fact, Lakis Rekor had never left Greece."

"Why did they kill all those people?" Professor Pericles Levi asked softly.

Pappas focused his attention on the professor. "Cuttler told me that once Major Vassos fired at them, they couldn't stop. You see, Professor, there are some people who enjoy killing."

"Merciful God. All those poor people," groaned Pericles Levi, sinking further into his seat.

"Continue, Dimitri," Vitos said, ignoring Levi's distress.

Pappas went on to tell the group about his first meeting with the Turk, the theft of the Rubens, and the old boy intelligence network that Iskur used to move his stolen art. Pappas noted that when he mentioned the intelligence background, General Tsimas, the head of CIS, was suddenly busy studying the tabletop. Pappas wondered if CIS had used Iskur in some fashion. That could be trouble.

When Pappas finished giving his report, the minister asked, "What do we know of the three Americans, Cuttler, Simmons, and this Denny McKay?"

"Nothing," Pappas answered.

"What?" Vitos shouted. "You did not request a background check from the FBI? Why, Dimitri?"

"Because both Simmons and Cuttler are dead, and—"

"Cuttler died?" Vitos said in a surprised tone.

"Yes, several days ago," Pappas said, shuffling papers inside the folder. "An unfortunate accident. It appears that he fell off his bed and several ribs punctured his lungs. Internal bleeding, I'm afraid. I took it upon myself to have the Americans notified that Cuttler and Simmons were innocent tourists killed in the terrorist attack. I explained away the delay in notifying the American authorities by saying that they were unidentified; they did not have their means of identification on them. I've arranged for our government to extend condolences to the Americans."

"Why, Colonel?" General Tsimas asked slyly.

"Because I think it is safe to assume that both Cuttler and Simmons have extensive criminal records, as does their New York contact, Denny McKay. I do not believe knowing the details of those records would be of any help to us now. And since McKay is the only surviving link to the people responsible for the massacre, I think it wise that we do not let anyone outside this room know that we know about McKay. I'd like very much to keep Denny McKay alive."

"Why?" General Tsimas asked, looking at the colonel with open suspicion.

Pappas looked down the table to the professor and said, deadpan, "While we were searching Orhan Iskur's shop, one of my lieutenants discovered an amphora that was half-filled with black sand. It appeared to be genuine, not one of Iskur's fakes, so I had it delivered to Professor Levi at the museum."

Heads turned toward the elderly professor.

Pericles Levi stirred. With his right hand he reached into the folder, took out a glossy nine-by-ten color photograph of the amphora, and held it up so that all the men could see it. The others reached into their folders and removed their copies of the photograph. Colonel Pappas extracted a mechanical pencil from the breast pocket of his uniform blouse and began to sketch the mourning Athena on the cover of his folder.

"If you will look at the scene that is painted on the amphora," Levi began, "you will see that it depicts the struggle of Herakles and the centaur Nessos." Pointing, he continued, "You can also see that the three Gorgons and the Medusa have already been beheaded by Perseus." He sighed. "This amphora, gentlemen, is genuine. We know from original sources that two amphorae were made in Athens in 600 B.C. by the painter Demaratus. The sister of this amphora is on display in the museum. The one in the photograph had been considered lost. We know that a silk merchant from Luxor bought it for his mistress and brought it back to Egypt around 400 B.C." His lips trembled. "I suspect this amphora was used to store an irreplaceable part of our heritage, something that has now been stolen from us."

The sound of tires crunching over gravel outside broke the heavy silence.

Pappas drew pleats into the mourning Athena's chiton.

With a weary sigh, Minister of Public Order Vitos asked, "What has been stolen from us?"

Professor Levi studied his audience, his eyes going from man to man.

Pappas sketched the temple of Poseidon next to his other drawing.

Professor Levi slowly clasped his hands in front of him, and began to talk about Alexander the Great. He lectured on how Alexander's father, Philip, had sent to the island of Lesbos for Aristotle, son of Nicomachus, to teach his son. Aristotle taught the prince about the stars and about navigation. He also taught him many languages and explained the truths of justice, rhetoric, and philosophy.

Levi's frail body produced a surprisingly forceful voice as he told how Aristotle and his pupil spent hours reading the epic poems of Homer, poems called the *Iliad* and the *Odyssey*, poems that were at least three hundred years older than Alexander. Levi spoke about Alexander's belief that the blood of Achilles coursed through his own veins, and how Alexander had implored his teacher to make him a copy of the *Iliad*. And this Aristotle did for the young prince. Aristotle did not employ scribes; he wrote the text out himself and personally presented it to the prince on his birthday. This gift Alexander valued above all his other possessions. Years later, when Alexander had taken the field against his enemies, it was said that he used to sleep with his *Iliad* and a dagger under his pillow, calling the *Iliad* his journey-book of excellence in war.

During the second year of the Persian War, at the battle of

Issus, the most precious of the great King Darius's treasure chests or caskets was captured and brought to Alexander. The king decided that he would store his precious *Iliad* in the chest, and from that moment Alexander's *Iliad* became known as the "casket-copy."

"We know this from the writings of Callisthenes, Aristotle's nephew, who was with Alexander in Persia. And from Eumenes and Ptolemy, who were also there and served as Alexander's chroniclers," Levi said, "and from other surviving sources. And secondary sources such as Plutarch."

Levi reached out and poured water into his glass. Using both his hands to steady it, he drank slowly. He put the glass down on the silver tray, looked up at his audience, and said, "On May twenty-ninth, 323 B.C., outside Babylon, Alexander gave a party for Medius, his friend from Thessaly. The king stood before twenty or so guests and recited extracts from Euripides' play *Andromeda*. He drank wine to his guests' health and fell to his knees, ill." It soon became clear that Alexander the Great was dying. Levi told them how Alexander had written his will, given his ring to his friend, Perdiccas, and designated him Successor. In the throes of death Alexander placed the hand of his wife, Roxane, in Perdiccas's, and with a nod and a final smile, commended him to her.

The Great King was dead.

Pericles Levi sat forward, his elbows on the table, palms up. "Alexander lay in a golden coffin on a golden bed, covered with purple embroidery on which rested his armor and a Trojan shield."

Levi told how a weeping queen had placed Darius's treasure chest containing her husband's beloved *Iliad* at the foot of the coffin. He paused to wipe his eyes with a handkerchief.

Pappas thought, the old bastard is good. He has them hooked.

Ptolemy, Alexander's boyhood friend and now pharaoh, intercepted the funeral chariot on the road outside of Babylon, Levi recounted. "He secretly set off to Egypt with the chariot. Ptolemy had it put on display in Memphis and later had it moved to Alexandria."

"What happened to the chariot?" asked General Politopoulos, stroking his thick, bushy peasant's mustache.

Levi's face crinkled in an expression that seemed to say: who knows? "We do know that Augustus saw the chariot when he visited Egypt three hundred years later. Most scholars assume that the chariot was destroyed in the city riots of the late third century."

"But not you," said General Tsimas, his cold eyes fixed on the professor. Levi ignored the interruption. "Apollonius of Rhodes was the chief librarian in Alexandria in A.D. 246. One of the few items to survive the fire that destroyed the library was one of Apollonius's records of library holdings wherein he described removing the casket-copy from Darius's treasure chest and storing it inside an amphora. He described the storage jar in great detail. There is no question in my mind that the amphora found in Orhan Iskur's shop is the same one that Apollonius of Rhodes used to store the casket-copy."

"And the Iliad, what happened to it?" asked General Tsimas.

"Nothing was heard of the funeral chariot and its contents for more than twenty-one hundred years," Levi responded, reaching out for a bottle of mineral water, pouring, and drinking a glass before going on. "Until the collapse of the Ottoman Empire. By the early twenties refugees were streaming out of Egypt and the rest of the empire. They came carrying family treasures on their backs. Treasures that had been in their families for centuries; treasures they hoped would buy them a new, secure life.

"And the vultures came too. Collectors and art dealers from around the world flocked to the Mediterranean ports with one purpose uppermost in their minds: to cheat these desperate people out of their possessions. Most of the antiquities proved to be of minor importance. But some were price-less. And many of the collectors made fortunes."

"And Alexander's funeral chariot reappeared?" General Politopoulos asked hopefully.

"Alas, no," Levi said. "I'm afraid it is still lost."

"Then what has been stolen from us?" asked Vitos.

"In June of 'thirty-nine, a collector named Paolo Matrazzo wired his partner from Thíra that he was on the verge of making a great acquisition. Matrazzo instructed his partner to wire him two million U.S. Matrazzo's partner wired back demanding to know the nature of the acquisition," Levi said.

"And?" demanded the minister.

"Matrazzo wired back: 'I have found the casket-copy.' "

"And then what happened?" asked General Tsimas, leaning forward.

"Matrazzo's partner wired him the money." Levi shrugged. "Word leaked out that Matrazzo was after the casket-copy, and some of the vultures started to circle over Thíra. Anyway, the draft arrived from Rome on a Thursday. It was never cashed. Paolo Matrazzo was found dead in his hotel on Saturday. An apparent heart attack."

"And the casket-copy?" asked General Politopoulos, the head of the Hellenic Police.

Levi shrugged.

"A swindle," announced General Tsimas.

"I think not, General," Levi retorted. "Matrazzo was then one of the world's foremost dealers, specializing in Greek antiquities from three hundred B.C. to four hundred A.D. It would have been almost impossible for him to have been deceived by a fake. And he would, without question, have had the artifact authenticated before he wired Rome for the money."

Pappas held up his pencil to ask a question. "Professor, is it your opinion that the casket-copy had been kept in the amphora that we found in Orhan Iskur's shop?"

"Yes," Levi answered.

"Then why not take the amphora? Why would Iskur's killer leave it behind?" Pappas asked.

"Amphorae are not rare. True, this one is worth a considerable sum, but it is not priceless. And it is big. Perhaps whoever killed Iskur did not know it was in the shop."

Playing with his pencil, Pappas asked, "Do you believe that the casket-copy was taken out of Greece and transported to the United States?"

"Circumstances force me to that conclusion, Colonel," Levi responded. "The killers of the two policemen, and of all those other poor souls, were from New York City. One must assume that the person who hired them was also from the United States."

A hush fell over the room.

General Tsimas slapped the table. "You and the professor expect us to send someone to the United States, don't you, Colonel Pappas?"

"I want to see the casket-copy back in Greece. And"
—Pappas leaned forward in his seat, pointing his pencil at General Tsimas, his voice heavy with rancor—"most of all, I want the people responsible for Voúla punished."

"Proof," General Tsimas shouted across the table, slapping his hand on it in anger. "Where is your proof? We cannot send someone off on a wild-goose chase. Tell us the connection between the two policemen and Iskur. Proof, Colonel."

Pappas pushed his chair back and stood up. He put his palms down flat on the glistening table and looked directly at Tsimas.

"Proof, General? When I questioned Kostas and Thanos Koukoudeas, the brothers-in-law of one of the murdered policemen, Lakis Rekor, they confessed that Rekor and his partner, Tasos Lefas, had discovered something of great value in the ruins of Akrotiri on Thíra. I had the logbooks checked. Akrotiri was within their patrol zone. Kostas Koukoudeas, the older of the brothers, told me that Rekor and his partner used to park their patrol car outside the ruins at night and roam about searching for undiscovered treasure. As I'm sure you are aware, excavations were begun at Akrotiri in May of 'sixty-seven, and they are still not complete. Well, one night in the fall of 1984, in the Temple of the Egyptians, Officer Rekor noticed a depression in the ground and began to dig. They dug for most of the night while the watchman slept in his shack. They found something of great value.

"Thanos Koukoudeas told me that they quickly contacted Orhan Iskur, and he arranged the sale of the object to an American collector."

"And did he also tell you what this precious object was, Colonel?" General Tsimas asked.

"No he did not," Pappas said, lowering himself back into his seat. "Lakis Rekor told his brothers-in-law that they were better off not knowing."

"I see," said General Tsimas. "And did you speak with the other dead officer's family?"

"Yes, I did," Pappas answered. "At first they denied any knowledge. But after I carefully explained their situation to them, they confessed. And their story was basically the same."

"Colonel, you still have not presented any proof. Hearsay is not proof," Tsimas said, a thin smile compressing his lips.

"Alexander's *Iliad* was in that amphora," Professor Levi said sternly, his face set in a stubborn look.

"And how do we know that?" General Politopoulos demanded.

"The black sand tells us," Levi answered with authority. "Sand keeps moisture out and helps protect ancient writings from rot and decay. The ancients used it as a preservative. They knew that water was the main destroyer of parchment and papyrus. That was why Apollonius of Rhodes removed the *Iliad* from the casket and stored it in the amphora, which, I am positive, was filled with sand from the desert. Whoever brought the casket-copy to Thíra put the island's volcanic sand into that amphora to preserve Alexander's *Iliad*."

"If what you say is true," Antonis Vitos, the Minister of Public Order, said, "are we then to assume that Alexander's *Iliad* would be intact?"

Professor Levi's lips fluttered. "I don't know. No one can know the answer to that question with any degree of certainty. Perhaps it is a fragment. A scroll or two. Perhaps more. But think of it, gentlemen, the *Iliad* written in Aristotle's own hand for Alexander."

"If your somewhat imaginative conjecture is correct, Professor, then please tell me why this elusive American would go to such extraordinary lengths to arrange the deaths of two Greek policemen and an antiquities dealer," asked Antonis Vitos, crushing out the stub of a cigarette in an ashtray.

Pappas answered: "Because the two dead policemen had overextended themselves in business and thought that they could go back to the well and draw out more water. But, unfortunately for them and the people of Voúla, whoever this person is did not want to pay again for what he had already paid for once."

General Tsimas furrowed his brow. "Then why kill Orhan Iskur?"

"To sever all connections with himself," Pappas answered.

"Why?" asked General Politopoulos. "This American had whatever he wanted. He was safely back in the States. Why not tell them to go to hell? What could they possibly have done to him?"

Professor Pericles Levi chuckled. "You are not a collector, General, or else you would understand. Collectors are paranoid when it comes to their collections. Their acquisitions are kept secret from the world. Why do they do this, you ask? Because they know that other collectors are as crazy as they are. They know that other collectors will commit murder to possess certain pieces; pieces that they have spent most of a lifetime aching to possess, only to have someone else acquire them. Have you, General Politopoulos, ever heard of the Treasure of Priam?"

"Of course," answered Politopoulos. "It was the treasure that Schliemann unearthed at Troy. It was housed in the Berlin Museum and was destroyed during a bombing raid during World War Two."

"Correct, General," Pericles Levi said. "A treasure that caused Schliemann to send his famous telegram to the King of Greece: 'I have gazed on the face of Agamemnon.' Only the collection was not destroyed. It was stolen. Three of the museum's guards removed the collection during the raid. Later they sold it to a Canadian who now lives in dread that someone will steal his prized collection. He knows that there are those of us in the art world who *know* that the Treasure of Priam exists. And he knows that there are many who would kill to possess that treasure.

"And that, gentlemen, is exactly what your two dishonest policemen had to sell this elusive collector, their continued silence. Because if they, or Orhan Iskur, had revealed his name, then he, too, would have to spend his life in mortal fear."

4

New York City
July 1987

The furry head poked out from behind the tree trunk. Darting out onto a branch, the black squirrel reared up.

"Good morning, Ajax," Teddy Lucas said, standing near the kitchen window of his second-floor Stuyvesant Town apartment, located off Manhattan's First Avenue. He was spreading peanut butter over a cracker. "Sorry I'm late this morning." He broke the cracker and put the halves out on the sill. Stepping back, he picked up his coffee mug and watched the creature run out to the end of the branch and leap onto the windowsill.

Ajax reared, nostrils twitching, his bushy tail curling around his body. The squirrel scooped up a half and began to nibble away at the cracker. Dressed only in undershorts, Lucas sipped his coffee and talked to his friend. "So? How goes it, Ajax? You getting much?" Lucas wryly reflected on how surprised his men would be if they heard their tough boss talking to a squirrel.

Ajax's teeth champed into the peanut butter.

Teddy Lucas and Ajax had been friends for three years. Their friendship began the day Lucas moved into the one-bedroom apartment. He had been unpacking dishes in the kitchen when the squirrel appeared on the windowsill. When he noticed the squirrel watching him, Lucas leaned up against the kitchen counter and began to talk to the creature. It was someone to talk to, to confide in, maybe even be friends with. And for no special reason, he named the squirrel Ajax, after the hero of the Trojan War.

The next morning Ajax reappeared. Lucas put some peanut butter on a cracker and left it out on the sill. They'd been friends ever since. It was nice to have someone to talk to, another living creature to help break the loneliness of the morning.

At forty-seven, Teddy Lucas was trim and muscular, although he was beginning to notice some extra baggage around his middle. High black eyebrows added intensity to his dark eyes, and a forelock of black wavy hair fell down over his brow. Flat cheekbones, an olive complexion, and finely defined features combined to make him an unusually handsome man.

Ajax finished the crackers. He quickly brushed his mouth with his paw, looked up at Lucas as if to say thanks, and hopped back onto the branch. Lucas rinsed out the mug and balanced it on top of the pile in the dish rack. He walked through the living room into the bedroom and got dressed: tan slacks, brown loafers, a blue shirt with a white collar, no tie. He took a beige sports jacket from the closet and tossed it on the unmade bed. Going over to the oak dresser, he opened the middle drawer and, reaching under his socks, took out his holstered .38 Colt detective special and slipped it into his trousers, clipping it securely over his brown leather belt.

As he pushed the drawer closed, he spotted the small icon tucked away in the back. His mother used to pray to the damn thing every day. He remembered her giving it to him, telling him that it would protect him. He asked himself why the hell he was saving it; was it a part of his life that he wanted to hold on to? He reached into the drawer, took out the painting of Christ, and set it up on top of the dresser. He stepped back, studying the golden aureole that illuminated Christ's melancholy face. The sight of the icon brought back painful and embarrassing remembrances: fights with neighborhood kids who would make fun of his Greek-speaking parents; his mother having to clean other people's homes in order to make ends meet; his proud father's struggle to support his family in a foreign land.

Teddy Lucas was born Theodorous Loucopolous on September 2, 1940, in the northern village of Kilkis, close to the Yugoslavian border. He had picked a bad time and a bad place to make his entrance into the world. The Italians invaded Greece in 1939, then came the Germans, and then in 1943 the civil war broke out, pitting communist and royalist guerrillas against each other.

The civil war raged throughout the northern part of Greece. Of his childhood memories, fear ran through the most vivid ones. He could remember his mother clutching him tightly as she ran up the side of a hill with Melina and Thalassa, his two sisters, in tow; they were desperately trying to escape the shelling. He remembered the houses in his village aflame, and the explosions, and the dead, and the wounded begging for water. He remembered his mother and his two sisters cowering behind boulders, praying to the icon to spare the family. He had no recollection of his father during that period of his life. He was to learn years later that his dad had been in the hills fighting on the side of the ELAS, the communist guerrillas.

The Germans were driven out of Greece in 1945 and the civil war ended in 1949, a civil war that was to cost six hundred thousand Greek lives.

Teddy was nine years old when his parents gathered the family together in the living room of their whitewashed house and told them that they were moving to America. He could still vividly recall his father's weathered face and sad eyes as he explained that he wanted his children to grow up away from the ravages of war, safe and secure in a land of plenty: America. Although Teddy felt sad at the thought of leaving his beloved grandparents behind—they would continue to live in the family's house—he was glad to be leaving Greece. He had nothing but bitter memories; memories and the anxious fear that someday the bombs would begin to fall on them again.

The Loucopolous family settled in the Greek section of Astoria, Queens, in New York City. Their new home was in the basement of a three-family brick house. One room acted as their kitchen, bedroom, and living/dining room. At night a thick brown blanket separated his parents' bed from the one in which his two sisters slept. Teddy slept on a cot in the boiler room.

The beginning years in America were hard. His father worked double shifts in a factory that made cardboard boxes. Both his sisters helped their mother clean people's houses. Their new home had a small backyard; the landlord gave permission for the Loucopolous family to grow vegetables in it. The family garden became Teddy's responsibility. He enjoyed working the soil; he liked the smell of the earth and the feel of cold dirt under his feet. Teddy felt safe in America. He had looked forward to shedding his Greek ways and becoming an American. He wanted to immerse himself in the culture of his new homeland. But that was not to be; the part of Astoria where the Loucopolous family had settled was predominantly Greek. Instead of experiencing a new culture, he found himself living smack in the center of a kind of transplanted Greece.

By the time he was eleven years old he could speak English haltingly. After school he would deliver orders from Mr. Skoulas's grocery store. Although he had trouble speaking the language, he was able to read and understand it quite well; he devoured mystery stories. He loved to play soccer with his friends and was quite good at the game. Playing soccer developed his powerful legs and gave him an acute awareness of their strength and fluidity that most American boys his age lacked.

When he was fourteen years old his parents changed their last name to Lucas, took every cent that they had saved, and bought a "handyman's special" in Ridgewood, Queens. Teddy had never before heard the term handyman's special. He was to learn that in this case it meant a frame house that was attached on both sides and had an old, leaky roof, a wet basement, and a frayed electrical system along with a boiler held together largely by hope, faith, and patchy repairs.

Ridgewood was a vastly different neighborhood from Astoria. Mostly, the people were of Italian, German, and Irish stock. The few Greeks who did live there were completely assimilated into the culture and refused to speak Greek, except in private.

The neighborhood kids in Ridgewood used to make fun of the new Greek family who dressed differently and did not speak English well. Teddy in particular became the butt of their hazing. Many times the tough guys would lie in wait for him after school. They'd taunt him, making fun of his short pants and sandals. Sometimes they would circle him and shove him from one to the other. It was during these awful times that the memories of the war flooded back into his thoughts and he would feel helpless, a peasant fleeing for his life, not understanding why he was being punished. Their vicious insults made Teddy want to strike out with his powerful legs and hurt them.

But he could do nothing. He could not react to them because peasants do not strike their betters. Peasants learn early in their lives to be subservient, to cast their eyes downward, to bear the humiliation, to endure. Teddy was positive that if he ever did strike back and hurt any of the cowards, they would call the police. Then the police would come, and the foreigner would automatically be at fault, and the police would deport his whole family to Greece. Then all that his family had struggled so hard to achieve would be lost because he had not been strong enough to endure the taunts of cowards. During those times he would steel himself against his tormentors and vow that he would shed everything about himself that was Greek. He was going to become a true American—then he and his family would be safe.

He worked hard and his English gradually improved. He read everything in English that he could find. When the weather was nice he would work in the garden of their new home and whenever he had the time he would travel back to Astoria to play soccer with his Greek friends.

One spring day Teddy was working in the yard, hoeing his garden. He was barefoot and wearing gray short pants that his grandmother had sent him from Greece. He heard snickers behind him and tensed, resisting the temptation to turn. He continued working, but when the laughter grew louder he did turn around and saw six of the toughest neighborhood kids leaning over the fence in the rear of the yard watching him. They started yelling obscene insults at him. "Fucking foreigner, go back to your commie country."

Four of them leaped over the fence and rushed into the garden, trampling the vegetables, tearing them out of the earth and tossing them around the yard. Teddy stood by, doing nothing to stop them, tears of shame burning his eyes. Suddenly he heard Melina's frantic voice and he turned in time to see his sister running up out of the basement. She shouted at the tormentors to stop, yelling that they should be ashamed of themselves. The jeering kids circled Melina. They began to manhandle her. She fought back, slapping and kicking and cursing them in Greek. One of the youths made a grab at her breast. She kicked him. He punched her in the face, sending her spinning onto the ground.

Teddy saw his sister lying in the dirt. He screamed at the tormentors and threw his hoe at them. They hesitated, briefly taken aback by Teddy's unexpected bravery. Then they began to laugh at him, standing their ground with adolescent bravado.

Teddy rushed at them, targeting the biggest one, a tall burly boy with husky shoulders and big biceps. He could feel the power surging through his legs as he struck, arching his right foot up into the boy's face, knocking out teeth and toppling him onto his knees. Teddy wheeled and smashed his foot into the boy's stomach, splaying him backward onto the ground.

The other boys backed off, but Teddy's fury propelled him forward. He kicked another of them in the groin, and when he doubled over, he struck out with his foot, splattering the boy's nose like a crushed tomato. The ferocity of his attack caused the others to break and escape over the fence. Teddy helped his sister up off the ground and into the house, leaving the remaining two rolling in the dirt. His worst fear never came to pass: the police never came to his home; that was not how things were settled in Ridgewood.

That night when Teddy and his sister told their father what had happened, the father smiled, ruffled Teddy's hair, and said, "You did right."

Teddy was never again bothered, nor was any member of his family, after the incident in the backyard. As he grew older, Teddy became more attuned to his new way of life. He would refuse to speak his native tongue unless it was absolutely necessary to do so. At some point he decided that he wanted to be a policeman. Policemen were safe from the taunts of others and they helped other people, peasants, immigrants, and others in need of help. There were still times when he would get that anxious peasant feeling, and it was then that he remembered the bombs and got scared.

Staring at the icon, he saw his mother and sister praying behind the rocks. He grabbed it off the dresser, tossed it back into the drawer, took his lieutenant's shield off the top, and left for the office.

Chief of Detectives Tim Edgeworth, a big man with a heavy, overhanging brow, cold blue eyes, and thick lips, lit his pipe, unpinned the communication referral slip from the UF49, and tossed the pin into a glass ashtray. Another heavy, he sighed. The pink slips come down the chain direct from the police commissioner. He scanned the rows of endorsements; each one summarized the report and gave conclusions and recommendations. Some of them continued on the back of the official letterhead.

C of D Edgeworth removed the translation of the communication the NYPD had received from the Hellenic Police. One Major Andreas Vassos, Athens Security Prefecture, was being sent to New York City to investigate the murder of two Greek police officers.

"Fucking cop killers," Edgeworth muttered, thinking of the six cops who had recently been shot in El Bronxo. He studied the report from the State Department. State requested that the NYPD render all possible assistance to the Greek police. He read it a third time and frowned. Tossing it on his desk, he leaned back in his chair and looked meditatively at the ceiling. It didn't make any sense: why would the feds step aside on something this sensitive? Normally they would have insisted on assigning a small army of FBI and State Department people for liaison, rather than just the one man listed as a federal liaison contact. His name was Hayden. Instead here they were, handing the NYPD this one on a silver platter. Or was it on the end of a long, dirty stick?

Edgeworth picked it up gingerly and read it through again. The original Greek request had been filed with the U.S. embassy in Athens. It was approved and sent on to the Bureau of Diplomatic Security in Washington, D.C. Hayden's agency. Washington approved the request and forwarded it along with accompanying documents to the Diplomatic Security field office in NYC.

The request had been hand delivered to the PC. The First Deputy Commissioner's recommendation: APPROVAL. Chief of the Department: APPROVAL. Deputy Commissioner, Administration: APPROVAL. Deputy Commissioner, Legal Matters: APPROVAL. Edgeworth read the PC's final endorsement:

Major Andreas Vassos, Hellenic Police Department, will be extended every courtesy by members of this department. He will be assigned to a subordinate command within the Detective Division. The CO of that command will be responsible for the major's supervision and control. Major Vassos should, if possible, be assigned to a command where one or more members are fluent in the Greek language.

Forwarded to the C of D for implementation and report. Recommend: APPROVAL.

C of D Edgeworth studied the printout listing Greek-speaking detectives and their present assignments. Thirty-seven members of the Detective Division had demonstrated some proficiency in the language. Lieutenant Teddy Lucas, the Whip of the Sixteenth Detective Squad, spoke Greek. Edgeworth leaned back and fondly recalled the eight years he had spent in the Sixteenth Squad. They were great years, the best. Was it possible, really possible, that that had been over twenty-five years ago?

He snapped forward in his seat and pressed one of the buttons in the row on the right side of his desk. Sergeant Jacobs, Edgeworth's lead clerical, came in with a stack of folders neatly tucked under his beefy arm. "Yes, Chief?"

"Did you look over the forty-nine on this Major Vassos?"

"Yes, I did," he replied, settling comfortably into the chair on the side of the desk with the relaxed air of a confidant.

"Will Vassos be cross-designated?" Edgeworth asked.

Jacobs stacked the folders on his lap. He pulled one from the pile and spread it open. Glancing at the contents, he said, "I checked with the Legal Bureau, Chief. Only U.S. law enforcement personnel can be cross-designated from one agency to another."

"Will Vassos have arrest powers?" asked the C of D.

"No, sir. Any collars will be taken by our people. The

arrest will be made on the complaint of the Greek government. The perp will be arraigned in federal court and held pending extradition."

The C of D smiled. "I assume that we have an extradition treaty with the Greeks."

"We do. I checked."

"Will the major be permitted to carry firearms?"

"Technically, no. But since he'll be traveling under a diplomatic passport, he'll be able to carry a weapon, if he wants to."

"What about his living accommodations?"

"The Greek consul general is responsible for making those arrangements."

"Going on the assumption that they'll quarter him in Manhattan, I guess we ought to assign the major to a Manhattan command."

Sergeant Jacobs held his pencil at the ready. "Which one, Chief?"

■　　■　　■

Teddy Lucas read the report typed under "Details of the Case" on the bottom of the DD5 Supplementary Complaint Report, commonly called simply the five, the detective form used to report all phases of an investigation. He checked the crime classification code to insure that the fairy tale complied with department policy and procedures and, satisfied that it did, affixed his signature in the space provided on the bottom of the report.

I've become a goddamn fiction editor, he thought, reaching into the tray for another five.

The undersigned interviewed the complainant, who stated that she could add nothing further to aid the investigation. A recanvass of the place of occurrence met with negative results. Pending further developments, the undersigned requests that this case be marked: CLOSED, NO RESULTS.

The Squad's caseload last year had been 2,240 cases. These were divided among fifteen detectives, which meant that each detective had to spend a good part of each tour in front of a typewriter banging out fairy tales. But clearances must be maintained. The Palace Guard does not care how you do it; in fact, they don't want to *know* how you do it. Just be sure that your clearances are up and your paper is current.

Burglary complainants usually got a phone call, a fast PR job, and sympathy. Robbery complainants got to look at mug shots. If they were unable to pick out the perp, the case would be marked active for a few months, a few fives would be added to the case folder for color, and then the case would be marked: CLOSED, NO RESULTS.

Precious street time had to be spent on the heavy ones: homicides, felonious assaults, maimings, rapes, and any incident involving a diplomat or a famous person. The Job was uptight when it came to publicity. Stroke 'em, gently, and make sure that they don't come in your face, Edgeworth constantly reminded his borough commanders.

As a boy growing up, Lucas used to fantasize about becoming a cop. He wanted to match wits with master criminals; become Astoria's Maigret or Holmes. He was going to destroy criminal cartels, protect the downtrodden. He had been on the Job eleven months before he realized that nobody really cared about the downtrodden. And he was in the Detective Division two years before he realized that there was no such thing as a master criminal. There were only mutts—and their wailing lib-blab lawyers who had learned to master an inane, archaic criminal justice system.

Lucas pushed back from his desk and got up. He walked over to the fan on top of the library cabinet and turned it to high. Another scorcher, he thought, ungluing his shirt. He glanced around his office, his home away from home. The rows of clipboards: DD64b Recapitulation of Detectives' Arrest Activity, DD60 Detective's Report on Lost or Stolen Property, DD52 Wanted File, Special Operating Procedures, department bulletins. The green leather divan flush against the wall, the splotches of dirt, the file boxes and trays. The maps: Sensitive Locations, Crime Prone Locations. It wasn't perfect, but it was where he wanted to be: the Whip of a detective squad. He still longed to make like Maigret or Holmes. At this point he'd even settle for making like Kojak.

He reached for another five.

Detective Ivan Ulanov stuck his big Slavic face into the office. "Your ex is on the phone."

"Tell her I'm patrolling the east coast of Tahiti."

Ulanov nodded and disappeared back into the squad room.

The red telephone on Lucas's desk rang. "Lieutenant Lucas."

"Lou, this is Sergeant Jacobs from the C of D's office," the voice said, using the diminutive of lieutenant that was routinely used throughout the Job. "The bossman wants to see you, forthwith."

Grabbing his sports jacket off the coatrack, Lucas grumbled, "Everything in this job is 'forthwith.' Why can't they once say 'Report at your leisure'?"

C of D Edgeworth was studying July's recapitulation of force figures when Lucas entered.

"Sit down, Lou," Edgeworth said. "I'll be with you in a second."

Lucas watched the C of D's frown at the column of numbers. The massive shoulders and strong hands gave a hint of the man's brute strength. He looked out of character sitting behind a desk.

"There just ain't enough bodies to plug all the gaps," Edgeworth said, tossing the printout into a file tray. He leaned back, a sly smile tugging at his lips. "So? How goes it with your squad, Teddy?"

The old fox knows damn well how I'm doing. But Lucas would stick to the approved ritual: always have an answer ready, make up any numbers to show that you're on top of things. More important, make the boss feel important. "Everything's pretty good, Chief. My robberies are down twenty-two percent this quarter. Homicides are down thirty percent. I've reduced overtime forty percent—overtime was a biggie—and Inspections gave the Squad an above average rating last time around. And I'm sitting here wondering what you got in store for me."

A sunburst grin broke across Edgeworth's face. "Right to the point, Teddy. That's one of the things I always liked about you, you're a no-bullshit guy." He flopped his hands on top of his desk, leaned forward, "How'd you like to get away from the paper and play detective for a while?"

Lucas gave the expected good-soldier reply: "I'll do whatever you want, boss."

"Washington just threw us a heavy, and I need a Greek-speaking detective to run with it."

"Who'll run the Squad while I'm out playing Kojak?"

"Your Second Whip. Roosevelt can look after things for you, like he does when you're out getting laid or on vacation."

"What's the case?"

Edgeworth told him about Major Vassos and the two murdered Greek policemen.

"What do I do if I need some detectives to hit a flat or kick some ass?" Teddy asked.

"Use your people. Take them off the chart if you have to. And if things get hectic, get on the horn to me and I'll fly some men in to cover your chart."

"What authority will this major have?"

Edgeworth explained the nuances of cross-designation and why Vassos would not be cross-designated or authorized to make arrests but would be permitted to carry a weapon. "You'll have to make out a ten card for him. The Greeks will want to know how many hours a week he worked. Carry him on your roll calls. And Teddy, you're responsible for his control and supervision."

"How far do you want me to go with this thing? Do you

want me to go through the motions, or do you want me to be for real?"

"All the way. Do whatever is necessary to bring the case to a successful conclusion. The Greeks are going to be conducting a parallel investigation. You'll keep each other informed."

Lucas nodded curtly. "When is the major arriving?"

Edgeworth looked at his desk calendar. "Monday, July thirteenth. That's today. Olympic Flight 812, arriving Kennedy at four thirty-five. So you've got just about five hours to fill your Second Whip in on what's going down before you get out to Kennedy and pick up your new partner."

"If I'm coming off the chart, I certainly don't want to catch any borough duties. Are you going to send down a telephone message taking me out of the chart?"

"I don't want to go that route. I'll telephone your borough CO and tell him that you're on a special assignment for me and not to be looking for you for any other jobs."

"Who do I report to?"

"To me. I want a phone call every day."

"What about wheels and expenses?"

"You've been assigned a confiscated car with Jersey plates. A Buick. You can pick it up in the garage when you leave." He slid an envelope across to him. "The registration and the keys are in here along with two hundred dollars, compliments of Uncle Sam." He passed him two signature cards. "Sign these. You'll be getting credit cards in department mail. Keep receipts."

Lucas signed the cards and got up. As he was making for the door, Edgeworth called to him. "Whenever the feds ask me to conduct an investigation for them I get this tingling sensation in my balls, like I'm about to get fucked."

Reaching for the knob, Lucas answered, "I know the feeling, boss."

Portable steel barriers formed a funnel through which travelers had to pass when exiting the customs area of the International Arrivals Building. People jammed up against the barricade watching the trickle of passengers come out from behind the frosted glass doors, their anxious eyes scanning the crowd for a familiar face. Black-capped chauffeurs, holding up cardboard signs bearing the names of clients, clustered at the neck of the funnel.

Teddy Lucas edged his way through the waiting crowd into the isolation area. A customs inspector rushed over to him. "You're not allowed inside here, fella."

Lucas showed him his police credentials. "Inspector Cutrone is expecting me."

"You here to pick up the VIP from Greece?"

"Yes."

The customs man pushed open the heavy doors. "To your right, up two flights, and then go left."

The observation deck ran the entire length of the inspection area and was enclosed behind a wall of one-way glass. Agents perched on stools, scanning the deplaning passengers through binoculars. Four agents sat in front of a panel of TV monitors.

"Cutrone?" Lucas asked the first agent he came to.

"Through that door," said the agent.

Cutrone was a surprisingly small man with a southern drawl and oversized yellow-tinted aviator glasses. "How y'all doin'?" he said, pumping Lucas's hand while one eye remained fixed on the television monitor. "You're going to have to bear with me for a bit. We got something going down, down there." He folded his arms across his chest and intently watched the monitor. Lucas stood beside him.

Hidden cameras zoomed in on a couple moving up to the inspection stand. The bearded husband wore a fur cap and had long side curls. The woman's head was covered by a kerchief. Lucas's trained eyes spotted the male and female undercovers inching up to the unsuspecting couple.

"That little ol' gal down there got a diamond-filled prophylactic stuck up her pussy."

The husband tossed one suitcase up onto the counter. Suddenly they were surrounded by agents who hustled them off through a door on the side of the inspection area.

Cutrone turned his attention to his guest. "Now to your problem. Your friend landed six minutes ago. He'll be here shortly."

Eleven minutes later the door opened and a customs agent stuck his head inside. "Here's our guest."

A blue nylon bag was slung over Vassos's right shoulder, and another was in his hand.

"Welcome, Major," Lucas said, moving to greet him, noticing both the European cut of his clothes and his grief-stricken eyes. "I'm Lieutenant Teddy Lucas, NYPD."

Shaking hands, Vassos answered in Greek. "I'm pleased to meet you. I'm Andreas Vassos."

"I prefer not to speak in Greek. Do you speak English?"

Vassos's eyes grew chilly. "Yes, I do speak English."

"Let me help you, Andreas," Lucas said, taking the hand-grip and waving a thank-you to Cutrone.

A jumbo jet lumbered up off a runway, its nose straining to gain altitude as they walked out of the terminal. Lucas's assigned car was double-parked at the curb. The Port Authority cop he had asked to look after it stood nearby.

"Thanks," Lucas said to the cop, pulling the back door open and tossing the suitcases onto the seat. He stepped off the curb and walked around to the driver's side. Vassos was already in the passenger seat when Lucas squeezed in behind the wheel.

"At last I can see for myself," Vassos said, watching the PA cop give directions to a group of women.

"See what?"

"On television and in the movies your police always carry so much equipment I do not know how they can move about."

Lucas looked out the windshield at the cop. "Revolver, holster, twelve-extra rounds, handcuffs, traffic whistle, mace, billy, flashlight, memo book, summons book—all normal equipment, Andreas," he said, sticking the key into the ignition. "What do your people carry on patrol?"

Vassos said, deadpan, "Their revolvers."

"Nothing else?"

"No, nothing."

"They're lucky." Driving out onto the roadway, Lucas asked, "Where to?"

Vassos handed him a slip of paper. "My address in Manhattan."

They drove in silence, Lucas paying attention to the traffic; Vassos was absorbed by the scenery. The car glided up the ramp leading off the Van Wyck Expressway onto the Long Island Expressway. Lucas braked and merged into the traffic. "Where did you learn your English?"

"At Police College. It is not possible to obtain promotion without fluency in another language."

"Good idea," Lucas said, inching the car into the middle lane.

"I was told that a Greek-speaking officer would be assigned to work with me."

"A foul-up. I haven't spoken Greek in years."

"But you are a Greek, yes?"

"Greek-American."

"Your name is not Greek," Vassos observed, watching the driver.

"I was born Theodorous Loucopolous. My father had it shortened to Lucas."

A grimace. "Here everyone has to be American, yes?"

Lucas eased the Buick into the curb in front of the Hotel Olympian's blue-and-white canopy on Eighth Avenue near Thirty-second Street. The digital clock on the dashboard read 7:26. The hotel was a second-rate affair pressed between an abandoned movie house and a glass office building. Lucas tossed the vehicle identification plate onto the padded dashboard and slid out of the car.

Standing on the curb, Vassos watched homeless men gathering under the marquee. Shopping carts crowded with paper bags and bedrolls were lined up against the boarded-up doors of the movie house.

Lucas opened the car's back door and yanked out the luggage. He tossed one to Vassos. "Catch."

Snagging it with both hands, Vassos inclined his head toward the homeless people. "Are there many such persons in New York?"

"Enough. And in Greece?"

"None."

The hotel's oval vestibule had a vaulted ceiling. Painted wall panels depicted fishermen casting nets under a cloudless sky. The lobby was long and narrow, and led to a desk cage made of brown marble and faded brass. Two settees were the only furniture; they were worn and shiny.

"Do you have a reservation?" the desk clerk asked, looking up from his racing form.

Lucas put down his bag. "Vassos."

The clerk ran his finger over the reservation tray. He slid out a card, read: "Andreas Vassos. Direct billing to the Greek Consulate, Press Information, 601 Fifth Avenue."

"That is correct," Vassos said.

The clerk handed him the necessary form to fill out and then passed him his plastic keycard. "Room ten-ten."

Plastic pie-shaped light fixtures lined the ceiling of the long hallway. Vassos slid the plastic keycard into the slot above the knob. The light on the right of the lock turned green and the door opened. They walked into an ice-cold room. Vassos rushed over to the window, threw the curtain aside, and pushed the window up as far as it would go. Manhattan's sounds and moist, hot July air rushed into the room. The major looked down at the strange city. "I hate air-conditioning. It is unnatural." He looked around, found the temperature control, and fiddled with it until the flow from the air-conditioning vent stopped.

Lucas tossed the bag onto the bed and looked around the small, rather drab room. A night table, writing desk and chair, and a pay television with two movie channels. The remote was on the night table. One wing chair by the window.

Lucas sat on the lumpy bed and leaned back to the wall. "What do you think of the city?"

Vassos turned. "It is big and noisy."

Lucas noticed the blue of his eyes. They were the eyes of a truly homeless man, forever sad.

"Thank you for meeting me, Teddy."

"My pleasure, one cop to another." Vassos removed his sports jacket and slung it over the back of the chair.

Lucas's attention was immediately drawn to the automatic that was stuck into the slide holster on Vassos's hip. "That's some piece of equipment you're carrying."

Vassos glanced down at the weapon. He slid it out of the holster, pressed the release button that dropped the clip into his hand, extracted the chambered round, and handed the gun to Lucas.

"Nice balance," Lucas observed. "A nine millimeter Beretta. You don't see too many of these in New York."

Vassos sat down next to him. "It has some unusual features. This is a 93R model. On the left side of the frame there is a fire selector switch that allows the weapon a three-round burst capability." Reaching under the barrel, he slid down front handgrips. "When the weapon is on full automatic, it is advisable to hold onto the grip."

"It's a little heavy," Lucas said, hefting it in his palm.

"One point twelve kilograms. That is about two pounds."

"How many rounds in the magazine?"

"Twenty."

"Not bad," Lucas said, looking down at the two extra magazines protruding from the leather slip pouch snapped around Vassos's belt. "You're lugging sixty rounds around with you. I think that it might be a good idea if you fill me in on this investigation of ours."

Vassos took the weapon back and laid it on top of the night table. He unzipped the smaller of the two nylon bags and took out a bottle of scotch. "Black Label, duty free," he said. "Will you join me?"

"Why not?" Lucas said, getting up and going into the bathroom and returning with two glasses.

Vassos poured. He lifted his glass to Lucas. "*Giassou*, Teddy."

"Cheers," Lucas replied.

"Why won't you speak Greek with me?" Vassos asked.

"Why don't you want to tell me about the case?"

Vassos smiled, watching Lucas over the rim of the water glass. "It began nine weeks ago in Voúla . . ."

When Vassos finished telling about the shooting and the casket-copy twenty-six minutes later, Lucas looked at him and asked, "Why did they send you?"

"Are you married, Teddy?"

"Divorced. My ex decided that marriage with me was not for her."

Shaking his head, Vassos said, "I heard American women were rather unpredictable." Moving over to his sports jacket, he reached inside the breast pocket and removed his passport. He flipped open the cover, reached inside the leather case, and removed a photograph. Stepping back across the room, he passed it to Lucas. A beautiful woman posed with a toddler clinging to her shoulder.

"My family. They were among the dead at Voúla." He looked out the window at the gathering summer twilight. "If only I had not acted as a policeman that day, they might still be alive." He turned back to Lucas. "What sort of a policeman are you?"

"The kind that believes in justice," Lucas said, sipping the scotch.

Vassos gave him a hard look. "Real justice?"

"Yeah, the real kind, where the bad guys get it put to them and the good guys are the heroes."

"We believe that the people responsible for killing my family are here in your city. Will you help me?"

"My orders were to render all possible assistance. And if that means helping to nail the people who killed your family and returning some book to Greece, you got it." He slapped his hands over his knees and pushed himself up off the bed. "We might even get to bend a few rules together."

"We bend rules in Greece too, every now and then."

"Get some rest. We'll start in the morning."

When Lucas had gone, Vassos locked and chained the door. He moved to the telephone, read the instructions under the night table's glass, pressed six, and hearing the tone, dialed.

The voice came on the line after the third ring. Vassos spoke in Greek. "Professor Pericles Levi asked me to telephone you."

At 10:45 the following morning, a Buick with New Jersey license plates turned left onto East Sixty-seventh Street from Third Avenue and parked in front of the Sixteenth Precinct station house. Lucas put the car in park as Vassos, carrying a briefcase, slid out of the passenger seat and stared across the street at a dirty building that had all its shades drawn. Police barricades lined the curb in front of the building, and a sergeant and six officers guarded the entrance.

"What is that building?" Vassos asked, pointing with his hand.

"The Soviet Mission to the United Nations," Lucas said.

"Ah, yes, we too must guard certain locations." He turned and looked over at the station house's facade. "Renaissance with some Romanesque details," he observed.

They hurried up the station house steps and crossed the threshold into the precinct's muster room. Vassos moved slowly about, watching, fascinated: the cop on telephone switchboard duty; policemen moving around; a screaming prisoner with a gauze turban around his head; the high, ornate desk; the radio rasping out police calls; a blackboard covered with hastily chalked notifications; a civilian cleaner polishing the brass railing in front of the desk.

The Desk sergeant called out to Lucas, "Hey, Lou, something came for you in department mail. You gotta sign for it."

Lucas introduced Vassos to the sergeant and the cop on the switchboard. The sergeant handed Lucas a white envelope that had three 49a's stapled to it. Lucas ripped off the receipts, signed two of them, and handed them back to the Desk officer. The third one he slid into his pocket.

The Desk sergeant stapled one of the receipts into the property receipt book. And, holding the second one in front of him, he made an entry in a long, thick ledgerlike book with a gray cloth cover. He noted the time and date of delivery, the name and rank of the member of the force to whom he delivered the envelope, the page number of the property receipt book wherein he had filed the other receipt, and the serial number of the communication.

"What is that book called?" Vassos asked.

"The blotter," Lucas said, tearing open the envelope and taking out two credit cards. "It's used to record the chronological assignments, activities, and developments affecting the command."

"We call ours the service book," Vassos said, following Lucas out from behind the desk.

"Hey, Major," the telephone switchboard cop yelled, "how much does a Greek cop make a month?"

"About three hundred U.S.," Vassos called over his shoulder.

They walked upstairs and stopped in front of the wooden railing leading into the second-floor detective squad room.

Lucas draped his hand over the gate, reached down, and pushed open the release latch. "Welcome," he said, sweeping his hand through the air to include the entire squad room and announcing to the detectives, "This is Major Andreas Vassos of the Hellenic Police Department."

"I'm Ivan Ulanov," the huge detective said as he got out of his chair. "Glad to meet you, Major."

Shaking the king-sized hand, Vassos said, "Ulanov is a Russian name."

"My parents came from Kiev."

"Welcome, Major. I'm Detective Frank Gregory."

Vassos measured the strong Serbian features, the flat cheek-bones. "Where did your parents come from?"

Gregory grinned. "I was born in Dubrovnik on the Dalmatian Coast."

"Yugoslavia," Vassos commented, "but Gregory is not a Slav name."

"We shortened it from Goregorievitch."

Mildly confused, Vassos said, "For some reason I thought that your department was composed of Irishmen."

"We got plenty of them, Major." Ulanov laughed.

"Please call me Andreas. " He looked to Lucas. "You are fortunate to have men who speak so many languages."

"I don't speak Russian," Ulanov said, going back to his desk.

"And I don't speak Serbo-Croatian," Gregory announced with an expression of mild annoyance.

"Did I say something out of place?" Vassos asked Lucas.

"Not at all," Lucas said, darting a warning glance at Gregory and Ulanov.

Sergeant Roosevelt Grimes came out of his office. Lucas made the introduction. "Roosevelt is my Second Whip."

Vassos's face showed confusion and then understanding. "Ah, yes. We would call Roosevelt the Second Terror. I am the First Terror."

"It's all the same J-O-B, Major," Grimes said, and walked over to Gregory to ask him about one of his fives.

Vassos moved up to the squad room's wall maps. "What are the pins for?"

Lucas said: "The greens are foreign missions, the whites are foreign consulates. There are over forty-five diplomatic missions within the confines of the Sixteenth."

"And the red pins?" Vassos asked.

"They're the Soviet Mission, the Yugoslavian Mission, and the PLO Mission. We maintain around-the-clock details at those locations."

Turning in his seat, Ulanov asked, "How is your department organized, Major?"

Gregory and the Second Whip stopped what they were doing to listen.

"Our department covers the entire country and is commanded by a four-star general who reports directly to the Minister of Public Order. The country is divided into fifty-three prefectures. Each one is commanded by a colonel, except for the Athens and Salonica Prefecture, where a two-star general commands."

"And where are your detectives assigned?" Gregory asked.

"We do not have detectives in the same sense as you do. Our department is divided into three branches: Uniform, Security, and Traffic. A two-star general commands each one. All of our investigations are conducted by the Security branch. This includes criminal, intelligence, and street crime patrol. The men assigned to the Security branch are rotated between the various units."

"I'm sorry to interrupt," Lucas said, stepping over to Vassos and taking his arm, "but Andreas and I have work to do." He led the major into his office.

The Whip's cubicle had a stale smell. Lucas pushed the one window up as high as it would go, turned the fan on high, and pushed the blackboard next to his desk away from the wall. "Correct me if I make a mistake," he said. Taking a piece of chalk, he began to outline the case on the blackboard.

Rolling the chalk in his palm, Lucas said, "Tell me about Iskur."

"Colonel Pappas discovered his body at around two P.M. on the day of the massacre. The pathologist placed the time of death between ten-thirty and eleven o'clock."

Lucas added, "And if I remember correctly, your Colonel Pappas was told by Cuttler that Iskur had visited them in their hotel room that morning."

"That is correct. As I told you last night, Iskur arrived at the hotel at around eight forty-five and remained about one half hour, then left."

"What killed Iskur?"

"One bullet from a 7.65 automatic."

"Is it possible that Cuttler or Simmons killed Iskur?"

"We do not believe that to be possible."

"Okay. Tell me why."

"Several reasons. Iskur was their only hope of escape if something went wrong. That is what Cuttler told Pappas. Therefore, we do not believe they would kill Iskur. There is also the fact that Iskur was killed in his office in Plaka. The old city. Narrow, winding streets. Both Cuttler and Simmons were strangers to Greece. How would they be able to murder someone in Plaka and then drive to Voúla? Impossible. And we suspect Iskur was killed perhaps a bit before the shooting started in Voúla. We know that Iskur provided them with detailed maps of the drive from Athens to Voúla. He even insisted that they make several rehearsal trips. Cuttler told this to Colonel Pappas." Vassos came over to the other side of Lucas's desk and opened his briefcase. "Our forensic investigators discovered fingerprints on Iskur's billfold that did not belong to the victim." He removed copies of the latents and passed them to Lucas. They showed an enlargement of three blurred fingerprint fragments. Individual characteristics were noted on the side of the blowup. A total of nine common characteristics had been discerned among the three fingers.

"We need twelve points for a positive I.D.," Lucas said.

"So do we." Vassos went on to tell him how Cuttler had told Colonel Pappas about the taxi driver who was to have been waiting for them three quarters of a kilometer outside of Voúla. The driver was to have taken them to the Athens airport. Upon hearing this from the prisoner, Colonel Pappas had rushed a detail of men to the location outside of Voúla.

Farmers in the area were questioned. Several of the locals remembered the taxi waiting on the side of the road with its blinkers flashing. A description of the taxi and its driver was obtained. A shepherd recalled a partial license plate number.

It took two days of canvassing every taxi driver who worked the Athens area before the correct one was found. His name was Leykam. Investigation showed that he was an innocent pawn who was hired to pick up a man named Aldridge Long at the Athens airport on the morning of the massacre, drive Long to Iskur's office in Plaka, and then drive to Voúla and pick up two men who would meet him outside of the village. He was to drive these men directly to the airport.

Leykam had worked with a police artist to develop a composite sketch of Aldridge Long. Vassos removed the sketch; it was slipcased in plastic. He handed it to Lucas. "Our men checked the immigration control cards. They quickly found Long's. His passport number was checked with Washington. His address was a convenience postal box that was closed out soon after the passport came. He arrived in Athens on Flight 605 and left the same day on Flight 793 for New York."

Lucas studied the pencil sketch of a middle-aged man with a receding hairline. His nose was thick; he had bushy eyebrows and a heavy chin. "Our Aldridge Long appears to be a careful man who knows how to enter and leave a country undetected." He looked up at Vassos. "I think such a man would take precautions against anyone recognizing him. He'd take steps to see that no one would remember his face."

Vassos dipped into his briefcase and pulled out an eight-by-ten color photograph of a man. "And here's what his passport photo looked like. Your State Department provided this copy." He handed it to Lucas, who studied it with a frown of puzzlement.

"Well, there's a big difference between the man in the composite and the man in this photo. Maybe the sketch shows him in some kind of disguise. Look at the different hairlines."

Vassos pounced on the point quickly. "And it is entirely possible that the man in this photograph is not Aldridge Long, but a substitute. It could be anyone. The man at your embassy in Athens who got this for me explained that in your country you can get a passport through the mail. The photograph on the passport merely has to match the bearer. But if the man who actually traveled on this passport sent in pictures of someone who looked vaguely like him and then used some makeup and whatever to match up exactly with the man in the photograph . . ."

Lucas looked thoughtfully at Vassos. "So we don't know exactly what this guy Long looks like—just that he is a little like the composite sketch and a little like the passport photo."

"And the fingerprints on Iskur's billfold?" Vassos asked. A wily smile came over Lucas's face. "Even dogs and cats gotta get lucky sometimes."

The telephone rang.

The Second Whip was calling from his next-door office. "Lou, this thing that you're doing for the C of D, you going to want a sixty-one number?"

Sergeant Roosevelt Grimes had just made the minimum height requirement for the Job: five feet eight inches. He was a thin man with a bony face, coal-colored skin. He wore his hair flat on his head, and his deep brown eyes seemed too large for their sockets. He was known as one of the best second whips in the Job, with a rare combination of street smarts and paper smarts. Many a detective had been jammed and dumped back into uniform for conducting unauthorized investigations; the only difference between authorized and unauthorized was a piece of paper. If a copy had a sixty-one number assigned to a case, it certified that the case was kosher and the cop's ass would be covered. "Make out a complaint report and give it a number," Lucas said into the mouthpiece.

"And the crime classification?"

"Confidential Investigation/FOA."

"For Other Authorities?"

"Yes. And Roosevelt, thanks."

"You got it, boss."

Lucas hung up and returned his attention to the blackboard. "Andreas, give me the story again, from the top."

When Vassos finished his account, Lucas said, "You really don't have much, do you? Some partial prints that are worthless, a composite that some Athens taxi driver made, a dubious passport photo, and Professor Levi's assumption that Alexander's *Iliad* was found and spirited out of Greece. Not a lot to go on."

Vassos turned solemn. "We also have the sudden, unexplained rise in the standard of living of two policemen and their families, and we have the statements of those families. We also have the amphora and the careful record that Apollonius of Rhodes made out when he stored the casket-copy inside the amphora."

"Ancient hearsay and wishful thinking is all you have, my friend." Lucas slid up onto the edge of his desk; he looked questioningly at Vassos. "Do you have any idea how difficult it is to extradite a person from this country to a demanding country, especially when that person was not in the demanding country at the time of commission of the crime?"

"Difficult, I would imagine," Vassos said quietly.

"Difficult? It's almost impossible."

"My family was taken from me, Teddy, and I want the people responsible purged."

"Punished," Lucas corrected, studying the board. He took

in a deep breath, let it out slowly. "Maybe you're right, I don't know. What have your people come up with on Paolo Matrazzo?"

"An important art dealer who died after sending his telegram."

"But the bank draft that his partner sent him from Rome was not used, right?"

"Correct."

"Anything else on Matrazzo?"

"No, only that his body was shipped back to New York."

"Why here?"

"Although he had offices in Rome and London, he was an American and lived in New York City."

Thoughtfully rubbing his hands together, Lucas asked, "And Iskur?"

"Worked for Allied intelligence. Since the war he's roamed the art world buying and selling stolen works."

"Did your people contact the intelligence community about him?"

"Yes, we did. And we were told that they never heard of him."

Walking over to the two lockers that were up against the wall, Lucas said, "Bullshit, those guys wouldn't know the truth if it reared up and bit them on the ass. But I know someone who might be able to help." He worked the black-faced combination lock of the locker that had the word *Supplies* stenciled across the door. He lifted up the handle and opened the door. A small refrigerator was on the floor and two cases of Stolichnaya vodka were stacked on top. Lucas took out two cans of cold beer and passed one to Vassos.

The major peeked into the locker, a look of admiration lighting up his otherwise somber face. "Policemen always find ingenious places to hide their 'supplies.' "

"We drilled a hole in the back for the plug."

"I see that you have a good stock of Russian vodka."

Lucas pushed down the tab and drank. "We have a friend

across the street," he said, brushing the back of his hand across his mouth. He leaned over the desk, opened a side drawer, and put the beer can inside the drawer.

Vassos did likewise and pushed the drawer closed. "We do the same thing," he said, smiling at Lucas, "in case a watch commander comes snooping around."

"Do your guys eat on the arm?" Lucas asked.

"I do not know that term."

"You know, a friendly restaurant owner, you work his sector . . ."

"Oh that, of course, they eat on the arm. It is only natural, yes."

"Of course," Lucas said, mimicking his partner's accent. "Did anyone think to ask Professor Levi what the casket-copy is supposed to look like?"

"Papyrus scrolls."

"More than one?"

"They think so, yes. The *Iliad* is composed of twenty-four books, and the experts think that there must have been more than one scroll."

"How many?"

"Nobody knows for sure. In the middle of the nineteenth century a scroll containing the twenty-fourth book was unearthed in Egypt. It was from about the same period. It had survived and was in excellent condition."

"I don't know anything about scrolls," Lucas said, rubbing his jaw, studying the black slate, "but it's my guess that you don't get them unrolled at your local stationery store. Which means that our boy has got to go to a specialist, someone trained to unroll them, and that means that he is going to have to come out into the open to get it done. That's one avenue we're most definitely going to have to look at."

"Any other recommendations?"

"I think that we should take another look at Iskur and Matrazzo. There is a chance that whoever stole your book was connected to one or both of them, somehow, somewhere in the past." He reached over the top of the desk, opened the drawer, and took out the two beer cans. He passed one to Vassos.

They drank beer, studied the blackboard.

"You are beginning to talk as though you believe the casket-copy exists," Vassos said.

Lucas responded quietly, "Dead bodies don't lie. You got yourself a homicide, that I don't question. I just doubt that some book could have survived down through all the centuries. But, it's your game; you threw the ball into play and I'll run with it."

"Will we also examine the criminal records of Cuttler, Simmons, and this Denny McKay?"

"Of course. There has got to be a link there. But you know, Andreas, one of our biggest problems is going to be getting hold of an expert on ancient writings. Someone who can keep his mouth shut."

Vassos brushed his mouth with the back of his hand. "I can help with that. Professor Levi gave me the name of a reliable scholar to contact, an expert on ancient writings. I telephoned last night after you left the hotel room. We have an appointment at three o'clock today."

"Who is this guy?"

"*She* is curator of Ancient and Medieval Manuscripts at the Pierpont Morgan Library."

"Good," Lucas said, and then called out, "Ivan."

Ivan Ulanov sauntered into the office. "Yeah, Lou?"

"See if our friend can meet us in ten minutes, the usual place," Lucas said.

Ulanov picked up the telephone on the Whip's desk and dialed an outside number. When someone answered, the big detective began to speak in flawless Russian. Ulanov spoke for about four minutes, interspersing his conversation with laughter.

Ulanov hung up. "Twenty minutes," he said to Lucas as he strolled from the office.

"I do not understand," Vassos said, making circles with his hands. "He does not speak Russian, then he speaks Russian. Gregory is born in Yugoslavia and he does not speak the language. You are Greek, you do not speak Greek. It is all very strange."

Lucas drained his can, bent it in half, put it into the waste-basket, and pushed it under the trash so that it was hidden from sight. "You have to understand the Job, Andreas. We have a problem when it comes to foreign languages. Most of our supposed linguists are assigned to the Intelligence Division. They get extra money, they have weekends off, they don't generally pull night duty; it's a sweet detail. Only problem is, they don't speak the languages that they're supposed to. They are the lovers and relatives of important people in and out of the Job. But when someone is needed to speak Russian, or Serbo-Croatian, or Greek, the department has to reach out into the trenches."

"And the people in the trenches conveniently forget to speak their mother tongue unless they are asked to by someone in the same trench," Vassos said. "That is sad."

Ranks of flowers bathed Park Avenue's center mall in a rainbow of summer colors. Taxis honked their familiar symphony; rushing people packed the sun-drenched streets; office workers ate their lunches, lounging around outside the fountains of glass office towers. To the south, the golden spire of the Helmsley Building looked down on the magnificent avenue.

Andreas Vassos stood in the lobby of the Chemical Bank Building in awe, trying to absorb the full impact of the lush, exotic greenery. "I have never seen so many plants inside one building," he said to no one in particular, moving over to where Lucas and Ulanov were standing, watching the passing parade. "Who do we wait for?" Vassos whispered to Lucas.

Before the Whip could answer, Ulanov said, "There he is," and quickly moved off, leaving the building.

"He's going to meet a Soviet cop," Lucas confided, standing in the lobby, watching the detective melt into the crowd.

"KGB?" Vassos whispered.

"A cop like us," Lucas said. "He's our liaison with the mission."

"Why do you have such an elaborate method to meet?"

Lucas shrugged. "They have their ways, and we have ours. We get along fine; occasionally we do each other small favors."

"Such as Russian vodka?" A sly twinkle brought his eyes to life, and he added, "On the arm."

Vassos smiled, proud of his correct use of NYPD slang.

"Something like that," Lucas added, smiling back at him.

Ulanov mixed in with the crowd waiting for the light to change. When it turned to green, he was immediately caught up in the surging mass of pedestrians.

Lucas followed his bobbing head across the avenue.

"Where is the Russian policeman?" Vassos asked.

"Mixed in with the crowd."

"What are you asking him to do for you?"

"Dig up whatever information he can on Matrazzo and Orhan Iskur."

Ulanov reached the other side of the avenue. He did an about-face and waited for the light to change. When it did, he crossed back across the avenue.

"Message delivered," Ulanov said, coming over to them. He shook out a cigarette and offered one to Vassos.

Vassos was about to take one when a memory burst into his consciousness. Soula and Stephanos had always been after him to stop smoking. "Greek men and their damn cigarettes," Soula would complain. Stephanos would leave him drawings of birds, each with the same note scrawled on it: *Daddy, birds don't smoke.* His eyes brimmed over. Pinching the lids together, he turned away and said, "No, thank you, Ivan. I do not smoke."

5 ═══════

anagement Information Systems Division was on the seventh floor of police headquarters at One Police Plaza, near Wall Street and City Hall. Rows of pentagon-shaped machines lined the glass-enclosed office. In the adjoining room technicians sat in front of consoles, typing in access codes, demanding information from the silent warehouses of data. Lucas signed the visitors log for both of them, and Vassos had a sticker pasted on the lapel of his jacket that read: VISITOR. The duty officer then assigned a thin, bookish fellow who wore a small yarmulka pinned to his thinning hair to assist them.

They stood behind the technician, watching him type in the necessary codes. Within seconds the printer to the right of the console started churning out reams of paper.

"Are all of your criminal records on tape?" Vassos asked.

"Practically everything in the Job is on tape. Even our roll calls are computerized."

The technician ripped off the printout and passed it to Lucas. "Here are the arrest records, Lou."

Lucas studied them. Frank Simmons and George Cuttler had extensive records. He passed them to Vassos.

The major looked them over and passed them back. "I am not familiar with your terms."

Taking them back, Lucas said, "Simmons had eight previouses: robberies, burglaries, a couple of felonious assaults. He did three years on a seven-and-a-half-year sentence for armed robbery. Cuttler had six falls and did eight years inside for manslaughter. Both of them have falls for homicide and manslaughter."

"They do not appear to have been the arty type, do they?" Vassos observed.

"They certainly do not," Lucas agreed, turning to the technician. "Are the nineteens on tape?"

"Yes, Lou."

"Dig out their associates on each collar," Lucas said.

The computer man swung around and danced his fingers over the keyboard.

Watching the bright green screen, Vassos asked, "What's nineteen?"

"A Prisoner's Modus Operandi and Pedigree Sheet. Every time someone is arrested, the arresting officer prepares one. It lists how the perp committed the crime and any special characteristics of his MO, along with his physical description and his associates on that collar."

"That is our S six form," Vassos offered.

The printer chugged out paper.

"What is the difference between your UF and DD forms?"

"UF stands for Uniform Force, and DD for Detective Division. I suppose that your S forms are used by Security Division."

"That is correct."

The technician handed Lucas the printouts.

"Is there someplace where we can work?" Lucas asked the civilian.

Next to the console area was a bare, cheerless room, with one long table and several chairs, walls and ceilings muffled by acoustic tile, floored with black-and-white linoleum, and windowless save for a half-silvered window on one wall that afforded a view of the work area.

Lucas placed the spread sheets on the table. He took a lined pad out of the folder and started to write down the names of associates who had been arrested with Simmons, Cuttler, and Denny McKay. This done, he left the room and gave the list to the technician. "I'd like their records too."

The computer man adjusted his yarmulka. "And then you're going to want the associates of the associates."

"War is hell, kid," Lucas said, going back inside.

Each of the criminal records came with several sheets of grainy, black-and-white photographs of the prisoner. Lucas arranged the records alphabetically. He wrote the names on the pad, along with each date of arrest, the crime, and the names of associates listed on that arrest.

Vassos examined the list of names. "They appear to be mostly Irish names. Does that mean anything?"

A deathly pallor came over Lucas's face and his lips set in a hard line. "Denny McKay is the boss of the Purple Gang."

"Who are they?"

"Scum! The gang evolved from a mob founded in the twenties. Mostly Irish hoods who went in for strong-arm stuff. Our department intelligence people reported that sometime in the seventies they began to do contract killings. They were recently discovered by the newspapers, who dubbed them the "Westies" because they come from the West Side of Manhattan."

Vassos was standing, his palms flat on the table. "Do you think they would take an overseas job?"

"If the money was right and the right guy gave the order, yes."

"You seem to hate them."

"I do," Lucas said, shuffling through the sheets, pulling out Denny McKay's folder.

An unasked question formed on Vassos's lips.

Lucas said, "McKay is fifty-six years old; he's taken two collars. His first one when he was twenty-one, right after the Korean War." He pulled out McKay's nineteens. "On his first

arrest he presented his army separation papers as identification." He read from the report, "U.S. Army, serial number,
served active duty May nine, 1950, to January fourteen, 1953.
First Cavalry Division.

"Strange. He gets out of the army and takes his first fall for
a burglary when he stole quote 'a seventeenth-century medal-
lion pendant studded with rubies and inlaid with cloisonné
enamel.' Appears McKay acquired an interest in art soon after
he got out of the army." Lucas wrote something on a piece of
paper and turned his back to Vassos. He took out his roll of
expense money, palmed two tens and a five, and left the
room. He found the computer man having a private conversation with a female computer person near the water cooler.
Interrupting, Lucas slid his arm around the computer man's
shoulder and steered him away from the woman. "I'd like the
sixty-ones on these arrests." He handed the man a sheet of
paper listing the arrests of McKay, Simmons, Cuttler, and
their associates.

"You want the Complaint Reports on all of these?" the
technician asked with typical civil service reluctance to do
any more work than the rules required. Lucas discreetly
slipped the expense money into the waiting palm. "Here, let
me buy you lunch."

Closing his fingers around the money, the technician said,
"And then you'll be wanting the sixty-ones on the associates
of the associates."

"Exactly. Send them to me through department mail."
Lucas gave the clerk one of his cards and then stuck his head
back in the room. "Andreas, let's you and me go see our scroll
expert, and after that, we'll pay Denny McKay a visit."

Her white linen suit had padded shoulders, a V neckline,
and hidden buttons. Her honey-colored hair was pulled back
to form a single braid that started near the crown of her head.
She wore long black-and-white summer earrings. Her sleek

hairstyle, high cheekbones, piercing green eyes, and exquisite mouth gave her face a classic look. She was quite tall and had a striking figure.

"Andreas Vassos?" she asked, extending her hand. She had been waiting for them near the coatroom of the Morgan Library.

"Yes," Vassos said, taking her extended hand and introducing his partner. "This is my colleague, Lieutenant Teddy Lucas."

"Hello to both of you," she said. "I'm Dr. Katina Wright, the Morgan's manuscript conservator."

"Nice to meet you," Lucas said, guessing that she was in her late thirties.

"Shall we go downstairs?" She made a sign to the security guard, who opened the door directly in front of the coatroom. Her basement office was a glass cubicle filled with books and rolling tray cabinets. Two small plants and a stuffed panda adorned her desk.

Lowering herself into her chair, she motioned them into seats and said, "Dr. Levi's telephone call and letter intrigued me. I gather you gentlemen are on the trail of the casket-copy."

"Yes," Vassos said, asking, "Didn't Dr. Levi explain everything to you?"

"He did, but I'd prefer to hear it again from you two. Professor Levi has a tendency to speak and write in rather oblique terms."

Vassos got up from his seat and closed her office door. He returned and told her the story of Voúla and about their search for Alexander's *Iliad*.

"Matrazzo's famous telegram was the last hint that the casket-copy might have been found," she said.

"Could it have survived all those centuries?" Lucas asked.

She looked at the New York City detective. "Of course it could have survived. The Dead Sea scrolls survived, and they were written between the first century B.C. and the first half of the first century A.D. An entire library of scrolls was unearthed in Herculaneum in 1754."

"How many scrolls made up the casket-copy?" Lucas asked.

"We have no way of knowing for sure. They only wrote on one side of the papyrus and the scrolls were not very long. Maybe fifteen scrolls, who knows? Maybe one for each book." She looked at Vassos. "Did you see the amphora that was found in Orhan Iskur's shop?"

"Yes, Professor Levi insisted that I examine it," Vassos said.

A slight smile crossed her face. "Yes, he would. Tell me about it, everything that you can remember."

Vassos described the tall storage jar in detail. "It was half-filled with black sand, and the inside was lined with some kind of thick materials."

"Cartonnage," she said to herself.

"What is that?" Lucas asked.

"Papyrus paper," she said, looking up at them. "It's made from layers of papyrus that have been stuck together, sort of a papier-mâché. The Egyptians used it as mummy casing. They would take it from the garbage dumps. Cartonnage is a wonderful preservative because it is airtight and therefore makes the contents immune to the effects of moisture. The ancients went to great lengths to preserve their scrolls. They were aware that papyrus was vulnerable to insects and moisture, so they used cylindrical containers of wood and ivory to store their scrolls. They treated papyrus with cedarwood oil as a preservative and insecticide." She again turned her attention to Vassos. "Did Professor Levi conduct tests on the black sand?"

"Yes. He told me that the sand definitely came from the island of Thíra," Vassos said.

Lucas sat forward with his hands clasped between his legs. "Katina, I'm a cop and I think like a cop, so please bear with me."

"I shall forbear, Teddy," she said with a pleasant smile.

"If we should get lucky and get our hands on the casket-copy, how can we be sure that it's not a forgery? I read where the Egyptians used to make phony trinkets to sell to the Greeks and Romans."

"There have always been dishonest antiques dealers. Tomb robbery is the world's second oldest profession, and forging antiquities is the third," she said, "but today we have many different techniques to establish provenance. Alexander's *Iliad* would almost certainly have a colophon, an inscription at the end that identified the scribe and the date and place where it was written. And, more than likely, it would also have a sentence or two stating that it was prepared for Alexander, son of Philip, King of Macedonia."

"Are there samples of Aristotle's handwriting that we can use for comparison?" Lucas asked.

"Unfortunately, none of the originals of his works are extant," she said.

"Then we still cannot be sure it is not a forgery, can we?" Lucas asked.

"The critical principle when establishing the provenance of a writing is to compare the rhythmical patterns of the meter to the corpus of the author's work."

"What about carbon dating?" Vassos asked.

"It is not precise enough," she answered. "Carbon dating can only place a thing within a few hundred years. There are more exact techniques."

Lucas glanced at his Greek partner. "If someone did come into possession of the scrolls, how would he go about getting them unrolled?"

"Any major museum or library. And there are private laboratories."

"But he would want to have the job done without anyone knowing about it, wouldn't he?" Lucas said. "If he went to a museum or a library, the word would be out that he had the casket-copy."

"You keep saying 'he,' Teddy. A woman might have them,

did you ever think of that? And yes, I suppose that the person who did have the scrolls would want to be discreet."

"Is there some special machine that is used to unroll them?" Lucas asked.

She smiled. "Yes. Would you like to see what it looks like?"

"Very much," Vassos answered.

She led them from her office along the aisle that ran be-tween the high workbenches. Four young women sat on stools peering through large magnifying glasses, laboriously restoring ancient parchments and codices. The policemen paused to watch them. One woman was gingerly brushing flaking vege-table pigments off a papyrus. Another was restoring the ink of an ancient script. Katina looked over the policemen's shoulders. "Martha is working on a manuscript by Poggio that was written in 1425."

Martha looked up from her work and smiled.

"Hello," Lucas said.

"Hello," Martha replied, looking back down through the glass at her work.

Katina led them to the end of the restoration area and stopped before a bench crammed with the tools of her trade. "Here is our scroll unroller," she announced, placing her hand on the machine.

"A humidifier?" Lucas said, unable to hide his surprise.

"A *super*humidifier," she corrected. "We added a hose so that we can direct the vapor into the scroll."

"How does it work?" Lucas asked.

She thought for a moment and answered, "When papyrus is kept dry it has remarkable powers of survival. But it be-comes brittle when desiccated, and then it has to be moistened in order to regain its flexibility so that it may be safely handled, flattened, and mounted in permanent form.

"Since it is so brittle in the dry state, the first thing that we have to do is to relax it by moisture before any attempt is made to unroll it; otherwise the scroll would break into many pieces. We start the relaxing process by wrapping the roll loosely in several layers of damp blotting paper and then setting it aside for an hour or so on a sheet of glass. By that time the outside of the scroll has become sufficiently limp so that we can manipulate it without having it crack; then the unrolling can begin. We then put them on blotting paper to absorb excess moisture. There's a lot more to it, but those are the basics." She shrugged her shoulders and smiled. "This process is very, very slow and it must be done with the utmost care. But, after umpty-ump centuries, what's a little more time?"

"Wouldn't the water run the ink or get absorbed in the blotting paper?" Lucas asked, unable to conceal his fascination.

"Not at all," she said. "We immerse manuscripts completely without that happening. Carbon inks present no complications and even the fugitive iron inks leave a tracing of rust when they decompose that is unaffected by a slight degree of moisture." She studied the policemen. "Any more questions?"

Shaking his head no, Lucas thought: beautiful and smart.

She continued: "Once the papyrus is flat it must be dried without delay by changing the blotting paper several times in the course of a few hours. As a protection against molds we sterilize the papyrus by pressing it with thymol-impregnated blotting paper for several days. After that is done it may be mounted passe-partout between two sheets of glass."

"Does it have to be glass?" Lucas asked.

"Absolutely," she said. "Acrylic gives off static electricity. Papyrus is composed of cellulose and under magnification looks a little like shredded wheat. The electricity in acrylic compounds would pull the fibers apart and destroy the document."

"If I had the casket-copy," Lucas asked, "and I wanted to sell it secretly, how would I go about doing it?"

"Well, since you obviously would not have the necessary export papers, that would eliminate the auction houses, mu-

seums, and important libraries; you would be left with a handful of rare book dealers accustomed to dealing with pieces of
such magnitude. And, of course, private collectors."

"How many dealers?" Lucas asked.

"In New York, five or six, and an equal number in London
and Rome."

"Would you be able to provide us with their names?" Vassos asked.

"Of course," she said.

Lucas leaned against the workbench, watching the restorers
peering through their portable glasses. "Katina? How much
would the casket-copy be worth in dollars and cents?"

She shook her head in dismay, studying the policemen.
"You both have no idea what it is that you're looking for, do
you?" She turned and hurried back to her office.

The policemen looked at each other, turned abruptly, and
followed her.

Her back was against a tray cabinet, her hands out at her
sides tucked into the tray's thin handles. One leg was crossed
over the other, the linen outlining her shapely legs, molding
her ample breasts into the white material. "Please sit, gentlemen."

She reminded Lucas of a teacher about to lose her patience,
but her calm voice reflected her easygoing logic. "Teddy.
Andreas. Alexander's *Iliad* would be the greatest archaeolog-
ical find ever unearthed. It would be worth more than all the
treasures dug out of Egypt; worth more than all the property
looted from Etruscan tombs; worth more than all the booty
stolen from the Americas." Her hands came out of the handles.

"Why would it be so valuable?" Lucas asked quietly, taken
aback by the force of her beauty.

"Several reasons," she said, sitting down. "Anything connected with Alexander and Aristotle would inflame people's
imaginations and give the item great intrinsic value. But the

main reason would be the ancients' tradition of oral history."
She crossed one leg over the other.

"I don't understand," Lucas said.

"The concept of silent reading was unknown during classical times. Everyone read aloud."

"You're telling me that when Alexander read his *Iliad* to himself, he read aloud?"

"That is exactly what I'm telling you. Silent reading was an invention of Christian monasticism in the fifth century A.D. Homeric poems were handed down orally through several centuries. The first written text of the *Iliad* was made in Athens in the middle of the sixth century B.C. And copies were not duplicated or circulated, they were used only for references." The phone on her desk gave out a muted ring but she ignored it and continued.

"In ancient times there was little if any punctuation or word division. Texts were read aloud and often did not indicate a change of speaker. This meant that the reader had a difficult time and in many cases made up characters or changed lines as he went along. The first formal Greek grammar was prepared around 130 B.C., and Latin did not begin as a written language until the third century B.C. Formal grammar throughout the rest of Europe did not come about until the Middle Ages."

"Katina," Lucas pleaded, "what has grammar got to do with the value of the casket-copy?"

"Don't you see?" she asked impatiently. "We know that Aristotle tutored Alexander between 343 and 336 B.C. Which would mean that the casket-copy would have to have been copied down during those seven years."

"So?" Vassos asked.

"It is believed that the *Iliad* that has come down to us today is not the same one that Homer wrote, or even the same one that Aristotle copied for Alexander. What we have today is a corrupted version of Homer."

Lucas looked puzzled. "And why is that?"

"Texts copied by hand are prone to corruption. If four policemen were to copy your police regulations from memory, not one of them would be correct; each copy would be slightly different. It's the same with the *Iliad*. Storytellers would add their own words and thoughts, scribes who did not like a passage would make up their own; if an ancient reader found a passage difficult to understand, he'd change it. Every time the *Iliad* was told, it came out differently." She took in a deep breath. "All scholars consider the *Iliad* to be one of the most important works ever written. It is, without question, one of the essential underpinnings of our literary tradition. To have a copy, or even a portion of a copy, that dates from the fourth century B.C. would be a priceless find."

Vassos cast his eyes downward. "Katina, you understand we intend to return the casket-copy to Greece?"

"Yes, I know that," she said.

"Will you help us?" Lucas asked.

"Help you," she echoed. "That was decided before you arrived here. You see, gentlemen, Professor Levi is my father." She stood up, the look on her face saying no further glimpses into her private life would be allowed. "Would you like me to go with you when you visit the book dealers?"

"Yes," Lucas said, "you could be of help. Most of the dealers know you, don't they?"

"Yes, they do," she said, paging through her appointment book. "I have nothing I can't change scheduled for the remainder of this week. When would you like to start?"

"As soon as possible," Lucas said.

"I'll prepare a list of the dealers and telephone for appointments," she said.

"Will they see us?" Lucas asked.

She smiled. "It would be most unusual for any of them to decline to see the Curator of Ancient and Medieval Manuscripts of the Morgan Library."

• ■ ■

The Den was located on the west side of Ninth Avenue, between Forty-eighth and Forty-ninth streets. It was on a dilapidated block of abandoned tenements and boarded-up storefronts. Lucas parked the Buick three blocks away on the east side of Ninth Avenue.

McKay's hangout was a dingy West Side saloon on the ground floor of an abandoned four-story tenement with boarded-up windows. A pizzeria was one door uptown from the bar. Two derelicts shared a pint of muscatel in a nearby doorway. Cars continuously pulled up in front of the bar and double-parked; men rushed into the bar, stayed some minutes, and rushed back out to their cars.

"A lot of activity," Lucas observed, slumped down behind the wheel. He slid his arm over the back of the velour-covered seat, observing the foreign cut of Vassos's suit. "How'd you like to take a look inside that bar, let me know what's happening. If any of them so much as got a whiff of me, they'd make me for a cop."

Vassos reached inside his jacket and unsnapped his holster and ammo pouch. He stuffed them under the passenger seat. "I'll see you soon, partner."

Lucas grabbed his arm. "Andreas, observe and report, nothing more, okay?"

"You have it, Lou."

"You got it, Lou," Lucas corrected him, smiling.

Vassos reflexively shuddered at the artificial cold of the air-conditioning as he entered the darkened bar. The smell of beer mixed with a thick fog of cigarette smoke. Music blared from a jukebox. To the left of the entrance was a long bar; on the right, six leatherette booths.

Vassos moved inside and over to an empty stool at the end of the bar near the entrance, ignoring the inquisitive looks coming his way. Several men stood at the bar drinking and talking in lowered tones. The bartender, a grungy man with a day's growth of beard, came over to Vassos. "What'll it be, pal?"

Putting on a heavy Greek accent, Vassos ordered a beer, the same brand he'd consumed earlier that day at the precinct. He leaned forward, resting his arms on the bar, looking straight ahead, minding his own business. An open door at the end of the bar led into a kitchen. Vassos could see black pans hanging on the wall and part of a large commercial stove. A wide aisle separated the bar from the tables.

The bartender put down a beer and moved off.

From the corner of his eye, Vassos recognized a face from the mug shots he'd seen at police headquarters. Denny McKay, the head of the Purple Gang, was sitting in the last booth. Four other men were crowded into the booth with him. Although McKay was sitting, he looked much bigger than he did in his police photographs. Half-glasses were perched on his nose and wisps of gray hair fell untidily over the collar of his shirt. The pocket of his short-sleeved shirt was stuffed with pens; he wore white socks and sandals.

Brawny men kept coming into the saloon, each of them stopping to pay respects to McKay. Some of these men walked past McKay into the back room, stayed several minutes, came out, and left.

Vassos saw the bartender make eye contact with McKay. The man behind the bar picked up a towel and began to wipe his way over to the policeman. "You from around here, pal?"

"I am from Greece," Vassos announced in an accent.

"You, er, live in Greece or over here, in the States?"

"I live in Kaloni, a small village on Kriti," he said, using the Greek word for the island of Crete.

"What brings you to the States?"

Vassos saw McKay watching, chewing on his cigarette's filter. "A woman. She was beautiful, the kind of woman you want to do it to the moment you see her. And she was a virgin."

"What happened?"

"What happened?" Vassos echoed with a philosophical shrug of shoulders. "I wanted to fuck her so I became engaged to marry her, and after I did it to her for a month, I got bored with her and broke the engagement. Her brothers are hunting me, and I must stay out of Greece until my family makes things right."

The bartender made the universal money sign with his fingers. "It's gonna cost you."

Vassos nodded.

The bartender moved off, looked over at McKay. Vassos saw the bartender's head tilt and McKay's facial expression relax.

Vassos slid off his stool and, making his way along the bar, asked the bartender, "The toilet?"

"Straight ahead," the man behind the stick said, drawing a draft beer.

Moving past the entrance to the kitchen with his non-threatening eyes cast downward, Vassos entered the back room. There was a shuffleboard in the center of it and groups of men sitting in booths. Conversation stopped. Tough, hostile-looking men studied the policeman. There were two doors on his left. Vassos opened the first one and discovered a large closet with a skeletonized staircase leading upward. The banister, risers, and stringers were intact, but the treads, the steps one normally stood on, had been removed.

"What the fuck you looking at, pally?"

Vassos turned. Two ugly men were staring him down. "I need the toilet, please."

"Next door, pal," the uglier of the two barked.

The tiny, ill-lit bathroom reeked of urine. Vomit splattered the wall and sink, and soggy cigarette butts clogged the urinal. Vassos stepped up to the trough and urinated. He zipped up and meekly pushed past them out into the saloon. The dank bar was a welcome relief after the stench of the toilet.

He finished his beer standing up, left two dollars on the

bar, and walked out into the sunlight. He turned left, passed a group of men and the open-front pizzeria, and walked three blocks north before turning east.

The Buick came to a stop alongside some parked cars. Lucas leaned across the seat and pushed open the door. "Well?" he asked as Vassos slid inside.

Vassos gave him a brief report and told him about the closet with the staircase without stairs.

"That's an old trick used by narcotics dealers," Lucas said. "They removed the treads so that any cops who visit them will have to grip the banister with both hands and climb up on the risers or the stringers that support the banister. The bad guys wait on top." He glanced at the man in the passenger seat. "I'd say McKay's got something going on up there that he doesn't want the good guys to know about. Well, we're just going to have to make it our business to find out what."

Sergeant Roosevelt Grimes, the Second Whip of the Sixteenth Squad, had a steel plate in his head compliments of an overzealous white cop who had enjoyed cracking black heads with his nightstick during the Columbia riots. Before the black undercover officer could utter the code word that would have identified him as a member of the force, the uniformed cop beat him unconscious.

It ain't easy being a black undercover in *Nueva York.*

Grimes was sitting behind his cluttered desk massaging his forehead when Lucas came in and flopped into a chair.

"You got pain, Roosevelt?"

"It's the heat, Lou."

"And in the winter it's the cold. Why the hell don't you throw in your papers and sail off into the sunset? No more fives, no pressure."

"I got two more kids to put through college." He opened the side drawer, took out a bottle of orange pills, popped two into his mouth, swallowed, and asked, "What's up, Lou?"

Lucas, lifting up out of his seat, handed his Second Whip

a slip of paper. "I want you to get me a copy of Denny McKay's army record and have a couple of our guys try and locate any relatives of a guy named Paolo Matrazzo. He went DOA on a Greek island that the Greeks call Thíra, but the rest of the world calls Santorini."

"When did this Matrazzo guy pack it in?"

"Nineteen thirty-nine."

Grimes looked at the paper and then up at the Whip. "This caper connected to the CI you're doing for the C of D?"

"Yes it is, but I can't fill you in on it yet."

"You want a list of McKay's duty stations too?"

"I want everything."

"You got it," Grimes said, sliding the paper into the border of his desk blotter.

Detective John Leone, a handsome man with black hair, dreamy eyes, and a bushy mustache he referred to as his carpet sweeper, had a partner named Jack Owens who stood a hair over six feet and whose chest and shoulders flowed smoothly into a broad expanse that resembled a minor league dam. Owens was a black man who the guys in the Squad called Big Jay. When Lucas came out into the squad room ten minutes later, he found Leone pontificating to Vassos, Ulanov, Gregory, and Big Jay.

"You guys ever wonder how women piss in them little cups?" Leone asked. "I mean, they got nothing to aim with. I've been thinking about that ever since I took my physical last week."

"How do you figure they do it?" asked Big Jay.

"Well," Leone began, "they must hold the cup under their pussy and sort of get the range, maybe spritz a few drops, and then, when they're on the target, they give it a good squirt."

Ulanov turned back to the typewriter. "This place is funner than *Mad* magazine."

Big Jay placed a gentle hand on Ulanov's shoulder. "Don't

you find yourself always thinking about women? How you're going to score the next one, how she's going to open her legs for you?"

Ulanov looked up into the smiling black face. "Naw," he said seriously, "pussy makes me sneeze."

Lucas motioned Vassos into his office. The Whip flipped open the case folder and saw that Grimes had inserted a copy of the complaint report marked: Confidential Investigation/ FOA. He thought about his Second Whip and wondered what it must be like to have children to worry about, to work so hard to help them get a start in life. He decided that it must be wonderful. He jotted reminder notes on the inside flap: *1. Russian info re: M and I; 2. McKay's army record; 3. Old 61's on Purple Gang; 4. PM's relatives.*

When Vassos came into the office, Lucas said, "I want to do some research on the casket-copy. I'm going to the public library. Want to come with me?"

"I would like to, Teddy, but I must report to my embassy. They want to see me to make sure that I am alive and well." His finger traced the figure eight on the edge of the desk. "Would you like to have dinner with me tonight? The night clerk at my hotel is a Greek and he has told me of this restaurant in Astoria."

Lucas checked his watch. "What time would you want to go?"

"Late. Around ten."

"I'll pick you up at nine-thirty," Lucas said, moving out from behind his desk.

She slid out of the bed and padded into the bathroom. The warm golden glow of a summer evening slipped through the blinds and threw bars of light on her naked body. Lucas watched her lissome form move gracefully over the carpet. Long legs, well-developed figure, creamy skin, auburn hair. Her first name was Joan. Her last was Karsten. Six months ago Lucas had been in the supermarket reaching for a jar of peanut butter. She had been reaching for grape jelly. He did not want involvements; she wanted a weekly matinee. It had seemed like a perfect arrangement at the time.

He raised himself up on his elbows and watched her come back to the bed. He liked her goose pimply nipples and her delicate brown pubic hair. She stepped silently into her underpants and hooked on her bra. Her glum expression told him that something was on her mind. She lowered herself onto the edge of the bed and caressed his face.

"Teddy," she began, "you're a nice man, and you've been up front with me from the beginning, so please, please don't misunderstand what I'm going to say."

He fluffed the pillow up under his head, sat up higher, and waited.

Her eyes fell on the sheets. "I think that from now on we should use condoms. I have no way of knowing how many others you are seeing or who they are seeing, and, well, it just gets so complicated. . . ."

Looking into her anxious eyes, Lucas thought: we've fucked up our criminal justice system; we've fucked up our ozone layer; we've fucked up our ecological balance; and now, we're fucking up sex. Only man could be such an asshole. He brushed a strand of hair from her brow. "Do you make your husband use a condom?"

She laughed. "Mr. Wonderful? No need to worry about him. Mr. Wonderful's interests, in descending order, are: making money, football, basketball, baseball, and expensive cigars. Once every month or so he'll roll on top of me, grunt, and roll off."

"Why don't you leave him?"

"Because I'm forty-seven years old and scared. And because all the Prince Charmings have been taken, except you." She reached out and gave his penis a playful squeeze. "You wouldn't by any chance be interested in a more meaningful relationship?"

"I hate that word."

"Which one, meaningful or relationship?"

"Both of them," he said, reaching over the side of the bed, groping for his underwear.

"Will I see you next week?" she asked, a concerned edge to her voice.

Sitting up and heaving his feet onto the floor, he answered, "Yes."

"Teddy, may I ask you a personal question?"

Unsure eyes darted to her. "What?"

"Why me? You're a handsome man. You're a gentleman. Why get yourself involved in a dead-end relationship? There are a lot of available women out there looking for a man like you."

Joan was not the first woman who had asked Teddy Lucas that question. His stock answer was that his wife had left him because she felt that marriage was stifling her. He didn't think he'd ever tell anyone the truth; it was still too painful. Before he could give her his standard reply, Joan fell on her knees between his legs and hugged him around his waist. "I look forward to our weekly rendezvous."

"Me too," he said, pressing her head to his stomach. "Are you pressed for time?"

She looked up at him and smiled knowingly. "I have a few minutes," she said, pushing him back down on the bed.

After Joan left, he spread the sheet out over the bed, went into the bathroom, and showered. He dried himself off and telephoned the Forty-second Street branch of the public library. It was open until 8:45 that evening. He picked up the phone and dialed the C of D's direct number at One Police Plaza.

Edgeworth's gruff voice came on the line. Lucas brought him up to date on the conduct of the investigation.

"What's your feel for the case?" Edgeworth asked.

"I'm still not sure if I'm investigating a flight of fancy or if there is a real case to be made. But I'll tell you this much,

Chief, we're a long way off from handing anyone up for extra-dition to Greece."

"What kind of a guy is Vassos?"

"He's a good guy. Seems to know his stuff."

"Well, be sure to keep me informed."

"Ten-four, boss," Lucas said, using the affirmative police code signal.

"Yes, sir," C of D Edgeworth said into the telephone. "That is correct. Lieutenant Lucas just reported in to me, and he was not very optimistic about the course of the investigation. . . . Yes, Mr. Hayden, I most certainly will keep you posted."

Edgeworth thoughtfully replaced the receiver. He stared at the instrument, then snapped it back to his ear and dialed the PC's centrex number. "This is the chief of detectives. Is the boss still in the building?"

Police Commissioner Franklin Vaughn's ruddy complexion brightened when his C of D entered his office. He waved Edgeworth into one of the chairs arranged in front of his desk. "Your people did an outstanding job on that Rabbi Goldstein homicide, Timmy."

"A hanger, boss. Four local Jew haters got their loads on and went hunting. They left enough physical evidence behind for us to track them to Mars and back."

Vaughn reached into the bottom drawer of his desk and came up with a bottle of scotch. "Want a taste?"

"No thanks," Edgeworth said, watching the PC pour some into his coffee mug. A tingling sensation stung his lips and mouth. Maybe just one? No! He hadn't picked up a drink in four years and he wasn't going to today. He quickly checked the time: six-thirty. Shit! He'd miss the 7:00 P.M. meeting at St. Claire's. Now he'd have to rush uptown.

Vaughn drank, clutched the mug to his stomach. "You still on the wagon, Timmy?"

"Yes. One day at a time."

Vaughn shook his head. "Ya gotta be able to control the hard stuff, Timmy. I can stop any time I want to stop. I only take a few short belts now and then to help me relax. I think better with a few under my belt."

"Right, boss." He watched the PC take another swig.

"What's on your mind?"

"It bothers me that we have to report to this guy Hayden at the State Department on the conduct of one of our cases."

"The Greek thing?"

"Yes."

Pouring more scotch, Vaughn said, "The white-shirt boys are interested in this one, Timmy. Big diplomatic hullabaloo."

"We could be jeopardizing the integrity of the case by reporting to them. They're whores. We have no way of knowing what they're doing with the information we're feeding them."

"It's their case, Tim ol' boy."

"That's my point. Why toss it to us when there are at least six federal agencies with jurisdiction? It doesn't make sense."

"Who knows? Who cares? Maybe they felt that we could handle it more expe . . . ex . . . faster." The word was out in the Job: the PC was on the sauce. The sharks smelled blood and were circling; the sniping had started. Vaughn had been dubbed the King of Nowhere.

The PC's head shot up. "Keep me informed."

"Right, boss."

Edgeworth started to stand. Vaughn said, "Wait a minute," and passed him a slip of paper that he had taken from under his desk blotter. It contained the name, shield number, tax registry number, and present command of a female detective.

"When you get the chance," Vaughn said, "move her into the Bond and Forgery Squad."

"B and F is three over their quota now."

"The lady is Congressman Berns's girlfriend."

Edgeworth frowned in an effort to keep his face from showing the disgust he felt. "I'll take care of it."

Major General Philippos Tsimas, the head of Greece's Central Information Service, had five agents-in-place in New York City. Their main duties were to gather economic and political information and to sow as much harmful disinformation about Turkey as was discreetly possible. The station chief in New York was a short, feisty, sixty-year-old woman with a throaty voice and an affinity for man-tailored clothes, gold bangle bracelets, and gaudy rings. Her name was Elisabeth Syros; she was Vassos's control. Her cover was that of a secretary in the consul general's office.

"How do you like working with the American police, Major?"

Vassos continued to stare down at the black statue in front of Rockefeller Center. "They are like us in many ways."

"Have you made any progress?"

Vassos turned from the window and moved to the couch against the wall. "The investigation is just beginning. The lieutenant who has been assigned to help is competent and we work well together."

She lowered herself down next to him. "Your primary purpose is to return the casket-copy. I hope you understand that."

"And the people responsible for murdering my family?"

"I think we have to be realistic about our chance of extraditing an American citizen back to Greece to stand trial for murder."

"You think it impossible?"

"I think that any expectation of success is, at most, unrealistic." She gently searched his face. "Andreas, why do you think you were chosen for this assignment?"

He met her scrutiny without flinching. "Because of what happened to my family, and because I am a policeman."

"Yes, those are reasons. But not *the* reason. You were sent because it was felt that you would have the proper motivation, and the courage, to do whatever was required to return the casket-copy to us." She shrugged. "As for the people responsible for the Voúla massacre, we have no objections if you consider that a *personal* matter."

He looked out the window at St. Patrick's Cathedral's north tower. "I would prefer to handle the matter on a personal basis."

Detectives Ivan Ulanov and Frank Gregory huddled in front of the Sixteenth Precinct's computer console located in the muster room, behind the Desk. The days when the dogged detective had to spend a good part of his tour knocking on doors and seeking out information had gone the way of the truncheon and the *Police Gazette.* Today, by keying identity codes and access codes into police computer banks, detectives were able to retrieve a broad spectrum of facts about anyone. "Gimme their name and social security number, and I'll own 'em for life," Ulanov said to Gregory as he keystroked the Matrazzo name into the automobile registration bank.

"What is it with this Matrazzo caper and the Greek major?" Gregory asked, looking over his partner's shoulder.

"Don't know," Ulanov said. "The word is that the boss is doing a confidential for the C of D."

A list of Matrazzos who owned cars registered in New York State appeared on the lime green screen. Ulanov pressed the PF 8 button. The printer on the side of the console came alive, pushing out computer paper.

Frank Gregory tore off the spread sheets and slipped them into a folder. Ulanov typed in the access code for the boat and aircraft bank, then entered the Matrazzo name.

The precinct roll call man, a skinny guy with thinning gray hair, walked behind the Desk and glanced over at the detectives. "Hey, Frank, how's your love life these days?"

Gregory looked at his old radio car partner. "It don't go up so often."

"Yeah, but it do last longer," the roll call man said, putting the roll call sheets for the third, first, and second platoons down on the desk.

Gregory tore off the sheets that had just been ejected from the printer and slipped them into the folder. The police radio on top of the Desk belched out a 10:30 in progress. He picked up the telephone and, looking up at the list of telephone numbers taped to the wall over the console, dialed New York Telephone security. An appointment was made for later that day. He made other appointments with Consolidated Edison security and the Burgerwade Credit Company, Ltd.

Ulanov typed in his tax registry number and signed off the machine.

"Where do you want to go first?" Gregory asked as they stepped out from behind the Desk.

Ulanov glanced up at the wall clock. "Why don't we call it a day? We can hit the Board of Elections tomorrow and see how many Matrazzos vote."

Anna Grantas bustled around the restaurant dimming lights while her husband Spiro played backgammon in the lounge with two of the waiters. The last of the American patrons had left five minutes ago. The Greeks would be arriving shortly. The night was winding down; the clock behind the bar read 10:24. The bartender slowly turned the pages of a newspaper.

Zorba's was located on Thirty-sixth Street, three blocks west of Steinway Street in Astoria, Queens. The trendy Manhattan crowd usually arrived there early in the evening. They'd cross the Triboro Bridge in their cars and drive into the Greek section of Astoria to eat exotic foods, listen to exotic music, watch waiters dance, and break plates on the floor, the cost of which was added to their bills at a markup of six hundred percent. Breaking plates was good business.

The dining room was to the left of the entrance, down four short steps. It was a large room decorated with garish gold wallpaper; a vaulted ceiling with golden rococo molding framed swirling white clouds against a blue sky. A huge crystal chandelier dangled over the parquet dance floor; spaced at regular intervals were glittering glass candelabras set in niches in the walls.

At 10:46 five men sauntered through the glass doors. Anna Grantas called to the waiters to turn up the lights as she and her husband rushed to greet their guests. The new arrivals shouted greetings in Greek to the waiters and bartenders. One of them rushed to reach across the bar and shake hands. The band climbed back onto the bandstand.

More men arrived, coming in groups. Each of the male guests made a peacock's stroll into the restaurant. Soon couples and families began to arrive. An unmarried daughter of the owner ambled over to the steps to look into the restaurant, her eyes evaluating the available men.

Lucas and Vassos pushed their way through the door. Spiro and his wife greeted them warmly. A waiter escorted them to a table on the edge of the dance floor.

"Do you want me to order?" Vassos asked, seeing that the late-night menu was in Greek.

"That'll be fine," Lucas said, glancing around the room. Nothing had changed since his father had brought him here on his sixteenth birthday. Mr. and Mrs. Grantas looked the same; the waiters still wore white shirts open at the collars and black flared trousers to hide their elevator shoes. The late-night patrons still spoke Greek and the men still wore clothes with a European cut. Many of the men still carried handbags tucked under their arms. The ashtrays were forever filled with the butts of strong Greek cigarettes.

Lucas felt strange being there after so many years. He had the uncomfortable feeling of not belonging. He wondered why Greeks clung so tenaciously to their culture, why they held on to the past so longingly. Then a waiter appeared and began to put down plates of appetizers. Another came and put down two water glasses and a pitcher of the house *retsina.*

Vassos poured the homemade wine. "Giassou," he toasted. They raised their glasses to each other.

It had been many years since Lucas had tasted retsina. His grandfather used to make it out in a shed behind the house back in Greece. He hadn't thought of his grandfather in years. He pictured the old man's stern countenance, his upswept mustache, his warm embrace and loving heart. Suddenly he was enveloped in a wave of guilt because he so seldom thought of his grandfather, or his grandmother.

"Was your homework at the library a success?" Vassos asked.

Lucas cut off a slice of bread and scooped up cucumber salad. "Moderately. I didn't have much time but I learned that there is a lot to learn. I also learned that the plural of papyrus is papyri, that it comes from Egypt, and that when Alexander was a boy there was a shortage of the stuff because of the Persian occupation of Egypt." He sipped some of his wine. "Alexander's dad, the king, ordered a special supply of papyrus be sent to Aristotle so that he could copy the *Iliad* for his son."

"Yes, I know," Vassos said, trying to decide on an appetizer.

Lucas sipped retsina.

As heavy bouzouki music blared from the amplifiers the waiter brought more appetizers: rice-stuffed grape leaves, pies of cheese and spinach, fried squid, souvlaki. Lucas made wet circles with his glass, waiting for the waiter to leave. When he did, Lucas said, "The last time there was any mention of the casket-copy was on June tenth, 323 B.C., when Alexander went DOA." He ate a round of squid. "I don't believe that your people were killed over some papyrus fragments."

"What are you trying to say, Teddy?"

"I'm suggesting that there might be a different motive behind the massacre."

"Such as?"

"I don't know."

Vassos leaned across the table and said, "Teddy, you spent a little while at a library looking in a few books. Do you really think that you could have even begun to know such a subject in so short a time?"

"Of course not. And I certainly don't think that I'm any expert on Alexander. But I read enough to know that I've good reason for my skepticism." He watched as Vassos poured more of the amber wine into their glasses.

"Teddy, before you make up your mind concerning the existence of the casket-copy, I ask you to please wait until we speak to the book dealers."

Lucas picked up a grape leaf, studied the green blade dripping with lemon juice, popped it into his mouth, and said, "Fair enough."

The music grew in intensity.

A man leaped up onto the dance floor, his shuffling feet and flailing arms keeping time to the music. Another man ran up and danced, twirling his body over the parquet. The tambourine rattled louder. The steel guitar and the bouzoukis played in melody with the *Udte*. Three men linked arms around each other's waists and danced. The waiter came over to their table and put down plates of lamb heads.

"*Kefalaki*," Lucas said. "I haven't eaten lamb heads in years." He speared one onto his plate. Using his pinkie, he gouged out an eye and, impaling it upon his nail, sucked it into his mouth, savoring the cold membrane. He chomped down slowly until it squished, splattering inside his mouth.

Watching Lucas eviscerate the head with his knife and fork, Vassos commented, "And you tell me that you are not Greek. You eat *kefalaki* like a Greek." He laughed, a dry, mirthless hacking sound, then suddenly slammed his glass down on the table and leaped up onto the dance floor, slowly spinning around on one foot with his arms outstretched at his sides, his head thrown all the way back.

Lucas's hands and feet tapped to the beat of the music. He realized that he had eaten Kefalaki the Greek way, and he also realized that for the first time in many years he felt Greek.

Patrons began to toss plates. Waiters rushed to keep tabs on the wreckage.

Vassos twirled around the floor.

Lucas gulped down more retsina. He felt light-headed, full of fun. He tossed a plate out onto the dance floor. Vassos saw him do this and laughed as he twirled around. Spinning back into his seat, gasping for breath, he said, "I saw you throw that plate." Still fighting for breath, he smiled, shook a finger in his partner's face, and said, "We have a saying, my friend: a man cannot erase what is written on his blood."

Lucas drank wine. "And we have a saying too: A guy who goes through life with one foot in yesterday and another in tomorrow is bound to shit all over himself."

"Giassou, Teddy."

6

Sunlight streamed through the grated windows, casting a diamond netting of shadow over the detective squad room. A cleaner moved about emptying wastebaskets into a plastic trash bag. He scattered cleaning compound on the floor and swept up a night's worth of butts and dirt with a long-handled broom.

"Is he a policeman?" Vassos asked, standing in the doorway of Lucas's office.

"A civilian cleaner assigned to the precinct. The precinct CO is responsible for the building's housekeeping."

Floor fans hummed in the morning heat. Vassos turned and looked into the office, watching Lucas sitting on the edge of his desk, studying the blackboard. "You did not dance last night."

"It's not the custom here for men to dance by themselves or with other men."

"One day you will dance." Vassos moved into the office. "Thank you for paying the bill last night."

"The Job picked up the tab," Lucas said, turning to look at the sixty sheet, or the UF60 Chronological Record of Cases. He was relieved to see that nothing heavy had come in during the night. He might be off the chart, but it was still his squad, his cases, his clearances.

The metallic cadence of police calls droned through the squad room. Lucas looked at the wall clock: 9:32. He telephoned downstairs and asked the desk sergeant if the mail had arrived. It was being sorted, he was told. Moving into the squad room, he saw that Ulanov was typing a report. Gregory was interviewing a complainant over the telephone and Big Jay Owens was studying the case folder of an unsolved, seven-year-old homicide. John Leone had his feet up on the desk and was reading a newspaper.

"John," Lucas said, "do me a favor and go downstairs and get the mail."

"Right, Lou," Leone said, putting down the newspaper.

Leone returned in ten minutes with a wire basket brimming with mail. He moved to the pigeonhole lockers and began to sort the mail into slots.

"Anything for me?" Lucas asked.

Leone foraged through the basket searching for mail addressed: CO 16 Sqd. He handed the Whip a bunch of envelopes and went back to his newspaper.

Taking the handful of multiuse envelopes and folders back into his office, Lucas began to go through the pile, looking for anything from Central Records. He found what he was looking for in three double-packed folders. He untied the flap and slid out the contents: printouts of all the complaint reports that Denny McKay and his friends had collected over the years. He put them aside and opened the case folder and removed the arrest reports that he had brought back from Central Records. He took his time matching up the complaint and arrest reports. That done, he arranged the arrest reports alphabetically by name of prisoner. Most of the collars had been made for burglary, robbery, and felonious assaults. With the arrest reports arranged by names, he wrote down the names on a lined pad and beside each one listed the crime, as well as the details of the crime. Looking over the arrest report on a Bucky McMahon, Lucas noticed in the Property Information box: "one old book by Aristarchus. Value: $500,000.

Property not recovered at scene." He jotted down the sixty-one number and the complainant's name and address.

Vassos was studying the blackboard.

"An old book was stolen during the course of a robbery by one of McKay's men. It happened eleven years ago, and the complainant was a Mr. Belmont E. Widener. The property was never recovered."

Vassos turned from the board. "Do you think there's a connection?"

"I don't know," Lucas said. "It's one more thing we're going to have to take a look at. In fact—"

"You fucking cunt!" a frantic voice screamed out in the squad room.

Lucas and Vassos rushed outside in time to see a man come sailing over the wooden railing.

A hatless policewoman, heavyset, with a head of thick black hair, threw open the gate and stormed inside. "Get in that cage, asshole."

The man leaped up, yanked down his fly, pulled out his penis, and screamed, "Suck my prick, you cunt."

Ulanov continued to type.

Gregory covered the telephone's mouthpiece with his hand.

Big Jay turned in his seat, draping his arm over the back of his chair.

The Second Whip closed the door to his office.

John Leone casually moved to the police radio and turned up the volume, then strolled back to his desk, shaking his head disdainfully at the man as he passed him. The insolent prisoner's well-defined muscles shaped his dirty T-shirt. He stood in the middle of the squad room snarling at the police-woman, casting unsure glances at the detectives.

The policewoman's partner, a sloppy man in his early for-ties with a ponderous gut and a small waxed mustache, calmly walked past the prisoner and opened the door to the detention cage. He waited for his partner to make her move.

"I'm not about to tell you again, asshole, get into that cage."

"Suck this, you Puerto Rican douchebag."

Rolling her eyes with bogus irritation, she walked over to the prisoner, suddenly pivoted to her right, hunching down, and whirled around, throwing a right directly into the man's genitals. He gasped and doubled over in pain. The police-woman struck again with a left hand that caught him flush on the temple. He crumpled onto the floor, rolling onto his stomach.

Big Jay sadly shook his head. "You should be ashamed of yourself, letting a woman beat the shit out of you." He turned back to his case folder.

The policewoman straddled her prisoner, reached down, grabbed him by his belt and, scissoring him up off the floor, dragged him across the room into the cage. Her partner slammed the detention cage door, slid the locking pin through the steel bar, and moved to a vacant typewriter to help with the paperwork.

Vassos's lips pursed in approbation. "Are all your women officers that efficient?"

"We have some that don't row with both oars in the water, but most of them are okay, and a few, like Josey, are damn good."

"What am I being arrested for?" the prisoner shouted, struggling up on shaky legs.

"Possession of a big mouth," Josey said, rolling an arrest report into the machine.

The man sitting across from Trevor Hughes in the Oak Room of the Plaza Hotel waited for his guest to butter his roll. Hughes's feigned cheerfulness had not deceived his host. "How goes it in Athens, Trevor?"

"Fine," Hughes said, his gaze sweeping the intimate, cozy restaurant, its dark oak walls and groined ceiling. "As you know, Greece can be quite civilized," Hughes added.

"Did Nancy come with you?"

"No. She stayed on Paros. We rented a house there for the summer. I manage to pop over some weekends and whenever I can sneak away from the embassy."

"How are the children?"

"Grown and scattered all over the place, doing their own things."

"Well, I guess that's the way of it all." The host raised his water glass. "What brings you to New York?"

Hughes placed his butter knife across his bread plate and looked across the table at his host's ring. "I've always loved that ring."

"Yes, it *is* special," he said, sliding it off his finger and passing it to Hughes. "Emperor Caracalla had the coin struck around 215 A.D. from the imperial mint at Ephesus. Alexander is on the obverse, and on the reverse is a scene showing him hunting boar with Meleager."

Rolling the heavy gold ring over his palm, Hughes observed, "It must be quite valuable."

"Not really. There are many coins and medallions around from that period."

Hughes brushed a crumb off the tablecloth. "There was a massacre in Greece. In Voúla, a village outside the capital." He watched the waiter roll the dessert cart past their table.

"I read about it in the newspapers. Those damn terrorists are getting a bit out of hand, I'd say." The host forked some Caesar salad into his mouth.

"Terrorists were not responsible," Hughes said, dabbing his napkin at the corner of his lip.

"Really. Who was?"

"Two Americans. They were hired in New York City to murder two Greek policemen."

"Incredible. How do you know this?"

"I read the intelligence reports that are sent to the ambassador. And our FBI liaison has good sources within the Hellenic Police. The terrorist thing was a cover story that the government let out."

"I see."

"Cuttler and Simmons were their names."

"Whose names, Trevor?"

"The killers'."

A crash of dishes caused people to look up from their plates.

"Simmons was killed at the scene trying to escape." Hughes broke off a piece of roll and buttered it. "Cuttler was taken alive."

A muscle at the corner of the other man's jaw began to twitch. "I imagine that the Greek police must have some unique interrogative techniques." He lifted his wineglass to his mouth and drank.

"Actually not. They're concerned about civil rights and that sort of stuff."

"I'm glad to hear that they're so enlightened."

"Cuttler died in the hospital." Hughes cut his pan-blackened swordfish steak. "But not before he talked."

Maneuvering lettuce onto his fork, the host asked, "Did this Cuttler say who hired them?"

"He didn't live long enough."

"Pity."

"They're sending someone."

"Who is sending someone?"

"The Greek police. One of their men is coming here to try and find the people who hired Simmons and Cuttler and to find out why these people wanted the two policemen killed. He'll be working with someone from the NYPD." Hughes's face set in a disapproving scowl.

"Why the look, Trevor?"

"Orhan Iskur was murdered the same day as the massacre."

"Orhan probably had his spoon stuck in somebody else's pudding."

"You're more than likely right," Hughes said, cutting more

fish. "On the other hand, Simmons and Cuttler would have needed a contact in Greece, to help move things along."

"Yes, I suppose they would."

"Orhan would have made the perfect point man. Don't you agree?"

"Yes, I suppose he would have."

"But then, *our* Orhan would never have been persuaded to undertake such a task without explicit orders from you, would he?"

Both men sipped wine, their inquiring eyes peering over the rims. Silence grew between them.

Hughes lowered his glass. "I'm planning on retiring next year. I've bought a chalet outside of Bern."

The host smiled. "Sounds idyllic."

"I've enjoyed our occasional entrepreneurial adventures."

"Yes, they have been mutually rewarding."

Hughes blurted, "I'm leaving Nancy."

The man with the golden ring was surprised. "You've been married for over thirty years."

His guest looked somewhat sheepish as he explained, "I'm in love. For the first time in my life, I'm really in love." The host looked at his guest with a weary expression. Hughes added nervously, "She's younger, of course. She's twenty-four."

"Trevor! You're fifty-seven years old. What in the name of—"

Hughes angrily pointed his knife at his host. "I don't want to hear any of that. I'm trim and in excellent shape. She loves me and she excites me."

The man sitting on the other side of the table shrugged in indifference, raised his wineglass to salute his guest, and said, "I wish you the best of luck and happiness."

"Thank you. My new situation does, however, present me with certain problems. Problems that I had hoped you might help me solve." He relaxed, slowly twirling the stem of his wineglass.

A nasty undercurrent infiltrated the host's voice. "And what problem is that, Trevor?"

"As you well know, Nancy has all the money. Oil and railroads and real estate, mostly. I was always the charming poor boy from Harvard. I'll have my pension, of course, and I've managed to put the money from our private enterprises to work."

"Well then, you should be able to live in relative comfort."

"But you see, old friend, I've become accustomed to a certain life-style; without Nancy's wealth behind me, well, I'll be hard-pressed to live the way I want to. What I need is a cushion."

The host's eyes narrowed into a hard look. "Naturally."

"I've been thinking of starting a private newsletter."

The host stroked the back of his ring with his thumb. "A newsletter?"

"The Greek policeman will be working with the NYPD under the authority of the State Department's Bureau of Diplomatic Security. Reports will be required topside, the ambassador will have to be informed of the current standing of the case, prevent any embarrassment to Washington, that sort of thing. I'll have access to all of these reports."

The host smoothed down his end of the tablecloth. "How many subscribers do you envisage?"

"Oh, it would be a restricted membership. There'd be no annual or monthly dues. Only one lifetime subscription fee."

"You've become quite the businessman, Trevor."

"I've had some excellent teachers."

"Yes, I suppose you have." His eyes narrowed. "How much?"

"A half million U.S. should do nicely, I think."

The snow leopard basked in the afternoon sun while her cubs frolicked among the rocks. Peering through the thick glass, Denny McKay watched the spotted cat, wondering if he'd be able to take it out in a one-on-one fight. He imagined himself making like Tarzan, armed only with a knife, and the cat, crouched up on a Ninth Avenue fire escape, baring its fangs, ready to pounce. I'd take her fucking eyes out, he thought, turning away from the viewing glass and pushing his way out of the crowded grotto.

Five minutes later Denny McKay tossed away his cigarette and entered the Bronx Zoo's World of Darkness. Day was suddenly night. This is a scary fucking place, he thought, watching hundreds of bats streaking around their glass cave. He took in the outlines of people moving about the display of nocturnal animals. He had picked a strange place to meet, he reflected while he looked for the rendezvous point. He made his way over to the display of sugar gliders. He felt queasy standing so close to them. He saw an owl eyeing him and looked away.

A low voice startled him. "Hello, Denny."

"Where are you?" McKay whispered, an edge of desperation in his voice.

"Behind you."

McKay turned and saw the outline of a man standing in the corner. "Why'd you pick this spooky place to meet?"

"Because it's safe."

"What's so important?" McKay asked, watching the kit foxes.

"Cuttler talked before he died." The man pushed away from the wall and moved along the darkened passage, examining the displays.

McKay moved with him, anxious to see the light of day. They exited from the World of Darkness and McKay lit up a cigarette. They moved along the path leading to the house of the giant panda.

"Cuttler told the Greek police why they were sent there," the man with the golden ring said. "Fortunately, he did not live long enough to tell them who had sent them."

"George Cuttler was a standup guy; he wouldn't talk."

The man walking next to McKay smiled. "The vernacular

of the lower classes never ceases to amaze me. Standup, I believe, applies to a person who is willing to go to jail, even die, rather than betray his friends."

"Yeah, that's right."

"Well, Denny, let me enlighten you. Your Mr. Cuttler was not standup. Most people aren't."

McKay bit down hard on his cigarette's filter. "What did he tell them?"

The man recounted the high points of his lunch with Trevor Hughes.

Denny McKay was concerned. "A stranger showed up at The Den the other day. A Greek. He checked out okay, I'm sure it was a coincidence. Nothing to worry about."

"Then why mention it? If he returns, kill him."

"There ain't no way that they could be onto us. Cuttler and Simmons didn't know a thing."

"You're wrong, Denny. They knew that you hired them."

"But you just said that they didn't tell that to the cops."

"Correct. But then, the police might be keeping that bit of information to themselves, mightn't they?"

McKay shrugged and moved off to buy cotton candy. He returned with a stick of the puffy pink sugar. "Want some?"

The man with the ring looked disdainfully at the fibrous candy. "No, thank you." They walked along the path. "You're sublimely unconcerned over the possibility that the Greek police might know about you."

"I've been on the wrong side of the law most of my life. And I know that if they don't catch you with the gun in your hand, they don't got shit. As for a job going down in Greece? Forget about it. Ain't nothing to worry about." He took a big bite of the candy. "What about our next shipment? Do we send it?"

"Yes. Go ahead as though nothing had happened."

"What about Orhan's replacement? How we going to work it without him there?"

"I've already seen to that." He slid his ring down his linen lapel. "Denny, we're going to have to build a moat around ourselves and fill it with hungry piranha."

McKay's questioning eyes fell on the man with the golden ring. "You mean what I think you mean?"

"Exactly. Take out Trevor Hughes. Do you have any problems with that?"

"Of course not. Come on, let's go see the giraffes."

Lucas and Vassos pushed their way through the press of people engaged in conversation in the crowded bar area. The cuckoo sprang out of its tree house behind the bar and chirped seven times. Dirndl-clad waitresses rushed about inside the restaurant. Heidi's was decorated with Victorian bric-a-brac, antique clocks, and stained-glass windows.

The restaurant's location, on the northwest corner of Second Avenue and Fifty-third Street, made it a perfect watering hole for the detectives of the Sixteenth Squad. Far enough east to be away from the midtown limelight, yet close enough to the station house for a detective to rush back if any 10:2's —forthwiths—were telephoned to the cop phone Heidi had installed behind the bar.

"Over here, Lou," Big Jay shouted, his big hands waving over the heads of people at the bar.

John Leone, Ulanov, Gregory, and Big Jay pushed back to make room. Slipping in next to the detectives, Lucas gestured to the bartender for a round of drinks. The ferret-faced man working the stick began to set down six weiss beers on the bar.

Lucas saw that the Second Whip was among the missing. "Where's Roosevelt?"

Big Jay's eyes drifted down to the forest of tall tulip glasses with slices of lemon bobbing inside of them. "Sergeant Grimes had a moonlighting job to go to, a wedding, I think."

"You got watering holes in Greece, Major?" Leone asked.

Vassos's brows furrowed. "Watering holes?"

Sipping beer, Lucas explained.

"Ah, yes, we have them," Vassos said. "Some of the larger police districts have their own clubs."

A waitress squeezed past the detectives holding a tray of drinks out in front of her. Leone made an obscene squeal, looked at Gregory, and said, "I met this broad last week and still haven't been able to score her. She's harder to get into than Fort Knox."

Lucas wiped beer suds from his mouth with the back of his hand. "Maybe you're not making the right deposit."

Vassos shivered from the air-conditioning.

Ulanov inched up close to the Whip. "Gregory and I checked out the Matrazzo family this morning."

Lucas threw back his head, draining the glass. "And?"

"We came up with a cousin," Ulanov said, sticking a slip of paper into Lucas's shirt pocket.

"How do you know they're related?"

Ulanov shrugged. "I called and asked."

"Any word from your Russian friend across the street?" Lucas asked.

"Not yet," Ulanov said, watching a towering, square-faced woman push her way through the crowd. Her massive bosom rose and fell under an extra-large man's shirt.

She rushed up to the detectives and bear-hugged Lucas up off the floor. "Teddy, *mein Liebling*," she bellowed.

"Heidi, you're breaking my ribs," Lucas gasped.

"You are so handsome that you make me go wild," she said, kissing him repeatedly on his face. "One day we will do it, ja?"

"What about Hildegard?" Big Jay said, a big grin sparkling across his black face.

"We will not tell her," Heidi said, releasing Lucas. "I will cheat, like all *men* do." She brushed back her mannishly styled hair.

"Andreas, this is the famous Heidi. Heidi, this is Major Andreas Vassos. He's a Greek policeman," Lucas said.

She tipped her head back, looking directly at Vassos. "You are from Greece?"

"Yes, I am."

Heidi turned serious. "Is it true that Greek men all want to do it in the behind?"

Vassos smiled self-consciously. "Some do, yes. But it is the same here, no?"

"Once, many years ago when I still did it with men, I let a man do it to me there. I hurt!"

John Leone looked at her with his dreamy eyes, licked his mustache, slid his arm around her waist, pulled her close, and said, "I'd be gentle."

Breaking away from him, Heidi said, "Men don't know how." She caught the attention of the man behind the stick and shouted something in German.

The bartender came over and slipped six coasters onto the bar in front of the detectives. "Whenever you're ready, Heidi would like to buy you a round."

Big Jay toasted the owner. "A rare treat!"

Heidi quaffed her *Kirschwasser* and moved off to greet another group of regulars. The detectives spent the next forty minutes drinking beer, asking Vassos about the Job in Greece, and taking turns going to the bathroom. Skating his glass through a lagoon of spilled booze, Lucas said to Vassos, "Once we start interviewing the book dealers the investigation will be out in the open."

"I've thought of that," Vassos said. "Perhaps it's better that way. Let them know we're searching for them. Fear is a policeman's colleague."

"Did you know Katina was Greek?" Lucas asked.

"Katina is a Greek name, but I was surprised when she said she was Professor Levi's daughter."

"How's your hotel?"

Vassos shrugged indifference. "A place to sleep, and think." He looked at the American lieutenant's unsmiling face. "Hate and I have become friends these past months, Teddy. I know what it looks like, feels like. I saw it on your face when you told me about the Purple Gang and Denny McKay."

Lucas looked down into his tall glass and gave a single emphatic nod. "McKay killed a friend of mine."

A street lamp beam illuminated the deserted playground. Lucas looked out his living room window. The charcoal sky was full of bruised purple clouds. He turned abruptly and went into the bedroom, peeling off his clothes as he went, throwing himself onto the unmade bed. Linking his hands in back of his head, he stared up at the shadows, listening to the darkness. Vassos had made him think of Cormick McGovern and his hatred for McKay and his crew. He closed his eyes and let his thoughts slip back into the past.

Patrolman Cormick McGovern had rosy cheeks, a thick neck, and a Derry brogue. When Probationary Patrolman Lucas was in recruit school, department policy required rookies to be sent out into the field for one weekend a month in order to acquire practical experience alongside a seasoned cop.

Lucas's first tour in the street was in the Six-seven, a four to midnight. The rookies, in their starched gray uniforms, stood smartly at attention behind the outgoing shift, called a "platoon"; each one of them anxiously awaited assignment to a field training officer. They were eager to start their march to glory. A silver-haired Desk lieutenant called the roll, assigned each member to their posts. He gave them ringing times to call the station house, meal hours, and announced special post conditions.

After the roll had been called, the lieutenant assigned the rookies. "Probationary Patrolman Lucas."

"Here, sir," snapped the recruit, his enthusiasm evident on his spanking young face.

"Lucas, you're assigned with Patrolman McGovern."

A ripple of laughter swept through the platoon. "Knock it off," hissed the Desk lieutenant.

Assignments made, the lieutenant barked, "Sergeant, post the platoon."

"Yes, sir," the sergeant said, giving him a salute with his nightstick. He executed an about-face, called the platoon to attention, and marched it out of the station house. Once outside on the high stoop, the sergeant ordered, "Take your posts."

The platoon broke ranks. Members of the second platoon immediately appeared from doorways and rushed up the precinct steps to get at the sign-out book.

Seeing all the policeman suddenly appear from nowhere, not waiting on their post relieving points as required, Lucas realized for the first time that the Job wasn't the way they said it was in the Academy.

"Lucas? Lucas?"

He turned to face the humorless stare of Cormick McGovern. "Here, sir."

"Come with me, lad," McGovern said, a mellow smile suddenly lighting up his large face.

Lucas marched route step beside his field training officer. Up Snyder Avenue, left on Flatbush, past Albemarle Road, past Tilden Avenue, and directly into the grandiose lobby of the Loews Kings movie palace.

Cormick McGovern strutted past the ticket taker with the regal arrogance of a knight, his subservient squire in tow. Lucas followed his leader up the darkened back staircase to the last row of the balcony.

"Laddy, this is your post for the remainder of your tour. You're to stay here and do nothing. I'll be back to get you."

"Yes, sir," Lucas said, feeling his ardor sinking.

"Your first lesson in the street is to follow orders and don't get involved," McGovern said. "Do you know why you're spending your first tour here?"

"No, sir."

"It's so that you won't get into any kind of trouble that could jam you up while you're on probation and cause you to lose your job."

Lucas looked around the balcony and saw several classmates contentedly watching the movie.

During the next five months Lucas and the other recruits spent their field duties stashed away in movie houses, garages, and firehouses.

Graduation.

Chief Clerk Flynn read out the names off the assignment sheet. "Lucas, T."

"Here, sir."

"The Six-seven."

Lucas ran into McGovern on his second tour.

"Teddy, now that you're out of the Academy, how'd you like me to teach you the real Job?"

"I'd like it a lot."

Cormick McGovern commenced his in-service training course. He showed Lucas how to maintain two memo books, one for the bosses and a protector, a book that contained altered versions of each entry, designed to cover your ass. He demonstrated the correct way to search a prisoner, warning him not to be squeamish about searching women. "They can kill you just as dead."

McGovern gave him his trust/no trust list. Trust: Italians, wiseguys, Jews, Greeks, Irish, WASPs, Hispanics, except Puerto Ricans. No trust: hookers, junkies, dealers, FBI, newsmen, West Indians, all lawyers, girlfriends. Golden rule: never tell your wife, your girlfriend, neighbor, relative, friend *anything* about the Job, especially how much money you earn. He told Teddy about one of his friends who had died. When the grieving widow went to the pension bureau to inquire about Patrolman Bill Murphy's pension, she was advised that no Patrolman Murphy had died. However, a Lieutenant Bill Murphy had recently expired. "Now there was a cop who knew how to keep his mouth shut," McGovern said.

Cormick McGovern's public relations tenet: send the following cards to businessmen on your post—Christmas, Hanukkah, bar mitzvah, Holy Communion, confirmation, weddings, get well, and condolences.

Three years later Lucas was transferred into one of the department's plainclothes gambling units. McGovern's final lesson was: "Teddy, my lad, never go back."

Six years later Lucas found himself the Second Whip in Second Homicide. The district took in the Ninth, Tenth, Thirteenth, and Fourteenth Precincts. He and his old field training officer had kept in touch through occasional telephone conversations, met at a local watering hole, had dinner together once or twice a year. Lucas was surprised one day when he read in the Personal Orders that Cormick McGovern had been dumped out of the Six-seven and into the Fourteenth during one of the Job's mass corruption upheavals.

Lucas telephoned his friend. "What happened?"

"A lad with a year in the Job bragged to his girlfriend about the Christmas list and then a month later stopped seeing her. I don't know what they're taking into the Job these days."

"Are they taking care of you at the Fourteenth?"

"'Tis a lovely house to work in, Teddy. The roll call man and I are old friends. I'm out there meeting people and sending out my greeting cards, making friends."

The following June, Second District Homicide found itself swamped with homicides coming off the docks in the Fourteenth and Eighteenth Precincts. Lucas looked up his old friend. They met in the back of Roth's liquor store. Sipping Irish whiskey from a mug, McGovern said, "It's Denny McKay and his bunch."

"What's going on?" Lucas asked.

"A leprechaun who drives a forklift on the dock whispered into my ear that some young turks are trying to wrestle control from McKay."

"Will you nose around for me, see if you can dig up anything that will stand in court?"

"Will do, Teddy. I'll give you a call in a day or two," McGovern said.

Three days later Cormick McGovern's body was found lying face up at the end of Pier Thirty-eight. His features had been pounded into gore; fourteen bullets had mutilated his body; someone had defecated on his face. His shield had been torn from his uniform and was missing. The word that seeped through the pall of silence that fell over the docks was that Denny McKay had ordered McGovern killed because he had found out something about the killings that had been done on McKay's orders. But Teddy Lucas did not have to be told that. He knew that his friend had died because he had been poking around asking questions, speaking to the people to whom he had sent greeting cards.

Lucas did not get his chance to get at McKay. The district commander had the Second Whip transferred. The forty-nine read: "His personal friendship with the victim precludes objectivity."

Ten years and some months later, despite a maximum effort by the NYPD to nail McGovern's killers, the case folder was stored with the rest of the unsolved homicides in the old record room of the Second District Homicide Squad. And like the rest of the homicide folders, it was weighed down by the perfunctory addition of semiannual DD14 Resumé of Homicide Case forms.

Lucas would visit the old record room from time to time and sit in a musty corner with the McGovern folder. He would read through the file, looking for any additional facts; there never were any. He'd study the crime scene photos of his friend's battered body and recall the vibrant man who used to stash him in the Loews Kings. Time had distilled Lucas's rage into pure and abiding hatred for McKay and his people. C of D Edgeworth's assignment to work with Vassos had given Lucas another shot at McKay. The Job has a strange way of giving you another turn in the batter's box, he thought, turning onto his side and closing his eyes.

Tomorrow was a big day.

Trevor Hughes walked out of the lobby of the Plaza Hotel and stopped on top of the steps to admire the urban view laid out before him. Hansom cabs and taxis cluttered the street; a stream of people flowed along Fifth Avenue; stylish mannequins stood in Bergdorf's windows; a reggae band played in the plaza.

Hughes took a deep breath and let it out slowly. Everything was going as he had planned; he felt wonderful. With half a million dollars, plus his pension and investments, he could continue to live the good life without his wife. He adjusted his tie and moved down the steps, wondering why the man with the ring was so insistent on meeting him now, at eleven o'clock at night. Just like him, he thought. Secretive to a fault. "Wear a bright yellow tie and walk north along Central Park West," he had said when he telephoned an hour earlier. "Sit on the thirtieth bench along the park wall. I'll meet you there tonight at eleven, and we'll make arrangements for the delivery of the initiation fee."

"Why not come to my hotel?"

"Walls have ears, Trevor, or have you forgotten? I stretched a point by having lunch with you there."

He went west on Central Park South and then turned at Columbus Circle. Walking north along Central Park West, Hughes painstakingly counted park benches. When he reached the right one, he sat down. A bicyclist whooshed past, blowing his whistle, startling him. Eerie night sounds floated out of the park. More than a little spooked, he looked around. The park side of the street was dark. On the other side people strolled in much brighter light. On his side he could see people moving north a long way from him. A black man on a skateboard wove his way toward him.

Hughes felt terribly isolated and vulnerable. A chilling thought popped into his mind. He was alone; why couldn't they have met in the lobby or in some other public place? My God! I've allowed greed to overcome my common sense. He leaped to his feet. A rustle behind him caused him to whirl, his scared eyes searching the shadows in the bushes on the other side of the low stone wall. Seeing nothing, he turned to cross to safety on the other side of the street. He started to run. The skateboarder wove in front of him and pivoted to an abrupt stop, blocking his path.

Hughes saw only a mouthful of flashing white teeth. He heard a pop and felt himself backpedaling, his arms flailing out at his sides. He crumpled onto the bench. Clouds were forming over his eyes, but he was able to make out the smiling black face that looked down at him.

"You've killed me," Hughes said, and died.

The skater lifted his brightly colored shirt and tucked the nickeled .38 caliber S & W Chief into his waistband. He pulled a gravity knife from his back pocket and popped the blade out. Bending over Hughes's body, he cut out the trouser pockets and dumped them and their contents into a paper bag. He stripped off the dead man's wristwatch and wedding ring and added them to the collection.

He looked around. A lone taxi sped past. The skater pushed off on his board. At Seventy-second Street he jumped the curb into the roadway and whirled to stop on the driver's side of a double-parked automobile.

Denny McKay rolled down the window.

"A piece of cake," the skater said, passing McKay the bag.

He opened it and looked inside. "Is it all here?"

"Yeah, it's all there."

"You didn't get stupid and grab a souvenir, I hope."

"M'man," protested the skater, "I bees a motherfuckin' professional."

"See ya 'round." The window slipped up and the skater danced off into the night.

7

olonel Dimitri Pappas braked for the red light on Amalias Street. Morning traffic was heavy; the cloudless sky seemed an infinity of blue. A broad grin pulled up Pappas's lips when his gaze fell on the graffito on the wall of St. Paul's Anglican Church. "Long live Rudolf Hess" was bracketed between two swastikas. The subtleties of Greek political life, he thought, are endless. Prime Minister Papandreou was a politician with a socialist kink; the graffiti artist had an obvious neo-fascist twist. The meaning of the urban art: Fuck you, Papandreou.

Driving along Vassilissis Sofias, Pappas passed the gardens and slowed the car so that he could look up at the huge flag billowing atop Lykavitos Hill. A sense of pride surged through him, as it always did whenever he looked up at Athens' highest hill and saw the emblem of Greek sovereignty.

Seventeen minutes later Colonel Pappas was walking up the steps of 173 Leoforos Alexandras, headquarters of the Hellenic Police Department. It was a square building constructed entirely of white marble, with a bank of doors made of silvery one-way mirrored glass. Pappas went inside through the only unlocked door and was fed into the security cordon that funneled him to the control desk manned by four officers, three males and one female. The sergeant in charge of the checkpoint recognized the colonel and entered Pappas's name, rank, and the time in the service book.

Pappas stopped at his office and read the night's situation reports. One shooting in Piraeus, four stabbings in Kolonaki, a rape in Athens, and one armed robbery in Glifádha. We're becoming like New York, he thought, ripping off the top page of his desk calendar. It was Monday, July 13.

He left his office and took the elevator to the thirteenth floor. Interpol, Minister of Public Order, was written in French across the glass doors. He pushed inside the suite of rooms. Eight A.M., the change of tours. Tired men and women gathered in offices to pass on information to the day team. The communications room, a large space crammed with sophisticated equipment, was on Pappas's right. The rancid smell of stale cigarettes seeped into the hallway. Pappas walked quickly down the corridor to the end and entered the suite occupied by Colonel Teddy Tritsis, the minister's representative to Interpol.

Tritsis nodded Pappas into a chair while he spoke on the telephone. There was a large painting of Christ baring his bleeding heart on the wall. Pappas absently stared at the other man's thick, bushy white hair; it had an almost startling band of black around it just over the top of his ears.

"Dimitri, how are you?" he asked, hanging up the telephone.

"Good, Teddy, and you?"

"Busy as hell. Everyone wants their information yesterday. Want some coffee?"

"That would be nice."

Tritsis pushed the intercom button and spoke into the machine. "So? How goes the Voúla investigation?"

"I need a name, Teddy. One name. Someone who was close to Orhan Iskur."

The head of Interpol leaned forward. "Was his murder tied in with Voúla?"

"We think so, yes. But that is confidential."

Tritsis raised his palms. "Of course." He signed regret. "I might not be able to help you on this one, old friend."

"Why the hell not?"

"This assignment puts me in an awkward position sometimes. I'm a Greek policeman, assigned by the minister to run Interpol's Greek station. The job guarantees me promotion, but it also guarantees me a lot of headaches. I've got to do a balancing act between our regulations, Interpol's, and my own loyalty to the department. I'm required by this assignment to operate within sets of rules set down by both organizations."

"So?"

"The damn problem is that Interpol is prohibited from getting involved in any investigation with a racial, religious, military, or political angle. Voúla, from everything I know, was the work of terrorists, which would make it political." He leaned back, drumming his fingertips on the top of his desk.

Pappas noticed how deeply Tritsis's cheeks had sunken over the years. Then a tall man entered the office carrying a Turkish *aski*, a tray, suspended on three chains, holding two small cups of coffee and two glasses of water. Raising the tray's chains, the man removed the coffee cups and set them down in front of each man. The water came next.

"How was the traffic this morning?" Tritsis asked, watching the man turn to leave.

"You need the eyes of Argus to drive in Athens," Pappas said as the door closed. Tritsis sipped his coffee.

"Voúla was murder, pure and simple," Pappas said. "The terrorist thing was a ploy we used so that we could conduct the real investigation without having the newspapers crawling up our asses."

"Who was the intended victim?" Tritsis asked, lowering his cup.

"Takis Milaraki, the café owner," Pappas lied. "We think that Iskur and Milaraki had narcotics deals going that turned sour."

Grinning broadly, Tritsis shook his finger at Pappas. "You old fox. That terrorist story sounded phony to me from the beginning." He got up and moved out from behind his desk. "I anticipated that someone would be around to ask about Orhan Iskur, so I telephoned Paris and asked them to send me whatever they had on him." He crossed the room to the row of locked file cabinets. He punched in the combination and the top drawer of the middle file opened. He took out a folder, opened it, and removed a sheet of paper. Walking back to his desk, Interpol's station chief said, "Iskur was always a very careful man."

Two kilometers outside of Vouliagméni, on the coastal road leading toward Voúla, a thin road branched off and seemed to go nowhere. The artery twisted and turned under an umbrella of cypress trees that at night created a tunnel of darkness. The landscape on either side of the road sloped up the sides of hills, and here and there a light sparkled in a distant farmhouse.

Suddenly, when you least expected it, the tunnel burst into a street of glitter and noise known as the Vari district. It was a long block of *hassapo* tavernas, meat restaurants, each one with a butcher shop attached to it where patrons could make a leisurely selection for their main course from the rows of lambs, goats, and pigs.

Each taverna was aglow in flashing lights and had its own man in the roadway, thrusting his body in front of moving cars, beckoning drivers into his taverna. Many of the tavernas had strands of cowbells hanging from posts and young boys to shake them in a further attempt to lure customers.

George's was the gaudiest of the tavernas and was famous for its wine room, a damp, earth-floored space in the rear where patrons wandered among the rows of casks, sampling the homemade wines, choosing the brew that most tempted their palates. George's was also famous for its desserts, especially the homemade *meli*, a platter of thick yogurt smothered with golden honey.

Yiannis Yiotas, a small, weasel-faced man with two brown moles on his nose, had just finished eating a platter of goat meat and french fries. He poured the last of the retsina from the pitcher and settled back to enjoy his cigarette and people watch before he ordered his meli.

Yiotas was a thief and a bigamist. A thief because the thought of working for a living made him sick to his stomach. A bigamist because he loved to screw fat women, and because there were so many of them and they were so easy to get into bed and they were so grateful and motherly, he just couldn't break their hearts by leaving them, so he ended up getting married to them. Having more than one wife added a pleasant dimension to Yiannis's life. He loved leading a life of lies, living on the edge.

He looked around the restaurant—a mixed bag of Greeks and tourists. Children ran up and down the aisles; cats crouched near tables, waiting for scraps; a butcher was chopping up a lamb. Yiannis finished his wine; the homemade brew had a heavy pine-resin taste that caused him to smack his lips. He yelled out to the rushing waiter, *"Pahrahkahlo."*

The waiter paused long enough to look his way.

"Meli and retsina," Yiannis yelled.

The waiter nodded and rushed off.

He lighted and drew hard on a cigarette, pulling the relaxing smoke in deep, savoring its tranquil cloud. He thought about Niki, the fattest of his four wives. She lived in Filothei and thought her loving husband was a deckhand aboard a cruise ship. He thought of her pretty face and her big, wrinkled ass. And he thought of the sounds she made when he stuck his prick up her ass and played with her pussy at the same time. A warm flush spread through his groin, and he decided that he would visit Niki tomorrow. No! Tomorrow was Tuesday, bad luck for a Greek to plan anything. This had been so since that Tuesday in the fifteenth century when Constantinople fell to the Turks.

The waiter rushed over to his table, set down the meli and wine, and rushed off. Yiannis crushed his cigarette out in the tin ashtray, poured wine into his small glass, picked up the spoon off the platter, and began to stir the yogurt and honey into a pink mixture. The sound of bouzoukis and tambourines floated across the night.

Yiotas was enjoying his solitary pleasures when a feeling of dread came over him. He sensed a presence lurking behind him, watching him. He tensed, ready, if need be, to leap up and run. Continuing to stir the dessert, he began to cast his eyes from side to side without moving his head in an attempt to see who was standing there. He heard movement and saw the torso of a man come from behind him and go around to the front of his table. A chair scraped back. The stranger sat down. Yiannis continued to mix the meli. When he had steeled himself, Yiannis shyly raised his eyes up to look at the intruder. He blanched and suddenly felt sick to his stomach.

"Hello, Yiannis," Colonel Pappas said, pulling a spoon from the glass in the center of the table and scooping up Yiannis's meli. "I love this, it's my favorite." Licking the spoon, he added, "How have you been, Yiannis? I haven't seen you—let me see, it's been over ten years. I arrested you for a payroll robbery in Plaka."

Yiannis Yiotas had a sudden urge to go to the bathroom. "Hello, Major," he said, forcing courage into his voice.

"It's Colonel now. What a pleasant surprise, running into you at George's."

"I eat here a lot, Colonel."

A raw edge came into Pappas's voice. "I know." He picked up the pitcher and poured wine into one of the empty glasses on the table. He offered the copper wine pitcher to Yiannis, who held up his glass and uneasily watched the colonel pour retsina.

Pappas put down the pitcher and laughed. "I read in the newspaper this morning about a prison riot in New York City. A place called Rikers Island. The prisoners were upset because there were not enough telephones for them to use." He scooped up more meli. "Can you believe that? Telephones for prisoners. They even have televisions on this Rikers Island."

Yiannis laughed nervously. "I can't believe that, Colonel. It sounds more like a hotel."

Pappas drank wine. "It doesn't sound like a Greek prison, does it, Yiannis?"

"No," Yiannis snapped.

"Here we know how to treat prisoners. We make them pay for their clothes and food. We don't go out of our way to make their miserable lives easy. Isn't that true, Yiannis?"

"Yes, sir." Yiannis's legs were shaking.

"How old are you now?"

"Forty-six."

"Forty-six," Pappas echoed solemnly. "You're lucky that you have given up your old way of life. Prison would be difficult for you now, very difficult."

"Yes, sir, it would be," Yiannis said, sliding his hands under the table and grabbing his knees in an attempt to stop the shaking.

"It's too bad that your boss got himself murdered," Pappas said, licking the spoon's underside.

"Boss? What boss?"

"Orhan Iskur."

"I didn't work for him. I used to run errands for him sometimes, that's all. I know nothing about his business."

Pappas spread his hands in disappointment. "Yiannis, it's not nice to lie to a police colonel. It upsets me."

"I never worked with him, I swear."

Waving his spoon at the thief, Pappas said, "Let me tell you a story. Sixteen years ago in London, two men with Greek passports tried to sell a fake antiquity to an American. The American happened to be a dealer, and he recognized the statue as not being genuine. He called the police, and the two men were arrested. A few days later, for reasons we'll never know, this American decided to drop the charges against the two men. Constable Wade, who was the arresting officer, was a conscientious policeman, so he went back to his station and prepared an Interpol intelligence report. The duplicate copy remained at his station; the triplicate went into the central file, and the original made its way to Paris, where it remained until an inquiry was recently made by the Hellenic Police Department." He stabbed the spoon at the thief's sweating face. "Yiannis Yiotas and Orhan Iskur were the two men arrested."

"I forgot all about that," Yiannis blurted. "It was a mistake, I swear. We didn't know that it was a fake."

"Of course you didn't." Pappas drank some more retsina. He lowered the glass and made wet circles on the paper tablecloth. "Did Iskur have a mistress?"

The thief's eyes widened. "How did you know about her?"

Pappas smiled. "Men like him have either a mistress or a young boy."

Yiannis was so relieved at the shift in direction that he took a deep breath and went on to tell Pappas about Nina Pazza. A tall, strikingly handsome woman, Iskur had met her in Rome ten years ago, when she was sixteen. He fell in love with her and brought her back to Athens with him, installing her in a fashionable apartment on Aristodimou Street.

"What can you tell me about her?"

"Nothing, really. I used to chauffeur her on some of her shopping trips. But she never talked to me about anything. Just park here or there and wait for me."

Yiannis Yiotas's legs still would not stop shaking.

Pappas looked hard into the thief's eyes. "Why don't we talk about the Voúla massacre?"

Yiannis's mouth fell open; he began to tremble violently.

"We know it was you who got the car that was used by Cuttler and Simmons. We also know that it was you who followed officers Tasos Lefas and Lakis Rekor and learned their routines, and it was you who took the photographs of the officers to give to their killers," Pappas lied, following nothing more than an educated guess.

Panic filled Yiannis Yiotas's face, and Pappas knew that his dart had hit the bull's-eye. He had to keep up the pressure, not give the thief time to think, increase his panic, and then when there was no hope, to throw him a lifesaver. "You're going to spend the rest of your miserable life in prison." Then he smiled at the thief. Yiannis was shaking so much that Pappas thought he might faint. Now was the time to play nice guy. "Of course, if you cooperate, we might be able to work something out so that you don't have to go to jail, maybe not even be arrested."

Yiannis clutched the lifeline. "You won't arrest me?"

"I'm not interested in you. I want the people who planned Voúla. If you tell me everything you know, I'll see to it that you don't go to prison."

Yiannis Yiotas covered his face with his hands and wept. People at nearby tables turned and looked at him in open astonishment.

Pappas needed an admission of guilt. "You didn't know why Iskur wanted you to do those things, did you?"

"No. I swear, I didn't know, I didn't know."

"It was you who made the arrangements with the taxi driver to pick up Aldridge Long, the American, at the airport and drive him to Iskur's shop, wasn't it?"

Yiannis absently nodded his head. "Yes."

"Were you with Iskur when Long arrived at the shop?"

"No. He made me leave before he got there."

"Had you ever met Long?"

"No."

Pappas glanced around the taverna. This was not the place to conduct an interrogation. He had opened the door a little; he'd open it a lot more on the top floor of 173 Leoforos Alexandras. He motioned to the waiter. "My friend would like to pay the bill."

Watching the waiter add up the tab, Yiannis happened to notice that the wall clock inside the butcher shop read six minutes after midnight. It was now Tuesday, a bad luck day.

8

Teddy Lucas walked out of his building's lobby and stopped. The air was crisp and vibrant with the sounds of Manhattan. He looked up at the green canopy of trees and saw Ajax perched on a tree trunk. He moved jauntily down the steps. In a nearby playground, toddlers dashed under the shower's gentle spray while their mothers relaxed on benches next to it.

Lucas turned right, moving onto the wide concrete path that wound through Stuyvesant Town's carefully maintained shrubs, down the steps, and onto the sidewalk, which led to the city streets.

"Teddy," a familiar voice called out.

He stopped, aware of the immediate pounding of rage inside his head. He turned and saw her stepping out from behind a tree, a nervous smile on her lips.

He warned himself to stay calm.

"Hello, Teddy," she said quietly. "I didn't mean to ambush you, but you wouldn't answer any of my calls."

He glared at his ex-wife. Heavy brown leather sandals, loose-fitting Indian cotton dress, long hair swept up behind her head with a leather thong. No makeup, pallid skin, and dark circles under her otherwise pretty eyes. He tried in vain to recall some intimate detail of the life they had once shared. Only hurt and deceit came out of the grave of his memory.

"What do you want, Ellen?"

"Just to talk."

He heard a slight catch in her voice and found himself walking in silence beside her to a bench. Ellen sat, slapped the folds of her dress between her spread legs. Watching kids run under the spray, she said, "We wanted children once, remember?"

Stay cool, he thought. "Why don't you get to the point?" A memory floated into his head. The sad look of disappointment on his father's face when he announced his plans to marry Ellen. "But she's not Greek," his dad had said as his mother squeezed her husband's arm in a mute plea for silence.

"As you can see, I'm back in New York."

"I'm busy, Ellen. What's the problem?"

"Well, you see, I'm working in this boutique on Columbus Avenue and I've gone back to college. I'm majoring in psychology. I don't get home till eleven at night and I have to be up at six to make an eight o'clock class." She shifted uneasily on the bench, fanned her calves nervously with the hem of her dress, and slapped it back down between her legs. "I have a tiny apartment in Bensonhurst; it's the pits. My life would be so much easier if I could live in Manhattan, but I can't afford the rents. So, I was wondering"—she ran her finger over the design on her dress—"if you might let me come and stay with you. I'd sleep on the couch and pay my share of the rent. I'd cook and clean; it would just be until I got on my feet again." She seemed to run out of words and looked down at her lap, her ears bright pink from embarrassment.

He laughed and said, "You always did have a big pair of balls. You run off with another man and then reappear five years later asking to move back in because you can't afford Manhattan rents. Where's your boyfriend?"

"Gone. He left me for a nineteen-year-old."

He shrugged and looked away from her. "You're out of my life. I have no intention of letting you worm your way back into it."

"Teddy . . ."

"Listen to me, lady," he said, his angry eyes boring into hers. "I married you because I loved you. And I was a pretty good husband." He stopped and frowned. "I admit, I did spend more time at work than I did with you. So maybe I didn't think enough about what you needed."

She nodded in embarrassed agreement.

"You wanted to join the community school board, so I didn't object. And that was how you met the love of your life. . . ."

"Teddy, please . . ."

"Listen," he said, pressing his finger against her lips. "You left me for a forty-year-old creep with a beard who never worked a day in his life. He'd mastered the art of stroking colleges and corporations out of grants so he could spend his worthless life studying some language that only two people in the world speak. Well, you made your choice—live with it." He got up to leave.

"Your damn male Greek ego won't let you forget that I left you for another man, will it?" she snarled.

"You're wrong, lady. I could have forgiven unfaithfulness. But what I won't forgive, what I can't forgive, is that you used to go to his apartment and wash his goddamn socks. That kind of a commitment I'll never forgive." He turned and moved off to the sounds of her sobs.

At ten minutes before ten o'clock that beautiful morning, the blue Buick slid into the curb in front of the Pierpont Morgan Library. Lucas tossed the vehicle I.D. onto the dashboard and he and Vassos got out of the car.

Katina was waiting for them inside the vestibule. She was wearing a pink linen suit, bone-colored sling-back shoes. Her long legs were bare. "Good morning," she said cheerfully, and turned to lead them down the gleaming mahogany staircase into the basement work area. Walking into her office, she picked up a sheet of paper from her desk and handed it to Lucas. "The book dealers that I've contacted."

Lucas studied the list. "Widener Books? Widener?" He looked at Vassos. "Where do we know that name from?"

Vassos leaned forward in his chair, suddenly intense. "Belmont E. Widener?"

Lucas's voice went up several notches as it came to him. "Hey, he was the complainant who had a book stolen by one of McKay's boys in 'seventy-seven."

"The book by Aristarchus," Vassos said.

"Aristarchus of Samothrace?" Katina said, crossing her legs.

"Dunno," Lucas said, and proceeded to tell her everything that he could remember about the 1977 robbery. "Have you heard of this guy, Aristarchus?"

Her smile bore a trace of impatience. "Yes, Teddy, I've heard of him."

"Fill us in, will you?" Lucas asked.

"Aristarchus lived between 217 and 145 B.C. He was one of Alexandria's great librarians," she began, going on to tell them how Ptolemy had ordered that a complete collection of Greek literature be gathered and stored in the great library. This had never been done before so the librarians had to develop catalogues of the texts to be copied, and then they had to rent or borrow the texts from other kings so that the scribes of Alexandria might copy them. In order to protect against forgeries, the librarians were forced to develop new principles of textual criticism. In order to properly copy Homer, for instance, the librarians had to first decide which text passages were accurate transcriptions of oral recitations and not merely the writings of some unknown actor or scribe. They would study Homer's work and then write commentaries indicating which verses they considered fraudulent or corrupted by scribal emendation. Aristarchus used marginal notes to point out what he considered irregularities or spurious verses."

"Where were these notes made?" Lucas asked.

"On the text itself," she said. "He developed an entire system of marginal scholia."

"Then Aristarchus, after he made his notations on the original text, would write up his report, which you call a commentary," Lucas said.

"Yes," she agreed.

"Were these commentaries made part of the original text?" Lucas asked.

"No, they weren't," she said. "Since they were meant to be read only by scholars, they were prepared in separate texts. The librarians would hold weekly meetings to discuss the commentaries and try to agree on what changes the scribes should make in the texts that were being copied."

"Then it's safe to assume that Aristarchus prepared commentaries on the *Iliad*?" Lucas asked.

"On the *Iliad* and the *Odyssey*. Aristarchus was fascinated by Homer and he became the library's resident Homeric scholar." She got up, smoothed her skirt. "Would either of you like a cup of coffee?"

"No, thank you," Lucas said, suddenly aware of a strong aroma of coffee.

Vassos shook his head.

She left the office and returned shortly holding a delicate cup and saucer.

Lucas waited until she was seated to ask, "Katina, if I remember correctly, the casket-copy was stored in the library during the time Aristarchus wrote his commentaries."

"Yes, that's true," she said, taking a sip from her cup.

Her lipstick left a thick impression around the rim.

"If I were Aristarchus and I was preparing a commentary on the *Iliad*, I would certainly use the casket-copy as an authoritative and established text."

"I do not see how he could have failed to do such a thing," Vassos said, awaiting her pronouncement.

She returned the cup to the saucer and placed them on her desk. She picked up a pencil and began tapping it over the green blotter. "Yes, I believe that he would have done that."

"And if he did," Lucas said, feeling the strong glow of excitement stirring in his chest, "then he would have made marginal notes on the casket-copy."

His comments stilled her hand. She let the pencil fall, regarding him with newfound respect. "I agree with your reasoning, Teddy."

Lucas continued: "Aristarchus's commentary, along with the marginal notes that he made on the casket-copy, would go a long way toward authenticating Alexander's *Iliad.*"

Vassos leaned back in his chair, his eyes drifting over to a poster on the wall of a gondola gliding down a Venetian canal.

"There's a flaw in your reasoning," she said.

"What?" Lucas demanded.

Vassos kept his stare fixed on the shimmering black canal flowing under the stone bridge.

"Aristarchus prepared commentaries on other authors besides Homer. The commentary that was stolen from Belmont Widener in 1977 might have been on any number of texts, not necessarily the casket-copy," she said.

"Did many commentaries survive?" Lucas asked.

"Perhaps ten out of six hundred," she said, reaching for her cup.

A summer breeze swept across Manhattan, seasoning the air with the salty smell of two rivers. Widener Books was quartered in a slender, five-story building jammed between two glass skyscrapers on Seventeenth Street between Park Avenue South and Broadway. The building's cream-colored facade was brightened by window boxes overflowing with summer blooms. Muses and caryatids garnished the roof's balustrade.

Belmont E. Widener was waiting for them. A man of medium stature with pointy ears, he had sagging ivory bags under deep-set eyes and thick wavelets of brown hair swept back over a rather large head. The yellow silk bow tie that he wore was patterned with tiny pink butterflies.

He rushed forward to greet Katina. "Dr. Wright, what a great pleasure. I could hardly believe my ears when my secretary told me that you were coming to pay us a visit. And with the police, no less." He clasped his dainty hands to his chest and looked innocently at the policemen.

Katina made the introductions.

A salesman's grin spread across the book dealer's face. "Are you two gentlemen interested in purchasing rare books? If you are, I've recently come into possession of a Voloretti codex."

"We're here to ask you some questions concerning a robbery that took place in 1977," Lucas said.

"Eleven years ago? Really? That's yesterday's news." His bright, curious eyes examined Vassos. "You're not with the NYPD."

"I am a major in the Hellenic Police Department. Here on special assignment."

Lucas thought that he detected a fleeting expression of fear on the book dealer's face.

"I see," Widener said, and turned brusquely to Katina. "Dr. Wright, before we discuss whatever police business brought you here, I would love to show you my prized possessions."

"I'd be delighted," she said, asking for her companions to be patient by lifting an eyebrow.

Widener guided them up through three floors of books. Brass chandeliers illuminated dark parquet flooring covered with brightly colored oriental rugs. There were rows upon rows of rosewood bookcases, the contents of which were protected by fine black metal mesh. The musty scent of books and the comfortable smell of worn leather pervaded each floor. Widener was a joyous child showing off his treasures. He brought out ancient vellum manuscripts, maps, tomes of Barcherlo and Stair. He twirled a great Cussennelli globe signed and dated 1587. Finally he led them single file into the fourth-floor vault, a stainless steel monster with massive locking pins.

"My best stuff is here," he said, and proceeded to show them a tenth-century Bloomberg missal, a first edition *King Lear* dated 1608, a set of three Shakespeare folios. His last treasure was a first edition of de Reuyter's *Voyage to Foreign Lands*, dated 1579.

"May I?" Katina said, holding out her hands. "I love to listen to the music of the old paper."

"Oh, yes, so do I," Widener said, with an air of excitement bordering on sexual arousal. He placed the book into her waiting hands. She held it up close to her ear and gently flipped the pages, sounding each one with a sharp push of her fingers. Her head was tilted slightly into the book so that she might better hear the music, her eyes lifted in concentration.

Lucas watched her fingers caress each page, sending them past with a snap. They were exquisite hands, the beautifully cared for nails glowing with polish. His eyes drifted down to her bare legs, and he fantasized about the dark mysterious treasure at their apex.

Widener moved between her and the policemen. "Each page should give an authentic rag paper crackle," he explained.

She added, "If it's not a forgery." She snapped the last page and handed the dealer back his book. "A wonderful collection."

Widener beamed. "Thank you. Now. Shall we go to my office on the second floor and discuss this eleven-year-old crime?"

The office looked out at the colorful mixture of architecture in the area. A carved walnut desk with high-relief scenes of Hercules and the Sphinx dominated the richly furnished office. A golden tapestry depicting the Adoration of the Magi hung on one wall.

"Please sit," Widener said, moving behind the desk and lowering himself into a carved walnut armchair. His expression became serious. "Why are the police suddenly interested in this crime?"

Vassos took out and fingered his jade worry beads, the ones that Colonel Pappas had taken off of Iskur's body and then given to Vassos for good luck.

"Mr. Widener, we have some reason to believe that your stolen commentary might be connected to the theft of an antiquity from Greece," Lucas said.

A flush came to the dealer's cheeks. "What antiquity?"

"The casket-copy," Katina said dryly.

He looked at Vassos. "Your government has sent you here to try and recover it?"

"Yes," Vassos said.

"And you, Dr. Wright, have been enlisted to render whatever technical assistance that the police might require?"

"Yes," she said.

"I see." Widener slumped, his shoulders sagging under some invisible weight. "The casket-copy," he said reflectively. "The collector's ultimate dream."

"Was your Aristarchus commentary on the *Iliad?*" Katina asked, holding her breath.

"Yes," Widener answered.

"Would you tell us how you came to own it?" Lucas said.

Widener sighed. "The Duke of Siracusa was selling his private library back in September of 'seventy-five. The sale was to take place at the duke's castle in Lichtenstein." He sighed at the memory of it. "I went, of course, and bought some interesting things. Late one afternoon, I was browsing in the east wing of the library when I saw a scroll sticking out from behind a stack of books. I bent down and removed it. It was obviously quite old. I rushed to check the card index but there was nothing on it. So, I did the next best thing and asked the duke. He informed me that his great-grandfather was notorious for buying things and sticking them on library shelves without bothering to enter them in the index." A sly smile. "The duke and I engaged in some genteel haggling. He asked an outrageous sum, citing the scroll's antiquity. I pointed out that it might contain worthless business records, or even be blank, or illegible. I also told him that I'd have to spend a considerable sum on restoration and deciphering."

"But you did buy it?" Lucas said.

"Yes, and for not a lot of money," Widener said smugly.

"When did you realize what you had bought?" Lucas asked.

"Not for several months," the dealer said. "As soon as I returned home I entered into negotiations for a manorial land grant by William the Conqueror. That piece of business kept me occupied for the better part of three months. I stuck the scroll into the bottom drawer of this desk and forgot about it for a while. Five months later I had it unrolled and deciphered."

"What did you do when you discovered what you had bought?" Lucas asked the dealer.

"I did nothing," Widener said. "I knew that the scroll's value was not going to decrease."

"You didn't show it off to any of your friends or colleagues in the book business?" Lucas said, a disbelieving edge to his voice.

"In this business, Lieutenant, you wait before revealing your treasure. A smart dealer first makes sure that there is demand for his find." He tugged at his ear. "The greater the demand, the higher the price."

"And you create the demand," Lucas said.

"Exactly," Widener said, adjusting his tie.

"How do you do that?" Lucas asked.

"By going to dinner parties given by the right sort of people. Dropping tantalizing tidbits about Aristarchus of Samothrace and the great library at Alexandria."

"And after you've created demand?" Lucas wanted to know, catching Katina looking at him, a haze in her eyes. When he looked at her, her gaze dropped away.

"Then you let it be known at some cocktail party that you've located one of Aristarchus's commentaries, but that, unfortunately, the owner refuses to part with it," Widener said.

"And the word spreads," Lucas said.

"With the speed of light," Widener said. "Within days I had collectors and dealers calling me from all over the country. There was so much interest that I decided to hold an auction. So I announced the offering in my next catalogue."

"Was there any unusual interest?" Katina asked.

"There was a lot of interest, but nothing unusual," Widener said.

"Tell us about the robbery," Lucas said.

"A few days before the auction I received a telephone call from a Mr. Dwight Roget. He wanted an appointment for the next day so that he could examine the commentary. I told him to be here at eleven o'clock."

"Wasn't that unusual?" Lucas asked.

"Not at all," Widener said. "Most collectors want to see an item before bidding on it."

"Did you know this man?" Vassos asked, closely watching the rare book dealer.

"No, I didn't. But then, one does not know every dealer and collector, does one?" Widener said, adjusting his tie.

Vassos became agitated. "I think it very strange that you could show such a valuable thing to a person without making an identification of him first."

"The man with whom I spoke, Major, knew the rare book business. He knew the jargon, what was currently available. I had no reason to be suspicious," Widener said, a trace of anger in his shrill voice.

"You made the appointment, then what happened?" Lucas asked.

"The next day, at the appointed time, two well-dressed men appeared. One of them, a stocky fellow, introduced himself as Dwight Roget. The other one didn't say very much, as I recall. Just grunted hello. I escorted them upstairs and asked them to wait while I went into the vault to get the commentary. Suddenly, they were inside with me, the quiet one pointing a gun at my head." He clutched his chest in painful remembrance. Beads of sweat appeared on his nose. "They handcuffed me inside the vault and left with my commentary."

Vassos persisted: "I still find it very strange, sir, that you would see such persons without knowing them."

"Major, we in the art world are not accustomed to being confronted by gangsters with guns. It just doesn't happen."

Katina interceded in Greek. "He's right, Andreas."

"You're handcuffed inside the vault, then what?" Lucas asked.

"Luckily, they didn't close the door. So as soon as I saw them get into the elevator, I began to scream. It was early in the morning and no one else was on the floor. But fortunately, Mrs. Wooley, my assistant, was walking up from the next floor when she heard my screams. She ran up, saw me chained like a dog, and, thank God, had the presence of mind to press the alarm. One of your police cars was passing at the time. They caught one of the bandits, but regrettably, not the one with the commentary."

"Bucky McMahon was the man the officers arrested," Lucas said.

"Yes, that was his name. After eight months of interminable court postponements, he was permitted to plead guilty to robbery in the second degree," Widener said.

"Were you shown mug shots in an effort to identify the other one?" Lucas asked.

"Hundreds of them," Widener replied. "But I was unable to pick anyone out. They were all disgusting-looking people."

Katina slipped off her earring and laid it down on top of her pocketbook. She glanced at Lucas with a look that said: my turn.

"Mr. Widener, I must confess that I have always been fascinated by your two specialties."

Widener sparkled. "I have one of the world's greatest collections of incunabula and letters from nineteenth- and twen-tieth-century revolutionaries."

"I hear rumors," Katina confided, "that the Soviet govern-ment is negotiating for your collection of letters by Lenin and Trotsky."

Widener crimsoned. "That's a damn lie. I'll never break up my collection. Never! The Russians would love to get their grubby hands on those letters, but they never will."

A smile spread across Katina's lovely face. "See how ada-mant collectors are about their collections."

Lucas smiled back at her.

"Who unrolled and deciphered the scroll?" she asked.

"Edmonds at Columbia deciphered it and Goodman at the Met unrolled it," Widener replied.

"Mr. Widener, does the name Orhan Iskur mean anything to you?" Lucas asked.

"No, it doesn't. Should it?" asked the book dealer.

"No," Lucas said.

Vassos took out the composite sketch and the passport photo of Aldridge Long and handed them to Widener. "Do you know this man?"

The rare book dealer studied the photo and the drawing for a long time. Finally he said firmly, "No, I don't believe I do."

"Did you have much of a conversation with the men who robbed you?" Lucas asked.

"As I recall they didn't say too much," Widener said.

"Mr. Widener, can you tell me if either of them was the same man who telephoned you to make the appointment?" Lucas asked, watching the book dealer.

Widener's mouth dropped open; his eyes grew wide. "Good heavens, it was a long time ago." He sat pondering, his hands clutching the ornate arms of his chair. "It wasn't the same man," he announced with sudden vigor. "The man who tele-phoned was educated, articulate, and he knew the business."

"Then why did you let two men, neither of whom sounded or looked quite right, into your shop?" Vassos demanded.

"I . . . I didn't realize until just now. No one ever asked me," Widener explained.

Vassos's face betrayed open disbelief. He got up abruptly from his chair and said, with no pretense of courtesy, "I think we have heard quite enough. There are other people who can tell us what we need to know."

9

A roll of fat bulged around the fingerprint man's waist. Acne scarred his face and his flamboyant, greasy black mustache was grossly unkempt. He sat in front of the print scanner examining the latents from the Iskur crime scene. Lucas and Vassos stood behind him, studying the magnified impressions on the screen. Katina stood off to the left, her curious eyes taking in every detail of the Latent Unit's fifth-floor office.

They had left Widener's thirty minutes before. Lucas decided to stop off at One Police Plaza before continuing on to the rest of the dealers; he wanted the prints from Greece examined by an NYPD technician.

"What were those lifted off?" asked the technician, as he slid the latents around under the glass, obviously attempting to note all the characteristics.

"The victim's billfold," Vassos said.

"What can you tell us?" Lucas asked.

"Right up front I can say that there are not enough points to make a positive I.D. I can only make out nine points among the three fingers, and as you guys both know, we need twelve in each finger."

Katina drifted over to the machine. "What does that mean, enough points?"

Lucas said: "There must be twelve similar points of comparison before any two fingerprints can be positively identified as coming from the same person."

"What must be similar?" she asked.

"The ridges that form the fingerprint pattern," Lucas answered.

The technician picked up a pencil from the workbench. "This is a bifurcating ridge," he said, pointing. "See how it runs along and then forks into three branches?"

She leaned in between the two men to get a better look. As she did, she brushed against Lucas. He felt a charge of electricity course through his body. Embarrassed, he stepped back in order to make room for her.

". . . this ridge we call a divergence. Notice how the two ridges run parallel and then spread apart."

"Yes, I see them," Katina said.

"When we can point out twelve similar characteristics in another finger, we have a positive I.D.," the technician said.

Lucas found himself standing behind her, watching her as she bent toward the machine. The scanner's illuminated screen backlit her skirt, revealing the vague outline of her thighs. Vassos picked up on Lucas's hungry stare, and his face crinkled in a knowing smile. Katina backed away from the machine.

Lucas took her place, placing his hand on the man's shoulder, leaning forward as if to study the screen, whispering, "What can you tell me, unofficially?"

"Educated guesswork, Lou," he whispered back.

"I'm listening." Lucas became painfully aware of the man's rancid body odor.

"Well, for one thing, they're the prints of a man. Women have smaller, narrower ridges. And the array of the fingers show that they're from the middle, ring, and pinkie, most probably of the right hand," the technician said.

"Why the right hand?" Lucas asked.

Using the pencil as a tracer, the fingerprint man said, "The ridges of the pinkie enter on one side of the impression, recurve, and flow down the other side."

"I see that," Lucas said.

"We call that kind of an impression a loop. There are two kinds: ulnar loops, which flow out toward the ulnar bone, and radial loops, which flow out toward the radial bone. The overwhelming percentage of pinkie loops are ulnar, which would mean that the chances are pretty good that this pinkie came from the right hand."

"But not a certainty."

"That's right," he said. "The ring and middle fingers appear to be tented arches, which would narrow down the search considerably, *if* we were going to search the files. Another thing, see how the ridges at the bottom of the ring finger appear to have been ripped apart, how they have a jagged white line running through them?"

"Yes," Lucas said.

"That's a permanent scar."

Lucas glanced around at Vassos and tossed him a "get lost" look. Vassos answered with a nod, took Katina's arm, and waltzed her over to the wall display of blown-up marked fingerprints made for jury presentation in notorious trials.

Lucas leaned in close to the seated man. One of his zits was oozing pus. "Would you check these latents out against a list of B numbers for me?" he whispered, referring to the permanent identification number prisoners receive when they are first arrested.

"No problem, Lou. But you gotta understand, there just ain't no way I can give you a positive. The best you can hope for is a maybe."

"I'll take it. What about checking out the criminal and civilian files for me?"

"Lou," the technician moaned, "we ain't allowed to search the civilian files on a criminal matter. You wouldn't want me to violate some taxi driver's constitutional rights, would you?"

"Hey, perish the thought," Lucas whispered, asking, "Where's the john?"

The technician jerked his thumb over his shoulder. "Behind me and to the right." He shut off the humming machine and got up.

Passing Vassos and Katina, Lucas gestured to the major to keep her busy ànd moved down the aisle between machine-laden desks. As he moved past one desk he spotted a book of matches and picked it up.

Entering the white-tiled bathroom, Lucas stepped into an empty stall and locked the door. He reached into his left trouser pocket and took out the expense money that the C of D had given him. He peeled a fifty from the wad, folded it in such a way that Grant's portrait showed, and slid it behind the red-tipped forest of matches in the open book. He closed the book's cover, securing the lid behind the flap, and left the bathroom.

This was the part of the Job he hated. Years ago it was a cop's job. You did for each other out of a common sense of loyalty, a common purpose. No more. Civilization had come to the NYPD. The department was awash in political patronage, a pork barrel full of boa constrictors, each one with its mouth open.

The technician was at the photocopy machine duplicating the Iskur latents. Lucas walked up to him and handed him the list of Denny McKay's men that he had taken from Vassos on his way back from the bathroom. He gave the list to the technician and asked him to make a dozen copies.

The fingerprint man said, "Sure, Lou. No problem. Everybody's out to lunch so I don't have to worry about tying up the machine," and lifted the machine's rubber mat cover, laid the paper on top of the glass, blanketed the mat back over the paper, and pushed a green button.

The machine sprang into life, spewing out sheets of white paper into the side tray.

Lucas leaned against the copier, watching the light glow each time the top slid back and forth. "Would you check those latents against the fingerprints of the men on that list?"

"Sure, Lou," the technician said, switching off the machine.

"If you come up dry, would you also check the criminal and civilian files for me?" He slipped the book of matches into the technician's shirt pocket. "Here are your matches back."

Tucking in his chin, the fingerprint man looked down into his pocket. He stuck two fingers inside the pocket and pried open the cover. Pushing the row of matches forward, he spotted Ulysses Grant's dour face and smiled. "Lou, them civilian rights? I fuck 'em where they breathe."

Shielding his eyes with his hands, Lucas scanned Police Plaza for an empty bench. He spied four women getting up from a stone square. "Andreas, why don't you and Katina grab that seat and I'll go get us lunch."

Lucas returned shortly, gingerly balancing three cardboard plates holding hero sandwiches overflowing with crimson onions. A cardboard holder for sodas was clutched in his other hand, straws protruding out of punch-in cans. He eased the sodas down on the bench between them and handed them both a plate.

"How much do I owe you?" Katina asked, reaching into her pocketbook.

"Nothing, you made a score," Lucas said.

"What does that mean?" she asked.

"It's on the NYPD," Lucas said.

"Thank you, NYPD," Katina answered, gracefully nibbling onions. She looked at Vassos. "Have you ever eaten a hero sandwich before?"

"In Greece such a thing would be called souvlaki, and we use pita bread." He smiled. "But Pericles Levi's daughter must surely know that." He chomped into the hero.

"What do you think of police work?" Lucas asked her.

"It's fun," she said, her eyes sparkling. "It can get a bit boring patching up ancient parchments. Do you think we've accomplished anything?" she asked, wrapping her lips around the straw.

"I hope we've started some people worrying," Lucas said, looking at her wet lips.

She looked around the sun-drenched plaza. "Do most of these people work for the police department?"

"Most of them," Lucas answered, putting his plate down on his knees and looking at Vassos. "What did you think of Widener?"

Vassos made a noncommittal shrug. Katina responded instead: "He's got a slightly murky reputation. I think he is definitely hiding something. Maybe he's no victim at all."

Paul Mastri was a handsome man in his sixties, tall and well built, with a sinewy body that moved with the graceful assurance of success. Mastri Associates was located in a triple suite of interconnecting rooms on Madison Avenue north of Fifty-sixth Street. A male secretary led the trio into Mastri's office. The large room's white marble floor and walls gleamed softly.

"Dr. Wright, what a pleasure," Mastri said smoothly, moving out from behind his desk to kiss Katina on both her cheeks.

Katina made the introductions.

Lucas noted that Mastri's handshake was firm, his clothes jaunty: he wore a tie of bold blue stripes against a blazing orange background, a blazer of white linen, a fluffy orange handkerchief in the pocket, blue trousers. "I must have gotten a dozen telephone calls so far this morning telling me about your visit to Widener Books," Mastri said, carefully spreading the folds of his jacket to avoid sitting on them and wrinkling it. He lowered himself into his carved and gilded throne of a chair, which was covered with scarlet velvet.

"That's some chair you've got," Lucas observed.

"Thank you," Mastri said. "It's Venetian, circa 1730." He turned his attention to Katina, wiggling a finger at her. "You've tantalized the industry, Dr. Wright, with your inquiries concerning the casket-copy."

"Word travels fast," Lucas said.

Mastri leaned forward, sliding his elbows onto the desk. "Has the casket-copy really been unearthed?"

"We think so," Katina said.

"Think? Only think?" Mastri relaxed back into his seat. "Hasn't anyone seen it? Established provenance?"

"No, not yet," Katina said. "The entire matter is a bit confused.

"Confused?" Mastri said. "What is the Morgan's interest in all this?"

"Absolutely none," Katina said. "The police requested our help and we agreed. The library is not involved in any other way."

"Not involved?" Mastri said, a disbelieving smile evident on his smooth face. "One of the greatest finds ever, and the Morgan is not involved. I find that a very difficult morsel to swallow, Dr. Wright."

"Nevertheless, it's the truth," she said.

"Mr. Mastri, if someone were to bring you the casket-copy, would you be able to sell it?" Lucas asked.

"I wouldn't touch it without the necessary export papers," Mastri said.

Lucas leaned forward on the low-slung white sofa, his hand making tiny circles. "Just suppose that everything was in order."

An insincere smile exposed Mastri's capped teeth. "The legendary casket-copy? I would be able to dispose of it within the day."

Vassos was subdued and thoughtful. "At what price?"

Mastri fixed his eyes on the ceiling. "Truthfully? I don't know. Prices in the art world have come unglued since Van Gogh's *Irises* went at auction for fifty million dollars. There is no limit anymore, no rationale. What price? I would make up some ridiculously absurd number. And I would get it." He looked at Katina. "Dr. Wright, I would just love to show you my latest acquisition." He got up and went over to the book-case. Cabinets lined the bottom. He opened one of the doors and removed a book, its green cover heavily embossed with gold. He went over and handed it to her, then stepped back.

Katina placed the book on her lap and turned back the cover to reveal an ancient script written in silver ink on purple paper. Slowly turning each sheet, she took in each decorated page with muttered approval. Toward the end of the book she looked up at the policemen and explained, "This is a translation of the Bible into the Gothic. Sixth century, I think."

"Very good, Dr. Wright. You know your subject," Mastri said.

Carefully closing the cover, she handed the book back to the dealer and said, "Magnificent."

"Thank you," Mastri said, beaming proudly.

"Before today, had you heard of any interest in the casket-copy?" Lucas asked.

"No, I hadn't. The last I heard of it was when I heard of the famous Matrazzo telegram. And frankly, I just do not believe that it could have survived all those millennia. Fragments perhaps, but the complete *Iliad?* I can't believe that," Mastri said.

Lucas got up and moved aimlessly around the room. "You don't appear to have any alarm system in place, Mr. Mastri."

"We're well protected, Lieutenant," Mastri said. "There's all sorts of state-of-the-art gadgetry hidden about. Insurance regulations require it."

Vassos asked, "Do you know Orhan Iskur?"

"No, I don't. Is he in the trade?"

"Not really," Lucas said. "He deals in cheap imitations."

"I wouldn't know such a person," Mastri said dismissively.

"Mr. Mastri, did you know that Belmont Widener had

come upon one of Aristarchus's commentaries on the *Iliad?*"
Katina asked.

"My dear Dr. Wright, the entire trade knew once he announced it in his catalogue." He smoothed back his stone-
colored hair, taking great care that all the strands were tucked
neatly behind his ears. "I, of course, knew long before he
announced."

When Lucas asked him how he knew, Mastri tossed him a
patronizing look and said, "I've been in this business long
enough to spot a dealer who is making the rounds drumming
up demand."

Pompous ass, Lucas thought, smiling thinly at the dealer.

"Mr. Mastri, are you aware of any dealer or collector with
a special interest in ancient material relating to the development of silent reading?" Katina asked.

"You are confusing scholarship with collecting, Dr.
Wright. A collector desires to possess some great object from
antiquity, but . . ."

Lucas saw the fire blazing in the dealer's eyes. He'd seen
the same look on the faces of other men. He'd seen it on a
gambler's as he waited for the last card to be turned; he'd seen
it on an alcoholic's as he hurried up to the bar to get his first
drink of the day; he'd seen it on Andreas Vassos's whenever
he spoke of his murdered family. Driven men, consumed by
emotions they did not fully understand, each with an unalter-
able passion, and an uncontrollable one.

". . . a scholar seeks answers to questions. How did civilization progress from point A to point B? And why? A collector does not concern himself with such matters."

Vassos dumped his worry beads into his shirt pocket and
took out the composite sketch. "Do you know this person?"
he asked, passing the sketch and photo to the dealer.

A minute passed. Mastri handed them back. "No, I have
never seen this gentleman before."

"Would you let me know if you should hear anything about
someone offering the casket-copy for sale?" Katina said.

"You can count on it, Dr. Wright," Mastri said, standing.

Katina moved up to the desk to admire a black lacquer box. A hunting scene in a medieval forest was painted on the lid. She noted that the painter had made the blood of the dying boar all too real.

The air-conditioning in C of D Edgeworth's unmarked Plymouth had not been repaired, despite assurances from the Wagon Board that a new condenser would be installed "forthwith." This had not particularly improved his humor during the long, very hot drive up to midtown Manhattan from One Police Plaza. His driver stopped in front of the heavy stone facade of the Millennium Club, the iron bars over its windows and the heavy, dark-wood double doors of its entrance offering a rather forbidding welcome for the uninitiated guest.

Inside, the large marble-floored lobby afforded a cool refuge from the blazing afternoon heat. Edgeworth was met by a dignified black man in a gray uniform and courteously directed to an uncomfortable bench, very like a pew, that stood on one side of the lobby. "Mr. Borden hasn't arrived yet," he was told. Asked if he wanted to "freshen up," Edgeworth merely grunted a negative response and plumped himself down on the bench reserved for strangers. While he waited, with mounting impatience, he read a long and thoroughly puzzling article in the *Journal of the National Association of Chiefs of Police* written by a chief from a small western city, a prodigy who had a Harvard Ph.D. The article discussed ways of building department morale; Edgeworth found it as exotic and as irrelevant as a book by Margaret Mead on courtship in Samoa that he had read, under duress, while an undergraduate at Hofstra.

He was attempting to understand what his fellow cop meant by something called "male bonding" when a beautifully shined pair of handmade shoes appeared in the lower left quadrant of his vision. He looked up to see the bright blue eyes of Gerald Borden regarding him indulgently, his hectic red complexion set off by a waxed white mustache; a gray, pin-striped, unwrinkled summer suit, blue Brooks button-down, and a jaunty bow tie wrapping up the package.

"I'm grateful that you made time to see me, Tim. And that you came up my way. I have to catch a six-fifty train, and we need some time to catch up."

Edgeworth was wondering about what precisely they had to talk about as Borden led him up the wide staircase to the second floor, where they sat down in deep, leather-covered chairs. Large yellowing oil portraits decorated the walls; below them were bookshelves crammed with multicolored bindings. Edgeworth was making a cop's thorough mental inventory of the place when he saw Borden writing out an order for drinks while a waiter hovered deferentially nearby. "And you, Tim?"

"Just a soft drink, Gerry; whatever they got that's real cold."

Borden pushed back in his chair and looked over the low round table between them. He took an immaculate white handkerchief out of his breast pocket and blew his nose vigorously.

"I believe you have been in touch, er, more or less, with one of my former associates?"

Edgeworth regarded him sourly and said, "Is that what all this fuss is about? I thought Hayden was State Department, not one of your gang."

Borden took the bourbon old-fashioned that the silently reappearing waiter offered him on a silver tray, then picked up a tall glass of ginger ale and handed it to Edgeworth, who downed half of it in one gulp.

The waiter left and Borden continued in a lower tone of voice. "Strictly speaking, he isn't one of us. He was a contract employee, a paramilitary type. Police background, not too scrupulous about what sort of jobs he would take on. We put his talents to good use in Laos, back in the days of the great crusade."

Edgeworth sat forward, hands on his knees. "Just what sort of jobs did he do for you?"

Borden smiled benignly and said, "That comes under the great blanket of 'national security'—and I don't think you have a need to know." His eyes suddenly turned cold. "The Agency cut him off a long time ago. In fact, we helped him get a job with State because we wanted to get rid of him."

"And keep his mouth shut, too, I bet," the C of D said with a tiny smile.

"Ah, yes, we did ensure his . . . uh . . . discretion. Unfortunately he got used to working with some of my colleagues out there, some of my former friends who were a little too enthusiastic about helping the Hmong get their poppy crop to market."

Edgeworth had first met Borden when both men were on a joint Agency, DEA, and NYPD task force in the Golden Triangle engaged in antinarcotics operations with the less than enthusiastic authorities in Thailand. He knew Borden hated dope and anyone who made a profit out of the misery it caused. His son had gotten hooked on heroin while serving as a marine in Vietnam. Men like Hayden had helped to put the needle in the kid's arm. But Borden's son had kicked the habit the hard way. Six months after his return to the U.S., he shot himself in his bedroom in the Borden home in Virginia.

"These former friends of yours—are they still in the Company?"

Borden looked thoughtfully down at the polished oak floor. "No, the lure of private enterprise, as well as the suspicions of some of my DEA brethren, proved sufficient incentive to make them retire and go into other lines of work. Hayden is still their gundog, though. He'll clean up their messes, do the dirty jobs they won't touch." He reached over and put his hand on the sleeve of Edgeworth's rumpled tan suit. "Unfortunately Hayden is still on State's payroll. I hear that he finagled his way into a certain assignment so he could watch out for the interests of some of his old associates. And they have friends, very rich, very powerful friends. I expect I can find out more when I get back to Washington next week. I'll do a little nosing around, quietly. Don't want to alarm anyone unnecessarily, you know."

Edgeworth got out of his chair and looked at his friend without speaking for several moments. "I gotta go, Gerry. But you know my private number. My home phone is secure. I want to know a *lot* more. I got a bunch of damn good cops mixed up in something that's beginning to smell real bad. And I don't want any of the shit you guys deal in sticking to them."

As Edgeworth left the room, Borden was still wearily slumped down in his chair, looking at his feet. Edgeworth knew he had an ally. He just could not be sure how much Borden's pain and anger would overcome the ingrained tendency of any Agency person to protect the Company and its officers, even if they were rogue elephants.

The row house had brown curtains. It was in the middle of Markham Mews, an undistinguished block in the Red Hook section of Brooklyn. Adele Matrazzo was a registered Democrat and the sole occupant of the house with brown curtains.

Adele taught social studies at PS 181 until crippling arthritis forced her retirement. That was six years ago; now she passed her days confined to a shiny electric wheelchair. Her once-beautiful legs, which so many men had admired, were now motionless appendages hanging stiffly over the edge of her chair. And her graceful hands were now rigid, deformed claws with chestnut-sized knuckles straining the skin over them.

She had stationed herself by the parlor window after she received the telephone call from the police. A minor matter, the police lieutenant had said. Adele could feel the knot of anxiety in her throat as she thought about what the police really wanted to know. She had been preparing for such a visit for many years. She prayed that he was all right. Perhaps she should call him just to make sure that nothing had happened to him. She quickly decided against doing that. He had warned her many times never to call him unless it was some kind of emergency that she could not handle without getting him involved.

At a little before four o'clock a blue Buick stopped in front of her house. From behind the curtains, Adele could see two men and a woman get out of the car and stand on the sidewalk staring at her house. They made a handsome trio. She felt a strong desire to talk with them—and an equally powerful apprehension about the questions she feared they might ask.

"Number eleven," Lucas said, looking up at the house number as he lifted the metal bar. The gate hinge groaned, and almost as if on cue the front door opened.

"Yes?" asked the woman in the wheelchair.

Peering inside, studying the crippled woman, Lucas showed her his shield and made the introductions.

"Please come in," Adele said, reversing her wheelchair into the parlor.

"I hope we're not interrupting anything," Lucas said, following behind the wheelchair.

"As you can see, my dance card's hardly filled these days," Adele said, wheeling around to face them. She waved her crooked hand at the couch. "Please sit."

They sat, Katina in the middle.

"What is this all about?" Adele asked.

"We're trying to locate relatives of Paolo Matrazzo," Lucas said.

A surprised expression transformed Adele's heavily made-up face. "They're all dead, except me."

"How were you related to him?" Lucas asked.

"Uncle Paolo was my father's brother. Why in the world would the police be interested in any of the Matrazzos?" she asked, reaching into the candy box on her lap.

Lucas replied: "The Greek government has asked us to help them try and locate—"

"Alexander's *Iliad*," Adele interrupted, digging out a candy with a walnut on top.

"Yes," Vassos said, resting his hands on his knees.

Adele forced her hand up to her mouth and sucked the candy between her lips. After swallowing it, she said, "As a little girl I was forever hearing about Uncle Paolo's *Iliad*. No one in the family really believed it existed. I can tell you one thing for sure, if he ever did find it, no one in this family ever benefited. He died on Santorini, leaving his wife and two sons almost penniless."

"Paolo Matrazzo was a well-known collector," Katina said. "It's hard to believe that he did not leave a substantial estate."

"Believe it. He might have been a famous collector, but he was no businessman," Adele said sadly. "He squandered a small fortune running around the world searching for that wretched book. When he died, his partner told my aunt that there was almost nothing left in the business. Paolo's Folly, my aunt used to call Alexander's *Iliad*."

"Who was your uncle's partner?" Vassos asked.

"A man named Jean Laval. He bought out my aunt's interest in the business."

"Do you know what happened to him?" Lucas asked.

"He died in 1947," Katina said.

Lucas looked sharply at the beautiful woman sitting next to him. "How did you know that?"

Katina shrugged. "Art world trivia."

"I see," Lucas said, slowly turning his attention back to the woman in the wheelchair. "What happened to your uncle's family?"

"My aunt died in 1946. Anthony, the oldest son, was killed on Guadalcanal. Paolo Junior came out of the army a captain. He married, had two sons and a daughter. After he received his Ph.D. from New York University, he accepted a job teaching art history at NYU. He died of cancer in 1968."

"What happened to his wife and children?" Lucas asked.

Adele shook her head. "I don't know. We just sort of lost touch."

"Did you ever hear anyone in your family suggest that your

uncle might have smuggled the *Iliad* out of Greece before he died, or that someone was with him on Santorini when he allegedly sent that telegram to his partner?" Lucas asked.

Adele laughed. "No, Lieutenant. My uncle's obsession was his alone." She looked suspiciously at Vassos. "Why after all these years is there interest in the casket-copy?"

"We consider it a national treasure and would like to see it returned to Greece. My government, of course, would be willing to make any *necessary payments* to secure its return."

Looking at the stuffing leaking out of the couch's arm, Adele said thoughtfully, "I could certainly use some *necessary payments*, but I'm afraid that there isn't much hope of that."

"Does the name Orhan Iskur mean anything to you?" Vassos asked, opening his briefcase.

"No, I can't say that it does," Adele said.

Vassos got up and slowly walked over to the wheelchair. He held up the composite sketch and photograph of Aldridge Long. "Do you know this person?"

Adele squinted, her eyes close to both sketch and photograph, looking from one to the other, taking her time. An expression of fright and disbelief pulled back her mouth, causing dimples to appear. "He looks an awful lot like my Uncle Paolo. But that's impossible, isn't it? He's been dead since 1939."

10

Teddy Lucas walked into the Sixteenth's squad room and stopped dead. The detention cage was filled with shouting prisoners, many of whom wore silly-looking sailor hats. Detectives were busy at their desks, helping officers in uniforms prepare arrest reports and invoice property.

Lucas looked up at the wall clock: 5:20. The joint was jumping. He looked behind him at Vassos and Katina. "We'll go into my office." He reached over the gate and pressed the release latch. The prisoners spotted Katina; a chorus of hoots and whistles issued from the cage.

The two men convoyed Katina across the squad room into the Whip's office. Vassos closed the door. "You're busy this evening," he said, lowering himself down onto the department-issue green swivel chair.

"Seasonal trade," Lucas explained, rolling the blackboard away from the wall. "Rivergoing office parties that get out of hand. Happens every summer."

"In Greece such persons would be taken directly to court," Vassos said.

"Here too, normally," Lucas said, "but, according to our *Patrol Guide*, prisoners arrested on the navigable waters who can not be arraigned in court immediately must be brought to the nearest station house for search and detention. Those beauties outside won't be arraigned tonight; there's too much paperwork involved."

Vassos nodded in understanding.

Katina stood off from the men, looking around the Whip's office. Lucas picked chalk up from the runner of the blackboard and wrote the names of the people they'd interviewed, including the other dealer they had visited after leaving Adele Matrazzo's house.

Lucas stepped back from the board, his gaze fixed on the black slate. Out in the street a truck squealed to a stop; a cacophony of horns bubbled up into the squad room.

"They all have one thing in common," Lucas observed, leaving the rest of his thought unspoken.

Katina focused on the blackboard.

Vassos fingered his jade worry beads.

"In addition to being dealers, each one of them is also a collector," Lucas said.

"Most dealers are," Katina said.

"My gut instinct tells me that whoever has the casket-copy has one powerful urge to show it off," Lucas said, moving around his desk and sitting.

"Before you get the wrong impression," Katina said, "most dealers are also collectors, and many of them are secretive about their private collections."

Lucas made a dismissive grunt.

A detective out in the squad room screamed for quiet. The ruckus continued. The familiar sound of a swivel chair crashing against the bars of the detention cage caused a knowing grin to pass between the two policemen.

Lucas leaned back, his legs stretched across the desk's side table, studying the slate. "If Iskur did have a coconspirator in the States, they'd have to communicate with each other, wouldn't they?" He looked around at Vassos. "Were Iskur's transatlantic telephone calls checked out?"

Vassos muttered a curse in Greek. "I don't know, but I can

find out." He got up and went over to the squad commander's red telephone. He lifted the receiver, and dialed. He spoke for about one minute in Greek and hung up. "I must meet someone within the hour."

"How do you manage getting around the city?" Katina asked him.

"I have a book of maps in my briefcase," Vassos said, asking her, "What time does Bloomingdale's close?"

A benevolent smile crossed her face. She asked in Greek, "Have you ever been inside Bloomingdale's?"

"*Okhee.*" No, he said.

"I think they close at six-thirty tonight," she said.

Vassos turned the door knob. "Ten o'clock tomorrow, Lou?"

Lucas smiled. "Ten o'clock, First Terror."

After Vassos had gone, Katina said, "I hope that we accomplished something today."

"Time will tell," Lucas said, acutely conscious of her perfume. He looked into her beautiful face and wanted desperately to reach out and touch her, to ask her to have dinner with him. Don't be a putz all your life, Lucas. Ask her. All she can say is no, or I'm busy tonight, or I'm involved with someone. He slipped his feet off the desk and was about to ask her when he looked at the elegant, educated woman that fate had thrown in his path and imagined the unbridgeable gulf between them. So he merely smiled ruefully and said, "Come on, I'll drive you home."

Despite her sixty-two years and her infirmity, Adele Matrazzo's big black eyes were still capable of capturing a man's heart.

Adele enjoyed putting on her makeup every morning, pretending that today was the day he would visit her. She loved to paint her lips a glossy red and add a heavy streak of eyeliner, then brush mascara onto her long lashes. It was a painful struggle for her to do these things now, but she did them nonetheless. She relished her morning "get ready for the day" sessions; they gave her something to look forward to during the long nights. And, you never knew, today might be the day when he'd visit.

Adele's world consisted of the bottom floor of the two-story house: a parlor, bedroom, small kitchen, and a full bath with gripping bars on all the walls. She spent a good portion of her day watching the soaps on the twenty-five-inch television screen that he had gotten for her last Christmas. And there were her chocolates. Oh, how she loved chocolate. She loved the way the creamy pulpiness of the candy felt as it melted in her mouth, and the way it felt when she mushed it about with her tongue. There was always a golden box nearby.

Adele still received occasional telephone calls from old friends and colleagues. And there were her wonderful neighbors who would look in on her and even do her shopping. She was particularly grateful to Mrs. O'Rourke, who lived across the street. She would come by twice a week and have tea with Adele. They would watch "Search for Happiness," and Adele would smilingly endure the same worn litany of complaints against Mrs. O'Rourke's ungrateful daughter-in-law.

Sometimes when she was alone she'd make the radio music loud and play with her wheelchair's control box, spinning her cold metal throne about the room, pretending she was dancing with some remembered lover. She would close her eyes and dwell on the hardness rubbing up against her, and a shroud of lust would cover her loneliness.

But the high points of Adele's confined existence were his visits. She would never know when he would come by. There was always a telephone call first. "Adele, dear, are you alone?" She would say yes, and he would show up within the hour. She never dared question him about his other life; she knew better. He had always been withdrawn and secretive about himself, even as a child. She was thankful that they had been able to share a hedonistic life together. It had all begun when they were children. So long ago. A joyous shiver shook her shoulders as her mind replayed his last visit.

He had stood over her watching as she popped chocolates into her mouth. With her eyes locked on his, she put them in one at a time and rolled them about, turning them into delicious dark brown mud. He took out his beautiful thing and ran it over her wet lips, and when he told her to, she opened her mouth wide and took him into the chocolaty muck, ravenously sucking him until his hot juice spilled into her mouth.

Stepping back from her, his penis dripping with chocolate sludge, his arms suddenly went akimbo, his back arched, and he laughingly said, "Adele, dear, I've just made you a black and white soda. I do hope that you've enjoyed it."

"I did. I did."

Adele Matrazzo spun her wheelchair around to face her visitor. Her admiring eyes locked on him as he moved across the parlor and sat on her shabby sofa. He had come promptly in response to her phone call.

He leaned forward, watching her. "Adele, dear, do tell me all about your unexpected company."

She clawed a chocolate from the box and proceeded to tell him about Lucas, Vassos, and a woman named Katina Wright. When she finished, her visitor leaned back, his gaze fixed on a cobweb of ceiling cracks. Adele put another candy into her mouth.

"They know nothing about me?" he said.

"Nothing."

His lips pulled into a menacing scowl as his head came up off the back of the sofa. "Adele, did you ever mention me to any of your neighbors or friends?"

"I never mentioned you to a living soul. You've been my life's secret."

"Do you have any pictures of me, anything from the past that might tie us together?"

"There is nothing."

"Do you have me listed in your address book?"

"Of course not."

Her eyes widened with sudden realization; her deformed hands crushed the sides of the candy box. Her mouth quivered as she whispered, "You have it, don't you?"

A beam of sunlight pierced the dirty window and reflected off his golden ring. "Yes, I have it." He slid off the sofa and moved over to the wheelchair where he kneeled down next to her. He brushed a stray wisp of hair from her brow. "You've been a good, loyal friend all these years."

Her misshapen hand caressed his arm. "I've loved you since we were children."

"I know," he said softly. "Would you like me to relax you?"

She caught her breath, leaned her head against the back of her prison, and closed her eyes. "Yes."

He played with her breasts. She moaned.

Her thoughts drifted to other times, other places. Her young, healthy body was straddling his, lowering onto his straining cock. She felt the warmth of past ejaculations and her breath began to come in hard gulps. "Do my nipples."

He unbuttoned the front of her housedress and unhaltered her breasts. He took one into his hand, milking it. Bending forward, he sucked it into his mouth and gnawed the thick, brown crown.

"Harder," she demanded.

As he stimulated her, he looked up at her contorted face and saw that chunks of mascara had fallen on her cheeks. Her head lay still and she made mewing noises through her open mouth. She started to emit a hoarse, gagging sound, and her head began to rock back and forth. She stiffened. Her head came up sharply; she gagged several times and then screamed. She relaxed, slumping down into her seat.

Gripping the chair's arm, he pushed himself up onto his feet and, bending, buttoned the front of her dress.

"Would you like me to give you a blow job?"

"I have something else in mind," he said, taking a length of thin wire from his pocket; slipping behind the wheelchair, he held it over her head like a blessing.

"What is that?" she asked.

"The E string of a violin."

"What can we do with that?"

"The ultimate thrill, Adele, dear." He snapped the string around her neck, pulling tightly on both ends.

At first Adele Matrazzo did not scream or attempt to defend herself. She sat still, not understanding what was happening, not believing that it could happen. And then, as life-sustaining air fled her body, her alarm gave way to wide-eyed panic, and a terrifying, almost inaudible scream burst from her mouth. Her useless hands fought vainly against the E string. His powerful arm hoisted her up out of her seat, dark thick fluid drooling over her lips as her body convulsed in life's final dance.

Andreas Vassos walked into a wonderland of glass and black marble. Young, fashionably dressed women stood behind glistening counters, holding out perfumes in designer bottles. Weaving through the first-floor fragrance department at Bloomingdale's, Vassos became more and more conscious of the obscene display of luxury. Names shouted from the walls: Chanel, Saint Laurent, Givenchy. He thought of the modest and rather drab perfume stores in Greece, and as he watched an elegantly dressed woman pause to allow a saleswoman to dab a fragrance on her wrist, he thought also of how his mother and grandmother had labored in the fields picking tobacco, his grandmother until well into her sixties.

He stopped at a counter, looking confusedly at its contents.

"May I help you, sir?" She wore strange makeup: bluish eyebrows, purple eyeliner, and mauve lipstick. Her nails were painted blood red; she wore large pieces of jewelry around her wrists and neck so that she clanked every time she moved.

"I would like a bottle of Anaïs-Anaïs, please."

Her capped teeth gleamed. "You are Greek."

Bemused, he answered, "Yes I am."

The saleswoman clutched her chest. "I fell in love with your country. It's *sooo* charming, and the people are *sooo* friendly. My girlfriend and I go to Mykonos every year. In fact, we're going next month. We *always* go dancing at the Nine Muses; I mean, it's like a sacred thing with us."

His face a blank mask, Vassos thought, why are they always so dumb and so damn nasal? He made a few agreeable grunts, lingered a few seconds more, and said, "I must hurry, miss, I have an appointment."

"I'm sorry. I do run off at the mouth whenever I talk about Greece."

He watched her wrap his purchase. He paid; she returned his change. As he was leaving, she said good-bye. *"Ahndeeo."*

He smiled at her and rushed out of the store, anxious to escape the cloying bouquet that fouled the air. He looked around for a cab.

Ficco's was crowded. A fully extended orange-and-green awning sloped down over the sidewalk café's rows of tables, and a waiter trundled a gaily decorated cart from table to table, serving drinks. Vassos stood in front of the restaurant. It was directly across the street from Lincoln Center. He looked around carefully for his control. He spotted her sitting at a table in the last row. She waved at him. He acknowledged her by raising his briefcase. Squeezing through the cramped space, he reached her table and sat down across from her.

Looking across Broadway at the gushing fountain, Elisabeth Syros said in throaty Greek, "How goes it with you, Andreas?"

He shrugged and frowned at the same time, a gesture that meant "I'm not sure," and then he proceeded to bring her up to date.

A waiter glided over and took his order: ouzo and a plate of cheese and crackers.

"I want you to do something," he said.

"What?"

He checked out the people sitting near them. Leaning in close, he spoke softly in Greek. "I want a list of Orhan Iskur's overseas telephone calls for the past year."

"Only those made to the States?" she asked, her espresso cup poised before her lips.

Fascinated by all the rings on her hand, he managed to reply, "Every call made to anywhere outside of Greece."

The waiter leaned in from the row in front of them and set down his order. Pouring water into his ouzo, Vassos said, "Overseas telephone records are kept for two years so there shouldn't be a problem." He stirred his drink. "How long will it take you to get the information?"

"A day, perhaps two. I'll transmit your request to Tsimas tonight. He'll have it on his desk in the morning."

He had forgotten about General Philippos Tsimas, the head of the Central Information Service, Elisabeth Syros's boss. He wondered how Colonel Pappas was doing with his parallel investigation. Sipping the licorice-flavored drink, his eyes drifted over the tables. "Just suppose I do happen to come up with the . . . merchandise? What do I do about delivering it?"

She reached behind her and lifted her pocketbook off the back of the chair. Snapping it open, she took out a pad, removed the ballpoint attached to the side, and wrote down several addresses and telephone numbers. "You can deliver it to any of these locations at any time of the day or night. And, if you should ever need any help, call any of these numbers and tell whoever answers that you're a friend of the lady from Thessalonika."

Vassos arrived back at the Hotel Olympian at seven-thirty. Harry, the night desk clerk, greeted him in Greek. Harry was a small man who had had the misfortune of being born without a chin, so that his face resembled that of a fully grown rat. The thin mustache that Harry affected looked like a rat's twitching whiskers. Harry didn't know that his newfound friend from Greece was a cop, nor did Harry know about the gun that Vassos wore clipped to his belt.

As Vassos approached, Harry leaned across the desk, his face shrinking into a conspiratorial grin. "I've made those arrangements for you. Let me know when you're ready."

"Tonight," Vassos said, heading for the elevator.

Vassos tossed his briefcase on the wing chair and went over to shut off the air conditioner, amazed that a chambermaid would waste energy cooling an empty room. He pushed the tall window open; a strong current of hot air rushed in, bringing with it the clamor of Manhattan.

He unhooked the holster and tucked it under the mattress. He undressed, showered, stepped into fresh underpants, turned off the light, and sprawled across the sagging bed, listening to the harsh sounds of the city.

"Soula, Stephanos," he groaned, and then fell into an easeful darkness.

A soft knocking caused him to swallow his sorrow and call out in his own language, "Who is it?" He had lost track of time. He must have drifted off. It took him a moment to remember where he was.

"Harry sent me," she answered in Greek.

He rolled off the bed and padded over to the door.

She quickly brushed past him into the room. Early thirties, black hair, pretty face with a bit too much makeup, and a shapely body that was starting to add pounds. Crossing to the window, she said in Greek, "Harry told me that you wanted a woman who spoke our language, and that you had certain requests."

"Nai." Yes, he said.

She turned abruptly, shrewd eyes evaluating him. "No animals, no pain, and no bondage."

"My needs are simple."

"Sixty dollars for a straight lay, anything else is extra." She moved over to him and slid her hand between his legs, rubbing him. "Okay?"

He moved over to the briefcase and took out the perfume. He placed the bottle into her hand and told her what he wanted. The hooker softened; she kissed him on the cheek, nodded, and slipped into the bathroom.

He sprawled back across the bed, listening to the shower's muted roar. The sound of the water carried his thoughts back to the day he met the woman who would become his wife. Soula had been showering at Vouliagméni's pay beach that day. He sprinted across the sand and ran under the next shower. Turning under the sprinkling water, he thrust his face up and bent down at the same time to wash sand from his feet. He lost his balance and stumbled into the next open stall, toppling both of them out onto the grass.

"What's the matter with you?" Soula demanded, trying to untangle their arms and legs.

"I'm sorry," he said, feeling like an awkward and clumsy fool. At first he did not see her face, he was too busy trying to pick himself up off the grass. At some point he found himself staring into her saffron eyes, and then he was at a loss for words. He wanted to know this woman. The next seconds were lost in a mist of embarrassment. He remembered that he reached out to stop her from getting up so that he could ask her name. She turned abruptly; he reached over, intending to tap her on the shoulder, and somehow ended up with her bikini top dangling in his hand.

"You clown!" she screamed into his mortified face. Covering herself with her hands, she ran off into the ladies' locker room.

He jumped to his feet and pursued her through a gauntlet of laughter. Running into the women's locker room just behind her, he found his path blocked by the formidable body of the matron. "Cool your buns, young man, and wait outside," she said, grabbing the top out of his hand.

He slunk out of the brick building and waited just outside. A fig peddler passed. A peace reparation just might turn the tide in his favor, so he called out to the old man: "One kilo of figs." Realizing that he had no money, he ran around the other side of the building to the men's locker room, asked the attendant for his basket, took money out of his trousers, and ran back outside in time to pay the peddler four drachmas for the bag of figs.

A few minutes later Soula came out, her swim top repaired. When she saw him leaning up against the side of the building, she turned in a huff and hurried along the path leading down to the beach.

He ran after her. "I'm sorry. Please, wait one second and let me explain. Please." He stuck the bag in front of her face. "I've bought these figs for you."

Four meters away from them, some boys were playing soccer. One of them kicked the ball. It shot across the grass, passed people sunning on chaise longues, and caught Vassos between his ankles, causing him to go sprawling over the path in front of her, spewing figs all over the place.

Realizing all was lost, he picked up a fig and handed it to her. "I guess I'm not the suave type."

She took the fig out of his hand, peeled back the grainy skin, and said, "I think you're adorable."

The bathroom door opened. The naked woman switched off the light, made her way over to the bed, and lowered herself down next to him. She kissed his brow. "I love you, Andreas."

He pressed her close, intoxicated by the scent of Soula's favorite perfume. "Soula, I miss you so very much."

She stroked his hair. "I'm here, Andreas. I'll always be here for you, always, my darling."

Eddie Burke was what cops called a "predicate criminal." He was proud of the eighteen arrests on his yellow sheet; he was proud that he had never done an honest day's work in his life; proud that he didn't pay taxes, or have a social security number, or a credit rating. Eddie didn't exist, except in the criminal record files of the NYPD and the FBI.

He was a powerfully built man with wavy chestnut hair and a deeply lined face. He talked with a soft voice that sometimes bordered on a whisper. Burke liked to think of himself as a street guy with a heart of gold. He loved playing with children and watching the sunset. Eddie's buddies in the Purple Gang had a different opinion of him. Long ago they hung the moniker "Crazy Eyes" on Eddie because of the way his large tawny eyes popped out of his head whenever he got angry.

Whenever any of the Purple Gang got together their conversation would frequently make its way around to the time the late Frankie Airlake made a pass at Shirley Case, Eddie's live-in girlfriend. When Eddie heard about it, he threw an ax into a big shopping bag and went looking for Frankie Airlake. He found him in The Den, standing at the bar, talking to Louie D and Mush McCarthy. Eddie stormed over to the trio, shoved Louie D and Mush aside, buried the ax in Frankie Airlake's head.

As the dying man lay in a pool of blood, Eddie worked the ax free and began to chop open Airlake's chest. Placing one foot on the other side of the bloody trench, Eddie bent down and pried open the rib cage, reached into the warm gory mess, and ripped out Airlake's heart. Slapping the organ down on the bar, Eddie laughingly announced, "Ol' Frankie boy's done lost his heart to love."

Eddie Burke sat behind the wheel of the Plymouth Sundance watching a mounted cop slowly riding on his horse up Twelfth Avenue. He had rented the car earlier that day with some funny plastic. The motor was running; the air conditioner was on high, and the radio blared. Eddie's loose-fitting white shirt hid his muscular frame and his drawstring pants flared down over his stolen Bruno Magliloafers. He wore no socks; his only jewelry was a stolen Piaget watch.

Denny McKay had telephoned Eddie at his girlfriend's around eleven that morning and told him to get a car and meet him at nine-thirty that night at the northwest corner of Forty-fifth and Twelfth Avenue. Eddie wondered what was up. Probably a fast score to be made or some asshole who needed his legs broken. His eyes drifted to the dashboard's digital clock: 9:45. When he looked back out the windshield, he saw Denny McKay standing on the corner, fanning his open shirt against the oppressive heat, the familiar Marlboro cigarette clenched between his front teeth, his half-glasses perched on his nose, held there by a black cord stretched around his head. McKay's furtive eyes swept the scene, making sure no unwelcome parasites had attached themselves to him. A shower of sparks rained down from a wildcat construction job, causing McKay to jump back and scream curses up at the oblivious workmen.

Eddie Burke laughed.

McKay's gaze moved along the row of parked cars and locked on the Sundance. He gave a barely perceptible nod. Eddie Burke released the handbrake and let the Sundance glide to the corner, where he leaned across the seat and chucked open the door.

McKay lowered himself into the cramped space. "Couldn't you get a bigger fucking car?" he said, pressing his knees up against the glove compartment. He reached down and pushed the control lever back, sliding the seat to the rear. "That's better." He turned and looked at his friend. "How goes it with you, Eddie?"

"No complaints. Where to?"

"Pier Ninety," McKay said, crushing out his cigarette in the ashtray and lighting up another.

A few minutes later the Sundance's tires drummed over the pier's timbered entrance. The guard wasn't in his shack, so Eddie Burke drove out onto the wharf and parked the Sundance between two stacks of containers.

"Whadda we waitin' for?" Burke asked, watching two homosexuals holding hands at the end of the pier.

McKay cracked the window at the top and tossed out his butt. "I made a new coke connection."

"Colombian?"

"No. A Chink with a good source of supply. He'd tied in with the Wu cartel."

Eddie was impressed. "That's heavy-duty shit. How much can he deliver?"

"As much as we can buy."

"What's the price?"

"Thirty-five a key with a discount on anything over fifty keys."

"Sounds good."

McKay playfully punched his friend's arm. "Where you been hidin'?"

"I've been hustling a livin'. Made a good score in Jersey, a truckload of liquor."

"Hey, Eddie, remember how Sister Maria used to beat the shit out of us whenever she caught us fucking up?"

Burke laughed. "She was a tough old nun. She used to bang me around with that ruler she kept hidden up her sleeve. 'You two are no good!' she'd scream, remember?"

Nostalgia brightened McKay's face. "Yeah, I remember. Guess she's long dead, may her soul rest in peace."

"And remember Sister Rose?"

A lecherous grin perked McKay's mouth. "I always wanted to hit on her. I used to jerk off pretending I was fucking her."

"Me too." Burke laughed.

"Hey, Eddie, you remember a few years back you took off that book dealer for me?"

"That fucking queen squealed like a pig when I shoved the piece in his face." He looked at McKay. "I never could understand why you wanted that damn scroll."

"I got it for a friend of mine," McKay said, lighting up another Marlboro.

"Well, that favor cost Bucky McMahon eighteen months inside."

WILLIAM J. CAUNITZ ═══════════════════ 185

"You ever mention doing that job to anyone?"

"You said forget it, so I forgot it. Besides, it wasn't one of my more memorable scores. You only paid me two large for the job."

"I didn't make a dime on it myself. Like I told you, it was a favor."

Burke shrugged indifference. "No big deal."

"Bucky McMahon did the cop with you, didn't he?"

"McGovern? Yeah, he done it with me. I'll tell ya, that old cop was one tough Irishman. He went down fighting all the way. I carry his shield around with me for good luck." He looked at McKay. "Why you asking about the old jobs for anyway?"

"Aw, nothing. I was just—hey, here comes our man."

"Where?"

"On your left," McKay said, pointing.

Eddie Burke turned to look. He heard the explosion and dimly felt his head toppling onto the steering wheel. Blood gushed from his eyes, nose, and mouth. He didn't hear the second shot.

McKay tucked the .38 S & W Chief into his belt and tossed his cigarette out the window. He took out his handkerchief and wiped the seat lever. He placed the cloth over the door handle and got out of the car. He walked away, not looking back. The sight of dead friends depressed him.

Teddy Lucas had made his nightly report to the chief of detectives some time ago. He was still annoyed with himself for not being able to get up the courage to ask Katina to go out with him. He was going to have to shake that peasant out of his system and get on with his life. His tour had been over hours ago and here he was, hanging around the Squad drinking stale coffee and trying to decide what to do with the rest of the night. He could run over to Heidi's and have a few with the guys, but he wasn't in the mood to spend the rest of the night bullshitting about the Job and the way it used to be.

Joan had said she would stop by his place the day after tomorrow for a quickie before her ten o'clock dentist appointment.
He made a mental note to buy condoms. He hated those
damn things; they made a woman taste lousy afterwards. Aw,
the hell with it, he'd go home. He'd grab a bite at the new
Polish joint on Eleventh Street, do his laundry, and sack out
watching the late movie on the tube.

He started to get up out of his chair when Big Jay stuck his
black face into the office and barked, "We just caught a
homicide on Pier Ninety. A small-timer named Eddie Burke
got himself blown away."

Lucas tensed. The name Burke rang a bell. He reached out
and flipped open the case folder. Fishing through the thick
file, he asked, "Who caught it?"

"Leone. He's making the notifications now." Big Jay
stepped into the office and leaned against the side of the file
cabinet, watching the Whip go through the folder. "You
going to ride on this one?"

Lucas yanked a sheet of notes from the folder. He quickly
read through it, put the pages back in the folder, and slapped
the cover closed. "Yeah, I'm riding on this one."

Yellow CRIME SCENE signs swung from the orange tape that
corralled the Sundance between the stacks of freight containers. Two RMPs, radio motor patrol cars, were parked on the
edge of the pier, the strobe light on one of them hurling
colored streaks over the murky water. No boats were berthed
at the pier; no crush of people intent on sating morbid curi-
osities pressed against the police barricades. The Forensic
Unit's blue-and-white station wagon had its back door open;
black valises were stacked on the platform. Two attendants
stood near the ambulance chatting quietly with the patrol
sergeant. Big Jay and John Leone stood by the radio cars
interviewing the first crew that had arrived on the scene.

Lucas stood just outside the frozen zone, gathering first
impressions. Technically he was off the chart and not required

to be there. Both the *Patrol Guide* and the *Detective Guide* mandated an immediate notification to the Borough Command whenever a homicide occurred. If the Whip or the Second Whip wasn't aboard, then the detective supervisor covering the borough would respond to the scene and take charge of the preliminary investigation.

As soon as Lucas realized who had been offed, he telephoned the Borough Command and told the sergeant on the operations desk that he was present in the Squad and would respond to the scene. He had not forgotten Cormick McGovern or the casket-copy. He stepped over the tape and circled the Sundance, examining the outside of the car.

Big Jay and Leone came over to the barrier. "Lou, we got ourselves a virgin crime scene," Big Jay said. "The first cops to arrive on the scene roped off the area and prevented anyone from entering."

"What were they able to tell you?" Lucas asked, bending down to examine the small pile of cigarette butts under the passenger window.

Leone checked his steno pad. "They drove out onto the pier to have their coffee. They both spotted the DOA at the same time and got out of their car to investigate. Both of them recognized Burke as one of the Purple Gang crew. They secured the area and called us by land line."

"Good," Lucas said, pleased that the cops had used the public telephone at the end of the pier to make the notification, preventing the media from knowing that a homicide had gone down; it gave them time to do their jobs before the arrogant vultures descended on them.

". . . the guard wasn't in his shack when the RMP drove onto the pier," Leone said, a cynical grin curling one end of his mustache. "When he finally showed he told the cops that he was taking a dump in the portable toilet."

"A dump, huh," Lucas said, his voice full of scorn. "I think you two are going to have to give him an enema of the mouth."

"Be a pleasure, Lou," Big Jay said.

The patrol sergeant, a dumpy black woman with a puffy Afro, came up to the barrier accompanied by the two black ambulance attendants. "Lou," she began, "the stiff hasn't been pronounced."

Lucas glanced around at the body. Thick strands of blood hung down from the face; an exit wound had splattered blood and brain matter over what remained of the window on the driver's side.

Lucas looked at the two attendants. "Pronounce him at the morgue."

"Lou, we're required to pronounce at the scene," said the smaller of the two, a man of thirty with crooked teeth.

Lucas stepped back over the tape and slid his arms around the two attendants' shoulders and waltzed them back over to their ambulance. "Look, guys, this is a mob hit and I have a personal interest in seeing that everything is done right, so you can see why I don't want anyone inside that car until we're done doing our thing."

"Lou," Crooked-teeth protested, "we're supposed to check for vital signs before we pronounce."

"M'man, his vital signs bees all over the window," Lucas said, affecting an inner city drawl.

The other man was fat and had long dreadlocks. "Lou, we'd like to do the right thing, but suppose we pronounce him without checking his vitals and the man don't be dead? Shit. They'd have our asses for breakfast, lunch, and dinner."

Lucas slid his arms from around their shoulders, turned his back to them, and took out his expense money. He shaved a Grant off the wad and slipped it into Dreadlocks' shirt pocket. "Lemme buy you guys lunch."

Crooked-teeth smiled. He looked back at the crime scene. "That motherfucker sure bees dead to me." Thus Eddie Burke was pronounced.

Lucas snapped on plastic gloves and stepped back into the frozen zone. Turning around, he said to the patrol sergeant,

"Send your driver to the Hotel Olympian on Eighth Avenue and Thirty-second and pick up a Mr. Andreas Vassos and deliver him here."

"Right, Lou," she said, motioning to her driver.

Big Jay and Leone snapped on disposable latex gloves and followed the Whip into the frozen zone. Crime Scene Unit detectives waited patiently nearby. Their turn would come soon.

The Sixteenth Squad detectives moved cautiously around the Sundance, avoiding the pile of cigarettes. Leone had caught the case, so the collection and the preservation of the chain of evidence was his responsibility. He waved the photographer into the frozen zone. Big Jay maintained the crime scene log, listing the name, rank, and shield number, and the time each person entered the frozen zone.

Accompanied by Leone, the photographer snapped his pictures of the car's exterior; the pile of cigarettes was shot at several different angles to show its relationship to the passenger window. The outside of the car was divided into quadrants and searched, starting with the quadrant containing the driver's door and continuing clockwise until they had searched all quadrants of the car's exterior.

Leone crouched down next to the pile of cigarettes. Using a rubber-tipped tweezer, he picked one up, examining it. "Marlboro, with a chewed-up filter." He took out his pen and wrote his initials, shield number, and the date and time on the cigarette paper. He deposited the butt into a serial-numbered evidence bag. Big Jay noted the bag's number in the log.

The car door was open; the photographer snapped pictures of the body. Big Jay and Leone wrestled the corpse out from behind the wheel and laid it out on the ground. Burke's hands were immediately bagged; photographs were taken of the body.

Leone searched the body. Big Jay vouchered the contents of the clothes. Leone removed a shield case from Burke's trousers. Time had molded the contours of a patrolman's shield into the outside of the worn leather case. He looked down at it and then up into the Whip's grim face. He passed the case to Lucas. Taking it in his hand, Lucas heard Cormick McGovern's voice boom across time-worn memories. "Laddie, let me tell you how the Job works."

Bile rose in Lucas's throat. He snapped open the case. A silver patrolman's shield: NYPD 5593. He looked down at the corpse. "Burn in hell, you bastard." He slid the case into his pocket.

Big Jay asked softly, "Want me to record finding it, Lou?"

"Finding what?"

The interior of the Sundance was divided into eight search zones, starting with the driver's compartment floor. All areas under the seats were searched; the seats were removed and their undersides examined. All folds and creases in the upholstery were searched. The contents of the ashtray were photographed, invoiced, and initialed.

Their tasks completed, Leone motioned to the crime scene detectives. "It's all yours."

The fingerprint technician snapped open his valise.

Lucas, Big Jay, and Leone climbed out of the frozen zone and ambled over to the edge of the pier.

"Whaddaya think?" Big Jay asked the Whip.

"Hit up close by someone he trusted," Lucas said. "He wasn't carrying, so we have to assume that he didn't expect trouble."

Leone nodded his agreement. "The hitter smoked Marlboros and is in the habit of chewing the filters."

"No other brand of cigarette was found in or around the car and none were found on Burke, so we have to assume that the hitter was the smoker," Big Jay said.

Lucas said to Leone, "I want you to put a hold on the body. Get impressions of Burke's teeth and have the saliva extracted from the filters."

"I went that route once, Lou," Big Jay said. "The ME

doesn't have any forensic dentists on staff. Whenever they have occasion to use one, they farm it out to a few that they have on call. But the kicker is that we have to pick up the tab, which means getting the borough commander's approval for the expenditure of department funds."

"I'll call the C of D at home," Lucas said. "He'll approve it for us." He looked directly at the two detectives. "You two are off the chart. Stay with this one."

"Can you tell us if this hit is tied in with what you and the major are working on?" Big Jay asked.

Lucas watched a beer can bobbing in the river. "No can do, not yet. Trust me, okay?"

"Ten-four, boss," Leone said.

Six minutes later Andreas Vassos leaped out of the front seat of the RMP and rushed over to the detectives. "What is it?" he asked excitedly.

Lucas led him away from the others and told him what had happened and explained to him the course that the preliminary investigation had taken.

"You think the casket-copy is involved in this murder?" Vassos asked.

"I think that someone is scared that we might be getting close and wants to make sure that all we find are dead ends."

"The dental impressions are important, then?" Vassos said.

"They'll exclude Burke as the smoker, leaving only the killer." Lucas looked out at the dark river and continued, almost as if he were talking to himself. "When we find the perp we'll get a court order to take his dental impressions. That, with the saliva which will give us blood grouping, will nail him to the crime scene."

Somewhere in the distance a ship's forlorn horn sounded.

11 ═══════════

ddie Burke's body lay on a gurney surrounded by other cadaver-laden trolleys in the basement of the medical examiner's office. The steel ice boxes were filled; the dead were crowded in the hallways. Burke had been dead about twelve hours; the preliminary investigation had been completed. Lucas had telephoned C of D Edgeworth earlier. "I need a forensic dentist, now."

"Wait at the morgue; one'll meet you there," Edgeworth had promised.

Lucas and Vassos waited in a glass-enclosed office, drinking coffee and watching the double door with the black rubber piping, trying to ignore death's irritating odor. An attendant wheeled a body into the autopsy room; a radio blared Willie Nelson singing: "Won't you ride in my little red wagon."

A bronze-skinned blond woman pushed her way through the doors. Late thirties, dressed in tailored blue slacks, white blouse, carrying a medical bag. She had a distracted look on her face as she searched for the man she was supposed to meet. Lucas waved. She smiled, waved back, and made her way through the field of gurneys into the office. "Lieutenant Lucas?"

"Yes, and this is Andreas Vassos."

"Hi. I'm Dr. Helen Rodale. I apologize for taking so long.

The ME caught me just as I was leaving to take my son to his tutor." Her eyes roamed over the still forms. "Which one is yours?"

Lucas pointed out Burke. The body hadn't been washed. The distorted face was caked with gore.

They walked out of the office. "I'll need some water," the dentist said. Lucas went over to an attendant and asked him for water. Shoving gurneys aside, Dr. Rodale made her way over to her subject. She put her medical bag down on Burke's knees, opened it, and, reaching inside, looked at Lucas and said, "You understand, Lieutenant, that your department is responsible for my fee?"

"Yes, I'm aware of that, Doctor. What is your fee?"

"Fifteen hundred."

Vassos rolled his eyes.

She removed a chamois from the bag and spread it across Burke's chest. She reached back in and took out a paper pad, two tubes that resembled toothpaste, a horseshoe-shaped instrument with a handle, a metal putty spatula, and three plastic cups.

The attendant came over with a liter of water in a plastic bottle. "Hiyadoin', Doc?" he asked, working the bottle down between the cadaver's legs.

"Fine, thank you, Igor," she said.

When the attendant had gone, Lucas whispered, "Igor?"

"Yes, isn't that a pity?" She reached back into her bag and came out with a rectangular block of hard rubber. She snapped on a pair of latex gloves and pressed open the dead man's mouth. "Say ahhhh," she muttered, inserting the bite block between the back row of teeth, propping open the mouth. She opened one of the tubes and squeezed out a two-inch strip of paste onto the pad. She did the same with the other tube. Using the spatula, she mixed the two strips together.

The detectives gathered close to watch.

She explained: "One of the compounds is a rubber-based

polyester impression material; the other is a catalyst. We stir them together until we get a homogeneous mix." She worked the spatula. The paste took on a purple hue. "That should do it," she said, picking up the horseshoe-shaped instrument. "This is an impression tray," she said, loading the concoction into the tray's reservoir.

She inserted the tray into Burke's mouth and pressed the paste up into the top row of teeth, holding it firm with the pressure of her thumbs under the bottom of the tray while her fingers fanned out over the clay-cold face. "Do either of you have children?"

"Yes," Vassos said, then quickly correcting himself, "No, I don't."

"My older one is sixteen," she said. "We pay six thousand dollars a year to keep him in a fancy private school, and I still have to run around getting him tutored for the college boards." She removed her hands from the tray. The instrument remained motionless, cemented to the upper teeth, the handle protruding from the mouth.

She mixed more paste, troweled it into one of the cups she had taken from her kit, and asked, "Who has the cigarettes?"

Vassos removed the plastic evidence bag from his briefcase and handed it to her. She removed one of the butts and held it up to the fluorescent light. Using both hands, she carefully straightened the cigarette and implanted the filter into the paste. Turning her attention back to the cadaver, she took hold of the tray's handle and wiggled it free of the teeth. She removed the cast from the reservoir and put it down on the paper pad. She poured water into the basin and cleaned out the tray. That done, she mixed more paste and repeated the procedure on the bottom row of teeth.

After she had done that, she reached into Burke's mouth and removed the bite block, wrapped it in a disinfectant-soaked cloth, put it in a plastic bag, and tossed it back into her medical bag.

She opened a jar of wax and, picking up one of the molds, began layering wax around the outside of the impression.

"Why you doing that?" Lucas asked.

"In order to raise the base of the mold," she said. "This way I'll create a dam for the dental stone."

"Stone?"

"Dental stone is similar to plaster, only faster drying," she said. "We mix it with water and pour the solution into the holes that the teeth made in the mold. When it dries we'll have a replica of Burke's teeth."

Lucas looked down at the butt sticking up out of the cup. "Same procedure for that?"

"Yes," she said.

"How long will it be before you can tell us if Burke smoked those cigarettes?" Lucas asked.

"I can tell you that now," she said. "Those impressions were not made by the dead man."

Detective Ivan Ulanov was talking into the telephone, attempting to placate the moonbeam lady, a telephone regular who was convinced her landlord was attempting to regain her rent-controlled apartment by trying to kill her with moonbeam. "Yes, Martha, I know that it's rent-controlled, but I really . . ." He rolled his eyes at the Whip.

Frank Gregory was typing the unusual occurrence report on the Burke homicide, a need-to-know report that circulated up the chain of command.

Lucas asked Gregory, "Where're Big Jay and Leone?"

The Slav pointed his cheerless face at the old record room.

Passing the bulletin board, Lucas focused on the new flyer, one of many that regularly arrive in department mail, written by one of the Job's many anonymous authors:

SIX PHASES OF A POLICE DEPARTMENT PROJECT

1. Enthusiasm	4. Search for the Guilty
2. Disillusionment	5. Punishment of the Innocent
3. Panic	6. Praise and Honors for the Nonparticipants

Someone had written "The Job Sucks" across the bottom.

Lucas and Vassos entered the old record room, a cramped place that smelled moldy and was lined with green erector-set shelves crammed with department cartons containing the files of long-forgotten cases. Homicides were tucked away on the left side of the room; the victims' names and the dates of occurrence listed on the sides in bold, black letters.

A frail alcoholic was slumped in a chair. He looked sixtyish but was probably in his forties; he had a blooming complexion and bloodshot eyes.

Vassos inched his way along the shelves.

Lucas watched Big Jay's face. The black detective remained stoical, save for a subtle lift of his right eyebrow.

"Now, Eddie," Leone said wearily, "tell us again why you left the shack."

"I hadda take a shit," the watchman said. "How many fuckin' times I gotta tell ya?"

Big Jay's mock fury unleashed itself on the nearest carton, his fist punching through the side. "You're a fucking liar. You left cause you knew a hit was going down."

The watchman turned defiant. "Prove it."

"Prove it!" Big Jay bellowed. "You miserable little scumbag, I'll prove it." He clasped the bottom of the watchman's chair and lifted it up off the floor, tossing it against the shelf. The tops of several cartons came undone; the guard sprawled onto the floor.

"Hey! None of that stuff!" Lucas shouted. "Help the man up."

"Yes, sir," Big Jay said meekly.

Leone motioned to Lucas. "This is Inspector McCann, and this is"—he pointed to Vassos—"Captain Lopez. They're from the Mendicant Squad."

"Nice to meet you, sir," Vassos said.

"A pleasure," Lucas added, turning to Vassos and saying, "Captain, go to the supply locker and get something to relax Mr. Walsh."

Vassos nodded and left the room.

"Mr. Walsh," Lucas said, "we believe that you left your shack at that particular time because you were told to."

The guard waved a protesting hand at Lucas. "Naw, dat ain't it. I told ya, I hadda take a dump."

Vassos slipped back into the room with a bottle of vodka and a stack of pleated paper cups. Lucas motioned Leone and Big Jay out of the room. Vassos handed the guard a cup and passed one to Lucas. Big Jay and Leone left, closing the door behind them.

Vassos poured the clear liquid into the guard's cup, making sure to fill it to the brim. Lucas watched the guard toss down the drink and hold up his cup for another. "Edward, that is your name?"

"I ain't been called that in years," the guard said.

"My father's name was Edward," Vassos lied.

The guard looked squint-eyed at Vassos. "Dat's a funny accent you got. You from New York?"

"Puerto Rico," Vassos said.

"You know, Edward, you're not a bad guy, but you got yourself caught up in something that could jam you up," Lucas said. "We might be forced to hold you as a material witness."

The guard held up his empty cup to the fictitious Captain Lopez. Vassos poured more vodka. Walsh gulped down the drink, pulled a sour face. "Ya know, McCann, I never had any real ambition. I just wanted to go through life with enough fuck-you money in my pockets so I didn't have to take no shit from anyone." He shrugged philosophically. "But, dat didn't work out either. I'm a drunk who everyone dumps on."

"Some people put you in a whole lot of shit, Edward," Lucas said.

"Fuckin'-A right they did," the guard said, picking at a scab on his face.

Vassos poured more vodka into the guard's sloshing cup. "Did they telephone you or tell you in person?"

"Telephoned me in the shack."

Vassos looked at Lucas. "What did they tell you?" he asked the guard.

"To take a hike between nine and ten, and to keep my trap shut."

"Do you know who telephoned you?" Lucas asked.

"Naw. Some guy. On the docks you don't ask too many questions."

Disappointment showed on the policemen's faces. Lucas swung open the door. "Big Jay, drive Mr. Walsh home."

"What do we do next?" Vassos asked, sitting in one of the swivel chairs.

"Burke took several falls with a guy named Bucky Mc-Mahon. He's the one who was arrested for the Widener robbery." Lucas ransacked the top of his desk. "I sent a request to the Probation Department to try and locate McMahon. Their answer should have arrived in the department mail. Here it is," he said, pulling a multiuse envelope out of the basket. He opened it and read the slip of paper. "Shit! Bucky McMahon died three years ago." He balled up the paper and tossed it into the wastebasket on the side of the desk.

Ulanov sauntered into the office. "We're calling it a day, Lou. Wanna pop over to Heidi's for a taste?"

"I'm not in the mood."

12 ═══════════

unlight filtered through the bedroom blinds; the air still held morning's freshness. Dressed in undershorts, with his arm around Joan's shoulder, Lucas steered her into the living room toward the door.

She kissed him. "Thank you."

"Thank you," he echoed, reaching for the doorknob, anxious to get on with his day. She reached out shyly, touched his hair which was still wet from the shower, and put her arms around him. Hugging him tight, she savored what she suspected were their last moments together. "I'll miss you."

"Me too," he said, surprised to find, even as he said it, that he felt a pang of regret.

"What do I mean to you, Teddy?"

"You're a nice woman, Joan. I like you."

"A nice woman?" Her hands slid off his shoulder. "I'm available, I make no demands, and I'm a nice woman too. You got yourself a real bargain."

"Get off it, Joan. You understood from the beginning . . ."

She smiled and tilted her head back to look into his eyes. "I know, lover. It's just that I'm a hopeless romantic. But when reality sets in, I can cope." She reached down and gently bounced his scrotum in her palm. "Don't take any wooden nickels." She threw open the door and stepped out into the empty hallway. "By the way, I don't know who you thought you were doing it to just now, but it certainly wasn't me."

"Kahleemehrah." Good morning, Vassos greeted Lucas thirty minutes later.

"Kahleemehrah," Lucas said, going into his office.

Biting into a doughnut, Leone observed, "Not in such a great mood, our boss."

The Second Whip was in the Whip's office pawing through the morning mail.

"Anything important?" Lucas asked, scanning the sixty sheet.

Grimes pulled out a thick, multiuse envelope from the pile and handed it to Lucas. "Identification Section, addressed to you."

Lucas unstrung the jacket and slid out a clump of fives. The blue forms were pinned together. He worked out the pin and tossed it into the coffee can that dressed up his desk. A gigantic lollipop stuck out of the can. It read: "Winning isn't everything, but losing sucks." The fingerprint technician had prepared a five on each known member of the Purple Gang, summing up the results of the comparison of their fingerprints with those of the latents that had been lifted at the scene of the Iskur homicide.

Each report ended with NR, negative results. The technician had tacked on a personal note: "Lou, none of them came close. Sorry."

Lucas opened the bottom drawer of his desk and shoved the fives into the case folder. He glanced over at the composite sketch tacked onto the blackboard. Looking at Grimes, he asked, "Anything else?"

"A few things," Grimes said, pulling a stack of folders out from under the basket. "I've heard from the army on Denny McKay. He was a printer, worked in an intelligence unit that operated out of Japan during the Korean War."

"What were you able to find out about his unit?"

"I made a few phone calls. Seems he worked in a 'disinformation unit.' They used to print phony enemy orders, pay records, transfers, that sort of stuff. McKay remained there for the duration."

"Was he a printer before he joined the army?"

"He didn't join. He was drafted. It seems that he graduated from George Westinghouse Vocational High School where he learned printing." He passed the folder to the Whip.

"What else?"

"I've prepared our Quarterly Case Management Study," Grimes said, passing another folder to the Whip.

Lucas took out the report, a review of all active cases designed to insure increased supervisory direction and control of investigations. Glancing through the several pages, he thought: more fodder for the Palace Guard, that bureaucracy of self-preservation that had raised busywork to a managerial art form. "I'll sign this. What else?"

"That's it," Grimes said, leaving the office.

Lucas spun around in his chair and checked the list of important telephone numbers taped to the wall. He picked up the telephone and dialed the Legal Bureau. A civilian attorney answered. Lucas told him about the dental impressions and the result of the saliva test. The person who had smoked the cigarettes had A-positive blood.

"And you want to secure a search warrant that will enable you to forcibly take the suspect's dental impressions—and draw blood," the lawyer said.

Here we go again, Lucas thought, picking up on the attorney's bored and patronizing tone. "Correct."

"I'm sure that you're aware, Lieutenant, that allegations of fact supporting a search warrant may be based upon an officer's personal knowledge, or upon information and belief, provided that the source of the information and the grounds for the belief are stated."

"I know that, Counselor. I'm acting on information and

belief, an informer, one John Doe, a person whom I've used in the past, someone who has always proved reliable."

"Is this informer of yours registered with the department?"

"Come on, Counselor, you know as well as I do that most informers refuse to go into the register."

"Sure I know. But the courts are not interested in what you and I know. PD regulations require informers to be registered with the department. Now, if you try and play games with the court, you could end up having a mighty big problem."

"One of my detectives observed the suspect chewing on the same brand of cigarette as was found at the crime scene. And I know from the suspect's army record that he has the same blood type."

"Not enough, Lieutenant. You need something that tends to connect him to the scene."

"Thanks," Lucas said, slamming down the phone.

Vassos was in the doorway, watching him. Lucas told him what the department lawyer had said.

"You have strange rules, Teddy. In Greece we would drag McKay in and he would do what we told him to."

"Regrettably, we have different rules."

"Is there no way to get around these rules of yours?"

"There are several things we could do. But if we got caught doing them, there'd be a good chance that the case against McKay would go bye-bye. We'll wait. Good cops need a lot of patience. McKay is going to trip over his prick one day, and I'm going to be there when he does to make sure that he takes the fall."

Ulanov poked his head into the office. "Our friend from across the street just called. He wants to meet the both of us, now. Says he's got something for you."

Leaving the squad room with Vassos and Ulanov, Lucas asked Leone if they had come up with anything on the Burke homicide.

"Nothing," Leone said. "We traced Burke's movements back twenty-four hours before the hit but came up dry. His girlfriend, a debutante from Hoboken, told us that he had an appointment around nine, but she didn't know with whom. Claims he never talked business with her."

"Anyone on the pier see anything?" Lucas asked.

"Not even the seagulls," Big Jay replied.

"Let it slide then. Work on it when you have time," Lucas said, opening the gate.

Ulanov parked the unmarked police car on the west side of Park Avenue, in front of the Banco di Sicilia. Hands gripping the steering wheel, he people watched. Lucas, in the passenger seat, studied the golden statuary of Jupiter and Juno that adorned the golden clock of the Helmsley Building. Vassos sat in the rear of the car watching a bag lady scavenging for food in a refuse container.

The radio trumpeted police calls: 10:67, traffic condition, Madison and Five-six; 10:59, alarm of fire, Third and Four-seven.

"You're sure that he said he wanted to see both of us?" Lucas asked Ulanov.

"That's what the comrade said," Ulanov said, watching a long-legged woman with a very short skirt cross the avenue.

Leaning forward and draping his arms over the back of the front seat, Vassos asked Lucas, "Do you know this person well?"

"Colonel Sergei Nashin is the KGB's liaison with the NYPD," Lucas said. "Usually he only wants to meet with Ulanov. But I've met with him on several occasions. He's not a bad guy."

"There he is," Ulanov announced, "on the other side of the street, walking south."

"Wait in the car," Lucas told Vassos.

Nashin waited on the corner of Forty-sixth and Park until the two detectives had reached him and then crossed the street southward with the two policemen.

Nashin nodded to Ulanov. "Comrade."

"Colonel," Ulanov responded.

They strolled through Helmsley Walk East, an arcade that tunneled through the ground floor of the Helmsley Building. They exited onto Forty-fifth, crossed the street, and stood under the vaulted entrance to the Pan Am Building.

"I love this town," Nashin said in flawless English.

"Me too," Lucas said, admiring the KGB man's pressed, blue seersucker suit and open-collared blue shirt. Nashin's youthful face belied his forty-nine years, and his thick flaxen hair gave him a Germanic aspect.

"I hear the PC is getting out," Nashin said, his cagey eyes playing the afternoon crowd. He delighted in using NYPD slang when he was with cops.

"Rumors," Lucas said. "The police commissioner is always retiring, according to the grapevine."

Nashin smiled. "It's the same in my job. The latest rumor is that the Politburo is pissed off at the director because he was screwing an Olympic gymnast thirty years younger than he."

"Hey, that don't make him a bad person," Ulanov said.

Nashin laughingly agreed. "How's your son, Ivan?"

"Getting ready to go off to college," Ulanov said. "And your daughter?"

"She just finished her first year at Moscow University," Nashin said proudly. "She thinks she's smarter than her papa and her mama." He looked at Lucas. "You should visit the Soviet Union, really. I'd set the whole thing up for you. You'd have a ball, and I'd see to it that it was, ah . . . on the arm."

"Maybe someday," Lucas said.

A panhandler approached the trio. Nashin waved him off. "They always seem to have money for booze and cigarettes."

"You said that you had something for me," Lucas said.

"Let's walk," Nashin suggested.

They backtracked through Helmsley Walk East and strolled up Park Avenue, heading north. At Fiftieth Street they climbed the steps of Saint Bartholomew's Church and slowly walked through the plaza that ran between the church and its community center. Nashin peeled away from the other two and sat on the stone coping that ran above Fiftieth Street. He placed his hands behind him and leaned back, admiring the church's stone tracery and tiled dome. "I love church architecture. Either of you ever see the fan vaulting in King's College Chapel at Cambridge?"

The detectives said no.

"You ought to go see it; it's really incredible." Taking a small, elegant leather notebook out of his pocket, Nashin said, "Iskur worked for the Allies during the war. Mostly around the Mediterranean. During the Korean War he did some intelligence work in Japan. We don't know what he did, but we do know that he spent some time there." He looked at Lucas. "Why are you interested in Iskur?"

Lucas knew better than to lie to the Soviet policeman. "We have reason to believe that he was involved in smuggling antiquities into this country."

"From where?" Nashin asked.

"Greece," Lucas said.

Nashin turned serious. "Iskur has been murdered."

"How did you know that?" Lucas asked, trying to smooth the surprised edge of his voice.

"From the collators," Nashin said. "We have people in Moscow who spend their days cutting articles out of newspapers and magazines from all over the world. They translate them and then feed them into computers. Some of our people believe that it was no coincidence that Iskur was killed the same day as the Voúla massacre."

Lucas looked cautiously at Nashin. "Why do I get the feeling, Sergei, that you have a vested interest in what happened to Iskur?"

"We are extremely interested in Iskur and his associates," Nashin said.

"Why?" Lucas asked.

"We are a big country, Teddy, with thousands of churches

and monasteries scattered through the most isolated regions. All of them are crammed with ancient art. A criminal network is looting our patrimony; we have reason to believe that Iskur was involved."

"How do you tie him into it?" Lucas asked.

"Last year our border guards stopped a truck trying to enter Turkey at Yerevan. According to the papers that the driver and his helper tried to pass, they were delivering potash to Yerevan. For whatever reasons, the guards became suspicious and searched the truck. Hidden inside a false gas tank they found a Cyrillic codex from the eleventh century and a tenth-century Byzantine diadem. Both had been stolen from the monastery at Orsk."

"I assume that your people had a talk with the driver and his helper," Lucas said.

"Oh, yes. They are both serving thirty-year sentences in a most disagreeable labor camp," Nashin said.

"I wish we could send some of our mutts to one of your labor camps," Lucas said wistfully.

"Thank you, but we have enough mutts of our own," Nashin said. "The comrades told our interrogators that they had been paid by a man in Orsk, who sent them to a dealer in Yerevan. There they were provided with forged travel documents and the necessary export papers."

"Printed documents?" Lucas asked.

"Very good quality forgeries. We believe that the counterfeits were made in the States and shipped to the Soviet Union."

"Don't you have enough of your own forgers?" Lucas asked.

"Yes, we do. But our crooks do not have the high-tech electronic copying machines that you have in the West, nor do they have access to special paper. Our experts tell us that the documents came from the West, probably the States."

"What happened to the dealer in Yerevan?" Lucas asked.

"Some of our people paid him a visit. Some money changed hands and he confided that the eventual destination of the stolen art was Athens."

Lucas looked at Nashin. "Orhan Iskur?"

"You got it, kiddo," Nashin said.

"A network of art thieves with Iskur running the operational end," Lucas said.

"That is what we believe," Nashin said. "Turkey, Italy, and Spain have a similar problem."

"What happened to the man who hired the driver and his helper?" Lucas asked.

"He disappeared before we could arrest him. We'll catch him, eventually." Nashin watched several people climb the church steps. "I've been authorized to offer you whatever help you might need."

"Thanks. I'll stay in touch, Sergei," Lucas said, making a move to leave.

"There is something else," Nashin said. "Eight years ago a Greek Scylites manuscript depicting Oleg's campaign against Constantinople was stolen from Saint Andrew's Church outside of Kiev." He looked at Ulanov. "Your hometown."

Ulanov screwed up his face. "A long time ago, Sergei Sergeyevich."

Nashin smiled. "The manuscript resurfaced last year in Rome. A respectable dealer was offering it for sale. We ransomed back what had been stolen from us."

"Why didn't you go into court and sue to get it back?" Lucas asked.

"It was a political decision. The *nomenklatura* who decide such matters felt that it would not do for my government to go into a court in Rome and have to admit that we were unable to protect our national treasures. It would have shown, I believe the word was 'vulnerability.' " He sucked in a deep breath. "We were bamboozled. The manuscript was a forgery."

"They steal the original, make copies, and peddle them around the world," Lucas said.

Nashin continued wearily. "Our agents went back to the dealer and told him that it was a fake. He returned our money along with his apologies."

"Do you think he was in on the scam?" Lucas asked.

Nashin said carefully, "There is no way of knowing for sure. He claims that he, too, was taken in. Would you care to guess from whom he acquired the manuscript?"

"Iskur," Lucas said firmly.

Nashin nodded. "Let's stay in touch?"

"Absolutely," Lucas said.

The policemen walked away from the plaza. Two fashionably dressed women passed as they were descending the steps. "Good afternoon, ladies," Nashin said, smiling at them.

"Gentlemen," the taller of the two women responded good-naturedly.

"I have to get back to the office," Nashin said, shaking Lucas's hand; then, with a mischievous grin on his face: "Say good-bye to Major Vassos for me."

Adele Matrazzo's body had become a swollen black mass. Larvae squirmed over her lifeless eyes; insect eggs lined the corners of her mouth and nostrils.

Lucas, Vassos, and Ivan Ulanov stood amid the bizarre activity that homicide engenders. The stench of decaying flesh infested the house. Every ground-floor window had been thrown open; plates sprinkled with disinfectant crystals were scattered about. The big-screen television was still on, the sound turned down.

Seven-two Squad detectives gathered around the body; another day, another case. The heavy noon heat didn't make it any easier. Lucas suggested closing the windows and turning on the big window air conditioner full blast.

"What the fuck is it?" asked one detective.

"Looks like a long piece of wire," observed another.

A third announced: "It's a string from a stringed instrument. Most likely from a violin."

"No shit?" said the first. "It sure cut the hell out of her neck."

Sandy White, the Seven-two Whip, a lean veteran with a

craggy face, spotted Lucas and the others and came over to them.

"A friend of yours, Teddy?" White asked, pointing to the body on the floor.

"I interviewed her regarding a nothing case my squad is carrying," Lucas lied. "I left my card with her."

"I found it; that's why I called you," White said. "Why don't we get some fresh air?"

They abandoned the crime scene for the sunlit world of the living. Once outside, Lucas introduced the Seven-two lieutenant to Vassos and Ulanov.

"Greek, hmmm?" White said, eyeing the major.

"Yes. I am here on an exchange program," Vassos said.

"Exchange program?" White echoed disbelievingly. He turned to Lucas. "Why you interested in my murder victim?"

"We're looking for a cousin of hers in connection with a larceny," Lucas said.

"What's the hump's name?" White asked.

"Paolo Matrazzo," Lucas said.

White asked, "Is he connected?"

"An independent," Lucas said. "No tie-in with the wise-guys."

White silently ran the name through his memory, then said, "Paolo Matrazzo? Never heard of him."

Lucas asked White what his detectives had come up with on the initial canvass. White told him that the victim had been strangled, and that there was no sign of a forced entry into the house. "We figure she's dead maybe twenty-four hours, no more than forty-eight. It's hard to tell in this heat, they melt fast. We interviewed the people living in the immediate vicinity. The neighbors did her shopping, but none of them knew shit about her. A Mrs. O'Rourke"—he pointed to the green house across the street—"she and the victim used to have tea together a few times a week. She's the one who discovered the body. She don't know anything about her either."

Lucas glanced at the O'Rourke house in time to see someone duck behind the curtains.

". . . a retired schoolteacher with no known relatives. I've sent one of my men to the Board of Ed to have a look at her records," White said.

"No one saw anyone enter or leave the house?" Lucas asked, glancing across the street in time to catch a glimpse of someone ducking back from the same window.

"No one saw nothing," White said.

Lucas turned his head slightly so that his peripheral vision could take in the O'Rourke house. He could see a woman peeking out, watching them.

"Ya'know, Teddy, if you want this case, I'll be more than happy to bang out a five and transfer it to your squad," White said. "My intuition tells me it ain't going nowhere."

"Thanks, pal. But I'm carrying enough open homicides. I don't need another one to drag down my clearances." Lucas dropped his voice. "Any objections if I have a talk with the O'Rourke woman?"

"Be my guest," White said.

"Wait here," Lucas told Vassos and Ulanov.

"Mrs. O'Rourke?" Lucas asked when she opened the door. He produced his shield and I.D. card.

She was a short woman with gray hair pulled back and held in place with a rubber band. Her face was alive with barely suppressed excitement. She wore a peach-colored housecoat, white anklets, and sandals. She studied Lucas's photo identification card, comparing it with the smiling face in front of her. "I told the other policeman everything that I know."

"A moment of your time, please?"

"Well, I guess it'll be all right. After all, Adele was a dear friend. God rest her soul." She stepped aside to admit him into her house.

He walked into a cheerless room filled with overstuffed furniture swaddled in plastic. He lowered himself down into a yellow armchair. "It's a lovely neighborhood," he began.

"It used to be a grand neighborhood," she complained, "but it's changing, for the worse, if you know what I mean?"

"I think I do," he said, and for the next several minutes smilingly endured her rambling monologue before he felt she had relaxed enough for him to ask, "Have you lived here a long time, Mrs. O'Rourke?"

"Himself and I raised six children in this house. My husband passed on twelve years ago, God rest his soul."

"I guess you must know everyone on the block."

"Yes, I do," she said proudly. "Mrs. Cohen—she lives three doors down—moved in three years ago." Leaning forward, lowering her voice to a conspiratorial whisper, she added, "She keeps kosher, if you know what I mean?"

"Yes, I do."

"Once a week," she continued in her conniving tone, "a man who has those funny strings that religious Jewish men wear around their waists visits Mrs. Cohen."

"Those fringes are called *tsitsis.*"

"Well, I can tell you, I wouldn't be a bit surprised if he played with Mrs. Cohen's *tsitsis*, if you know what I mean?"

"I think I do, yes." Leaning forward in his seat, he went on: "I understand that you and Adele had tea together a few times a week."

"Yes, but we never discussed anything about her private life. I'm not one to pry, you know."

"What did you two talk about?"

"Mostly she listened to my problems. Adele was a very good listener. One of my daughters-in-law doesn't believe in cooking, working, or cleaning. Humph! The modern woman. I tell you, my Johnny is forever buying that no-account wife of his presents. No one ever buys me presents. And I'll tell you something else, Adele agreed with me. No one ever bought her presents either, except that one at Christmas. And I'll tell you something else, too—"

"What one at Christmas?" he asked, on the edge of his seat.

"The television. The one with the big screen in the parlor. Adele told me that it was a gift from her wonderful cousin."

"What cousin?"

"I don't know. She just said in passing it was a gift from her cousin. And then she added 'my wonderful cousin.' "

"Did she ever mention any other member of her family?"

She thought; shook her head no.

"Did you ever see anyone visit her?"

"I play bingo and go to exercise classes most days at the senior citizen center, so I'm usually not home."

Lucas retreated into his own thoughts. Adele Matrazzo had told him that she had had two cousins: Anthony, who had been killed on Guadalcanal, and Paolo Jr., who had taught art history at NYU and had died in 1968, leaving behind a wife and two children. He hadn't checked out any of that information. It hadn't seemed relevant at the time. He got up from his seat and thanked Mrs. O'Rourke.

Walking out of the house into the bright sunlight, he saw the morgue attendants carrying Adele Matrazzo's body to the meat wagon. Her shroud was a dark green body bag, compliments of the City of New York.

Waiting the following morning in front of the stone mansion on the northeast corner of Fifth Avenue and Seventy-eighth Street, Teddy Lucas watched the passing parade. First came a file of roped-together nursery-school children who were shepherded by several teenage girls. Next came a dog walker struggling with ten leashed canines.

He checked the time and saw that he was twelve minutes too early for his nine-thirty appointment with Katina. He had telephoned her late yesterday afternoon after he returned to the Squad from the Matrazzo crime scene. "Is there some way that we can check on Paolo Matrazzo Junior's academic credentials to see if he really existed?" he had asked her. She had said yes and they arranged to meet the next day.

Lucas had shaven carefully this morning. He wore a paisley tie with a white button-down shirt, a brown sports jacket, and his beige slacks. He wanted to look his best for her. The imaginary insects in his stomach began to buzz when he saw her hurrying along Seventy-eighth Street. He quickly admired her pale yellow dress and black leather pumps. Her large yellow earrings and the way her hair was pulled back in an arrangement that accentuated her beautiful, high-cheek-boned face. He wanted to rush up to her and tell her how wonderful she looked, but instead he just jerked his thumb at the stately building and said, "Some shack."

"The Duke Mansion," she explained, looking at the facade. "The family left it to New York University's Institute of Fine Arts. If Matrazzo Junior received his Ph.D. from NYU, his doctoral dissertation will be on file here."

They climbed the steps and entered the vestibule. She signed for both of them in the visitors' log at the security desk.

He looked around at the enormous marble reception hall just beyond the vestibule and felt like a tourist. An elaborate curving marble staircase with a gilt-and-black wrought-iron bannister dominated the hall.

"Shall we walk up, or ride?" she asked.

"Walk. I want to see as much of this place as I can."

A quarter of the way up he stopped to admire a wall relief of putty, cupidlike children without wings. Climbing farther, he paused to look at a tapestry hanging on the stairwell's wall. When they reached the second-floor landing, he leaned over the railing to get a better look at it.

The library was at the end of a long hallway. They moved inside and went over to the blue-labeled card catalogue. "Do you have any idea when he was supposed to have written his dissertation?" she asked quietly.

"No."

"They're filed by year and then alphabetically, by author."

"Adele told us that his brother Anthony was killed in the war. So why don't we assume that the brothers were about the same age and begin with 1935."

She slid out a drawer and flicked index cards to the year.

Some minutes later she had worked her way through to 1943. "He's not here."

"Adele might have lied to us."

"I did not have that feeling when she was talking to us," Katina said. "I thought that she was proud of Junior's accomplishments."

Lucas mulled over the problem. Researchers moved about the racks of books; others worked silently at long tables.

"Paolo Junior might have gone back to school on the GI bill after the war," he said.

"Makes sense," she said, flipping index cards up to the year 1949, her fingers dancing over the tops to the Ms. "Teddy, look."

The call numbers were typed on top of the card and were followed on the next line by the title of the dissertation: "In Defense of Alexander's *Iliad.*" By Paolo Matrazzo, Jr.

Five minutes later they were alone inside a small reading room, sitting at a square table. Above them three stacked circular catwalks lined with books led upward to a skylight of opaque gray glass. A faded lavender binder lay on the table between them. He opened the cover. Brown age marks stained the edges of the pages. She inched her chair closer to his; they read together while she turned the pages. She went on to tell him how some scholars considered the casket-copy to be apocryphal, a fable made up to add to the legend of Alexander.

Matrazzo's thesis defended the existence of the casket-copy. Katina gave Lucas a detailed explanation of original and secondary sources and told him how Matrazzo had cited Callisthenes, Aristotle's nephew and Alexander's official historian in Asia, as the primary source for the world's knowledge of the existence of the casket-copy.

Lucas looked up. A woman was on the lowest catwalk, consulting her call slip as her finger slid over the spines of books. Very quietly he asked, "Could the casket-copy be forged?"

"On papyrus scrolls?"

"Yes."

"I would think that very unlikely. The aging of the papyrus. The ink. And the scrolls? A fake would never be able to withstand scientific scrutiny."

"Suppose a buyer accepted it as genuine without having its authenticity verified?"

She shrugged in disbelief. "I cannot believe anyone would be that stupid."

"Greed makes the smartest people foolish, Dr. Wright. It's the con man's staunchest ally." He shifted in his chair to face her. One of his knees got between hers accidentally. "There are many people in this world who are heavy with money but also short on brains."

"That's true," she agreed with a warm smile.

"Let me give you a scenario. An art dealer with an impeccable reputation, and a captivating foreign accent, offers a one-of-a-kind antiquity, one that has, regrettably, been stolen from another country. So it lacks the necessary export papers; thus the prospective buyer can't have provenance checked."

"And this wealthy buyer thought he, or she, was getting a bargain."

"You got it," he said, aware of the tiny ringlets of fine hair around her ears. "How does the art world stay informed about stolen objects?"

"Trade publications, insurance bulletins, word of mouth. And then there are the flyers from the FBI and Interpol."

Lucas looked up at the skylight and did not speak for a minute or so, his expression serious and thoughtful. "I wonder."

"What?"

"I get the feeling that there is someone out there laughing at me. And I'm also wondering if . . ."

"If what?"

"Nothing, it's too farfetched. Can we meet later today?"

"It will take me most of the day to research his writings.

Why don't you and Andreas come to my apartment tonight around seven. I'll make us a light dinner and we can go over whatever I come up with on Dr. Matrazzo."

"Sounds good to me." Lucas watched her gathering up her notes. As they were leaving she asked, "Where is Andreas?"

"He had an urgent call from his embassy."

A gray cloud of pigeons landed around the fountain in Lincoln Center. Across the street in Ficco's, Elisabeth Syros sipped espresso while she sat in the front row. Her cowboy shirt had leather fringes running down the sleeve; her brown-and-white boots not only gave her an extra two inches in height, but also complemented her western-style jeans. Her wrists and fingers were gleaming with silver Navajo jewelry.

Sipping the strong coffee, her hungry eyes followed a long-legged beauty passing the restaurant. Caught up in a sudden erotic reverie, she licked her lips and unconsciously put her hand between her legs where a wonderful warmth began to spread out. Aroused, her nipples showed their points even through the thick denim of her shirt. Like her ancient ancestors, Elisabeth Syros loved both men and women, but she preferred the latter.

One hand gripping the railing, Vassos edged his way into the aisle and squeezed into the empty chair at her tiny table. Beckoning to the waiter on the other side of the railing, he ordered espresso. She slid a folded slip of paper over to him. "This arrived in the pouch. It's from Pappas. Iskur's telephone calls," she said in Greek.

Vassos unfolded the paper and studied the list of calls. They were printed out alphabetically by country, followed by the cities within the country, followed by the numbers called within each city. The listings covered calls made to England, Greece, Italy, Turkey, the Soviet Union, and the United States. The majority of the calls to the United States were to a 212 number in Manhattan. "Do we know whose telephone numbers these are?"

Elisabeth passed another slip of paper over to him. The waiter came and, stretching his arm over the railing, handed Vassos his espresso. When the waiter had gone, Vassos removed the hand that was covering the slip of paper, picked it up, and studied what was written on it. Each telephone number had the subscriber listed below the digits. The frequently called 212 number belonged to a Brandt Industries. It had the same address as The Den, Denny McKay's Ninth Avenue headquarters. He folded both slips and put them in his shirt pocket. "Anything else?"

They continued to speak in Greek.

"Pappas has located the man who did Iskur's legwork," she confided. "His name is Yiannis Yiotas. He's in custody and has admitted making the arrangements, but he denies knowing what Iskur was planning."

Vassos ran a finger over one of her rings, a silver band with a turquoise stone. "Iskur took his orders from someone in the States."

"Pappas has come up with a name."

His face grew stern. "Who?"

"According to Interpol, seventeen years ago in London Yiotas and Iskur tried to sell a fake antique to a tourist who turned out to have been a dealer. He had both of them arrested. Then, without any explanation, the American refused to go forward with the court case and the charges were dropped."

"The dealer's name?" he demanded.

"Belmont E. Widener."

Chief of Detectives Tim Edgeworth was standing by the window of his office contemplating the panoramic view of the Manhattan skyline when Lucas entered. He waved the lieutenant into a chair. "Any progress on the Greek caper?"

"Several things are beginning to take shape," Lucas said, sitting in one of the three chairs arranged in front of the desk. "I want to take four of my men off the chart to work with

Major Vassos and me. That's going to mean telling them the nature of the investigation."

Edgeworth turned away from the window. He looked tired and drawn. He moved over to his desk and sat down behind it. Picking up his pipe, he lit it with slow deliberation. A swirl of white smoke partly concealed his expression. "Do you have any disciplinary problems in your squad, Teddy?"

"All my men are solid, Chief."

"Well, I hope so. But if you do have any problems, get rid of them. If you don't, you'll take the fall with them. Did you hear what happened in the Five-three?"

"No."

"Two detectives are doing a night duty. They lock up a burglar and process him for central booking. But they have a problem. There's a precinct stag party in a local VFW hall that the two supersleuths want to attend. And they know that if they go to central booking with their prisoner, they'll be stuck there for at least three hours and will miss most of the festivities. So what do you think the two birdbrains do?"

Lucas swallowed a smile, forced himself to wear a grim expression. "They brought the burglar to the party."

"That's right! And it gets better," Edgeworth said, stabbing his pipe at the lieutenant's face. "They had *entertainment* at this soiree. The two birdbrains belted down a few balls and decided that they were going to be nice guys. So they chipped in and got their prisoner a blow job." He was banging his pipe on the desk; a few embers spilled out of the bowl onto the blotter. "We used to beat the shit out of prisoners. Now we're getting them blow jobs." He leaped up out of his seat and pointed his finger at Teddy. "That's the result of all that goddamn human interaction bullshit they teach at the Academy." He threw his pipe into the glass ashtray.

Lucas grabbed a folder from the desk and discreetly smothered the embers.

"Goddamn those men," Edgeworth shouted, slumping back down into his chair. "At the arraignment the next morning the legal aid lawyer asked the burglar how the cops treated him. 'Great,' the burglar said, and then blabbed about the party."

"What's going to happen?"

"Both detectives are being flopped back into the bag, along with the Whip, who wasn't even at the party. With authority—"

"—goes commensurate responsibility," Lucas chimed in.

Edgeworth pushed his chair back, bent down, and blew stray ashes off his blotter. "How many men did you say?"

"Four—Leone, Big Jay, Ulanov, and Gregory."

"Your squad working two-handed?"

"Generally, yes. Occasionally I'll have a three-man team covering a duty."

"Are these four guys partners or are you splitting teams?"

"Partners."

"How long do you think they'll be off the chart?"

"A month, maybe longer."

Edgeworth opened the top drawer of his desk and slid out the Force Figure Folder, a projected thirty-day analysis of the manpower pool available within the Detective Division. He studied the tear sheets. "With vacations and military leaves we're always short bodies in the summer. Let me see now, I'll fly in one detective from the Staten Island Robbery Squad and another from Queens Robbery." He flipped pages. "I don't want to pull any men away from the busy squads, but I don't want to send you any duds. Okay. Here are the other two, both of them from Manhattan North's Crimes Against Senior Citizens Squad."

"Thanks, Chief. I'll assign them to work with detectives from my squad until they familiarize themselves with the precinct."

"Can those guys of yours keep their traps shut?"

"I wouldn't have selected them if they couldn't."

"I hope so. We don't want the press getting wind of this investigation. Those bastards would turn it into a circus."

"I understand."

A veiled expression came over the C of D's face. "I have something that might interest you." He lifted up the desk blotter and slid out a report. He handed it to the lieutenant. It read:

From: Commanding Officer, Central Park Detective Squad

To: Police Commissioner

Subject: HOMICIDE OF U.S. DIPLOMAT WITHIN THE CON-FINES OF THIS COMMAND.

1.   On July 15, 1987 at approximately 2300 hours on the east side of Central Park West, thirty feet from the northeast corner of West Sixty-fourth Street, a white male, identified as Trevor Hughes, the political officer of the U.S. embassy in Athens, Greece, was the subject of a homicide under the following circumstances . . .

Lucas looked up at the C of D with a frown of puzzlement and then read the rest of the report. When he finished, he put the report back on the desk. "Any leads?"

"The detective who caught the case thinks it was a hit that someone tried to make look like a mugging."

"What makes him think that?"

"The perp employed a mugger's MO of cutting out the pockets. But only pack muggers do that. Two mutts will grab the victim and a third mutt will cut out the pockets. Hughes was shot. A mutt with a gun don't cut out pockets. He just shoves his piece into his victim's face and tells him to fork over his possessions."

"What have they turned up on Hughes?"

"He took a vacation and flew to New York. Checked into the Plaza. That's it."

"Was he married?"

"He left his wife in Greece."

"Any girlfriends?"

"None that they were able to come up with."

"Boyfriends?"

Edgeworth shrugged.

"Any alarm bells go off in the State Department when they were notified one of their people had been murdered?"

"Not a tinkle."

"Strange. A diplomat gets whacked and nobody in D.C. raises an eyebrow."

Packing tobacco into his pipe, Edgeworth said, "You'd expect a political officer to be a savvy guy who'd know better than to go strolling around Central Park at night. Unless he was looking to get bungholed, or unless he had an appointment." Putting the stem into his mouth, he added, "We think like cops, don't we?"

"That's what we're paid to do, isn't it?"

"Yeah, that's what we're paid to do." Edgeworth looked down at his desk and said in a low voice, "I'm gonna give you a little bit of unofficial guidance, Teddy. For your ears only— not a word to anyone else, especially Vassos."

The C of D got up and walked over to the window. "I can tell you now that we will be getting somebody to 'liaise' with us." Edgeworth spat out the phrase like he was getting rid of something foul tasting on his tongue. "You don't need to know anything more than that for the moment. Whatever shithead shows up, I don't care if his credentials have been signed by God Almighty, you give him nothin'. Don't trust him. Give him a hand job, blow smoke up his ass, and report back to me on everything he says, everything he does."

Lucas stared at the broad back of the C of D. "You make it sound like he isn't exactly on our side."

Edgeworth whirled around. "You said it, Teddy. We got to find out damn fast just *what* side he's on. So from now on, anybody who comes at you from Washington should be handled like a fucking cobra—because that's what they're sending us."

Forty-seven minutes later Teddy Lucas gathered his detectives inside his office. Leone, Big Jay, Ulanov, Gregory. The Second Whip stood in the doorway, his shoulder leaning against the jamb, a can of diet soda in his hand.

The rim of the blackboard was covered by crime scene photographs: Iskur, Burke, Matrazzo, Trevor Hughes; homicides linked to an ancient book. Lucas untacked one of the Voúla crime scene pictures. Sitting on the edge of his desk, he held the grim photograph up and said, "This is the kind of a case you dream of. It surfaced last year in Voúla, Greece. But it really began after the battle of Issus in 333 B.C. . . ."

The men listened as Lucas unfolded the complexities of the case. When he had completed the briefing he asked if there were any questions. At first no one spoke. Each detective seemed to be absorbed in his own thoughts. Finally, Big Jay said, "Why was Major Vassos assigned to the case?"

Lucas held up the photograph of the Voúla crime scene. "The woman and child in the spacecraft were Major Vassos's wife and son."

Lucas watched the faces of his men; he could see they were thinking of their own wives and children. "It's no secret in the Job that Cormick McGovern and I were close. It's also no secret that Denny McKay ordered the hit on Cormick. As I just got through explaining, McKay and his people are involved in Voúla. That means we got another turn in the batter's box." His angry eyes rested on each detective in turn. "I don't intend to strike out again." He removed the case folder from the bottom drawer and slapped it down on the desk. "Familiarize yourselves with the fives."

The detectives got up and gathered around the desk.

"I've got news from Greece," Vassos said, rushing into the office, shrinking back when he saw the detectives collected around the case folder.

"It's okay, Andreas," Lucas said. "From now on, they're going to be working with us."

"That is good," Vassos said, and went on to tell Lucas about his meeting with Elisabeth Syros. He gave the Whip the list of telephone calls. Lucas read the list. He moved to his desk and copied down several numbers and their subscribers. He passed the new list to Ulanov. "See that Nashin gets this."

Ulanov looked over the list of Soviet telephone numbers. "I'll see to it."

Vassos sat in the chair next to Lucas's desk and announced, "I want to bring in Belmont Widener for questioning." A flush of anger darkened his complexion.

Lucas tensed. "Why?"

Vassos related what his control had told him about Widener. "I never believed his story about how the Aristarchus commentary was stolen."

"Pappas got his information about Widener from Interpol?" Lucas asked Vassos.

"Yes. And despite my experience with Interpol, I would consider the information reliable for once. We should bring Widener in here right away and force him to tell us what his connection is with Iskur and Yiotas."

"Now is not the time," Lucas said gently, hoping to defuse Vassos's anger.

"Not the time. Why not! Iskur made telephone calls to Brandt Industries, McKay's headquarters. We now have a direct link between them. I cannot believe that you do not want to question Widener."

Becoming aware of the stares of the detectives, Lucas turned to them and said, "Will you men excuse us? The major and I have something to discuss."

They left the room; Grimes closed the door behind him.

Vassos was standing by the blackboard, clenching his fist.

"Andreas, I want to talk to Widener as badly as you do. But he's not the one behind this. He doesn't have the balls, and McKay doesn't have the brains."

Vassos's face rankled with discontent. "So we wait. Question more people while you build your endless chain of evidence."

"It's the smart move, Andreas."

"If it had been your family, would you say it was the smart move? I think not. You'd drag Widener in here and break his kneecaps if you had to." Driven by frustration, Vassos whirled and ripped a photograph of Voúla from the blackboard. "Look! That's my family. And you say to be patient?"

"Andreas, you told me that getting the people responsible and returning the casket-copy to Greece were the reasons you came to the States. If we rush out and scoop up Widener we'll blow the case. It's a different ball game over here, with different rules."

"You're a Greek who is ashamed to be a Greek. You could never understand how I feel."

His words stung. "I'm a cop, just like you are. So don't feed me that bullshit about not feeling Greek. We belong to the same fellowship, don't you forget that, my Greek friend."

Vassos looked at Lucas with cold resolve. He spoke in Greek. "If your way does not work, then we will do it my way?"

"Nai."

13 ═══════════

Didn't Andreas come with you?" Katina asked Lucas as he stepped into her eleventh-floor apartment which overlooked Gracie Square.

"He was unable to come and asked me to give you his regrets," he said, walking through the small marble foyer.

They moved into a tastefully decorated living room filled with American and English antiques and adorned with two large Victorian-era sofas. Teddy thought about the contrast it made with the Salvation Army decor of his own apartment.

Katina was dressed in white Bermuda shorts, a cotton tank top, and white espadrilles. "May I offer you something to drink?"

"No thank you," he said, noticing the sliding glass doors leading out onto the terrace. Moving over to them, he said, "Great view." He stepped out and looked down at the promenade and the East River.

"I was lucky," she said, coming out and standing close to him. "I moved in here six years ago when it was a rental. The building went co-op four years later, and I was able to buy it at the insiders' price. I could never afford to buy it today."

The darkened silhouette of the Queensboro Bridge loomed off in the distance; across the river in Long Island City, the

Pepsi Cola billboard cast a crimson glow over the lightly wind-ruffled water.

He felt her presence beside him and turned. He caught her looking at him. He had the urge to reach out and touch her, to bring her into his arms, kiss her wet lips. But instead he led the way back inside to the cluttered coffee table that stood between the two sofas. Long yellow legal pads and pencils were lying on photocopies of articles from academic journals. "I see you've been working."

"Yes, yes, I have," she said, summoned back from her own private thoughts. "I've made copies of some of Dr. Matrazzo's academic writings. I also telephoned NYU, where Adele told us he had taught. An old classmate of mine is chairwoman of the fine arts department. She looked up Matrazzo's employment record for me. It turns out that he only taught there for one semester. He left and that was the last they ever heard of him. On his employment application, he listed his marital status as single and Adele as the person to be notified in case of an emergency."

"She told us that he was married with two children."

"She sure did."

Bending forward, Katina began to gather up papers. As she did her breasts pushed against her tank top. Desire flowed through Lucas's body, causing him to want to reach out and caress her.

When she had gathered up the copies and put them on her lap, she leaned back and said, "Dr. Matrazzo was an intelligent man with varied academic interests. Most academics confine their inquiries to a narrow field of research. Matrazzo's writings show a much broader range—Greek history and literature, a keen interest in the technical aspects of the restoration of ancient materials." She broke off and smiled apologetically at him. "I'm sorry, Teddy, you must be hungry. I've prepared a salad and I've got a bottle of wine cooling in the refrigerator. Would you like to eat now or wait until we're done working?"

"I'd just as soon wait."

"Me too," she said quickly, a glow lighting up her face. "Back to work." She pulled out another article. "This is one he wrote on paleography, which is the study of writings on papyrus, wax, parchment, and paper. And this one is on the use of X-ray crystallography and ultraviolet spectrometry in the detection of spurious materials."

Lucas leaned forward, studying the glass top of the coffee table. "Do you think that he'd have the ability to unroll ancient scrolls?"

"I would certainly think so."

"In your opinion, would he possess the technical knowledge to forge antiquities?"

"Yes, I believe he would."

Lucas pushed himself up off the sofa and moved over to the sliding doors. "I'm just wondering what the odds are that Matrazzo is alive and well—and involved in this case."

Her hands rose and fell onto her lap. "I don't know."

He turned and faced her; their eyes held steady. She broke the spell. "Shall we eat inside or out on the terrace?" she asked.

A flickering candle illuminated their faces as they sat across from each other. Reaching across the table, he poured wine into her glass, then his.

"To Big Al," he toasted.

She tilted her glass at his. "To Alexander."

He picked at his salad, wondering how to get her to talk about herself. He wanted to know all there was to know; he felt the need to know. Something was happening between them; he wasn't exactly sure what it was.

They continued to eat in silence. Finally, he said, "Andreas and I were surprised when you told us that Pericles Levi was your father."

She turned her head and cast brooding eyes across the river. "We've been estranged for several years. When he telephoned me from Athens and asked me to help you, I was, well, frankly, I was overjoyed." She looked back at him. "I saw it as an opportunity for us to reconcile. I love my father." She hurriedly picked up her wineglass and sipped, watching him over the rim. She put down the glass. "My mother was born in New York. She met my father when he was teaching at Columbia. They fell in love, married, and had me. She died when I was fifteen. I'd lived all my life in the States, except for the summers we spent in Greece. When we lost Mother, my father and I decided that there were too many memories here, so we moved to Greece." She took a deep breath. "I came back to the States when I was seventeen to attend college." She sipped her wine, gathering the will to continue. "Papa could never forgive me for marrying a twice-divorced man who was twenty-six years my senior."

"I guess many fathers would have a similar problem."

"I suppose," she said, playing with her glass. "I met Kenneth on a dig in Vergina. They were excavating the Macedonian Royal Tombs. I had just finished my doctoral dissertation and had decided to spend that summer in Greece, trying to sort out what it was that I wanted to do with the rest of my life. I had dual citizenship so I had to decide where I wanted to live and work."

"What year was that?"

"June of 'seventy-nine. I had just turned twenty-five. I'd been home for about three weeks and had visited all my relatives and friends, and I was bored to tears. My father suggested that I go on the dig. Kenneth Wright, a colleague of his from Columbia, was in charge of the excavations. Have you ever been to Vergina?"

"No I haven't," he said, noticing the glimmer in her green eyes.

She lapsed into Greek. "Vergina is located in the shadows of the Piéria Mountains. The Aliákmon River flows nearby, and at night it's very romantic. The first time I saw Kenneth he was up on a scaffold studying the frieze of the Royal Tomb.

He was gorgeous," she said, looking down at the shimmering wine. "He was wearing shorts and sandals and he had on a floppy sun hat. In the next few weeks Ken and I worked closely together cataloging the contents of the tomb. At night we'd all walk into Vergina and spend the evening in one of the tavernas. Later we'd stroll back to camp. One by one the lovers would peel away from the rest of us, making their way down to the river." She stared at the flame, remembering. "One night Kenneth took my hand and led me off toward the river. He didn't say anything. He really didn't have to." She sighed. "We got married five weeks later. It was a civil ceremony. My father refused to attend. He called my marriage to Kenneth an act of immaturity, said that it could never work. I tried reasoning with him, but he refused to speak to me. Anyway, Kenneth and I moved back to New York. And then I accepted my position at the Morgan. We moved into one of Columbia's subsidized apartments on the Upper West Side."

"You never heard from your father?"

"He wouldn't answer my letters or take any of my phone calls. I was distraught over it, but there was nothing that I could do to get him to accept the marriage."

"And then what happened?"

Again her brooding eyes looked out across the river. "The first three years were wonderful. Then? I wanted a baby. Whenever I brought up the subject, Kenneth would say he was too old for parenting and we'd end up in a fight. I did a foolish thing. I stopped taking the pill without telling him. When I became pregnant, he was furious with me. He demanded that I have an abortion. I couldn't. I just couldn't.

"Overnight I became Kenneth's enemy. He accused me of ruining his life: all of a sudden I'd become a pariah. I couldn't believe it was happening to me.

"Then, when I was in my third month and miserable, I dragged myself home from the obstetrician one Saturday and found Kenneth in the living room with one of his graduate students." She brushed tears from her face. "He was screwing her, right there in *our* living room, on *our* sofa. I ran away from the house and never returned. I went to my aunt's in Astoria. Kenneth and I were divorced shortly after that."

"And the baby?"

"I don't want to discuss that, not now." A desperate cheerfulness perked up her face. "What's your story, Lieutenant?"

A faint smile turned up the corners of his mouth. "Your everyday American love saga: married and divorced."

"Children?"

"Regrettably, no." He checked the time. "It's almost eleven. I'd better get going."

They pushed away from the table. She walked with him to the door. "Thank you for dinner, and for the conversation." He went to shake her hand good night.

She stepped into his arms and kissed his cheek. "Good night, Teddy."

14

Belmont Widener looked down Seventeenth Street for a car with the familiar triple-X sign in the windshield. He had telephoned the car service at six and told them that he wanted to be picked up at eight. It was now 8:10. The heavy beat of rock music from a nearby club irritated him. Gramercy used to be a quiet and even genteel neighborhood, he thought. Now, with Yuppie restaurants opening on every other corner and condos blooming everywhere, its charm and atmosphere had been ruined.

Looking across the street at Union Square Park, Belmont thought that at least the real estate boom had gotten rid of the junkies. He checked his wristwatch again. His dinner date was for 8:30 and he did not want to be late. He had been surprised and delighted to receive an invitation from his dear friend to have dinner at Maison Blanche.

Belmont patted his hair, checking to see that his ringlets were still all in place. He had taken extra care dressing for this dinner. He wore his white silk suit, complemented by a blue shirt with bold stripes and an oversized blue bow tie.

As he waited Belmont remembered how they had met. In retrospect, he realized that their meeting eighteen years ago had not been a chance encounter. His friend's motive had obviously been to get him to drop the criminal charges against

Iskur and that disgusting man, Yiotas. But that was all in the past now; the important thing was that they had met.

Belmont had been sitting at the bar in London's Imperial Hotel, sipping a whiskey and soda, when he glanced to his left and saw him standing nearby. Belmont was immediately taken with the man's almost excessive handsomeness—then he saw the magnificent gold ring on his hand.

The stranger became aware of Belmont's interest and, taking his drink with him, came over and stood next to him. He put down his drink and slid off his ring, placing it down on the bar in front of Belmont, and said in a pleasant, mellow voice, "Emperor Caracalla had the coin struck around 215 A.D."

Belmont, his pulse accelerating, picked up the ring.

"The scene on the reverse shows Meleager and Alexander hunting boar."

Belmont was brought rudely back to the present when an Oldsmobile sedan stopped in front of him. "You're late," he said coldly, sliding into the backseat. The car drove off toward Broadway. A rented Ford sedan with Connecticut license plates backed out of a parallel parking space on the side of Union Square Park. Leone was driving; Big Jay sat in the passenger seat; perched in the rear, with his arms crossed over the top of the front seat and his burning eyes fixed on the departing taillights, was Andreas Vassos.

15

rustration gnawed at Colonel Dimitri Pappas. His investigation of Voúla had stalled at Yiannis Yiotas. No matter what avenue he went up, he kept dead-ending at Yiotas. There must be something he had overlooked, some witness he had failed to locate, something he had neglected to do.

He left home an hour early that morning to do what he always did whenever he felt discouraged by a lack of progress in a case: wander around ancient Athens, allowing his mind to sift the facts, searching for a new beginning.

Driving his unmarked car along Amalias Street in the center of Athens, he reached the part where the street opened into a large busy triangle and saw to his right the imposing columns of the Arch of Hadrian, the monument erected in 132 A.D. to mark the boundary of the ancient city and the start of "New Athens."

He steered the car through the heavy traffic, maneuvering it toward the curb. The traffic policeman, on duty in the middle of the avenue, saw him and watched with an expression of mixed incredulity and anger. When Pappas parked in the forbidden zone, the policeman snatched the white pith helmet off his head and ran screaming over to Pappas. "Are you out of your fucking mind? Move that car. Now!"

Pappas dug into the pocket of his trousers and came out with his credentials. "I won't be long."

"Yes, sir," the traffic man said, returning the helmet to his head and retreating back to his post.

Shoulders hunched, hands plunged deep into his pockets, Pappas strolled the relic's external boundary, pausing occasionally to kick a stone. One side of the arch bore the inscription in classical Greek: THIS IS ATHENS, ANCIENT CITY OF THESEUS; the other side was inscribed: THIS IS THE CITY OF HADRIAN AND NOT OF THESEUS.

Why had the case stalled? Pappas asked himself over and over again. Iskur's calls outside the country suggested the involvement of many more people in this confederacy of thieves. Why hadn't he been able to come up with any in Greece? He believed Yiotas had told him everything that he knew about Iskur. He also believed that Iskur was too smart to have confided in a person like Yiotas. Still . . . There had to be some unpicked morsels inside Yiotas's mind, something he knew without realizing its importance.

Pappas angrily kicked the dirt in the circle around the arch. He suddenly realized that the only person connected to Iskur who he hadn't interviewed was Nina Pazza, Iskur's mistress. He hadn't bothered with her because he'd assumed that she was just another one of Iskur's objects, to be used and displayed in public. Damn! She should have been questioned. How did he know what their relationship was? Policemen did not have the luxury of assuming anything. In all the years he'd been in the department, he still hadn't been able to overcome that damn chauvinistic Greek attitude toward women. That was a serious flaw in someone in his line of work. He'd telephone her this morning and go see her. But first he thought he'd go see Yiotas and replow some old ground, Pappas decided, wondering how Yiotas was enjoying his isolation cell in the basement of police headquarters.

■　　　■　　　■

Two hours later, after leaving an exhausted and frightened Yiotas in his cell, Pappas stopped at an open-front stand and ate three souvlakis and then drove to Nina Pazza's section of town.

Siesta was just ending and tourists were lining up for the funicular, which would take them to the top of Lykavitos Hill. Pappas parked his unmarked car two blocks away from the Aristodimou Street apartment and walked. It would not be smart to give a witness the opportunity to connect him to the small car that he drove.

He was anxious to meet Iskur's mistress, to see for himself if she was worth an apartment in one of Athens' more exclusive areas. She was. He had expected to see a beautiful woman in expensive clothes, but was not prepared for the sight of the Eurasian beauty who opened the door. "Nina Pazza?" he asked, unaware of the slightly stunned expression on his face.

She smiled. "Colonel Pappas, how nice to meet you."

Long black hair cascaded down her back. She had perfectly defined cheeks and almond skin; a white caftan flowed over her tall, ripe body, increasing her radiant sensuality.

He walked past her into a large room splendidly decorated in white wicker; carefully placed antique pieces—a late Roman head, a broken torso in gleaming black stone—were artfully placed around the room on small, low tables. "You were Orhan Iskur's mistress?" he asked, noticing the silk damask walls of the dining area and the Tabriz rugs.

"Yes, I was," she answered forthrightly, sitting in a wide-armed chair.

"You're an Italian citizen?" he asked, unable to stop staring at her exotic beauty.

"Yes, I am."

"Your passport, please."

An arched eyebrow, a sneering smile. "Of course." She shifted in her seat and reached into the pocket of her caftan, pulling out her official documents. "I thought that you might want to see it, so I had it ready for you. Policemen seem to enjoy examining passports. As you can see my other papers are there too, my visa and my resident card."

This one doesn't scare, he thought, checking her travel history. "Your Greek is excellent."

"I've had a lot of practice."

He managed a little smile. "I see that you don't have a work permit."

"I don't work, Colonel. Orhan was an exceedingly generous man."

"You've done a lot of traveling."

"We both enjoyed visiting other countries; Orhan did not like to travel alone."

"How long had you been with him?"

"Ten years. We met in Rome when I was sixteen."

"Didn't your parents object to you going off with a man so much older than you were?"

"They had no say in the matter, Colonel. My mother was a Japanese graduate student doing research on Castiglione when she met my father in Rome. He is an Italian philanderer and one of the most hateful men in the world. He never married my mother. She died shortly after I was born, and he consigned his mistake to a convent orphanage."

He handed her back her documents. "What can you tell me about Iskur's business dealings?"

"Nothing. I can only tell you that he was a kind, gentle man who trusted no one. Orhan confided in very few people."

"Evidently he trusted you."

"To an extent he did, yes. I guess I was the closest thing he had to a friend. But the only thing he ever told me about his business was that he made and sold souvenirs."

"What were his interests?"

"Classical art and literature. He was an extremely well-read man."

"And business associates?"

She shrugged.

"His family?"

"He had an ex-wife and three grown sons. He'd go to visit his children from time to time, but he never took me on such trips, of course."

Looking around the apartment, Pappas asked, "He lived here with you?"

"Yes, but I suspect he had another place somewhere."

"Why do you believe that?"

"Because sometimes he'd be gone for days and when he returned he would be wearing different clothes, ones I'd never seen before."

"Another woman?"

She answered with swift assurance. "I saw to it that he had nothing left for another woman."

I'm sure you did, he said to himself, then spoke aloud: "What did he tell you about his army days?"

"Sometimes when he had a little too much wine he'd reminisce about those days, his friends, and what it was like to do intelligence work, but never anything of earth-shattering importance. As I'm sure you *do* know, he was born in Turkey. His family moved here when he was a boy and settled in Macedonia, around Kavalla."

"I know. They came with the Turkish influx of the twenties."

"He served with the Greek forces in Korea. I don't know what he did during World War Two."

"Did he ever mention the names of any of the men he served with?"

"No, he didn't."

Pappas got up and wandered idly around the room. He stopped at a bust of a woman, a life-sized, elongated face with wide, seductive eyes.

"The Queen of Sheba," she said, coming over to him. "She ruled one of the five kingdoms that flourished in the thirteenth century B.C. in Arabia. It's said that she traveled to Jerusalem and gave Solomon a hundred and twenty talents of gold and spices."

Running his hand over the head, he asked, "Is it real?"

"A copy. Orhan was the king of the fakes."

Pappas moved back to his seat and took the sketch and photograph out of his briefcase. "Do you know this man?"

"No. Who is he?"

"Someone who took a taxi from the airport to Iskur's office the day he was murdered."

She restudied both. "I don't know him. I'm sure."

He reached back into the briefcase, took out the photograph that had arrived last night from New York, and showed it to her.

"No, I don't recognize him either."

"He's an American named Trevor Hughes. I thought you might have had some contact with him."

"I'm afraid not, Colonel. I've never met the man and I don't know anyone by that name."

"Do you know who killed Iskur or why he was killed?"

She remained quite composed under his steady gaze. "No, I don't." She got up and walked out to the terrace. Gossiping women talked from balcony to balcony. Their buzzing increased when Nina stepped outside.

Pappas followed her.

"I loved him, you know," she said, looking down at the narrow street.

"I'm sure that you did." He paused, and asked casually, "You didn't know any of his associates, but you did know Yiannis Yiotas."

"He's a chauffeur, an errand boy."

"I want to search your apartment."

"And if I refuse?"

"Then I would give you five days to settle your affairs and leave Greece."

A shadow of alarm passed over her face. "You can't do that."

"I can, and I would."

Her color deepened with anger. She tossed back her hair, smoothing it at the sides with her palms. "I'd be happy to let you search my home, Colonel."

For the next two hours he looked through closets, drawers, bookcases, vanities, and tables. He looked under the rugs and inside the appliances. He emptied closets, piling clothes on the bed, searching each article, including the shoes. Finding nothing, he pushed the pile aside and sat on the edge of the bed, absentmindedly opening the drawer of the end table. He took out the Athens-Piraeus telephone directory and the Blue Book, the business-tourist directory. Holding them, he looked around the bedroom. "You lived with a phantom."

Wearing a satisfied smile, she said, "That is exactly what I've been trying to tell you, Colonel."

He put the book down on the bed, got up, and slowly walked out into the living room, around the dining area, out on the terrace, and back into the bedroom. She's a cool one, he thought. No man, no matter how secretive he is, lives without personal articles in his home. She must have gotten rid of everything. Which means that there is something that she is trying to hide. I'm going to have to take a close look at this Nina Pazza, he thought, looking down at the book. He saw a white border showing between the blue pages of the Blue Book. He opened the book to the page and removed a black-and-white photograph. Three young men posed in front of a Shinto shrine. The lens had captured Japanese couples in the background strolling in a park at cherry blossom time. He showed her the picture. Her surprise was genuine. "I've never seen this before."

"That's Orhan on the right, but who are the other two?"

"I don't know."

And Pappas knew that neither of the other two men looked

like the composite sketch or the passport photo. So how on earth would he be able to identify them?

Piraeus was a city of three harbors and four police stations. It took Pappas the better part of an hour to make the drive from Nina Pazza's apartment to the station on Vassilissis Georgious 1. He could have telephoned in his instructions, but he had learned early on that if you wanted to make sure things were done the way you wanted them to be done, you had better make the arrangements in person.

Entering the station house, Pappas walked behind the watch desk and signed himself present in the service book. Lieutenant Kanakis's gangly body stiffened to attention when he spotted the colonel entering the third-floor office.

"You did a good job at the Iskur crime scene, Lieutenant," Pappas said, moving across the room to the double windows. "Finding that amphora with the black sand pointed us in the right direction." He looked across the wide boulevard at the passengers boarding the ferries for Aegina and Póros. "I have another job for you. I want you to use your best people, only those capable of instant amnesia."

"All my men suffer from that ailment when necessary, Colonel."

"Good. This is going to be a surveillance. I want you to make sure that your people can blend into any crowd."

Kanakis moved up behind the colonel. The sound of the busy port filled the airy room. "This harbor used to house the triremes of the ancient Athenian fleet; now it harbors the yachts of the rich."

They stared out at the luxurious boats, each man momentarily lost in his own thoughts. "Does this job have anything to do with the Voúla massacre?" the lieutenant asked.

"It's directly related, Lieutenant."

A humming, throbbing mass of people pressed through Plaka's narrow arteries. At the end of Ifestou Street a stone stairway wound upward to the slopes of the Acropolis. Along the way an intricate network of narrow byways branched off to form shop-lined streets.

Sitting under a pepper tree in one of the tavernas, Major General Philippos Tsimas sipped ouzo as he tried to pick out the passing women who were not wearing underpants. Dressed in brown slacks and a white pullover, he looked more like a tourist than the head of the Greek intelligence service. Fingering worry beads, he focused on the folds of a lanky blonde's skirt, on how it creased into her marvelous young ass. Sipping his drink, he spotted Pappas climbing the steps right behind the woman.

"Dimitri, good to see you," Tsimas said, inviting Pappas to sit next to him, watching as the policeman came into the café's garden. Bright, colorful flowers in borders surrounded the tables occupied by people having early evening aperitifs.

Without any preliminaries, Pappas poured himself a drink and added the water. "I received a request from Vassos for information on Trevor Hughes, an American diplomat stationed here."

"I know about Hughes. What information does Vassos want?"

"Whatever you can give him. Andreas sent me a photo of Hughes."

Tsimas picked up a slice of feta. Gnawing the edges, he asked, "How are things going in New York?"

"Your head of station is running Vassos, so you probably know more about that than I do."

Tsimas's face remained expressionless. He scraped his chair closer to the table. "Dimitri, I'm worried. No matter how much I want to, I can't bring myself to believe that the Americans will ever allow Alexander's *Iliad* to leave the country. The big museums would never permit it. They'd steal it outright if they could, or make up some false claim to get their greedy hands on it."

Pappas was startled by his colleague's outburst. "The investigation being conducted here, and the one in the States, are both covert. The American museums have no way of knowing about this case. We've been careful, very careful."

Tsimas added more ouzo to their glasses. "For a seasoned policeman, you're terribly naïve. Tell me, my friend, how was the New York end of the investigation arranged?"

"Through the American State Department."

"And the State Department is run by tight-assed American aristocrats, the same sort of people who run the museums. Do you really believe that word of the casket-copy hasn't been leaked to important curators?"

Pappas clenched his jaw. "I don't know."

"Those fucking people have stolen most of our national treasures." He slammed his glass down; ouzo splashed over the sides. "The people of this country would never tolerate it if they knew the truth about Voúla and the casket-copy. Their outrage would be such that I'm sure the government would be shaken." He leaned close and whispered, "If the casket-copy cannot be returned, it should be destroyed."

Pappas's mouth fell open. "You're serious?"

"No matter what the politicians of this country say in public, they know, as I do, that Greece's future is irrevocably tied to the United States." He took an orange from the bowl on the table and rolled it between his hands. "See how easy it is for me to do this?" Suddenly he slapped the orange and watched as it flew off the table.

Cats pounced on the fruit.

"I just knocked it into a different orbit. It is the same way with countries, Dimitri. All you need is the right pretext to tilt a country's policy. The casket-copy could be the vehicle to knock Greece into a much more Eastern alignment."

The whitewashed church set on the top of Lykavitos Hill glowed in the bright morning sunlight. Tour buses discharged their passengers in front of the funicular. Taxis cruised Aristodimou Street. At a little past seven that morning a gray van had parked at the end of the block; at nine o'clock plain-clothes policemen began their apparently aimless promenade around the area. Inside the van Lieutenant Kanakis waited by the communications monitor, arms folded, listening to negative field reports.

Meanwhile, three kilometers away at 173 Leoforos Alexandras, Colonel Dimitri Pappas worked at his desk, waiting for Kanakis to inform him that Nina Pazza had left her apartment.

Reading the report on Trevor Hughes, Pappas grudgingly gave Tsimas an A-plus for efficiency. The folder not only contained photographs and biographical data on the dead American, it also detailed every time he had left Greece, giving the date and time of departure, his destination, and the date and time of his return.

Pappas noticed that all of his trips were within Europe and of short duration; most of them had been made on weekends. A courier with a diplomatic passport would have been an asset to any smuggler. Pappas put the file down and telephoned his wife to tell her that he would not be coming home for Saturday lunch. She reminded him, in an unyielding tone of voice, that his name day was next week and that his daughters were planning a surprise for him. He was ordered to be home that night, no matter what. "I'll be there," he said, replacing the receiver just as the green phone on the confidential line began to ring.

Many fashionable cafés were located within walking distance of Syntagma Square. All of them were places where a person could inexpensively pass a day or evening watching the cosmopolitan life of Athens passing by; places where Greek men, wearing the latest American and Italian casuals, could stalk female tourists. The Everyday Café, located at 15 Standious Street, had shiny tube chairs with brown calfskin seats. Outside the tables formed an arch around the café's curved front.

At 1:10 Nina Pazza stepped from a taxi and passed the first two outside rows, choosing a table in front of the café's gleaming window. Driving away in his taxi, the "cab driver" reached under the seat and slid out a walkie-talkie. A gray van pulled up at the curb across the street from the Everyday Café. Policemen inside it aimed movie and still cameras through the one-way glass set in the side panel. Using the van's cellular telephone, Lieutenant Kanakis communicated their location to Colonel Pappas.

Twenty-three minutes later Pappas parked his unmarked car at the other end of Standious Street, far enough away so that the subject would not see him or the car. He quickly blended into the mass of people flowing along the busy shopping street, stopped by the side door of the van, and knocked. It slid open and Pappas climbed inside. "What's she doing?"

"Sitting and drinking tea," Kanakis said. "She might be waiting for someone."

"Why don't we arrange to eavesdrop," Pappas said.

Kanakis opened the supply drawer above the communication console and took out a magnetized M5A microtransmitter. "Paper-thin," he said, showing it to Pappas. He called over one of the six policemen squatting on the portable bench that folded down from the wall. The officer took the transmitter and left the van. Pappas and the lieutenant watched the policeman cross the wide street and saunter into the café.

George Dangas, a member of Kanakis's elite unit for the past seven years, moved across the Everyday Café's marble floor to the cashier, who was sitting behind her machine adding up checks and putting the register's tapes on the waiters' trays. Dangas told her that he wanted to see the owner. "Over there," she said, pointing with her head.

Dangas walked up to a short, bowlegged man and showed him his shield. "I need to talk with you a moment."

Five minutes later George Dangas, wearing a white waiter's

jacket and carrying a tray, reappeared outside; he worked his way along the rows, bussing the sidewalk tables. He cleaned the tin tops and emptied and wiped ashtrays. When he came to Nina Pazza's she gave him an indifferent glance and returned her attention to the people passing by.

When her attention was elsewhere, Dangas fastened the microtransmitter to the underside. He continued working along the row until he came to the end, where he turned and worked his way back to the café's entrance.

Inside the surveillance van the policewoman manning the console's sophisticated communications equipment flicked on the receiver switch and began monitoring instruments on the front of it. Loud fragments of conversations and laughter burst forth from the speakers. She painstakingly worked the controls until the clink of Nina Pazza's teacup was clearly discernible, at which point she looked up at Kanakis and said, "We're zeroed in, Lieutenant."

Leaning against the van's wall with his arms folded across his chest, Pappas asked the lieutenant, "Is the entire area covered?"

Kanakis nodded and picked up the hand mike.

A young man on a motorbike stopped in front of the café and called out to a passing woman. She hesitated, looking in the direction of the voice. "John," she called out, and rushed over to the bike, throwing her arms around him. As she did this, the policewoman said into the transmitter fastened inside her blouse, "Orange three on station."

Two women sat at a table in the row directly in front of Nina Pazza. They immediately leaned across the small space and began to gossip about a friend who was having an affair with a married man. As they talked, the redhead pulled a tissue from her shoulder bag and wiped a fleck of dirt from her eye. While doing so, she whispered, "Orange five on station."

■   ■   ■

Lieutenant Kanakis looked at the colonel. "I've got my people scattered throughout the café. I've also got some nearby motorbikes ready to go after her if she bolts on us."

They waited; fifteen minutes passed.

Kanakis was the first to spot the woman heading between the tables toward Nina Pazza. She was well dressed and had a designer scarf around her neck. She looked to be in her mid-thirties and had short auburn hair. An attractive woman, she moved with the grace and sureness of a professional dancer. Coming up to Nina Pazza's table she sat, speaking in English with a decided British accent, "I could not get rid of a silly customer."

"I hope you made the sale."

"Of course I did. How are you, Nina? You look wonderful. Widowhood appears to agree with you."

"It does." She leaned close and whispered, "Ann, a policeman visited me yesterday, a Colonel Pappas. He questioned me about Orhan's murder."

"What did you tell him?"

"What do you think I told him? The truth, of course."

"Of course."

"He searched my apartment and found a photograph of Orhan and two other men. One of them was his friend from New York, Denny McKay. I don't know who the other one was," she lied easily.

"Why on earth didn't you destroy it with the rest of his things? You should have anticipated a visit from the police."

"I didn't destroy it because I didn't know it was there. The old fool hid it in a telephone book." Nina sipped her tea. "I don't think we have any reason for concern. There is just no way that they can connect us to New York."

"Don't be too sure of that, Nina. Yiotas has been arrested and Trevor has been killed. I don't like it. Everything ran smoothly for years, but now unpleasantness is cropping up all around us."

"We have nothing to worry about. Yiotas knows nothing.

Besides, he was always getting himself arrested for one thing or the other. And people are always getting murdered in New York."

"And Orhan?" Ann asked, beckoning to a waiter. "That was no accident?"

"He more than likely had his hand in someone's pockets. You know how he was."

A waiter came up to them. Ann ordered tea with lemon. "Will you share a baklava with me?"

"I'll nibble," Nina said.

The waiter walked off.

"You don't think the police know anything about the business?" Ann asked anxiously.

"Absolutely not."

Ann sucked in a deep breath. "I can't help wondering if Orhan's death had anything to do with what happened in Voúla. It was the same day, Nina. Coincidences like that just don't happen."

"Of course they do. Don't let your imagination play tricks with you. Use your common sense."

"I suppose you're right."

The waiter came with Ann's order. He put it down and left. Picking at the honey-soaked pastry, Ann asked, "What are we going to do without Orhan?"

"They asked me to come to New York to discuss taking his place."

"Oh, Nina, that's wonderful," Ann said, leaning up out of her seat to kiss her friend's cheek. "I'm so happy for you. You're going, of course."

"I'm trying to book a flight sometime this week."

Ann squeezed lemon into her tea. "Do you miss him?"

"I guess so, yes. I miss his brains and the way he made me laugh. But I don't miss the other part, the pretending. Ugh. I hated it."

Ann inched her hand across the table until their fingers touched. "Do you enjoy it with me?"

"How can you ask that?" she said, brushing fingers over Ann's. "Would you like to come home with me?"

"Very much."

The surveillance on Aristodimou Street resumed at 2:31.

At 4:32 Ann walked out of the lobby of Nina Pazza's apartment and hailed a passing taxi. Standing on the curb, she turned and waved up at Nina, who was standing on her terrace dressed in her white caftan. Ann's lips puckered into a silent kiss. She turned and slid demurely into the taxi.

Eighteen minutes later Ann got out on crowded Othonos Street in front of the Pan Am ticket office. A few doors away two policemen, with machine guns strapped across their chests, guarded the entrance of the E1 A1 ticket office. Walking west, Ann passed the Albert Café, the Boutique Regina, and entered an exclusive-looking shop with a marble facade and the name *Delos Antiques* written in gold script in both Greek and English above the entrance.

A gray van parked across the street from the Albert Café. "Get someone inside that store and find out who this Ann is," Pappas said to Kanakis.

The lieutenant called a policewoman off the bench. "Areta, be careful," Kanakis said to the officer.

Areta opened the supply drawer and took out a microtransmitter. Turning away from the others she unbuttoned the front of her blouse and clipped the transmitter to her brassiere. She buttoned up, smoothed down the front of her blouse, and climbed down out of the van. Bustling city sounds echoed inside the surveillance van as Pappas and the lieutenant watched Areta enter Delos Antiques.

A door opening, a tinkling bell, the woman called Ann speaking Greek: "May I help you?"

"I'm just browsing, thank you," Areta said.

Silence.

Inside the surveillance van, Pappas leaned up against the communication console, his ears close to the speakers.

Ann, speaking Greek, said, "It's beautiful, isn't it?"

"Yes it is. My husband and I have been searching for a table for our entrance hall. This looks as though it would be perfect," Areta said.

"It's French, early eighteenth century. It's made of tulipwood and kingwood veneer and has ormolu mounts."

"How late are you open?"

"Until seven."

"I'll come back with my husband. Are you the owner?"

"Yes, here is my card."

"Ann Bryce," Areta read. "Your Greek is excellent."

"That's because I am Greek."

"Really?"

"My parents emigrated to the U.K. when I was three. I married an Englishman, but that didn't work out, so after the divorce I decided to come home to Greece."

"How interesting. We must talk more when I return with my husband."

Athens was quiet, the night clear, the cafés almost deserted. Two revelers walked unsteadily into the lobby of the George I Hotel. A garbage truck drove slowly along Syntagma Square, its crew gathering and emptying refuse cans. On Othonos Street two policemen lurked in the shadows of the E1 A1 ticket office.

A gray van rolled up onto the sidewalk in front of Delos Antiques. Two police cars appeared from nowhere and blocked both ends of Othonos Street. A fire truck skirted around the car blocking the east end of the street and drove up on the sidewalk, stopping behind the gray van. Firemen jumped down and began lugging hose out of the truck's bay. A man came out of the van and knelt down in front of the gate protecting the antique store's windows. He removed a set of manufacturer's keys from a black pouch and went to work on the padlock. Firemen tugged hose into the lobby of the office building that housed the antique store.

Inside the van Pappas and the lieutenant reviewed the plan. Working with a detailed diagram of the store that the policewoman, Areta, had made, it was decided that the antique store would be searched using the "wheel" method.

The search would be conducted outward from the center of the store, in straight lines out along the spokes of an imaginary wheel. Teams were assigned to each of the spokes.

"It's open," radioed the key man.

Pappas and the lieutenant entered the darkened store at 3:24 A.M. A team quickly followed them and installed a black cloth over the window.

The lights were switched on. The interior was long and narrow and crammed with furniture, clocks, stelae, and pedestal busts of gods and warriors. In the rear six steps led up to a balcony that served as an office.

Search teams entered and went about their tasks. One team climbed up to the office and began to empty the desk and file cabinets. A woman member of the team put a self-stick label identifying what had been removed in the exact spot where the item had stood. This was done so that the object could be put back in exactly the same spot. An aluminum table was set up and each item was removed, then photographed. Teams moved gingerly out along the radii, searching everything within the confines of the spokes. Pappas and Kanakis remained in the front of the store, observing the Special Operations policemen do what they had been trained to do.

One of the teams removed all the electrical fixtures; some members of the unit probed walls, ceilings, and floors with a magnetic box that registered hollow spaces. In the building's lobby the firemen relaxed, waiting for the word to return to quarters; their part of the charade was over.

A policewoman dressed in jeans and a UCLA sweatshirt and sneakers crawled between a chest and a commode, over to a long case clock topped by an allegorical bronze figure representing Time. She ran her hand over the front and around to the sides. Squeezing into the cramped space between the clock and the commode, she lay on her right side and stretched her arm between the wall and the back of the clock. Running her hand over the smooth wood she felt an almost imperceptible crack. A ridge? A joining? "Someone give me a flashlight," she requested. A policeman twisted his way through the furniture over to her and passed down a light. She aimed the beam behind the clock and made out the outline of a panel fitted into its base. Looking for a latch of some kind and finding none, she transferred the light to her left hand and, throwing the light over the back of the clock, tried to dig out the panel with her nails. "Shit, I broke a nail." She studied the panel, trying to determine how to get it open. "A nail file," she called out.

The policeman who had given her his flashlight repeated her request, and a policewoman came over to him and gave him a nail file, which he passed down to the policewoman lying on the floor. She worked the blade into the crack and began prying out the panel. After loosening it, she pulled it free and leaned it up against the wall. Maneuvering her hand inside the clock, she felt the stiff binding of buckram-covered ledgers. Contorting her body, she worked out three books. A big smile on her pretty face, she passed them up to Lieutenant Kanakis. The rapid clicking sounds of high-speed camera shutters soon shattered the eerie stillness that had fallen on the antiques store.

With the pages of the ledgers photographed and everything returned to its proper place, Kanakis ordered his men out. The blackout curtain was taken down and folded; the grill pulled across the front of the store, and the padlock returned to its rightful place.

Othonos Street was reopened to traffic at 4:45 A.M.

Colonel Pappas returned to his office to await the development of the film, and to try to get some sleep. He left instructions with the night duty officer to awaken him as soon as the film was ready, then collapsed on the leather couch and fell into a deep sleep.

A harsh sound roused him, causing him to spring up and dash barefooted for the phone. "They're ready, sir," a woman's soft voice said.

"Thank you." He fell heavily into the chair. "I'm too damn old for this kind of life," he muttered to his wiggling feet on the cold floor. He was uncomfortably aware that he had forgotten to bring fresh socks and underwear from home.

"I thought you might need some coffee," the duty officer said, coming in with a tray. She had pretty eyes and full lips. A sergeant at thirty. The new breed, he thought, watching her put down the coffee. I bet she has extra underpants and stockings in her locker. "Thank you."

She smiled and left the office, returning shortly with a clump of folders. She put them down on his desk, asked if there would be anything else, and left.

Pappas dumped the contents of the folders onto his desk, separating the business records from the photographs. He propped one of the surveillance photos of Nina Pazza and Ann Bryce against the desk lamp. Next to it he added one of Trevor Hughes and another of the three men posing in front of a Shinto shrine. The cast of characters was getting bigger, he mused, draining the bitter sediment from the bottom of his cup. For the next hour he studied copies of the ledgers. The entries in the first column appeared to be abbreviated names of artwork and countries. The next column listed the dates the items were shipped to the United States. He looked up from the page, wondering why they sent art to the States and then had it shipped back. The third column showed the date that the item was returned to Greece followed by a circled number, usually a 3, 4, or 5. He noted that in every instance the merchandise was sent from Greece to Brandt Industries in NYC. What did the circled numbers stand for? Fishing through the invoices, he found many recorded shipments of souvenirs and toys from Brandt Industries to Delos Antiques.

Trying to decipher unfamiliar business records with an exhausted mind just doesn't work, he thought. His tongue, sour from too much coffee, pushed grounds out of his teeth. His eyelids started to fall shut. Placing his head down on folded arms, he gave in to his fatigue. After a while he felt a soft warmth envelop him and he dreamed of the first time he made love to his wife. Pappas felt his prick stretching into a hard shaft. He asked himself if ancient policemen got as horny on night duties, wondered if he was awake or sleeping. Then he felt firm, relaxing hands caressing his shoulders. He was sure that he was not dreaming so he opened his eyes and saw the photos of records scattered all over his desk. He sat up slowly, conscious of the light summer blanket over his shoulders.

"I didn't mean to awaken you, Colonel," she said, "but I worried that you might catch a cold."

"Thank you," he said to the duty officer, gathering the blanket at his neck.

"I'll be outside," she said, leaving the room, her maternal instincts satisfied.

His improvised cape secured around his shoulders, Pappas reached out and pressed the start button of the tape recorder. Nina Pazza's latest telephone conversations flowed from the machine. Ann Bryce had telephoned to thank her for a wonderful afternoon. "It was marvelous," Nina agreed. "We must do it again, *soon.*"

"Please, please."

They laughed.

The next call was from a travel agent. Nina was booked first class tomorrow on Olympic Flight 641, leaving Athens at 12:55, arriving Kennedy 4:15 New York time. The agent informed her that she had an open-return ticket and that her reservation had been confirmed by the Plaza Hotel.

Pappas listened to the clicks as she made a transatlantic call. Outside he could hear people on the morning shift coming down the hall and passing his closed door. A man answered in English. "Hello."

"Belmont, it's Nina."

"Everything okay?"

"Yes," she answered, and went on to tell when her flight would arrive and where she would be staying.

"I'll meet you," he said, and hung up.

Just a curt conversation between friends. He'd been a policeman long enough to recognize the special intimacy of thieves. Scooping up the photographs that leaned against the desk lamp, he shut off the recorder and hurried from his office, dropping the blanket to the floor.

Yiannis Yiotas, his trousers gathered at his ankles, was sitting on the stainless steel toilet contemplating his laceless shoes when the cell door swung open and Pappas marched in.

In an embarrassed flurry Yiotas made a hasty effort to pull up his trousers.

"You needn't stand," Pappas said, lowering himself to the bunk. "We're pretty informal around here." Sniffing the air, he added, "I see you're using a new after-shave." He held out a photograph taken at the Everyday Café. "Who are these women?"

"The one with her back to the window is Nina Pazza, and the other one is the lady from the antiques store." Yiotas crossed his palms over his groin.

"What antiques store?"

"Delos on Othonos Street. On Wednesdays whenever Nina and Orhan were together I'd drive them there. I could see them talking to her through the window."

"What's her name?"

"I don't know."

"Did they ever meet anyone else in the store?"

"Sometimes the three of them would leave and meet a man in the Albert Café and have lunch."

"Who was the man?"

"I don't know. He wasn't a Greek. Maybe English or American."

Pappas showed him a photo of Trevor Hughes.

"That's him."

Pappas sprang up from the bunk and left the cell. Moving down the corridor toward the elevator, he heard the clank of the steel door closing and thought: One down.

Back in his office, he picked up the blanket and draped it around his shoulders, then sat behind his desk. He picked up the telephone receiver and dialed the international access code, the country code, the city code, and the number Andreas Vassos had sent him. After a series of metallic clanging sounds and a tidal wave of rushing air, he heard a ring and gruff voice answer, "Lieutenant Lucas, Sixteenth Squad."

So, Pappas thought gleefully, they have to work on Sundays, too.

16

P eople with American passports move to your left, all others go to your right," two immigration agents instructed the deplaning passengers from Olympic Flight 641. Coming off the moving stairs, the travelers flowed along a short passage that fed into the immigration checkpoint, an auditorium-sized room with manned booths.

A very short, slight man dressed in civilian clothes and wearing oversized aviator glasses with yellow tinted lenses moved among the foreign travelers. "Have your passports, visas, and landing cards ready," Inspector Cutrone said, sweeping his eyes over the line, searching for a Eurasian beauty named Nina Pazza.

Waiting just beyond the booths, uniformed as a customs inspector, Teddy Lucas waited along with the real inspector. He spotted Nina Pazza moving into the room and taking her place in line. Sexy, he thought, watching her. She was dressed in a raw silk suit with epaulets and beige open-toed, open-heeled shoes. She carried an overnight bag and had a large pocketbook slung over her shoulder.

Cutrone moved along the line checking documents. When he reached her, he slid the visa that she had obtained with some difficulty on short notice out of her passport, gave it a cursory examination, and handed it back to her. He continued along the line for a bit and turned, motioning Lucas and the other agent into the empty booth at the end of the row.

Lucas and the real inspector squeezed into the booth. Cutrone moved back along Nina Pazza's queue, arbitrarily broke it off four passengers in front of her, directing them to line up at the newly opened checkpoint.

"What is the purpose of your visit to the United States?" Lucas asked Nina Pazza, taking her documents.

"Holiday," she said.

Looking up from her passport and landing card, he examined her face casually and said in a bored tone of voice, "You're staying at the Plaza Hotel?"

"Yes."

Handing her back her papers, he gave her a worn smile. "Enjoy your visit."

When Pazza had exited the inspection area, Lucas hurried from the booth into the ground-floor supervisor's office in the front of the inspection area. Vassos was waiting for him. Lucas changed back into his street clothes.

Nina joined the other anxious passengers gathering around the baggage carousels. To her pleasant surprise she immediately saw her one piece of Hermès luggage sliding down the chute onto the shiny plates. Quickly passing through customs, she walked into the crowded lobby and brightened when she saw Belmont Widener waving to her.

A few feet away from the reunited couple, Detective Ivan Ulanov spoke into the transmitter clipped to his shirt pocket. "They're leaving, get ready."

Nina Pazza and the rare book dealer left the terminal and crossed the street to the parking meridian on the other side and a waiting sedan.

"We got 'em," Big Jay said into the radio.

John Leone, sitting in the rear of a taxi, rapped on the protective grill. "Don't lose them."

"Fuck you. I don't lose people."

■   ■   ■

Inspector Cutrone led Lucas and Vassos through a labyrinth of security doors. Exiting at the rear of the building, they were met by a wall of heat and the roar of engines. "There's your helicopter," Cutrone said, pointing to the blue-and-white police department craft.

C of D Edgeworth rose from his chair to greet his visitors. "Major Vassos, nice to meet you at last."

"Nice to meet you, sir," Vassos said, looking around the plaque-filled office.

Returning to his desk, Edgeworth asked, "Is Lieutenant Lucas looking after you, Major?"

"Yes, sir, very nicely."

"Good, good," Edgeworth said, filling his pipe with tobacco. He looked across the expanse of his desk at Lucas. "What's so important?"

"Yesterday we received a call from Andreas's boss, a Colonel Pappas."

"Yes, yes, I know all about that, you already told me," Edgeworth said.

"Today we received records and other material from the colonel. We've spent all our spare time going over it. We now believe that the case can be brought to a successful conclusion."

Drawing on his pipe, Edgeworth said, "Then you know who has the casket-copy."

"No, not yet, but I believe we're getting close."

A cynical smile showed through the swirl of smoke. "Am I then correct in assuming that you need just a little more help before you're able to drop the net?"

"Surveillance vehicles, electronic equipment, and men for tail work, preferably experienced guys from Narcotics or Safe and Loft."

Edgeworth frowned. "Equipment, okay; more men, impossible."

"Chief, the case is starting to go, I can feel it," Lucas said. "I need some people watched around the clock and I don't have enough detectives to do it. One of them is Denny McKay, the hump who ordered the hit on Cormick McGovern."

Edgeworth bit down on his pipe, flipping it up and down between his teeth, regarding the lieutenant with stern eyes. He removed the pipe from his mouth and thoughtfully placed it in the glass ashtray. "Teddy, I judge leadership by what a commander does with his resources at hand. Every squad boss in the Detective Division is yapping for extra manpower. There ain't none; I'd be guilty of malfeasance if I stole more men and gave them to you." He looked at Vassos. "I hope you understand, Major."

"I do, sir. We have the same problem in Greece."

"I'm sure that you do, Major," Edgeworth said, returning his attention to the lieutenant. "There is another reason why I can't give you more people. Security. The more detectives I fly into your squad, the greater becomes the risk of a leak to the press."

Vassos asked matter-of-factly if the C of D was keeping Washington informed of the progress of the investigation.

"I brief a Mr. Hayden. He's with State's Bureau of Diplomatic Security. At the moment he's here in New York."

Vassos's placid face hid his concern. He recalled Pappas's admonition to destroy the casket-copy if it should prove impossible to get it back to Greece. He knew that he could never bring himself to do that. Alexander's *Iliad* was going to be his memorial to Soula and Stephanos.

"The equipment?" Lucas asked.

"I'll make the arrangements," Edgeworth said, buzzing for his lead clerical.

A clap of thunder heralded the downpour. Within minutes the city's catch basins overflowed into the streets; traffic slowed to a crawl on all the major parkways. And then, as suddenly as it had come, the rain was gone, leaving a deep purple sky behind. Lucas stood on Katina Wright's terrace sucking in the cool, crisp air. The past days had been exhausting ones for the team. His detectives had been tailing Widener and Denny McKay, and each five on the surveillance ended with "nothing to report." Tonight his men had followed them to the Plaza Hotel, then waited outside and in the lobby until Widener left and returned to his home. Big Jay and Leone had stayed on Widener.

Every night since Monday, Vassos, Lucas, and Elisabeth Syros had been meeting in Katina's apartment to study and restudy the material from Greece. Lucas's expense money and credit cards bought the dinners. Vassos had never eaten Mexican food, so tonight Lucas had ordered camaróns, enchiladas, mole poblano, and nachos. Katina provided the soda.

Lucas had come to look forward to spending these evenings with Katina. He felt that being around her on a regular basis might give him the courage to say the things that he wanted to say to her. Once or twice he thought that he saw her looking at him and even imagined that he saw a certain receptivity in her glances. But he knew that that was only his wishful thinking. A woman like Katina does not let herself fall for a cop with only a high school diploma. On Friday night Lucas stole a look at Katina and clumsily tipped over a container of beef teriyaki, causing Vassos to look upward in an exaggerated gesture of prayer.

Tonight was to be their final meeting, the one where they were to sum up their findings before starting the operation that could lead them to the casket-copy.

Lucas stepped back inside. Paperboard cartons of food and dirty paper plates littered the table between the two sofas. One of the couches was covered with records and photographs; Vassos, Katina, and Elisabeth sat on the other one. The two women had gotten along well since Vassos first introduced them the previous Friday evening.

Katina, dressed in her usual off-duty outfit of Bermuda shorts, a tank top, and espadrilles, studied the photo of Ann

Bryce leaving Nina's apartment. "Colonel Pappas said they're lovers?"

"Yes." Vassos replayed the tape of Nina's conversation with Ann.

While the recorder was on, Lucas picked up the photo of the men standing in front of the Shinto shrine. "Iskur and McKay, but who the hell is the other guy?"

The tape played out and Vassos shut off the machine.

"I'm sure that the first column in those ledgers is a record of stolen artwork," Katina said.

"That we all agree on," Lucas said, "but that doesn't help us find the casket-copy."

Katina shook her head at the records. "I assumed all of this was going to lead us to Alexander's *Iliad.*"

"It will," Lucas said. "I would be surprised if McKay didn't know something about the casket-copy."

Elisabeth tugged at her cowboy boots. "I can't believe that Iskur would knowingly allow himself to become involved in something like Voúla."

"He didn't," Vassos said, his face a tortured mask. "I caused the massacre. Cuttler and Simmons were sent to Greece for the purpose of killing two policemen. If I hadn't taken action that day, they would have done what they had come to do and left, leaving all the others alive, my wife and son included."

Lucas jumped to his feet. "That's the craziest thing you've ever said. You're a cop, for chrissake. You think you're supposed to stand by and do nothing while two other cops are getting killed? What happened to you could have happened to any policeman in the world. Don't give yourself a guilt trip, Andreas."

They fell silent.

Katina was the first to speak: "Why would anyone want to kill Adele Matrazzo?"

"It was her uncle who rediscovered the casket-copy," Lucas said, closing one of the food cartons.

"But that was in 1939," Katina said. "He's long dead."

"Is he?" Lucas said, picking up another half-empty carton. Everyone looked at Lucas.

"You're not saying he's alive?" Katina questioned.

"What I'm saying is that the only connection Adele Matrazzo had with the case is through her family. And the only reason I can come up with for killing her was to prevent her from talking to us, to prevent her from identifying some member of the family."

"You can't be serious," Elisabeth Syros said. "Paolo Matrazzo would be too old to commit murder."

"Yes, he would be ninety-seven," Lucas said, "but he had two sons." He picked up a yellow pad and read: "Corporal Anthony Matrazzo, B Company, 1st Battalion, 7th Marines, killed on the night of October 24, 1942, during the battle of Bloody Ridge on Guadalcanal.

"Paolo Junior, the other son, the one Adele told us had died? Well, I can't find any record of his death. And army records show that he served in Japan during the Korean War. He was there the same time exactly as McKay and Iskur."

"Did the army send you a copy of his fingerprints?" Elisabeth asked.

"Yes," Lucas said. "So I had our fingerprint man compare them, and the best he could do was a possible maybe. There were not enough points of comparison in the latents lifted at the Iskur scene to make a positive I.D."

"What about a photo of Paolo Junior?" Katina asked.

"The army didn't have one and I can't find any," Lucas said. "We traced the guy all the way back to high school. He didn't pose for the yearbook, nor did he pose for anything during his college days. Seems to me that Paolo Junior was a very shy type." Lucas rummaged through the material on the sofa and came up with an artist's sketch. He compared it to the unknown member of the trio posing in front of the Shinto shrine. "Just doesn't look like the same man," he observed.

Elisabeth took them from Lucas and compared them. "They might be the same person."

"How?" Lucas questioned.

"Plastic surgery," Elisabeth suggested.

Katina added, "If I wanted to disappear and still remain in New York, that would certainly be an option I'd consider."

"Widener knows who our third man is," Vassos said. "Give him to me for a few minutes and we'll know too."

"That's not the way to go, Andreas, not yet, anyway," Lucas said.

"I still do not understand why your detectives prevented me from following Widener into that restaurant," Vassos complained.

"They did it because Maison Blanche is one of the more fashionable joints in this town. You can't get in without a reservation and you can't get a reservation unless your name is known," Lucas explained. "If you had tried to push your way inside, some blow-dried headwaiter would have tried to stop you and we would have had a commotion that could have alerted Widener to the fact that he had a shadow."

Vassos made a disagreeable face.

"We're going to be tailing a lot of people during the next few days," Lucas said. "It's too bad we don't have enough troops to cover the clock."

Vassos picked up his pad. "I've been worried about that so I've worked out a plan."

Lucas squeezed in next to Katina. "I'm listening."

"The best way to cover Pazza, Widener, and McKay is with a fluid surveillance. With your four detectives and the two of us, we have six officers. I'll be able to supply six additional men," Vassos said, watching the Whip.

"And from where will you get these six bodies?" Lucas asked.

"From me," Elisabeth said, "so, counting me, it will be seven additional bodies."

Lucas looked at Vassos's control, heaved a sigh, and thought: do what ya' gotta do, but do it right. "Are your people reliable?"

Vassos grinned. "I would think so."

They spent the next hour arranging schedules. When they had completed that, Vassos said, "There will still be a hole after two A.M."

"I'll take care of that," Lucas said, adding, "You understand, Andreas, that your people are to observe and report, nothing else."

"Of course," Vassos said, gathering up his notes.

"Andreas, nothing else," Lucas said.

"I understand," Vassos said, checking his watch. "It's after midnight."

"I'll drive you back to your hotel," Lucas said, starting to get up.

A gleam of humorous wisdom showed in Vassos's eyes. "Elisabeth can take me. Why don't you stay and help Katina clean up?"

Katina accompanied them to the door. She touched her lips to Elisabeth's cheek and said in Greek, "Thank you for all your help."

Elisabeth smiled and said good night.

Katina closed the door behind them to find Lucas carrying cartons and dirty plates into the kitchen.

She followed after him.

"Where's the garbage?" he asked.

"Under the sink," she said, bending to open the cabinet, and taking out a plastic bag. She held it open in front of her and watched as he dumped the refuse inside. "Why don't you like to speak Greek?"

Without replying, he stepped around her and moved back into the living room. She hurriedly placed the plastic garbage bag in the sink and followed him. She found him sitting on the sofa sorting through papers. "I didn't mean to pry. I'm sorry," she said, sitting beside him.

He looked at her and then went on stacking the papers in a neat pile, all the time brooding over the maddening inhibition he felt when he was close to her. "I'd better get going."

"Please stay."

Her warm hand came to rest on his arm and he felt a sudden thump in his heart. He returned her gaze and slowly, haltingly, moved to meet her lips with his.

Lucas sat up in the bed, gazing out the window at the orange sun pasted high in the sky. Recalling their night of unreserved lovemaking, he looked down at her naked beauty. For the first time in many years he felt really wanted and secure. He kissed her head, whispered, "You're wonderful."

"So are you," she mumbled, stretching. Suddenly her eyes went wide with disbelief, and she quickly gathered the sheet over her body. "I can't believe what I did last night. I . . . I actually asked a man to, to stay."

"I'm very happy that you did."

She tenderly brushed the side of his head. He took her into his arms and they made love again.

Afterward, as they were locked together on the rumpled sheets, she said, "I've been waiting a long time for you, Theodorous Loucopolous."

"Not as long as I have for you. How, may I inquire, did you know my Greek name?"

"I asked Andreas." She kissed his neck. "The last time we were together you asked me to tell you about my baby."

"I remember."

She shivered with a painful remembrance. "I miscarried in my fourth month. Kenneth didn't bother to visit me in the hospital."

He pressed her closer to him, pulling her leg across his stomach, and then, to his surprise, his own painful litany burst forth: his childhood, his self-image, his failed marriage.

When he finished he felt as though he had worked free of some awful curse. He kissed her and she kissed him back. "I'd better get going," he said softly.

She clutched him to her, "Just a few minutes more, please."

■　　■　　■

Andreas Vassos sat up, looking at his travel alarm clock for the time. His eye fell on the empty wine bottle on the writing desk. He looked down at the sleeping hooker next to him and came to the painful realization that his nocturnal fantasy could not stand up to the light of day. Her mascara had run and her hair was spread out over her puffy face. He didn't even know her real name, nor did he want to know it. His self-disgust rose. The driving force of his life now should be vengeance, not self-pity. He closed his hands over his face and spoke to Soula and Stephanos, telling them that he missed them and promising them their memorial.

He felt a warm hand on his back. "I love you, Andreas," she said in Greek.

"I have to get to work," he said, playing out his macabre part.

"Make love to me, please."

"You know I can't do that."

"No one has ever loved me the way you love Soula. Just once I want to be made love to that way, just once, even if it is make-believe."

"I can't do that," he said, pushing up off the bed and going into the shower.

Businessmen entered the atrium on the Fifty-sixth Street side and walked through into the lobby of the IBM Building. Homeless men and women had already gathered around the atrium's windows to eat their inadequate breakfasts and watch Madison Avenue's human traffic. Colonel Sergei Nashin, dressed in jeans, penny loafers, and a Konstantin chamois shirt, lounged at one of the tiny wire tables, his keen interest obviously on a woman passing by in an orange sundress.

"Good morning, Sergei," Lucas said, sitting across from the KGB man. "Thanks for coming."

"I assumed it was important. Where is Comrade Ulanov?"

"On an assignment."

"We've never before met alone. Are you planning to defect?"

Lucas laughed. "Not today, comrade." He shoved a roll of photocopied papers across the table. "Here are copies of some ledgers the Greek P.D. came up with. They record the theft of art from various countries in Europe, including yours."

Picking up the roll, Nashin said, "Thanks."

"Now I need a favor."

Nashin's eyes grew wary. "If I can."

"I'd like to borrow some of your people for a surveillance job."

Disbelief was plainly evident in the Russian's face. "Your brains must have turned to borscht, my friend."

"The bad guys are the same ones who've been helping themselves to your heritage. I just thought that you'd want to be in on it in case we recover any of your goodies, including, maybe, the painting of St. Sava that's listed on one of the sheets in that roll."

Pointing the roll at Lucas, Nashin said, "Policemen stationed in foreign countries—i.e., your FBI and me—are not, repeat *not*, to engage in criminal investigations within the host country. Their function is to act as liaison in the expeditious flow of criminal information and to report on developments in investigative and forensic methods and techniques." He made a self-satisfied nod, smiled, and asked, "Why not use your own policemen?"

"My allotment's been used up. I can't trust the feds so I've got to improvise. All you'd have to do is observe and report, nothing else."

"Observe and report?"

"Correct."

"And if I see you or any of your men in a difficult situation I'm to walk away."

"Correct."

"*Хербьина*, which translated means *bullshit*."

17

arkness had spread over the city, sending a swarm of transvestites out onto the street, where they dominated their Ninth Avenue turf. A tractor-trailer turned into the avenue. A hooker hailed the driver, stepping out into the roadway, gesturing to him by sucking on her lip and reaching into her open blouse and squeezing her breasts together. The driver steered the semi to the curb and parked. The hooker ambled over. A brief conversation ensued; the hooker removed her spiked heels and climbed up into the cab.

"Love is wonderful," Lucas observed, maintaining his grim vigil at The Den. They had parked the surveillance van in front of the pizza parlor that was one door uptown from the bar.

Lucas and Vassos had been planted there for almost an hour, watching people going in and out of McKay's headquarters and the gaudily-clad hookers turning tricks. They had spent the day cooped up inside the van listening to field reports. Nina Pazza had left her hotel at eleven in the morning, spent her day shopping, and returned to the Plaza a little after six. Denny McKay passed his day closeted inside the bar. He left around seven and drove to his Christopher Street bachelor apartment, arriving there at seven-twenty. Belmont

Widener worked all day in his rare book store and retired upstairs to his living quarters a little after eight o'clock.

It was eleven P.M. when Lucas decided it was time to have a look inside McKay's headquarters. He slid off the stool and opened the equipment chest on the floor next to the communications console. He took out a pair of night surveillance binoculars, two ten-inch tubes that electro-optically amplified ambient light and used it to make green-phosphor images. It had a pistol-grip attachment, with a round, glass-fronted cylinder in front that gave out a powerful beam of infrared light and acted as a kind of invisible spotlight.

He rested the rubber eyepiece against his face and scanned the area. The building that housed the bar and the two adjoining buildings were in the same state of dilapidation. With the exception of the pizza parlor and the bar, all the windows and doors had been cinder-blocked.

Carefully scanning the area with the glasses, he saw the transvestite raise her head off the driver's lap, adjust her wig, spit a wad into a tissue, and toss the paper out the window. She climbed down out of the cab, put on her shoes, and joined her sisters on the stroll.

Lowering the glasses, Lucas turned to Vassos and said, "Those hookers make good watchdogs. I can't imagine McKay allowing them to work his turf without some kind of payback."

"McKay's Praetorians," Vassos said, watching out the other window, studying the sleazy scene. "How are we going to get in?"

"It's time to break a few rules," Lucas answered, taking an army knapsack out of the equipment locker, selecting items he thought he might need, and shoving them inside the sack. Then he moved over to the radio locker on the wall and removed two walkie-talkies, handing one to Vassos. "I'm going to need you here to protect my back. We'll communicate with these. Set the channel selector switch to three. I'm going to keep my volume control low in case there's anyone inside the building. If you have to communicate, press the transmit button three times." Lucas did that and both radios squawked each time he pressed.

Lucas returned his attention to the street. "I'll wait until all the 'ladies' are working and then make a dash for the pizza parlor."

"Why not go directly for the bar?"

"McKay is the type of guy to have some extra insurance, like a couple of hungry pit bulls. I'll go in through the pizza store, make my way up onto the roof, cross over, and go down the roof stairwell into the bar."

"How will you make it from the store up onto the roof?"

"That type of tenement generally has a door leading from the street level store into the building's vestibule."

Fifteen minutes passed.

The street had become a runway for cars and vans, for hookers getting in and out of vehicles.

"Aren't there any female hookers in this area?" Vassos asked, sitting on the stool, watching out his side of the van.

"We've got plenty of them, too," Lucas told him, "but this is a transvestite stroll. The women are around the corner."

Vassos looked out both windows. "They're all busy, go now."

Lucas remained seated. "I learned a long time ago that when you're all set to go, wait." As if to confirm his instincts, a hooker pranced out from behind a stoop and strutted over to a car that had just double-parked.

Lucas slid open the side door, turned to Vassos. "If you get anyone snooping around, press that button." He pointed to a black disk on the control monitor and slipped outside, dashing into the deeply recessed doorway.

Pressing back into the shadows, he fell to his knees and slid the knapsack off his shoulder. He took out a penlight and stuck it between his teeth, aiming the beam at the lock on the door to the pizza parlor in the ground floor of the building that stood next to The Den. He inserted a pick and began raking open the cylinder, smiling when he heard a hooker shout, "Don't hold my ears. I know my job."

The latch sprung open. He slipped inside, closing the door behind him. Reaching down to his belt, he pressed the transmit button twice.

His radio gurgled twice in response.

The dry smell of flour and rotten tomatoes filled the air. Moving cautiously, the beam roving ahead of him, he searched for the door that would lead out into the building's common stairway. Unable to find it, he knelt and threw the beam under a rack of ovens; there he saw the door. Realizing there was not enough space between the wall and the back of the ovens to squeeze through, he got down on his stomach and, pushing the knapsack ahead of him, crawled under the oven to the door. The scurrying sounds of rats made him silently swear never to eat pizza again.

There was not enough space between the back of the oven and door for him to reach up and try the doorknob. He pushed against the bottom of the door trying to get it open, but the paint of countless years had sealed it into the jamb. He opened the knapsack and, directing the penlight's beam inside, fished around until he found the fiberscope. He took it out and snaked the quarter-inch braided steel cable under the door. He fitted the eyepiece to his face and pressed the trigger.

The optical glass fibers inside the cable transmitted images from the other side. Taking hold of the bottom of the cable, he twisted the scope's optical tip. The illuminated images he saw were those of a deserted staircase cluttered with debris. He became aware of the dryness in his mouth, the annoying tickle of flour invading his nostrils, and the distracting beads of sweat rolling down from his hairline. He wiped his face against the canvas knapsack.

The pine door had a panel seven inches up from the bottom. He took out a serrated hunting knife and scored a line until he pushed the blade through the wood. He took out a battery-powered jigsaw, inserted the blade through the hole, and cut out the panel.

After dropping the satchel through to the other side, he wriggled through the hole and stood in the tomblike cold of the building's central stairway, breathing in the alkaline odor of cinder block. He punched his arm through the knapsack's harness, shouldered the load, and projecting the circle of light ahead of him, climbed the squeaking staircase to the roof.

He crossed over the parapet to the roof of the adjoining building. After checking the roof door for alarm wires and finding none, he took out the fiberscope, pushed it under the door, and cursed when he saw the cutouts in the walls and ceiling of the immaculately clean staircase. They were about the size of two packages of cigarettes, and they ringed the stairs in an infrared alarm system that sent out sensory feelers that measured movement and heat changes. No wonder the stairs are so clean, he thought. Mice could set off the alarm. Rummaging through the knapsack and not finding what he needed, he slipped the radio off his belt and pressed the transmit button three times.

Vassos answered in Greek, "Nai?" Yes.

To his surprise, Lucas found himself whispering Greek into the mouthpiece.

Leaving his equipment behind, he made his way back over and down to the pizza parlor and waited. Soon a shadow appeared, dropped something in the doorway, and was gone. Lucas reached out, grabbed the package, closed the door, and made his way back up to the roof.

He undressed down to his shorts and stepped into the neoprene wet suit, pulling the hood securely over his head and face. Neoprene, a synthetic rubber derived from acetylene and hydrochloric acid, was one of the few available ways to circumvent an infrared system, permitting a person to pass through the system undetected.

He stuck the penlight up his sleeve. He knew that he

wouldn't be able to use it because the heat from its tiny bulb would set off the alarm, but he decided to bring it anyway. He wouldn't be able to take the radio or his revolver because there was not room in the tight-fitting wet suit. Removing the hunting knife from the knapsack, he slid it up his other sleeve.

Working with the picklock and rake, he carefully unlocked the roof door leading to the staircase that went down to McKay's bar, but did not open it because he was afraid the ambient night light might be enough to set off the alarm system. Deciding he'd have to chance it, he opened the door just enough for him to slide inside. Holding his breath, he guardedly closed the door behind him. He remained perfectly still, forcing himself to adapt to his new environment. Soon he was able to make out the wall and the banister. He groped for the next step, and then the next, and the next.

He came first to the fifth-floor landing and discovered a steel fire door bolted shut. He continued down to the next level only to discover the same thing. He moved on to the third floor and was disappointed again. Groping in the dark toward the second floor, he became aware of the unmistakable odor of beer; he remembered Andreas's description of the closet in the rear of the bar that contained the staircase without stairs. Probing the space in front of him, he encountered some kind of soft material at the bottom of the flight of steps that led to the second floor. He stopped, gingerly patted the invisible material, and decided it was a curtain.

Sliding his hand over its softness until he reached the seam, he parted the material slightly, moved his hooded face to peek around to the other side, and saw that he was about to step down onto the second level above the street. It contained a landing with a bolted fire door and the stairwell of the skeletonized staircase leading down to the ground floor.

He stepped out from behind the curtain and saw that there was no alarm system. He squatted down and peered down into the light coming up from the back room of the bar. He could make out faint street sounds. The downstairs door to the closet concealing the skeletonized staircase was obviously partly open. He slipped out the penlight and cast its beam down into the stairwell, searching for an alarm system. Finding none, he got to his feet and, gripping the banister with both hands, slid his foot out onto the first riser's edge, starting down cautiously.

Reaching the bottom, he knelt, quickly assessing his surroundings. He slipped into a prone position and crawled out into the back room and then the front bar. Three transvestites were talking in the doorway just outside. There was enough light so that he did not have to use the penlight. Looking around, he could see no way of getting up to the sealed-off upper floors and decided to leave. He turned to crawl back to the staircase when he saw a dumbwaiter hatch on the wall at the end of the bar. He wiggled over to it. Lucas was about to reach up for the latch when he caught sight of something out of the corner of his eye and froze. A sudden urge to urinate caused him to stifle a moan. He lay in the unyielding stench of stale alcohol, his mouth open, his eyes wide in shock and disbelief. There, asleep on the bar's slatted floor, were the folded muscular coils of a huge boa constrictor. McKay's backup system. That crazy bastard, he screamed inwardly, recalling the street talk awhile back that some Colombian drug barons were flying in constrictors with their shipments to sell to other dealers who used them as persuaders.

Motionless, he watched the big snake, desperately trying to remember everything he knew about them. They kill their prey by crushing and suffocating them and then swallow them whole. They don't hunt often, maybe once a week or so, and most importantly, they don't move fast.

Lucas got up off the floor slowly and lifted the latch, opening the hatch and hunkering backward into the dumbwaiter.

The creature's eyes flicked open; its serpentine head coming up off its thick coil.

"Nice doggie," Lucas whispered, closing the hatch. Grabbing hold of the pulley ropes, he hoisted the cart upward.

"I gotta piss," he moaned quietly, working the ropes, positive that his bladder was about to burst.

Reaching the second-story hatch, he slid out the knife and worked the blade between the door and the jamb, pushing it upward until he caught the latch and kicked it up out of the gate. He opened the door and, peering out, saw no alarm system, so he slid out onto the floor. Working the rubberized zipper down his neoprene armor, he reached into the suit, hauled out his penis, and, emitting a long sigh, pissed into the dumbwaiter shaft.

Done, he zippered up and looked around. He was in a long narrow room that had been divided into several different work areas. Moving around the room, he saw a separate place for woodworking, another one for printing with the latest high-tech equipment, a painting section, and an area where marble was being worked on.

Brandt Industries, he thought, they steal it there and copy it here. Suddenly realizing that he had not signaled Andreas in a while, he reached for his radio but then remembered that he had been forced to leave it on the roof along with the other stuff.

His penlight beam hit a glass-enclosed office. Before entering it, he checked for wires. The big spenders wouldn't go for the money to protect every room, he thought, going inside. A rolltop desk, a filing cabinet, an illustrator's board, a photocopier, and an old-style telephone. He moved to the desk, lifted the receiver, and dialed Communications. When the police operator answered he asked to be connected to Citywide, the elite unit within the Communications Division that routes undercover and Detective Division transmissions.

"Citywide, Dolan," a gruff voice answered.

"This is Lieutenant Lucas, Sixteenth Squad. Pipe me through to surveillance van one-two-four."

"Hello?" Vassos's uncertain voice came on the line.

"How are things going?"

"Why are you telephoning instead of using the radio?"

"It's a long story. I'm inside the plant where they forge the art. They have enough equipment here to reproduce the Sphinx. How is everything on the street?"

"Busy. The prostitutes must be running a sale."

"I'm going to leave this line open while I look around," Lucas said.

Vassos spotted a pimp doing a sly sashay over to the van. He wore black leather trousers and a green shirt with the top five buttons open revealing a chest and neck bejeweled in a glittering array of nugget necklaces. The pimp tried the rear door. He opened the blade of a gravity knife and stuck it into the lock.

Vassos pushed the alarm button on the control monitor. The threatening growls of Doberman pinschers leaped from a speaker within the van; the pimp leaped back onto the side-walk and rushed away.

Lucas had found nothing of interest in the rolltop desk. The top three drawers of the file cabinet were empty; the bottom one contained a swing-hinge binder with Brandt In-dustries shipping invoices for the years 1986 and 1987. He unfastened the joints and removed the invoices. Placing four of them at a time on the duplicating machine, he spent the next forty minutes making copies. He rolled them up and stuck them into his wet suit, returned the originals to the binder, and, picking up the telephone, told Vassos that he was on his way back.

After checking out the other floors and finding nothing, he got back into the dumbwaiter and lowered himself back down to the ground floor. He opened the hatch and peeked out. "Baby" was resting behind the bar. Dozens of transvestites strolled the street; three of them were holding a conference in the bar's doorway. He knew that he'd never make it to the van without being seen. He looked at the dormant snake and thought: why not?

He slipped out of the dumbwaiter and skulked on all fours over to the door. He quietly slipped the bolt and, leaving the door slightly ajar, crawled to the back of the bar. He remembered that a shuffleboard was in the back room. He crawled into the back room and picked up four of the disks. Rolling one of them into the barroom, he crooned, "Meow, meow, meow." The metal disk thudded into the bar stool and toppled over onto its side. He rolled another one.

Without warning the serpentine head popped up over the bar, swaying in the dark, seeking out its prey.

Lucas rolled another one. The snake's homing system zeroed in on the disk and its long, thick body flowed over the bar to the floor, slithering toward the sound.

"That mother wanted me to take it in the ass for twenty dollars. 'Honey,' I said, 'my ass is worth fifty,' " a hooker with orange hair was telling her sisters.

One with a rhinestone-studded blouse and short shorts confessed, "I did my golden shower trick tonight. That man just loves it when I pass my pissin' dick over his face. And he told me . . . what's that on the ground? Oho-1-ooo-ooooo!"

"Nooooooooo!"

"Uuummmmmmmmm aaaaahhhhhhhnnnnn."

Their ghastly, panic-stricken screams reverberated across the avenue, setting off a wave of hysteria that sent the hookers fleeing, littering the street with an assortment of shoes, wigs, pocketbooks, and broken pint bottles of booze. The boa constrictor slithered out into the bar's doorway and arranged its muscular coils, its green diamond-backed eyes watching.

Steam misted the tiles. Lucas drew a line through the condensation and slipped deeper into the water, relaxing his head against the rim.

He laughed when he thought about the snake caper; it was the kind of tale that added to the Job's folklore.

After making his way back to the van, they had had to wait ten minutes for Emergency Service to come and gather up Baby in a snake bag for delivery to the animal shelter. Lucas was sure that McKay would blame one of his people for leaving the door open. Then they went back to the office so that Lucas could read the fives on the day's surveillances. All negative reports. But that didn't discourage him. Every cop bone in his body told Lucas that Nina Pazza was taking her time sanitizing herself; she'd come to New York for a meet and wanted to make sure she didn't have any guardian angels hovering nearby.

After going over the fives, Lucas and Vassos gave the surveillance units a "see." They were all on station. Elisabeth Syros and the Greek contingent were covering Belmont Widener. At 1:15 A.M. two Soviet policemen relieved Ulanov and Gregory at the Plaza Hotel.

At one-thirty in the morning, after parking the van in the Sixteenth Precinct's garage, Lucas and Vassos stopped off at Heidi's for a quick taste. They found the owner, Ulanov, Gregory, and Sergei Nashin together in a back booth doing a number on a bottle of Russian vodka.

A fast reading of the scene told Lucas that the impromptu party had all the makings of an all-night session. He had promised Katina that he would come to her place as soon as he was finished and fill her in on what happened. He had one fast drink and said good night, leaving Vassos and Sergei corkscrewing on the dance floor, whooping what he assumed were Cossack war cries. Making for the door, Lucas heard Vassos call out, "One day you will dance, my friend."

Katina had greeted him in a pale pink nightgown and panties. She rushed into his arms, her tongue searching his mouth. He pulled up her nightgown and they made love on the floor, and then they got up and went into the bedroom and loved again.

Afterward, locked in a lovers' embrace, he told her about his day and how he had bent the rules.

"I don't want to lose you, Theodorous," she said.

"You're not going to." Reluctantly, he got off her bed and went into the bathroom.

Lucas reached out and picked up a plastic bottle: ESSENCE OF LILAC BATH GEL. He unscrewed the cap and poured the contents into the tub, stirring the water to make bubbles and causing waves of water to splash over the rim of the tub and make puddles on the floor.

Reaching up, he yanked down two towels from the rack. He leaned over the rim, soaked up the water, and left the towels in a sodden heap on the floor.

A soft knock came to the bathroom door. "Theodorous, may I come in, I need my makeup remover."

"Of course."

"Theodorous!" she said, stepping inside. "You've made a flood."

He made a weak-hearted shrug and sank below the water. When he surfaced he found her on her knees mopping up the floor with towels. "You don't look like the Morgan's Curator of Ancient and Medieval Manuscripts."

"Lieutenant, we have to have a talk."

"I'm sorry," he said, grabbing down the remaining towel and, standing, drying himself. He stepped out of the tub and, kneeling down beside her, mopped. "Is this what they mean by a meaningful relationship?"

She hurled a look of feigned anger his way and said, "I think so."

He worked his way behind her and lifted her bathrobe and nightgown.

She stopped wiping, remained on her knees.

"You're beautiful," he said, guiding his finger over the crescent opening between her legs.

"You make me feel alive again," she moaned, resting her face on the toilet lid, undulating against him and gasping when he opened her body and mounted her.

18

Belmont Widener daintily spread his fingers and admired his fresh manicure while Claude, the owner of the exclusive and ridiculously expensive Madison Avenue salon, styled his hair. Widener paid no attention to the woman who slipped into the adjacent chair. Elisabeth Syros hitched up her jeans and crossed her legs, revealing the Mayan design carved into the sides of her cowboy boots. She threw up her arms, letting her many bracelets slide down to her elbows, and said to her stylist, "Just a trim, please."

Denny McKay crashed his fist on the table and shouted, "I lost my fucking snake because one of you dumb cocksuckers left the door open."

The two men sitting in the same booth with McKay looked at each other uneasily.

Three other men were sitting on bar stools nearby. One gazed vacantly into the faded mirror, the second hunched silently over the copper-topped bar, and the third, a man called Patty Guts, sat with his back to the bar, his arms folded across his stomach, watching McKay's every gesture.

"I'll get you another snake, Denny, a bigger one," the man known as Bubblebelly promised, wiping beads of sweat from his upper lip.

"Yeah, Denny, a bigger one," the other man in the booth said. His name was Pussy Lyne.

"Make sure that the door is locked from now on, understand?" McKay growled.

"Yeah, Denny, I'll see to it," Pussy Lyne said meekly.

McKay studied the two men. "The take from the docks is off this week. You guys wouldn't be playing games, would you?"

"No. Denny, I swear," Bubblebelly said. "A few of the longshoremen came up short with their vig."

"One of them is three weeks behind," Pussy Lyne added.

"Three weeks," McKay repeated, thoughtfully pursing his lips and nodding slowly. "I want you two to employ some modern collection techniques with the hump who is three weeks late. Chop off his leg below the knee."

"Below the knee?" Bubblebelly questioned.

"Yeah," McKay said. "That way they can stick a peg leg on and send him back to work so he can play catch-up with the vig."

"Good advertising too, Denny," Pussy Lyne said with real enthusiasm. "They'll think twice before they miss a payment."

McKay lit a cigarette and bit down on the filter. "I want you to ask around. I'm looking for a decorative painter who can do gold leaf, French lacquer, marbleizing, and graining."

Bubblebelly started to say something when the front door flew open. Beams of sunlight outlined the silhouetted figure of a policeman standing in the opening, his hat cocked rakishly to the side, his hand menacingly close to the grip of his service revolver. Conversation inside the bar ceased; only Julio Iglesias continued to sing "Ron y Coca-Cola" from the old-style jukebox. Obviously and regally drunk, the policeman walked into the bar, his head high and his steps carefully measured.

"He's drunk outta his fuckin' gourd," Bubblebelly hissed.

McKay said nothing. He sat chewing his cigarette, his suspicious eyes locked on the approaching policeman.

"I gotta take a leak," the policeman mumbled with a booze-thickened tongue and then stumbled, falling across McKay's table.

Pussy Lyne jumped out of his seat and helped the officer off the table and onto his feet. The policeman shook a wrathful finger at the bartender. "Your floor is dirty. I oughta give you one for maintaining a licensed premises in an unsanitary condition." He staggered into the toilet and slammed the door.

Standing before the urinal, the policeman pulled an evidence envelope from inside his summer shirt and deposited the cigarette butts he had palmed when he staged his fall. He remained inside the stinking room for another moment and then left, weaving slightly as he crossed the sawdust-covered floor. Outside a patrol car and a bored-looking driver waited for him. "Let's go," the policeman said to the other cop, sliding into the recorder's seat in front of the radio set. The cop behind the wheel eased the transmission into drive and the police car slid away from the curb.

The recorder picked up the handset. "Sixteen Adam to Central, K."

"Go, Adam."

"Time check Central."

"Twelve forty-six Adam."

"Ten-four." The recorder wrote the certified time in the space provided on the evidence envelope and radioed: "Central, Sixteen Adam has left the licensed premises. We're still ten sixty-one, precinct assignment. We should be back in service in about five minutes."

"Ten-four, Adam."

The blue-and-white cruised down Ninth Avenue, turning west on Forty-fifth, continuing until Tenth Avenue, where it pulled over to the curb where Teddy Lucas was waiting.

"How'd it go?" the Whip asked the recorder.

"I'm ready for the big time, Lou," the raw-boned cop said, giving the evidence envelope to the lieutenant.

"I'll give you a receipt," Lucas said.

The recorder pulled his black, leather-bound memo book

off the dashboard, wrote out a receipt under the last entry, radioed Central for the certified time, and made it a part of his entry along with their current location. He wrote down the names and shield numbers of those present and passed the official log out to the lieutenant.

Lucas signed his name on the consecutively numbered page below the officer's signature, handing the log back to him and asking, "What about the transmitter?"

The raw-boned cop casually tossed his log back on the dashboard. "When I fell I slipped it under the table."

"Thanks, guys," Lucas said.

"All part of the J-O-B, Lou," the recorder said, grabbing the handset and transmitting, "Sixteen Adam is now ten ninety-eight Central, resuming patrol."

"They're gonna chop off some guy's leg," Ulanov said, his big frame crouched on a stool in front of the surveillance van's communication center.

McKay's voice had come through the speakers with a slight scratch of static.

"Like the man said," Gregory intoned, "ye reap what ye fuckin' sow, bro."

The van was parked on Ninth and Fiftieth. Lucas drove back from his meet with the two policemen in one of the department's latest unmarked cars, a Jeep Cherokee. He parked on Fifty-first Street off Ninth and walked over to the surveillance unit. Entering the van by the side entrance, he stopped once he was inside. Glancing at Vassos's tired face, he asked, "How late did you guys hang out last night?"

"Too late," Vassos moaned. "That Russian loves to dance."

Threading a telescopic lens onto a camera, Gregory complained, "My head feels like there are a lot of strange things dancing around inside."

Lucas sat down on the bench that ran along one side of the van. "You guys pick up on the assault they're planning?"

"Yeah, we heard," Ulanov said. "Some guy's gonna lose a part of his leg because he didn't pay his weekly vig."

"Phone in a sixty-one on McKay, conspiracy to commit assault one. Maybe Sergeant Grimes will be able to turn one of them," Lucas said, not really believing it. He looked at the detectives. "Can you guys handle it from here on?"

"No problem, Lou," Gregory said.

"I want you to stay in radio contact with me. Andreas and I are going to be jumping back and forth between units. Do you have the list of call numbers?"

Ulanov consulted the pad in front of him. "You're Mobile One. Leone and Elisabeth are Mobile Two and they're covering Widener. Big Jay's Mobile Three and he's on Pazza. We're Mobile Four and we're on McKay. The comrades are Mobile Five and they're late-tour reliefs."

"Correct. Remember that Sergei and his crew do not come out until tonight," Lucas said.

"Do the Russians have radios?" Gregory asked.

"Yes," Lucas said, "I gave Sergei two sets last night." He leaned forward in his seat, resting his elbows on his knees. "Listen up. I split the other teams, assigning a Greek with Big Jay and Leone, but I kept you together because you're going to be on McKay. You're to observe and report, nothing more. No hero stuff. Understand?"

"We understand, Lou," Ulanov said.

"Do you have heavy weapons?" Lucas asked.

"Shotguns and Uzis," Gregory said, pointing to the weapons locker bolted to the wall.

"McKay and his friends are bad people. Don't take any chances," Lucas said firmly.

"We won't," Gregory assured him.

Ten minutes later Lucas and Vassos slid into the blue Jeep with the smoked windows.

"Where did you get this?" Vassos asked.

"Motor Transport. It comes equipped with all sorts of high-tech goodies."

"Thank you for going out on a limb and planting that transmitter in the bar. I know you could be making trouble for yourself, not having a search warrant."

" 'S'all right, we didn't need a warrant." He started the engine, checked traffic.

Vassos was confused. "I thought . . ."

"We can turn a public place into a Hollywood sound stage if we have to," Lucas said, driving out of the parking space. "Nina Pazza has a right to privacy in her hotel room, but The Den is a public place. The courts have held there's no expectation of privacy in a public place."

"All your laws aren't so stupid, are they?"

"Not all of them," Lucas agreed, turning up the volume control on the police band radio under the dashboard.

Belmont Widener bought a pair of loafers at Gucci. He left the Fifth Avenue store and walked north. At Fifty-sixth Street he entered Trump Tower's marble lobby and strolled through the gleaming center hall, idly glancing at the expensive things for sale in the gold-plated display cases on either side. He paused to admire the cascading waterfall, occasionally glancing sideways at the crisscrossing escalators.

Elisabeth Syros, who had changed into a white spaghetti-strapped sundress in the back of a Mykonos Fruit Store delivery truck, was examining a gold necklace in the Blantree and Company jewelry store to the right of the waterfall. Detective John Leone, riding the up escalator, had one eye on Widener and the other on the shapely ass of the woman standing in front of him.

Nina Pazza stepped off the elevator inside the Plaza Hotel's lobby and paused to look at a diamond necklace in the display window of Black, Starr and Frost, Ltd. She stared at the glittering gems for a minute or so before she made her way through the lobby to the entrance of the Palm Court, the hotel's unenclosed restaurant separated from the lobby by a low wall made up of flowers and palms set in large Chinese vases. She had a brief conversation with the maître d' and was escorted to a table.

A string quartet played Brahms against the background

noises of tinkling silver and glassware and the polite hum of muted conversation.

Big Jay, sitting in one of the lobby's armchairs, turned to Christos, his newly assigned partner, and said, "Looks like the lady is going to have lunch."

Christos, a fat little man squeezed into an ill-fitting, European-cut suit, leaned close to confide, "I'd love to feel her warm lips around me."

"Broads like that only suck cocks attached to wallets," Big Jay said, adjusting the tiny receiver in his ear. He inclined his head slightly and spoke into the microphone concealed by his jacket. "The lady is having lunch."

Lucas's voice came over the surveillance network: "Mobile Two, location of your subject, K?"

Leone, who had just followed Belmont Widener out into the street, radioed, "Leaving Trump Tower, walking north on Fifth, K."

Lucas: "All units, it's going down. Mobile Three, K."

Big Jay: "Mobile Three standing by, K."

Lucas: "Mobile Three, do you have a magnetic transmitter, K?"

Big Jay: "Negative, K."

Lucas: "Mobile Three, have your partner ten eighty-five this unit in three minutes at CPS entrance."

Big Jay: "Ten-four Mobile One."

Christos was standing on the hotel's steps when the Jeep Cherokee jerked to a stop behind a double-parked Rolls Royce. Lucas honked the horn. Christos rushed over to the Jeep, held a short conversation in Greek with Vassos, took the disk from Lucas, and hurried back up the steps, disappearing inside the hotel.

Big Jay surveyed the scene. The maître d' was busy checking the reservation book while a line of five people patiently waited to be seated. Nina Pazza was seated near the quartet, at a square marble-topped table.

"Wait here," Big Jay told his partner, and moved toward the restaurant. He passed the headwaiter, pretending to wave to a friend. Nina Pazza, elegantly turned out in a pink dress with matching accessories and a short-brimmed straw hat, was too busy watching the violinist to notice the man who stopped next to her table and tied his shoelace.

Big Jay: "Mobile One, K."
Lucas: "Mobile One standing by, K."
Big Jay: "Down and dirty, K."
Lucas: "Ten-four."

Lucas turned to reach into the supply box; he removed a receiver. He set it down on the console between the front seats and adjusted the sensitivity selector switch to screen out all low-level noises. He reached back into the supply box again and took out a maxi-powered mini tape recorder and plugged the attachment cord into the receiver.

"I have never seen one that small," Vassos commented.

Resting his head against the seat's headrest while he listened to the incoming transmission, Lucas said, "It weighs three and a half ounces."

"Nina, darling, you look absolutely stunning," Widener said, brushing her cheek with his lips.

"So do you, Belmont."

"Have you ordered?"

"I'm having the salmon."

"I think I'll have the grilled swordfish," he said, after studying the menu.

"Belmont, will you please tell me what is going on?"

"Whatever do you mean?"

"Orhan and Trevor. That is what I mean," she said angrily.

"I honestly don't know, Nina."

The waiter came to take their orders.

Elisabeth Syros walked into the hotel's main entrance. Leone entered on the Central Park South side.

■   ■   ■

Widener took his handkerchief out of his breast pocket and dabbed at his face with it. "The American and Greek police are interested in Alexander's *Iliad*."

Her eyes grew cold. "Are you sure?"

"They paid me a visit. A lieutenant from New York, a major from Athens, and a woman from the Morgan Library. They were checking out the major dealers to see if we'd heard anything about the casket-copy coming onto the market."

"And had you?"

"No. I was also questioned about my Aristarchus commentary. It was taken from me during a robbery a long time ago." Sipping water from his glass, he added, "One of the robbers was caught. Did you know that?"

"I'd heard."

"His name was Bucky McMahon. At his arraignment the DA informed me McMahon and Denny McKay were, er, friends."

She looked down at her place setting, perplexed.

"It would be a real coup for some collector to possess both the commentary and the casket-copy."

"Yes, I imagine it would be."

"I love your hat."

"Thank you."

"Would you know anyone who might be interested in both of them?"

"No one that I can think of," she said, reaching for her water glass.

He unfolded his napkin and carefully spread it out over his lap. "He wants to see you, tonight."

"How does he look?" she asked quietly.

"Don't be so gloomy, Nina. He looks wonderful, and he's anxious to be with you again."

"Where and when?"

"Your room, around nine. Ah, here comes our lunch."

19

obile Two, your location, K?" Lucas radioed.

Leone, who had tailed Belmont Widener to the Plaza, radioed back: "In lobby with Mobile Three, K."

Lucas: "Mobile Three, your subject's room number, K?"

Big Jay: "Four-oh-two, K."

Lucas: "Mobile Two and Three, buy me twenty minutes, K."

Big Jay looked into the Palm Court, saw Widener and Nina Pazza deep in conversation, and radioed: "You got it, K."

Lucas opened the Jeep's door. Vassos grabbed his arm, stopping him. "I'll go with you."

"I need you here to monitor transmissions and to see that the tape recorder is working," Lucas said.

"You're going to break some more rules," Vassos said with a knowing grin.

"One or two little ones."

"Then I will go with you."

"Stay here, *pahrahkahlo*." Please.

Vassos looked down at the slow-moving reel and said, reluctantly, "Nai."

■   ■   ■

Lucas got off the elevator at the fourth floor and walked quickly down the carpeted corridor checking room numbers. This was going to be one of those times when expediency dictated police action. Approaching Pazza's room, he saw the chambermaid's supply cart and brightened at the thought of not having to use the set of picklocks that he had brought along with him. The door to room 402 was open; the maid was busy vacuuming the bedroom, her back to the entrance.

Lucas slipped inside the room and ducked into the hall closet. Listening to the drone of the vacuum, he smelled a woman's perfume all around him. His hand groped in the darkness and encountered a light cotton raincoat that gave off a strong aroma of evergreen. He thought of Katina and realized how much he wanted to be with her.

The droning stopped. He heard movements outside, a rustling sound, a door closing, and then silence. He stepped outside and found himself in a small entry foyer that opened into an attractive suite of rooms. The pale pink bedroom was off to the right of the living room. He moved around, studying the layout, resisting the temptation to search. Walking into the bedroom, he thought: she's neat. Frilly undergarments hung drying above the tub.

Seeing what he had come to see, he left, rode the elevator down to the lobby, and, stepping out, walked straight over to the reservation desk.

"May I help you, sir?" asked the clerk at the desk.

"Yes, my wife and I are in town for a few days, and we wondered if room 400 was available for tonight. You see, we spent our wedding night there and, well, you understand," Lucas said.

"Of course, sir," the clerk said, looking down and punching keys on the desk computer keyboard. Watching the screen, he smiled and said cheerfully, "I can let you have room 400 for one night, but you'll have to be out tomorrow."

"That will be fine," Lucas said, sliding the department credit card across the counter.

▪   ▪   ▪

"Exigent circumstances" meant conditions requiring secrecy because there was a reasonable likelihood that a continuing investigation would be compromised if any of the persons under surveillance became aware of it. Lucas had looked it up in his manual on criminal procedure law.

After he left the hotel, Lucas went back to the Jeep and radioed all mobile units to stay on their subjects. He told Andreas to remain with the monitoring equipment and caught a taxi back to the Squad.

In the squad room he spent several minutes going over reports with the Second Whip. He then closeted himself in his office with copies of the *Code of Criminal Procedure,* the *Detective Guide,* and the *Investigators' Eavesdropping Handbook.* He did not intend to allow anyone in the Legal Bureau to tell him he didn't have sufficient probable cause for a wire, not this time.

He decided that he could claim "exigent circumstances," and went on to read the CPL's definition of probable cause. He read that an eavesdropping warrant could be issued only when one of the crimes designated in section 700.05 was being, had been, or would be committed by a particularly described individual. He read the long list of crimes, picking out several in his mind that applied to the case.

Lucas got up and went over to the form cabinet. He ran his finger over the dog-eared index thumbtacked to the inside of the door. Reaching into pigeonhole eleven, he pulled out Form 26:1—Eavesdropping Warrant.

He rolled the typewriter stand over to his desk, inserted the warrant application into the machine, spread out the case folder and the reference books on his desk, and, with a pencil firmly gripped between his teeth, started typing, saying aloud: "Once upon a time . . ."

At five-forty that evening a black van with a dish antenna on its shiny roof was parked on Central Park South, across the street from the Plaza.

"There they are," Lucas said, pointing to the van and pushing the Jeep's door open. He slipped around the end of a slow-moving, horse-drawn hansom cab and hurried over to the black van. When he got inside the department's special project mobile unit Lucas was met by two detectives dressed in dungarees.

"Lieutenant Lucas?" inquired the shorter of the two.

"Yes."

"I'm Covington, and this is Schwartz. Can I see your warrant, Lou?"

Lucas handed him the search warrant.

"Looks in order," Covington said, taking down a number four ledger from the shelf and making a long entry that included the date the warrant was issued, the name of the authorizing magistrate, and any time limitations specified in the warrant. "You understand, Lou, that you cannot record privileged communications. If the subject's lawyer or clergyman shows up, you must terminate."

"I understand."

"Sign here," Covington said, handing him a Receipt for Equipment form.

Schwartz picked up a suitcase from the floor and handed it to Lucas. "You know how to do the installation, Lou?"

"I know how," Lucas said.

Room 400 was the twin of 402. The detectives entered quickly. Lucas tossed the suitcase on the sofa. Vassos closed the shades and switched on the lights. Lucas opened the suitcase and removed a high-speed drill.

He inserted a bit into the chuck and looked around the suite, getting his bearings. The bedroom wall of room 400 was the living room wall of 402. He went into the bedroom, removed the lamp from the night table, and climbed up on it, turning to Vassos and saying, "Find out where she is."

Vassos: "Mobile One to Mobile Three, K."

Big Jay: "Standing by, K."

Vassos: "Subject's location, K?"

Big Jay: "Beauty parlor, K."

Standing on the night table, Lucas drilled a hole high up in the wall, pressing on the bit until he broke through the plaster on the other side. Vassos handed him the pinhole lens, an instrument about five inches long with an eighth of an inch lens at one end and telephone wires on the other. He took the jar of lubricant jelly from Vassos, greased the sides of the lens, and worked the instrument into the hole until it was about a sixteenth of an inch from the pinhole opening on the other side of the wall.

Vassos handed him a black box, a metal container about the size of a package of one hundred-length cigarettes that contained the camera's omnidirectional antenna. After he attached the lens wires to the box, Lucas got down off the table and went back into the living room.

He removed the microwave-receiving video recorder from the suitcase and set it down on the coffee table in front of the sofa. He switched on the machine and watched as the interior of suite 402 appeared on the screen.

Bubblebelly and Pussy Lyne strolled out of The Den, followed almost immediately by McKay and Patty Guts. It was after seven and the remaining sun gave no hint of the twilight soon to fall. McKay looked up and down Ninth Avenue, the others waiting silently and making a loose circle around him.

His instincts told him that something was wrong. His eyes narrowed as he scanned the street; McKay couldn't quite put his finger on what was out of place. Then he saw the van parked diagonally across the street, WARSHOW ELECTRIC COM-PANY stenciled on its side panel. He lit a cigarette, and stared at the dark glass set in the van's side. "Wait here," he told the others and strolled off by himself, looking across at the stationary vehicle.

"He's made the van," Ulanov announced.

"Looks that way," Gregory said, calmly taking two mini Uzis from the gun locker and handing one to his partner. The

detectives clicked thirty-two-round magazines into the guns'
housings, unfolded the metal stocks, and slid the selector
switches to full automatic. "Keep your eyes peeled," Ulanov
said, spinning around on the stool and transmitting, "Mobile
Four to Mobile One, K."

Lucas and Vassos were relaxing on the sofa when Ulanov's
transmission came over the network.

Lucas sprang forward, grabbing up the walkie-talkie from
the table. "Mobile One. Go, Mobile Four, K."

"They made us, K."

"You sure, K?"

"Pretty sure, K. Wait. Our boy is walking away, K."

McKay strolled back past his men, stopping at the open-
front pizza parlor. "Hey, Giuseppi, or whatever the fuck your
name is, how long's that van been parked there?"

The pie maker stuck his head out, looking. He studied the
van and made an open-palmed gesture: How should I know?

"Terrific," McKay growled. "I got a blind pizza maker protecting my rear. That's terrific." He ambled back to his men.
"Bubblebelly, I want you and Pussy to get a few of the boys
and make swiss cheese out of that van."

Bubblebelly and Pussy Lyne walked back inside the bar.

Watching through the one-way glass, Gregory said, "I believe they're planning a surprise for us."

Lucas: "Mobile Four, what is your condition, K?"

Before Ulanov could radio his answer, Sergei Nashin's
voice burst upon the network speaking in Russian. "Comrade
Ulanov, two of my associates and I are on the way, K."

"No unauthorized transmission," Central radioed. "This is
a restricted frequency. Stay off this frequency."

"*Пососи мой хуй!*" Nashin transmitted.

"Such language," Ulanov radioed in Russian.

"No unauthorized transmissions," Central blared.

"Mobile One to Mobile Four, hightail it out of there, K."

"Ten-four, Mobile One."

Bubblebelly, Pussy Lyne, and three other men rushed out

of the bar carrying shotguns hastily concealed in brown wrapping paper only to see the van driving off down Ninth Avenue.

"You want we should get our cars and go after them, Denny?" Pussy Lyne asked.

"Naw. Let 'em go. Me and Patty got something to do. You guys hang out until we get back."

Nashin: "Mobile Five to Mobile One, K."
Lucas: "Go Mobile Five, K."
Nashin: "We have McKay in view. Do you want us to stay with him, K?"
Lucas: "Affirmative, K. You're early."
Nashin: "We were bored, K."
Lucas: "Remember, Mobile Five, observe and report, nothing more, K."
Nashin: "Ten-four, y'all."

Denny McKay and Patty Guts waited in the West Fiftieth Street station for the E train.

Hearing the thundering rumble coming from the tunnel, they stepped back from the edge of the platform and watched the train come to a squealing stop. The doors opened; passengers pushing their way out of the train collided with the hordes shoving into the train. Patty Guts made a hole in the crowd for McKay and himself.

The door struggled closed; the train pulled out of the station. Twenty-one minutes later the E train stopped at the World Trade Center, and the two men joined in with the crowd flowing into the vast underground complex leading to the PATH trains and the twin towers.

They entered one of the arcade's open cafés and sat down, Patty Guts ordering cappuccino for both of them. McKay scanned the crowd, looking for a familiar face or a pair of eyes that wouldn't meet his.

McKay gulped down his cappuccino and said to Patty Guts,

"Wait here." Leaving his bodyguard, McKay walked into the massive lobby of One World Trade Center and took the elevator up to the 107th floor. Stepping out into the Cellar in the Sky restaurant, he moved down the steps into the cocktail lounge and sat at the bar. He ordered a scotch on the rocks.

Clinking ice cubes, he turned on his stool and examined the faces of people in the bar, pausing only once to look out through the glass wall at the panorama of the city far below. Satisfied that he had not been followed, he paid the tab and rode the elevator down to the first floor.

Working his way to the front of the car so that he would be among the first to exit, McKay rushed out on the ground floor, turning to watch the faces of the other departing riders. He waited near the elevator bank for five more minutes before he walked over to Two World Trade Center, darted into the oversized elevator car, and rode up to the 107th floor, where he stepped out onto the open-air viewing platform.

He moved slowly, momentarily absorbed by the breathtaking view. Then he spied a solitary man who was leaning forward on an ivory-handled cane. He was well dressed and wore a golden ring.

McKay slowly approached and stood next to him. "The cops were watching my place in a surveillance van," he whispered, gazing off into the distance.

"Is that unusual? I would think that they would always be keeping an eye on people like you."

"Yeah, that's true, but now, with all that's going on, and in a van, I thought it might be something to be concerned about."

"Anything else out of the ordinary?"

"A few minor things," McKay said. "Someone left the door of my place open and my snake got out. The counter on the copying machine was unexplainably high. I figure one of my guys used it for something personal."

"We've been careful, Denny. I don't think we have a problem. Still, it's wise to look over your shoulder now and then."

Two men moved up and stood next to them. McKay and his friend stopped talking. One of the newcomers took out a cigarette and lighted it with a gold-trimmed butane lighter that concealed a modified Minox 16mm camera. The other newcomer pointed to something off in the distance and said something in Russian. The one with the butane lighter nodded his head in acknowledgment and said, "Da, da."

Moving out of earshot of the two strangers, McKay said, "Whaddaya gonna do about our lady friend?"

"I'm going to debrief her about what is happening in Greece and then I'm going to offer her Orhan's job."

"Do you think she can handle it?"

"Yes, I believe she can."

"You're the boss."

He looked at McKay. "Yes, I am."

20

ina Pazza had returned to her room a few minutes past six. She undressed and padded into the bathroom and took a bath. Then she put her bathrobe on and moved into the bedroom. She set the clock for seven-thirty and fell asleep. When the alarm went off she got up and slipped out of her robe, dropping it on the foot of the bed. She admired her naked, gleaming body in the full-length mirror, turning sideways to look at her buttocks and deriving satisfaction from the firmness of her thighs. She spread her legs and pinched her inner thigh. "Disgusting," she said with an ironic grin. She went into the bathroom to wash her face and put on her makeup.

"That lady has a great body," Lucas observed, watching the video screen.
"She certainly has," Vassos agreed.

Nina went back into the bedroom and stepped into fresh panties. She took a bra from the dresser and was hooking the front together when she had second thoughts. She removed her brassiere and returned it to the drawer. Standing erect in front of the mirror, she caressed her firm breasts, gently kneading her nipples. Moving to the closet, she reached inside and took out a white cotton jumpsuit.

. . .

Lucas: "Mobile Three, your location, K?"

Big Jay: "In the lobby, covering exits, K."

Lucas: "Mobile Four, your location, K?"

Ulanov: "Parked across street, covering front entrance, K."

Lucas: "Mobile Two, your location, K?"

Leone: "We followed subject back to bookstore, K."

Lucas: "Mobile Two, leave that location and respond back here. Cover CPS entrance of hotel, K."

Leone: "Ten-four."

Lucas: "Mobile Five, your location, K?"

No response.

Lucas: "Mobile Five, do you read this unit, K?"

Static.

"Perhaps they're not in a position to transmit," Vassos said.

"I hope it's nothing more than that," Lucas said, watching Nina get up out of her seat to answer a knock at the door.

"How have you been, Nina?" he asked, giving her a perfunctory kiss on her cheek as he moved past her into the room. It was 9:03. He was always punctual.

She made no response other than to throw herself on the sofa and sulk. She drew her arms tightly across her stomach and glared at the tall, sinewy man as he moved around checking the room out with almost excessive caution.

"Damn!" Lucas exclaimed, watching Paul Mastri, the rare book dealer, lean his cane up against the side of the sofa and hand a gift-wrapped package to Nina.

"A present," Mastri said in a quiet, pleasant voice.

She looked away, avoiding his eyes. "No, thank you."

He gently turned her face toward him. "Please."

She unceremoniously snatched the gift from his hand and ripped off the wrapping to discover a small oil painting.

She sat down next to her. "A landscape by Il Grechetto. Signed and dated 1650." He leaned close to her, scratching his upper lip with his finger. "You do know who Il Grechetto was, don't you?"

She slapped his face. "You bastard!"

He grabbed her hand. "I thought you would like it, after all, Giovanni Castiglione was your mother's favorite."

She threw the painting down on the cushion. "I hate you." The tears came, and then the sobs, and she fell crying against her father's chest, remaining there while he gently stroked her hair.

Suddenly she recoiled from his caresses and ran crying into the bathroom. A few minutes passed before she returned, her makeup reapplied, hair combed. She lowered herself back down into her seat. "Why did you kill Orhan?" she demanded angrily.

He sighed and dismissed her question with a wave of his hand. "Orhan suffered from a life-threatening malady: greed. He wanted me to sell our birthright and share the money with him."

"And the Aristarchus commentary? I thought Belmont was your friend; but you told your goons to steal it from him."

"Friend? That is a middle-class word that does not apply to people like us. The commentary helps authenticate Alexander's *Iliad*. I've been collecting everything that has to do with the casket-copy since my father died. I had no intention of letting Belmont know I was interested in it. His big mouth would have blabbed it all over the art world."

"You trust him enough to do business with him."

"Business is one thing, our heritage is another."

"I want none of it."

He grabbed her shoulders, forcing her to face him. "Your grandfather spent his life and his fortune searching for the casket-copy. The world laughed at him. Well, I took up his search. I gave up my name, my own face, everything so that I could reclaim our birthright—and you dare to sit there and tell me you want none of it? I brought you into the family business because I thought you were intelligent enough to comprehend how important the casket-copy is to us. To me! Damn it, it's mine. I earned it!"

"Please," she said, removing one of his hands.

He opened his mouth to say something when he noticed a few whitish flakes on the floor. Mastri reached for his cane and rose slowly. Moving over to the wall, he knelt, examining the small mound of plaster on the dark red carpet. He stood, backing away from the wall. Using the tip of his cane as a pointer, he prodded the wall suspiciously.

"What is it?" Nina asked, concern growing in her voice.

Mastri's features clouded with anger. "I think the Plaza has mice, my dear." Suddenly he stuck the pinhole viciously with his cane.

"He might try to escape through the connecting door. You take that, I'll take the door to his room," Lucas said, transmitting as he ran, "Mobile Two, Three, Four—ten eighty-five, forthwith."

"Three on the way," Big Jay radioed as he and Christos made for the elevator.

"Mobile Two," Leone shouted into the mouthpiece, making for the stairs with Elisabeth.

"Mobile Four coming," Ulanov radioed as Gregory swerved the surveillance van across Fifth Avenue, down Fifty-eighth Street, and made a sharp right turn into Grand Army Plaza, followed by a hard left that made the van go partway up the hotel's steps. As shocked guests watched, Gregory leaped down from the van and ran into the lobby, followed almost immediately by Ulanov, who had lingered only long enough to lock up the van.

Lucas ran out into the corridor, his revolver drawn. With his back to the wall, he reached out and tried the doorknob of Nina Pazza's room. It was locked. "Open up, Mastri. Police!" Lucas backed away and smashed his foot just above the knob. It did not give, so he kicked it again.

At the same moment, Vassos threw open the connecting door of his room and tried Nina Pazza's. It was locked. Drawing his automatic, he ran back into the room to gain momentum and hurled himself at the closed door. His body struck just as the door was jerked open from the inside, catapulting the policeman into the room. The cane sword smashed its way into his mouth, then went clean through to the brain. Both his eyes filled with blood; gasping, he blew a spray of blood through his nostrils and out his mouth. Through a crimson haze he saw Soula and Stephanos waving to him. He called out their names and ran to meet them.

Paul Mastri rushed into the policemen's room. Ignoring the video setup, he stood by the door, listening, waiting.

Lucas finally crashed into Pazza's room, his weapon at the ready. An unexpected, numbing dread seized him; then a piercing howl exploded from his mouth when he saw Vassos. He stumbled over to his fallen friend, automatically feeling for a pulse; there was none.

He stared in mute agony at Andreas's body, at the head propped on the sword handle, the smeared blade sticking out of the back of his head, the blood pouring onto the carpet and pooling in a dark circle. He should have taken the connecting door, sent Andreas through the front. Slowly the cloud began to clear and he became aware of sounds behind him. He turned and saw Nina curled up on the sofa in a fetal position, wrenching sobs coming from her distorted mouth.

In a state of shock, he automatically slipped his handcuffs from his belt and, leaning toward her, cuffed her right hand to her left leg. Only then did he kneel next to Andreas and begin to weep.

Paul Mastri had waited until he heard a crash against his hotel room's main door; he ran out into the corridor, headed for the fire exit. Rushing down the stairs, he heard the commotion of people coming up so he darted out of the stairwell onto the third floor. He pressed for the elevator and serenely stepped into it when it arrived. He got off in the lobby to find it a sea of shouting confusion and calmly walked from the hotel, using the Central Park South exit.

• • •

Big Jay and Christos rushed into the room. "Oh, my God!" Big Jay exclaimed, falling to his knees next to Lucas. "Lou, you okay?"

The Whip ignored him.

"Lou! You okay?" Big Jay repeated, shaking the Whip's shoulder.

Leone ran into the room, followed by Elisabeth Syros. She screamed and ran over to the body. Kneeling, Elisabeth rhythmically nodded her head and made signs of the cross, chanting the prayer for the dead in a near-choking voice.

Gregory and Ulanov sprinted inside, stopped, their stares frozen on the macabre scene. "Shit!" Ulanov shouted.

Lucas leaped to his feet and ran into the next room. The VCR was still running; it had recorded the entire ghastly murder. He rushed back into the crime scene, picked up the radio from the floor, and broadcast, "All units on citywide patrol, wanted for the homicide of a police officer, three minutes in the past, Paolo Matrazzo, alias Paul Mastri, description as follows . . ."

His control regained, Lucas finished his radio message and picked up Andreas's 9mm Beretta from the floor. He stuck it into his belt and, reaching down, unclipped the magazine pouches from Vassos's belt. He held back his jacket and fastened them on his own belt. Moving to the sofa, he grabbed Nina Pazza by the handcuffs and dragged her contorted body into the next room. He tossed her to the floor. "Where did he go?"

She fearfully shook her head.

"Where?" he shouted.

"I don't know," she screamed.

Elisabeth Syros ran in and started to kick the prisoner in the face. Lucas stepped between them, shaking his head.

Syros knelt down next to Pazza and said with threatening calmness, "You're going to spend the rest of your life in a

Greek prison—and I'm going to be there to see that your life is a hell. Now! Where is he?"

"Ask McKay," she shouted. "He'll know."

Denny McKay took his time aiming the disk. He let it go, watching it slide the length of the shuffleboard, knocking Patty Guts's and Bubblebelly's off the board into the alley.

The muffled sound of a ringing telephone caught McKay's attention, causing him to look back into the barroom. His rule had always been no telephones in The Den, except for one locked in a drawer behind the stick. It was never used and it never rang. He went behind the bar and unlocked the drawer. Putting the handset up to his ear, he said, "Yeah," and listened.

"Park a couple of blocks away," Lucas told Gregory as the surveillance van turned into Ninth Avenue heading downtown.

Gregory drove to Fifty-first and parked the police department vehicle at a bus stop. Lucas took out the Beretta, slid out the magazine to check if it was full, and stuck the weapon back under his belt.

Big Jay, sitting on a stool, slid rounds into the chamber of a Remington Bushmaster pump shotgun. Ulanov handed Gregory an Uzi from the gun locker as he stepped into the back of the van. Lucas asked Ulanov if there had been any word from Nashin.

"Mobile Five is among the missing," Ulanov said. "Maybe his radio is dead."

"He could call us on the cellular phone," Lucas said in a worried tone.

"Maybe he can't get to a phone, Lou?" Gregory suggested.

Lucas nodded and removed six pairs of handcuffs from the supply locker, handing each of his detectives two sets. He unlocked the explosives box and tossed Gregory two stun grenades.

Before leaving the Plaza, Lucas had ordered Leone to take Nina Pazza to the station house and process her arrest reports. There was a lot of work to be done back in the squad room and he wanted Leone to take care of it. The video tape had to be invoiced as evidence, the "unusual" had to be prepared, notifications had to be made.

Elisabeth Syros had been unyielding in her demand to come with Lucas and his men until Lucas told her that he wanted her to tell her people throughout the city to be on the lookout for him. He was going after the casket-copy.

"You all know what to do?" Lucas asked.

The detectives looked around at each other. "Yeah, we know," Big Jay replied.

"Then let's do the sucker," Lucas said, shoving open the side door.

Denny McKay pensively returned the telephone to the drawer and looked up at the anxious faces gathered around him. "We might be having company. Pussy, clear out this place and tell whoever is hanging around outside to make themselves scarce. We're going upstairs to clean out some stuff, and then we're goin' to take a vacation."

Lucas got inside the pizza parlor, saw no customers, and closed the door. The pie maker's protests were cut short by the sight of the Beretta pointing at his stomach. "Don't hurt me! I'll give you my money."

"Close up this hole," Lucas ordered, reaching behind and locking the door.

The pie maker reached up and pulled down the accordion shutters. Going behind the counter, Lucas motioned the nervous man over to the oven rack and handcuffed both his hands to a stainless steel handle on the oven door. "Cry out and I'll come back and put a hole in your head."

The pie maker shook his head violently. "I won't. Only please, don't hurt me."

Lucas crawled under the oven, pushed out the door panel, squeezed through into the hallway, and made his way up to the roof.

Pussy Lyne and Bubblebelly stationed themselves on the landing of the second floor at the top of the stairway without stairs, each man cradling an automatic shotgun in his arms.

Patty Guts, his back to the other two and his shotgun held loosely in his hand, peered through the plastic cutout in the curtains, looking up into the staircase leading to upper floors and the roof.

Denny McKay hurried through the second-floor workshop into his office. Stretching his arm behind the rolltop desk, he pulled off a remote control module and rushed over to the file cabinet, shoving it aside. Getting down on one knee, McKay aimed the remote at a space on the wall, pushed the "on" button, and proceeded to punch in a code. A panel slid up into the wall, revealing a black dial safe.

Ulanov looked up from his wristwatch. "Now."

Gregory picked up the cellular phone and dialed 911.

"Police operator forty-two, may I help you?"

"Der guy who murdered the Greek cop in the Plaza Hotel is hangin' around right now in a bar called The Den, at Ninth and Forty-ninth," Gregory said into the mouthpiece, and hung up.

Big Jay wiggled a cigar out of its cellophane and stuck the unlit stogie in his mouth, clasping his hands behind his head, waiting.

"All units on patrol in the Sixteenth and adjoining pre-cincts," Central broadcasted. "Central has just received an anonymous call that the suspect wanted in connection with the homicide of a police officer, this date, in the Plaza Hotel, is at a bar within the confines of the Sixteenth, located at . . ."

Ulanov waited until Central had radioed the bar's location

and a description of the suspect before he transmitted, "Six-teen detectives to Central, K."

"Go Sixteen detectives."

"This unit is a block away from that location, Central. We're in surveillance van one-two-four. Request backup units, K."

"Sixteen Eddie on the way."

"Sergeant going."

"Adam-Boy going."

"Anticrime going."

Big Jay tapped Ulanov's shoulder and pointed to the cigar.

Ulanov nodded, and radioed, "Sixteen detectives to Central, K."

"Go Sixteen detectives."

"Advise responding units that there is a black member of the service with this unit. He's in civilian clothes; he's big, as ugly as sin, and he'll have an unlit cigar stuck in his mouth."

Responding units let go with a chorus of ten-fours.

Big Jay stood and locked the gates that sealed off the van's interior. Moving out front, he knelt between the seats and said, "All secure. Let's do it."

Surveillance van 124 screeched to a stop on the sidewalk, blocking the bar's entrance. Detectives leaped out and took up firing positions on both sides of the entrance.

Gregory tried the door; it was locked.

Standing off to the side, Big Jay fired a shotgun blast into the wood, sending the door flying open.

Gregory stepped into the doorway, aiming his Uzi into the deserted bar; Big Jay and Ulanov darted inside.

The detectives paused briefly to check out the area. A bar to the left of the entrance, a kitchen at the other end of the bar. Booths to their right. A sawdust-covered walkway sepa-rating the bar and booths, leading to a large back room with more booths and a shuffleboard. In this back room, Vassos had told them, was a closet that contained a stairway without steps.

The wail of approaching sirens filled the air.

The three-man fire team leapfrogged their way to the back of the bar, two covering while the third ran to take up a new firing position.

Bubblebelly and Pussy Lyne trained their weapons down into the stairwell.

Patty Guts tightened his grip on the shotgun's cold steel, his eyes fixed straight up in the direction of the roof door.

Denny McKay removed the .38 Colt from his belt and placed it on the floor beside him while he continued to sort through the safe, shoving money and records into a shopping bag.

Lucas flattened his back against the roof hutch that contained the top of the staircase that led down through the tenement to the bar. His eyes were fixed on the second hand of his watch as it swept around the dial.

Ulanov, standing with the others outside the tiny chamber downstairs that housed the stairless staircase, saw his second hand hit thirty and shouted, "Now!"

Gregory threw open the door.

Bubblebelly and Pussy Lyne fired down into the stairwell, splintering the door between the back room and the stairs off its hinges. The alarm system went off, emitting the sounds of klaxons. Gregory, standing outside the tiny room, stuck his Uzi inside and emptied the magazine up into the stairwell.

Big Jay pulled the pin on the grenade, holding the spoon down.

Ulanov stepped into the doorway, firing up the stairwell in the general direction of the second-floor landing.

Big Jay moved across the threshold and tossed the grenade up onto the second-floor landing. It exploded in a smoky roar, sending all three men reeling.

Lucas threw open the roof door, ran to the third floor, and fired three bursts down the stairwell. Patty Guts lurched forward, ripping the curtain from its rod, shrouding himself in black cotton as he fell dead. Rushing down the steps toward the second-floor landing, Lucas emptied his magazine, crouching down to reload.

Pussy Lyne, retaining the cover of the wall, stuck his shotgun around the wall and fired two blasts up the stairwell at Lucas, forcing him to dive prone on the steps. Pussy Lyne darted out from safety to fire at the lieutenant. Lucas, lying on the steps, fired first, exploding Pussy's face in a geyser of gray jelly and blood. The dead man remained standing, his finger frozen against the trigger, the shotgun discharging automatic rounds up into the ceiling of the stairwell. Lucas fired another burst; it sent the corpse and weapon to the ground.

Big Jay, with covering fire from Ulanov and Gregory, climbed up the risers, his hands clutching the banister, his shotgun thrust in front under his belt.

Bubblebelly extended his arm and fired four rounds blindly down the stairwell. Taking careful aim so as not to hit Big Jay, Ulanov and Gregory fired alternate bursts, watching as their partner continued his perilous climb up the treadless staircase.

Lucas, his back to the stairwell's wall, automatic thrust downward, stealthily placed his foot on the next step down to the second floor.

Reloading, Bubblebelly shouted, "Denny, they're creepin' all around me."

"I need another minute," McKay shouted back, hurriedly sorting through records.

Guns drawn, uniformed policemen rushed into the bar and charged into the back room. Firing a short burst, Gregory shouted for the new arrivals to stay back and do nothing. An overzealous rookie pushed his way through the crowd of policemen and recklessly fired two rounds up at the unseen criminals. Ulanov's ingrained response was to swing his Uzi at the rookie, striking him across his forehead and sending him staggering backward, blood streaming down his face.

"You fucking asshole," Ulanov shouted at the stunned policeman, "we've got our own people up there!"

Lucas was three steps away from the second-floor landing. Big Jay climbed to within a foot of the top. The alarm system continued to scream its head off at a deafening level; the acid-sharp reek of potassium nitrates fouled the air.

Lucas hunkered down, his sweaty hands tight around the grips. Bubblebelly saw the shadow fall over the floor. He leaned his shoulder into the stock, aiming at the hidden source of the shadow in the stairwell.

Big Jay stopped just below the top, balancing carefully on the risers, and slid the shotgun out of his belt, waiting to make his move.

Ulanov fired a burst.

Lucas raised his walkie-talkie above his head, silently counted to three, and heaved it out onto the second-floor landing.

Instinctively Bubblebelly pointed his shotgun in the direction of the sound of the radio hitting the landing, saw what it was, and swiveled the weapon back to aim at the staircase.

Big Jay popped up and fired a blast into Bubblebelly's stomach, sending the fat man crashing back against the wall. He slumped against the shot-pocked wall, gaping with bewilderment at the bloody hole in his dying body.

Lucas dashed out from the staircase. Bubblebelly's body had collapsed against the wall. Approaching cautiously, Lucas picked up the shotgun and tossed it away. Sticking his foot behind Bubblebelly's, he yanked the dead man's legs out from under him, sending the corpse crashing to the floor. Lucas moved to the stairwell, extended his hand, and pulled Big Jay up onto the landing.

The detectives fanned out in the workshop, moving warily, their weapons at the ready.

"Give it up, Denny," Lucas shouted. "You and I can make a deal. I want Matrazzo, not you."

McKay, clutching two bulging shopping bags and his revolver, crawled behind the printing press to take cover and consider his options. The blocked windows offered him no escape. Cops were all over the place. He'd never make it to the roof alive and staying alive was what it's all about. There would have to be a trial. That meant lawyers, and bail, and appeals. "I'm coming out. Don't shoot," he shouted, and stood up, hands above his head, his revolver dangling from his forefinger.

Ulanov rushed over and took the weapon from him. Big Jay frisked the prisoner.

Lucas, his face a mask of icy contempt, grabbed McKay's arm and led him away. "Denny, we don't have much time, so listen. You give me Matrazzo and the casket-copy, and you walk."

"I wanna call my lawyer," McKay snarled.

"You're going to be arrested and charged with murder in Greece. Your boy George Cuttler made a dying declaration before he checked out, naming you as the one who sent him and Simmons over to hit the two cops."

"I don't know what you're talking about. I've never been to Greece."

"After that, you'll be extradited to the Soviet Union and charged with the theft of government property. I don't think you're going to like it there, Denny. And after all that, if they don't kill you, I'm going to arrest you for homicide."

A shadow of concern crossed McKay's face. "What homicide?"

"Eddie Burke."

"Wheredja hear that shit? Eddie was my friend."

"You whacked him, Denny, and I can prove it. You left your cigarettes in the ashtray and outside the car. A forensic dentist will testify that it was your teeth that left the marks on all the filters. And the saliva we extracted from the cotton has your blood grouping."

"Circumstantial evidence," McKay said uneasily.

Lucas nodded in agreement. "But it's powerful evidence, Denny. Anyway, we got this new gadget in the lab. It takes bioforensic 'fingerprints.' That means it analyzes DNA, that's the stuff we all have in our genes. This machine measures several millionths of a gram of any body fluid. It's a positive I.D. just like prints. Your saliva is going to buy you twenty-five to life." He pulled him close and said grimly, "If the Greeks or Russians don't get you, I will."

McKay pulled away. Nodding his head at the two shopping bags on the floor. "There's two hundred K. Take it."

"Denny? When I came on the Job the theme song was 'The Best Things in Life are Free.' Today it's the *Ave Maria.*"

McKay shoved his hands into his pockets, regarded his shoes. "I walk?"

"You walk."

"I'm not sure where he is. He telephoned and told me to get out. I know he got a house someplace in Queens and another one out in East Hampton. It should be easy for you to find out where. My guess is that he's making for one of them."

"And Alexander's *Iliad?*"

"I don't know nothing about that. He had me send a couple of boys to take care of the Greek cops. Orhan did all the background work on the job. That's all I know."

Lucas turned to his detectives. "Read him his rights. Then book him for everything we got on him."

"You promised!" McKay shouted.

"I lied," Lucas said, walking away.

21

C of D Edgeworth was huddled in the back of the bar with the detectives, conducting a hurried rehearsal of the who, what, when, where, how, and why of the eventual official version of what had transpired. "Where did you get your reasonable cause for busting in here without a warrant?" Edgeworth asked.

"We were on patrol looking for the suspect wanted in connection with the Vassos homicide when we responded to a radio message that the perp might be here," Lucas said, casting a warning look at his men. "We entered, saw armed men running to the back, identified ourselves as police officers, at which point one of them turned and aimed a shotgun at us, necessitating the use of deadly physical force."

"Okay," Edgeworth said, nodding satisfaction. "Evidence?"

"We discovered two shopping bags filled with records," Lucas said. "We haven't had a chance to go through it all, but a cursory examination reveals records recording the theft, counterfeiting, and resale of art."

"No money?" Edgeworth asked.

"None," Lucas lied smoothly.

"Was this evidence obtained as the result of an illegal search?" Edgeworth asked as he walked into the closet with the stairless staircase.

Lucas and his men followed. "No, sir," Lucas answered. "It was in plain view when we arrested McKay."

"Did McKay make any statements?" the chief asked.

"Before we had a chance to read him his rights, he pleaded for us not to kill him and claimed that he sent Cuttler and Simmons to Greece only on Matrazzo's orders."

"Good. Good," Edgeworth said. "A *res gestae* confession, spontaneous and extemporaneous." He looked at Lucas. "The Greek ambassador telephoned me. They want no mention of Major Vassos in any of this. As far as anyone is concerned he was the victim of a robbery attempt."

Lucas said, "I understand."

"Anything else I should be made cognizant of?" the chief asked.

"No, sir," Lucas said, turning to look at Ulanov. "Ivan, the van is still blocking the entrance. One of our radios is still missing. Will you see if you can locate it?"

"Sure, Lou," Ulanov said, and quickly walked away.

Emergency Service trucks cordoned off Ninth Avenue between Forty-eighth and Fiftieth streets. The department's searchlight truck illuminated the building. Scruffy people leaned out of windows, watching the free show. Ulanov climbed up into the surveillance van and, bending, made his way inside, lowering himself to the stool in front of the communication console. "Mobile One to Mobile Five, K." Only static cracked in response from the speakers.

"Sergei Sergeyevich, where the hell are you?" Ulanov radioed in Russian.

Police Commissioner Franklin Vaughn arrived at the scene at 2:47 A.M. accompanied by two men. One of them was a big mean-looking man around fifty dressed in a single-breasted seersucker suit with pleated trousers; he casually twirled a Panama hat on one finger. The other one was tall and thin, midforties, dressed in a dark blue suit; he had busy eyes that missed nothing and blow-dried brown hair streaked with gray at the sides.

"You and your men did a good job, Lieutenant," the PC said, nodding his approval at Big Jay and Gregory. "I'm going to see that all the detectives who worked on this case get grade money." Motioning the two civilians over, Vaughn made the introductions. "This is Mr. Warren Cribb of the National Institute for the Fine Arts. And this is Mr. August Hayden of the State Department's Bureau of Diplomatic Security," the PC said, pointing to the man in the Panama hat.

Oozing forced affability, Hayden said, "You did a good piece of police work, Lou."

Hayden talked with the gruff sureness of a cop. Lucas studied him for a long moment and said, "You sound like you might have been on the Job."

"Georgia State Police for ten years. I left there for a stint with the U.S. Marshal Service. And now I'm with State."

Looking Hayden in the eye, Lucas said, "I've heard of Diplomatic Security."

Hayden gave him a thoroughly unpleasant smile.

Warren Cribb, the man from the National Institute for the Fine Arts, stepped forward to pump Lucas's hand. "Your country and your department can be proud of you, Lieutenant. You and your men have enriched our cultural heritage."

Lucas hurled a quizzical look at the C of D, who shrugged ignorance.

"I don't understand. Enriched what cultural heritage?" Lucas said, his mistrust growing.

"Alexander's *Iliad*, Lieutenant," Cribb said. "You've rediscovered a lost national treasure."

Lucas forced himself to remain calm. "I thought it belonged to Greece."

"That's a matter for the courts, Lou," Hayden said, "not a couple of cops like us. Besides, the Greeks think that they have a claim on everything ever dug up in their country."

"I see," Lucas said, stealing a look at his detectives.

Big Jay spit out the unlit cigar.

"Actually, my understanding is that Paolo Matrazzo legally purchased it in 1939 and surreptitiously shipped it into this country," Hayden said, twirling his hat.

Cribb burst out angrily: "We have legal justification for taking Alexander's *Iliad* into our possession. I can assure you, Lieutenant, that the National Institute for the Fine Arts is above reproach."

Bullshit, Lucas thought. Aloud: "I'm sure it is, Mr. Cribb, but you see, we don't have it."

"You don't have it?" barked the PC. "I was told that the case had been broken. What the hell is going on here?"

C of D Edgeworth stepped forward. "A communication foul-up. We got the perps but the big cheese got away. We'll have him before the day is out."

"Does he have the casket-copy with him?" Hayden asked.

Thinking fast, Lucas said, "I don't think so. He didn't have time to come back here to get it."

"Then you believe it's hidden somewhere in this building?" Cribb asked, rubbing his hands in anticipation.

"Yes, sir, I do," Lucas said. "Secreted upstairs, someplace."

"Didn't you search for it?" Hayden asked, watching the lieutenant's eyes.

"You should know better than to ask that, Hayden. We didn't have a search warrant. We put too much work into this caper to have it go out the window because we didn't take the time to get a warrant," Lucas said, meeting Hayden's searching stare.

"But your police commissioner told us that you retrieved a lot of evidence," Cribb said.

"We only seized what we saw out in the open," Lucas said, going on to explain, "Whenever a police officer makes an arrest he may take possession of any evidence that is in plain view but is required to get a warrant to search further."

"Well, we're not police officers," Hayden said. "How do we get upstairs?"

Lucas pointed to the staircase. "Put your feet on the risers, grab hold of the banister, and climb."

Hayden put on his Panama and began to climb the staircase without stairs. His face soon turned red and sweat began dripping off him. Lucas turned and moved out into the bar, followed by his two detectives.

"Two untrustworthy types," Gregory observed to Big Jay.

"Uptown we'd call them a couple of hoodoo cunts," Big Jay said, spitting out a snippet of tobacco. Lucas headed for the van.

"Mobile Five, do you read this unit, K?" Ulanov radioed, tapping his knuckles over the control board.

"Mobile One, pick up your land line, K," Central ordered.

"Ten-four." Ulanov looked around for the cellular telephone and, not seeing it, remembered that they had secured it in the locker before the raid. He got off the stool and retrieved the instrument from the locker. As soon as he switched it on it began ringing.

"Detective Ulanov."

The frazzled rush of air that came over the line was punctuated by clanging electronic sounds, then came an accented voice speaking in careful English: "Lieutenant Lucas, please."

"He's not here. Can I help you?"

"I am Lieutenant Suslov, and I am telephoning from Moscow. I have an urgent message from Colonel Sergei Nashin for Lieutenant Teddy Lucas."

Ulanov took out his pen and, reaching for the notepad, said in Russian, "You did say, Moscow?"

"Da. Moskva."

22

Manhattan's jagged profile shimmered under the rising morning sun as surveillance van 124 sped east on the Long Island Expressway. Ulanov steered it off the parkway at Woodhaven Boulevard and headed south at high speed. Lucas grinned nervously as Ulanov twisted the wheel, dodging around a taxi and a bus, arousing a host of angry horns as he fought his way through traffic. "You sure of the location?" Lucas asked.

"Yep."

"From Moscow?"

"Yep."

Lucas raised the radio to his mouth. "Big Jay?"

"Yeah?"

"They miss us yet?"

"Negative."

Lucas lowered the radio to his lap.

Ulanov made a sharp left turn on Myrtle Avenue and drove through Forest Park, exiting onto Park Lane South, continuing around the circle to Park Lane where he made a left up the driveway leading to the parking lot of the park's administrative offices. He made a sharp turn in the lot and stopped the van alongside a black Chevy Monte Carlo with diplomatic license plates. Lucas pushed open the door and got out, leaving Ulanov monitoring transmissions.

The parking lot was on a hill overlooking a section of Kew Gardens Hills, an exclusive enclave of well-manicured lawns and gardens and large expensive houses ranging in style from 1930s Tudor to ersatz Palladian. All was quiet in the clear light of the new day.

Sliding into the Monte Carlo's passenger seat, Lucas said, "Good morning, Sergei."

Nashin angrily shook the police department radio at Lucas's tired face. "Your radio stinks. I can receive, but I can't send."

"Happens, even in the Soviet Union."

Nashin's weary face betrayed his deep sadness. "I'm sorry about Andreas. He was a good policeman."

Lucas closed his eyes and sucked in a mouthful of cool morning air. "Yes, he was a good policeman. And a good man." He shifted in the seat, struggling to control his emotions. "What happened to you?"

"We followed McKay to a meeting at the top of the World Trade Center. I got pictures of him with Matrazzo. When they left the building, I decided to follow the new man, not knowing who he was at the time. We tailed him to the Plaza and watched him go inside. I assumed that you would be there for the meet with Nina Pazza, so I stationed myself on Central Park South, across the street in the taxi stand where I could watch both exits. When I heard you pull Leone off of Widener, I dispatched my two men to take his place."

"Good move," Lucas interjected.

"When I heard your emergency transmission and then saw Matrazzo leave the hotel and jump into a taxi, I did what any policeman would do; I followed him."

"Where is he now?"

Nashin pointed to a large stone house with leaded windows, rich ornamental details, and a slate-covered roof. The house was near the corner, at the top of a lawn that sloped down to the street.

Lucas reached inside his jacket and took out the Beretta. He ejected the magazine and checked the number of rounds in the clip. Satisfied, he shoved the magazine back into the housing and, leaning forward in his seat, reached behind his back and stuck the automatic into his belt, to the right of his spine. Reaching down in front, he drew his .38 detective special from its in-trouser holster, checked to see it was fully loaded, and replaced it. "What was with that call from Moscow?"

"I couldn't leave this location and there are no public phones around, so . . ." He reached under his seat and pulled out an instrument that was shaped like and about the size of a hardcover book, with a recessed computer keyboard and a four-inch-long liquid crystal display on the top. "A burst transmitter radio, direct to Moscow. I had to wait until four o'clock when our relay satellite comes into orbit. Moscow Center relayed my message to you."

Lucas looked at him, a sardonic smile on his lips. "Standard equipment for the cop on the beat. Our job's changing, my friend." He pushed open the door and turned when he heard footsteps approaching.

Ulanov, who had come over from the van, thrust a radio transceiver at him. "They're calling you."

"Big Jay?" Lucas queried.

"You've been missed. They're sending out the hounds."

"Ten-four." Lucas passed the set back to Ulanov. "Wait here with Sergei."

"I wanna come with you, Lou," Ulanov said.

"It's my endgame, Ivan," Lucas said.

Folding his big frame into the passenger seat, Ulanov said, "Good morning, comrade."

Lucas drove the van out of the lot and across the street, straight into the winding driveway of the house. Tires crunching on the gravel in the parking area, the van lurched to a stop. Lucas leaped out, heading toward the vine-covered entrance portico.

The heavy door was open, the sound of a Mozart divertimento coming from somewhere inside the house. He cautiously went inside and found himself in a ground-floor foyer that had a black-and-gray marble floor. He walked quietly over the carpet of the long hallway that led off the foyer, past heavy wood doors, and into a huge oblong room with a wall of French doors opening onto an emerald lawn with a towering weeping willow. A large tapestry, depicting a lush savanna and tropical birds, hung over a stone fireplace on the wall opposite the French doors.

Following the sound of the music, he moved through a formal dining room with two crystal chandeliers and found himself standing in front of a closed door. The Mozart was clearly coming from the room on the other side of the door.

Uncomfortably aware of the smell of his own unwashed body and the sweat pouring down his sides as well as the foul, "late-tour" taste in his mouth, Lucas drew his .38, threw open the door, and crouched inside in a firing stance.

On guard, he trained his revolver around the room. He had never been in such a strange place; the cavernous chamber had four granite pillars which reached up to support a vaulted ceiling. Sitting on a wooden folding chair next to one of the pillars, a tape deck played Mozart.

Display cases were arranged in a circle inside what was obviously some sort of shrine. All the tops were open; a dolly was on the floor inside the circle and strapped onto it were twenty-six unfurled papyrus scrolls encased between thick sheets of glass. His heart pounding, Lucas moved inside the ring, continuing to move his pointing gun around the room. Seeing that he was alone, Lucas knelt down beside the dolly.

Eyes wide with wonderment, he looked down at the ancient Greek words. He started to touch one, but jerked his hand back as though afraid of committing sacrilege. And then, slowly, reverently, he placed his palm on one and was immediately overcome by feelings that he could not have described.

The music stopped abruptly.

Lucas knelt in the sudden and ominous silence, apprehension freezing on his face. He turned to assume a prone firing position.

Matrazzo stepped out from behind a column in back of the policeman, a .45 automatic pointing at the back of Lucas's head.

"You might try and get a round off before I blow your head apart, Lieutenant, but you'll be dead before you turn around. Now! Put your weapon down and slide it back to me."

Lucas looked across the room at the silent tape deck.

"I pulled the plug," Matrazzo said. "Extension cords are so helpful, don't you think?"

Lucas hesitated, and then reluctantly put his revolver on the floor and pushed it behind him. Matrazzo picked it up and stuck it in his belt. "You may now get up, but keep your hands clasped behind your head."

Standing, Lucas said, "You know you're playing with half a deck, don't you?"

Matrazzo's hand holding the gun was shaking from the man's barely controlled rage; his eyes were icy. "Don't you dare call me crazy, you pathetic civil servant. My father was a great man. I devoted my life to reclaiming what was his and is now mine. Now! Push the dolly through that door." He motioned to a solid wood door between two leaded windows. "My treasure is going with me."

"You're going to forge the casket-copy and sell the fake," Lucas said, not moving. "And you're betting that a certain museum is so anxious to have it that they'll never even notice they're buying a fake."

"Very astute of you. It will take me about twenty months to do a good job. I'll make my own ink. I intend to sell both the casket-copy and the commentary. Thanks to your meddling, certain people in the art world are foaming at the mouth to get their greedy hands on the scrolls. I've already been in touch with some Japanese who fancy themselves collectors. They're willing to pay up to sixty million. And I'll get to keep the real ones. Now move the cart."

Bending, Lucas pushed the wheeled cart into a breezeway connecting the house and a stone garage.

"Inside the garage," Matrazzo ordered, treading softly behind the lieutenant.

A station wagon was sticking halfway out of the front of the garage. It was set back from the main house, at the end of a parterre, with an asphalt lane winding down into the main driveway. It was too far back and off to the side for Ulanov and Sergei to see his deadly predicament. Easy does it, kiddo, easy does it. Wait for the right moment, Lucas counseled himself, looking around the garage. Gardening tools and an aluminum ladder hung from the wall, and there was a lawn mower on the floor next to two red gasoline cans with yellow bands around their centers.

"Start loading them into the back," Matrazzo ordered.

Lucas held back. Matrazzo waved the .45. "I'll splatter you all over the floor and walls. Move!"

Lucas unbuckled the belt securing the plates on the dolly. He slid his hands under three of them and picked them up, commenting, "They're in a remarkable state of preservation."

"The ancients knew how to reserve their heritage. Now, stop stalling and load."

Lucas lugged the plates over to the back of the station wagon. Bracing his knee under the plates, he tried to open the rear door. "It's locked," he lied, struggling to get his load back to the dolly.

Matrazzo looked at the policeman. "Sit on the floor facing the wall with your hands behind your head."

Lucas carefully set the glass plates on the dolly and lowered himself down, his back to the dolly, the gasoline cans a few feet beyond his reach. Keeping his automatic trained on Lucas's back, Matrazzo slowly moved backward toward the driver's side. Lucas inched his torso back, winding it up for a forward leap, waiting for that instant when his enemy would be off balance. He tilted his head slightly to the right so that his peripheral vision included Matrazzo.

Reaching behind with one hand, Matrazzo felt for the handle. He opened the door. With his eyes riveted on Lucas, he transferred the automatic to his left hand and, bending at the knees, groped under the dashboard for the tailgate latch release.

Now! Lucas sprang forward, grabbing a gasoline can and hurling it at Matrazzo; then he dived for cover behind the dolly.

Matrazzo got off one round with an unsteady hand; it missed. The can struck his chest, knocking off the spout and dousing his front; he staggered back across the driver's seat. Lucas grabbed the Beretta and fired a shot under the dolly that struck Matrazzo's foot.

Screaming obscenities, Matrazzo grabbed the automatic with his right hand and pulled himself up into a sitting position. "Get out from behind my *Iliad*. Get away, you son of a bitch! Leave my *Iliad*," Matrazzo screamed, aiming for a clean shot.

Lucas popped out from around the side of the loaded cart, firing a round at the killer. The driver's seat exploded in a reddish blue fireball that engulfed Matrazzo and turned him into a flailing, thrashing gargoyle with blue and yellow streamers fluttering out his eyes and mouth. Lucas leaped up off the ground and hauled the dolly past the roaring fire out onto the driveway. He ran bent over, trying to put distance between himself and the garage.

The force of a violent explosion hurled Lucas across the dolly, toppling him and the cart over the lawn, spilling the plates onto the grass. Slowly regaining his senses, Lucas straightened up and looked back at the inferno. A deformed hand was sticking out of the hungry flames, a gold ring reflecting the savage light of the blaze. Then the hand disappeared in the fire.

The Monte Carlo came racing over the lawn and jerked to a stop. Ulanov and Sergei leaped out and ran over to him.

"Are you all right?" Nashin shouted.

"I'm okay," Lucas said, uprighting the dolly. "Help me pick up these sheets."

"Matrazzo?" Ulanov asked, picking up some scrolls.

"In there," Lucas said, jerking his thumb at the now blazing garage. Ulanov smiled grimly. "That's a conviction that won't be overturned."

"Where is he?" August Hayden, the man from Diplomatic Security, demanded. They were standing outside The Den, a cluster of police officials that included the PC, the C of D, Warren Cribb, the man from the National Institute of the Fine Arts, the Duty Captain, and two detectives from the Sixteenth Squad.

"I don't know where he is," Big Jay answered.

"Me neither," Gregory followed.

Repeatedly digging his forefinger into Big Jay's chest, Hayden warned, "You'd better tell me, Officer, or it'll be your ass."

Big Jay scowled down at the offending finger. "If you stick that thing at me one more time, we is gonna be rushed to the hospital. They's gonna be extracting my foot from your asshole." Since all of them had spent a sleepless night, tempers were ragged. The coolness of a new day did little to ease the tension.

Angrily snatching off his Panama hat, Hayden said to the PC, "You oughta instill respect for civilians in your men, Commissioner."

Police Commissioner Vaughn met Hayden's glare. "Fuck you," he said, turning away and walking over to his car.

Hayden glared at the C of D, who looked away from him.

"Let's get out of here," Hayden said to Cribb, and the two of them ran to their car.

Edgeworth looked at the two detectives and said, "You'd better get on the horn to your boss and tell him some uptight people are going to be looking for him."

23 ═══════════

Before noon August Hayden had set up a temporary command post in the garage on the Forty-fifth Street side of the United States Mission to the United Nations.

"This was to have been uncomplicated," Cribb complained.

"We can't always control events," Hayden said, pacing back and forth in front of the open garage door. "Obviously Lieutenant Lucas has his own plans for Alexander's *Iliad.*"

"Then you do think he has it?"

"He has it all right. But the question is, what is he going to do with it?"

"What do you mean?"

"He might want to sell it to the highest bidder, or he might want to turn it over at a full-blown press conference, get some publicity for himself and his men. Or . . .?" He let the word drop, glancing at his men lounging around the double-parked sedans on the street outside.

"Or what?"

"The lieutenant and Major Vassos were partners. I wouldn't expect you to appreciate the significance of that, but take my word, among policemen it means a lot." Hayden thoughtfully tapped his fist against his chin. "I think he's going to return it to the Greeks."

Cribb's mouth dropped open. "You must not allow that to happen. Kill him if you have to, but that *Iliad* must remain in this country."

"Kill an American cop?" Hayden said, his voice full of contempt. "I get paid to pull dirty tricks on people but I don't murder Americans, not for any price."

"But . . . but . . ."

"There are no buts, Cribb." Hayden called one of his men over and told him to go inside the mission and get a Manhattan telephone directory. When the man returned, Hayden put the thick book on the hood of the town car parked inside the garage and copied several addresses onto a page of his notepad.

"What are you doing?" Cribb asked.

"If I were Lucas, I'd go get the casket-copy and make for a Greek government facility in New York."

"Why? Why not some fish store in Astoria?"

"Because it's not extraterritorial, outside the territorial and judicial limits of the United States," Hayden said, reaching for the walkie-talkie atop the town car's hood. "And the Greek UN mission and consular office are."

Northbound traffic crawled along York Avenue from Fifty-third to the entrances of the Franklin D. Roosevelt Drive at Sixty-first and Sixty-third streets. Lucas thought: my luck is holding.

They had just finished loading the plates into the back of the Monte Carlo when the fire engines arrived at the scene. Traffic had moved briskly on the way back into Manhattan. Big Jay's transmission had alerted Lucas that the bad guys were looking for him. Figuring that Hayden wouldn't be able to gather enough people on short notice, he drove all the way east, hoping to slip through any cordon placed to intercept him. He looked out into the sideview mirror and saw the surveillance van behind him. Ulanov was driving; Nashin, copiloting. He prayed that Elisabeth had alerted her people.

Traffic agents worked cars into the northbound entrance at

Sixty-first Street. Lucas cut the car out into the far left lane, skirting around the packed mass of cars trying to get on the drive.

The light turned red; he gunned the engine and sped north, with the van staying close behind him. At Seventy-ninth Street, Lucas made a left turn off of York Avenue and double-parked. He got out and ran back to the van. Ulanov rolled down the window. Lucas told him that he was headed for the Greek consulate between Park and Madison avenues.

"Right behind you, Lou," Ulanov said.

Lucas looked at Nashin. "Sergei, why don't you grab a taxi back to your mission and report the car stolen? Stay out of it, you've done more than your share."

Nashin let go with a litany of Russian obscenities.

"What did he say?" Lucas asked Ulanov.

"You don't wanna know, Lou. But the bottom line is, he's coming with us."

The Greek consulate was located in a town house on the north side of Seventy-ninth Street. Three low steps led up to two arched doorways with ornamental ironwork, separated by a large window. Approaching Park Avenue, Lucas saw the blue-and-white Greek flag hanging over one of the doorways. He also spotted the crescent-shaped barricade of black sedans blocking the entrances and the men standing alertly behind the cars.

Hayden's read my mind, Lucas thought, hurriedly stopping at the curb and parking. He got out and stood between cars, looking into the next block, desperately pondering his next move. He knew that he had to get the casket-copy to a safe place where Hayden and his crew couldn't get their thieving hands on it. The only really safe place would be a diplomatic mission. If Hayden had thought to cover this location, he'd have the Greek mission and other places covered too. I don't want Andreas to have died for nothing, he thought. No! I'm not going to let that happen. He could see Hayden and Cribb

having a curbside discussion with three men. They're probably telling the Greeks that they are there to protect them
against an imminent terrorist attack, he thought; then the
surveillance van whooshed past him with Nashin leaning out
the window signaling him to wait where he was.

"Tighten your seat belt, comrade," Ulanov shouted, shooting the van across Park Avenue against a red light.

"This is almost as much fun as getting laid," Nashin said,
pulling the belt tight across his lap. Ulanov drove to the
middle of the block and spun the wheel, forcing the van up
on the sidewalk and plowing into the improvised barricade of
cars in front of 69 East Seventy-ninth Street, bulldozing the
front ends of two automobiles aside and making a hole.
Frightened men scurried for safety. Pedestrians stopped short,
unsure what to do.

"My neck," Ulanov shouted in pain. "I hurt my neck."

Nashin unbuckled himself and helped the detective out of
the driver's seat. He jumped behind the wheel and, grinding
the transmission into reverse, recklessly backed the van across
Seventy-ninth Street. "Here goes my promotion," he said,
ramming his foot down on the gas pedal and slamming into
low gear, aiming for the disarranged sedans. The police department vehicle smashed through the barricade and crashed
into the doorway, unhinging the grillwork and the door.

Once again throwing the van into reverse, its broken tail
pipe gouging the sidewalk and throwing sparks, Nashin at-
tempted, unsuccessfully, to shift gears but was unable to, so
he drove off in reverse, heading west. He got about fifty feet
away from the consulate before being boxed in by cars full of
angry men aiming an assortment of firepower his way.

Nashin rolled down the window and calmly announced,
"We are Soviet diplomats."

Lucas waited for the light to turn green. He stamped his
foot down on the gas pedal, propelling the Monte Carlo west-

bound on Seventy-ninth Street. He reached out and tightened the passenger seat belt around the stacked sheets of plate glass.

Reaching the smoking barricade, he spun the wheel and drove the car up onto the sidewalk, plowing into the doorway, wedging the vehicle into the threshold and sending chunks of concrete and mortar crashing down. He tried to get out but couldn't; the front doors were crushed shut against the building's doorjambs. He forced the window partway down on the driver's side and, placing his face in the gap, shouted to the people milling about inside the consulate that he had the casket-copy.

A man stepped out of the group of stunned and frightened people and asked, "You're from Elisabeth?"

"Yes. Yes," Lucas shouted back, turning to see Hayden and several men running his way.

Two men with fire axes rushed up onto the hood of the car and began chopping out the windshield. Lucas covered his face with his hands to protect himself from the flying glass. When the windshield was gone, the Greeks formed a human chain; Lucas passed the glass plates out to them.

"Open the fucking door," Hayden shouted, pulling on the handles of the back door. Lucas ignored him; he went on passing plates out to the two men standing on the hood.

Hayden grabbed a rifle from one of his men and smashed in the rear window. Reaching inside, he opened the door and jumped on Lucas's back, putting a headlock on the policeman.

Lucas dropped a plate on the front seat and hurled himself backward, smashing Hayden into the doorpost. The two men lashed about, Hayden maintaining his stranglehold, Lucas pounding his elbows into his assailant's ribs. Meanwhile one of the Greeks climbed through the windshield and resumed passing out Alexander's *Iliad*. Hayden was screaming curses into the policeman's ear. Lucas felt his oxygen-starved body going limp, a cloud of blackness sweeping over him. He thrust his hand behind him and grabbed hold of Hayden's testicles, digging in his fingers and crushing them.

Hayden yowled and, releasing his grip, lunged for the policeman's hand.

"We have them all," one of the Greeks said from the hood of the car. "Thank you."

Lucas collapsed on top of Hayden. "It's over," he gasped.

Retching as he held his hand over his aching balls, Hayden muttered, "How will I ever be able to explain all of this?"

Breathing deeply, Lucas answered, "You just begin your report with, 'Once upon a time . . .' "

24

The forklift's claws held the flag-draped coffin. An honor guard had formed just inside Olympic Airlines' freight hangar at Kennedy airport. C of D Edgeworth, Lucas, Sergeant Grimes, Big Jay, Ulanov, Gregory, and Sergei Nashin tendered a breast salute as the lift rolled past them on its way out to the waiting cargo jet. Katina and Elisabeth Syros stood together off to the side, both with tears in their eyes.

Elisabeth came over to the file of policemen and, working her way from man to man, thanked each one of them for all that they had done. When she reached Lucas she pressed a gold strand of jade worry beads into his hand. "Andreas would have wanted you to have these. And his Beretta."

"Thank you," he said, adding, "I'm glad you're taking him home along with the casket-copy." He reached into his pocket and took out Cormick McGovern's shield. Handing it to her, he asked, "Will you see that they're together?"

"I'll tell Colonel Pappas," she said, putting the shield in her pocketbook.

Lucas reached down and picked up Denny McKay's shopping bag. "This is for the people of Voúla."

She looked down into the bagful of money. "Thank you," she said, and kissed him.

Lucas turned to watch the forklift darting out onto the apron. He thought about the first time he met Andreas in the customs office at Kennedy. It all seemed so long ago. He laughed bitterly to himself as he thought of the newspaper headlines of two days ago: NYPD THWARTS TERRORIST ATTACK ON GREEKS. Andreas would have approved of that tale; there was a certain Greek panache to the lie.

Watching the coffin being lifted up into the aircraft, he brushed tears from his face and whispered, "Good-bye, my friend."

"Lou, we're going back to the Squad," the Second Whip said. "I've got a desk full of fives waiting on me."

Lucas turned and looked at the sergeant. "I'll see you in seven days. I hooked some vacation time onto my swing."

"I'll hold it down," Grimes said, walking off with the rest of the detectives.

Nashin came over to Lucas and asked, "How's your vodka supply?"

"Getting low."

"I'll take care of it."

"Did you have any problems with the car?"

"None at all. My superiors were delighted with the material you gave us. Our labor camp population is about to increase."

"See ya 'round, comrade."

"Ten-four, Lou." Nashin snapped back briskly and walked away.

Long after the Olympic 747 had taxied out and moved off to the runway, Lucas stood by himself, looking out at the busy airport but seeing, in his mind's eye, the faces of Andreas and his wife and son. He actually jumped, startled, when he felt a hand grip his arm. It was C of D Tim Edgeworth, looking unusually subdued and thoughtful. The two of them stood without saying anything for several minutes. Then Edgeworth cleared his throat with a cough and said quietly, "I don't think Hayden is going to be collecting a pension from State." He

rubbed his eyes wearily and continued: "I wouldn't be surprised if he ends up needing a good lawyer. A friend of mine
called from Washington this morning. Apparently Hayden is
facing an administrative review hearing. And I sent a memo-
randum of information to the U.S. attorney's office."

Lucas turned and stared directly at his superior officer. A
thousand possible questions ran through his head—and the
vision of a murdered Greek family stayed with him like some
awful retinal afterimage. His hand unconsciously felt for Andreas's worry beads in the pocket of his dark suit.

"Tim," he asked in a hoarse, strained voice, "who were
those two clowns working for?"

Edgeworth returned his stare without any change of expres-
sion. "In a strictly technical sense Hayden *did* represent the
State Department." He paused, looking off into the distance.
"But Teddy, they, I mean the guys at State, the feds in the
Bureau, the spooks at the Agency—they're a lot like the
department, like us. I get the same kind of paycheck you get.
And so do those assholes in our Intelligence Division. That
doesn't mean that we are all one big happy family. You got
Haydens everywhere. His paycheck came from State, sure,
but that don't mean his loyalty got paid back. This guy,
Cribb . . ."

"Yeah," Lucas interrupted. "I never heard of his outfit, this
fine arts setup. Katina says it was founded only a year or so
ago."

Edgeworth waved his hand impatiently. "Listen, OK,
Teddy? Just shut up for a minute." The chief looked like a
man expending considerable effort to control his temper.
"Cribb is a curator—I mean he *was* a curator for a museum
on the West Coast. A fairly new one, with a hell of a big
endowment but not a hell of a great collection. Anyway, he
got promoted sideways when this foundation was set up. The
old, established museums didn't want it, didn't need it. Seems
that a bunch of people in the government thought it was a
great idea. The foundation would represent the interests of

the new, smaller or poorer museums. The ones ready to cut a few corners. The ones with patrons and donors who own things that they got through . . . well, ways that weren't strictly kosher."

A jet howling its way out to the runway momentarily drowned out what Edgeworth was trying to say. He waited impatiently and went on after the noise of the plane receded. "I don't know all of the fine details, but Mastri, I mean Matrazzo, and Iskur, and even that poor bastard, that diplomat who got offed—well, they were all part of an old boy network. From what I understand, it all got started when people who chased around Europe after the war looking for art and stuff the Germans had stolen, guys in CIC and OSS and whatever, learned how much money could be made selling stolen art. So they went on working for all kinds of different parts of the federal government—damn it, they got paid, they got diplomatic passports—look at that guy in Athens."

"You mean the late Trevor Hughes," Lucas said bitterly.

"Yeah, him. He was a courier. Even put stolen stuff in the goddamn diplomatic pouch."

Lucas held the worn worry beads out in the sun. "And Andreas Vassos screwed up a nice thing for them, right?"

Edgeworth gave Lucas a hard look, one that told him to stop and not push any further. "Yeah, they killed a cop. A damn good cop. They are going to regret it—and not just the people who aided Matrazzo. Denny McKay got recruited back when he was stationed in Japan. He was a good printer and engraver. They picked him when he was working at a CIA base in Atsugi, creating stuff to help our pilots who got knocked down over North Korea use escape and evasion routes. There are a lot of McKays out there."

Lucas began to walk away, then stopped and turned to look at Edgeworth. "So who puts them away, *sir?*" The last word came out with irrepressible bitterness.

Edgeworth clasped his hands behind his back and, rocking slightly back on his heels, evaded Teddy's eye. "I remember an old scrap of Latin that every police supervisor should worry about." Edgeworth frowned and pronounced the words carefully: "*Quis custodiet ipso custodes?* It means: Who will police the police? Teddy, it stops here. We got the guys that pulled the trigger. On a good day, that's the best we can hope to do."

Spiro and Anna Grantas greeted their guests in their restaurant's gaudy lobby. It was a little after eight at night and the band was holding back, husbanding their energy for later, when the Greeks arrived. Lucas stood on top of the steps looking into the crowded restaurant.

Katina watched him walk down and go to the center of the dance floor.

"Music for a Greek," he shouted in Greek, jolting the musicians out of their lethargy. The men on the bandstand looked down at the stranger and, seeing his red, swollen eyes, understood his needs. The tambourine man raised his shallow drum, shaking the metallic disks as he beat the drum with his fingers. The bouzouki came alive, as did the steel guitar and the *udte*.

Lucas, one leg crossed over the other, his arms outstretched at his sides, swayed to the rising and falling sounds of the music. Katina, watching him from the lobby, felt tears come to her eyes.

Lucas slowly began turning his body, swaying to the music, shouting in Greek, "Andreas, look, I'm dancing. I'm dancing."

ACKNOWLEDGMENTS

Black Sand is the story of policemen solving an unusual case. It is not, nor does it pretend to be, an academic work. Any mistakes of a factual or scholarly nature are mine alone and not the responsibility of the many experts who gave their time so generously helping me with my research.

My preparation for *Black Sand* required extensive reading. Some of the essential books that informed many of the pages of *Black Sand* are: *Plutarch's Lives,* translated by John Dryden; *Alexander the Great,* by Robin Lane Fox; *A Rare Book Saga,* by H. P. Kraus; *The* Iliad *of Homer,* translated by Richmond Lattimore; *Scribes and Scholars—A Guide to the Transmission of Greek and Latin Literature,* by L. D. Reynolds and N. G. Wilson; *The Treasures of Time,* by Leo Deuel; *Gods, Graves, and Scholars: The Story of Archaeology,* by C. W. Ceram; *The Bull from the Sea* and *The King Must Die,* by Mary Renault; *The Harvest of Hellenism,* by Frank Peters.

I am deeply grateful to the following members of the Hellenic Police Department for their help and for reinforcing my belief that the "Job" is the same the world over: Brigadier General Stephanios Tsintziellis, Security Division; General Stefanos Tsetselia, Security Division, Greek Constabulary (Retired); Colonel Spyros Roikos, Antiquity Squad, Security Division; Major Theodore Charalampopoulos, Interpol, Ministry of Public Order.

I am also indebted to Mr. Yiortos Chouliaras and Mr. George Dardavillas of the Permanent Mission of Greece to the United Nations for helping guide my way through the government bureaucracy and opening so many doors for me; Mrs. JoAnn Tfoukos of the American Women's Organization of Athens, Greece, and my interpreter in Greece, Mr. Dentrios Mitsos.

Black Sand could not have been written without the generous help of scholars who gave me glimpses into their world of erudition. I am particularly grateful to Dr. Barbara Gail Rowes for pointing me in the right direction, and to Dr. Helen Evans of the Metropolitan Museum of Art for transporting me back in time to the days of Alexander the Great; to Joan Leibovitz of New York University's Institute of Fine Arts for her help with Ph.D. dissertations and for a tour of the Duke Mansion; to Dr. Marit Jentoft-Neilsen of the J. Paul Getty Museum for showing me how to unroll papyrus scrolls and teaching me the difference between Greek and Roman pottery; to Dr. William Voekle of the Medieval and Renaissance Collection of the Pierpont Morgan Library for his help with ancient texts.

To those experts at the Metropolitan Museum of Art and the Smithsonian Institution's Freer Gallery of Art who requested anonymity, thank you.

I want to thank Mr. John Ross, Director of Public Relations for the Metropolitan Museum of Art, for his help, and Dr. Warren Scherer, Director of Research, Department of Operative Dentistry, New York University's School of Dentistry, for showing me how to make forensic casts.

I am also grateful to Mr. Artur R. Katon of Issco, Westbury, New York, for teaching me how to use pinhole cameras, and to Mr. Allen Gore of Alert Management Systems for showing me how certain kinds of alarm systems function.

To my friend Mr. Albert Levi, who acted as my Greek translator in New York and who shared with me some of the rich tapestry of Greek life in New York City, I say, Giassou, Albert.

The following members of the New York City Police Department have been most helpful, and I thank them for their kind help and cooperation: Chief of Department Robert J. Johnston Jr., Captain Tom Fahey, Sergeant Donald O'Donnell, Sergeant Peter P. Sweeney, and Police Officer Peter Fokianos, President, Saint Paul's Society, NYPD.

I am deeply grateful to my agents, Knox Burger and Kitty

Sprague, for always being there for me, for their tireless help in working on the manuscripts, their suggestions and many worthwhile criticisms. Thank you for helping the dream continue.

To my editor and good friend James O'Shea Wade, whose magical pencil continues to work wonders, I say, thank you, Jim. And to the members of the Crown Publishing family, whose ceaseless efforts make it all work, I say, thank you, thank you, thank you.